A SIGNIFICANT TEST OF BLOOD

by

Glynnis Hayward

PublishAmerica
Baltimore

© 2007 by Glynnis Hayward.
All rights reserved. No part of this book may be reproduced, stored in a retrieval system or transmitted in any form or by any means without the prior written permission of the publishers, except by a reviewer who may quote brief passages in a review to be printed in a newspaper, magazine or journal.

First printing

All characters in this book are fictitious, and any resemblance to real persons, living or dead, is coincidental.

ISBN: 1-4137-6838-5
PUBLISHED BY PUBLISHAMERICA, LLLP
www.publishamerica.com
Baltimore

Printed in the United States of America

For two admirable women, Audrey and Lyn,
who faced adversity with courage and grace.

My thanks to:

The victims of rape who shared their stories and pain with me;

Drs. Carl Sgarlata and Desmond Bell, for their medical explanations and information;

Lindsay Rothwell, for the cover design;

Graham Belchers, for artwork used on the cover;

My husband, Brian, for insightful comments as he listened to my thought processes.

I am grateful for all this invaluable assistance that helped make the novel possible.

1

Funerals are emotional. A mother's funeral is grueling. Quarreling relations at such a time are unbearable. Wendy tried sipping a glass of wine, but found herself gulping it instead. Her childhood bedroom seemed comforting as she stared out the window at the first leaves drifting in the breeze, harbingers of the end of summer. It was a relief to escape from the crowd at her mother's funeral who meant only kindness but accentuated her loss; it was also a sanctuary from Howard and Isabella, her argumentative brother and sister. She felt tears welling in her eyes recalling happy, distant days spent in this small Californian town, Los Gatos. It was the epicenter of her childhood. With difficulty she pulled herself away from that sanctuary to face the present; her father was in Intensive Care at Stanford Hospital and she needed to go to him. He would be waiting for her, unable to move while suffering injuries sustained in the car crash that had killed her mother. His long life was nearly over; the story was no longer about him, he was merely waiting for the end.

She made her way to the hospital and walked quietly to his bed. He appeared to be asleep but when she touched his shoulder, he responded by reaching up and squeezing her hand. Their closeness often made words unnecessary. He turned his head and gazed at her questioningly. Knowing his concern, she whispered, "It was a beautiful service, Dad. The church was overflowing; they brought in extra chairs and there were even people seated outside in the narthex."

He nodded, grunting hoarsely, "I wish they would've unhooked all these tubes. It's ridiculous that I couldn't attend my own wife's funeral." He wiped tears from his eyes and sighed. "There's unfinished business I need to take care of, Wendy. Your mother and I agreed about everything, except for one big issue." He stared intently at his daughter. "Now that she's gone, I wish I could tell her that I think she was right." He shook his head disbelievingly. "She didn't suffer, did she?"

Wendy wiped her tears and patiently answered his repeated question. "No, Dad, Mom didn't suffer." She stroked his head gently. "You should rest and let your body recover. If there's something you need to do, I can help you."

He held her hand tightly. "Darling Wendy," he said, "you're so thoughtful." But he shook his head emphatically, adding, "No, it's something that only I can take care of; I need to speak to my attorney if you can organize that please." Pointing to his cell phone he said, "Ned Mackay; his number is in my directory."

Wendy got Ned on the line and discreetly left the room to let her father make his call privately. It wasn't long before a nurse came hurrying to answer his call button and to usher Wendy back to his bedside. He glanced at her, saying, "Thank you. I hope you won't judge me too harshly in days to come. Your mother wanted this, and now Ned will take care of it. It would've brought her happiness and closure...Our children meant everything to her, you know—all of them. What amazing people you are. All our children..." Wendy was puzzled, but said nothing as her father was clearly troubled. He looked up at the ceiling and his eyes seemed to peer into eternity before coming to rest on his daughter again. "And our grandchildren, too. She was so proud of them." He closed his eyes for a time and Wendy thought he was asleep, but suddenly he opened them and said, "I worry about Lauren in South Africa. There's such violent crime in that part of the world. It's all well and good being a Good Samaritan, but she's very vulnerable. That granddaughter of mine is young and beautiful. It's almost inviting trouble in a dangerous place."

Wendy looked anxiously at her father. "I'm sure she wouldn't be there if it were unsafe. Bella wouldn't have let her daughter go. Don't upset yourself, Dad." She stroked her father's head to calm his agitation. "I know she's on an Exchange Program, but what's she actually doing there?"

"She went as an affiliate to Cape Town University doing research into teaching English as a second language, but now she's busy with something else as well. She was supposed to be coming home at Christmas, but not anymore."

"Why?" asked Wendy.

"She persuaded us to pay for an orphanage to be built there, but it won't be finished until next year..." He sighed deeply. "Your mother wanted to go and visit her. It was something near to Edith's heart as well, but it was out of the question; we were much too old to make that long trip." Again he closed his eyes and Wendy noticed tears glistening on his cheeks. He stayed lost in his thoughts for a while and then once again returned to the previous conversation. Wincing slightly with pain, he said very softly, "Apparently something like eleven per cent of the population in South Africa is infected with Aids; you can hardly imagine the number of orphans and abandoned babies. I think Lauren felt for the little souls because she remembered losing her own father." Once again he squeezed his daughter's hand. "She's also helping in some kindergarten in a township that sounds like a ghetto to me. I'll be glad when she's home. It's too dangerous." He rubbed his forehead and then blew his nose. As he stuffed his handkerchief back in his pocket, he added, "She's like her grandmother in that respect. Darling Edith always loved children. Your mother was a wonderful woman. She always put her family first and she always did the right thing. Always. Never let anyone say differently," he whispered and closed his eyes. "I'm very tired now."

Wendy understood. He was entitled to feel tired. He had survived a war fighting Nazi Germany; he had grown from a lover to a responsible husband and father; he had founded a global computer company, Parker Keating; but he had finally suffered gradual diminishing of strength after a heart attack. She leaned over him and looked deeply into his tired old eyes, trying to forever imprint their gaze in her brain. She kissed him on the forehead and smiled wistfully at him. "It's OK, Dad," she whispered.

He nodded his head and closed his eyes.

2

Grief and guilt are close cousins that sap the soul; when they are unchecked by their antidote, support, they can overwhelm reason. Lauren Marlowe's Saturday hike up Table Mountain provided welcome solitude to mourn her grandmother, recently killed in a car accident in California. The distance between South Africa and the USA had never felt as great as it did at this moment, for in addition to the big time difference, her cell phone gave very patchy reception which made communication difficult. She longed to be with her family and regretted that she hadn't jumped onto the first plane to be at the funeral. It was too late now. She knew that it would have meant a lot to her grandfather if she had been there, but it hadn't been possible to get a flight to make the thirty hour journey back to San Francisco in time.

Her January arrival in Cape Town had been exciting, but it had also been a lonely time. Since she'd met Mike Rousseau in late May, things had been different. His keen sense of humor was as appealing as his boyish good looks. July had been spent traveling to Kwazulu Natal to observe orphanages there, but when she returned to Cape Town in August, they started seeing a lot of each other. She recalled their date last weekend; they'd spent the day walking on top of Table Mountain and then he'd cooked dinner for her at his flat. After much chatting, laughter and wine, they'd been on the sofa together when things started to happen fast. She remembered how her heart was pounding as she felt herself putting on brakes. "No, Mike, we have to stop," she'd said. He'd covered her mouth with kisses to try and keep her quiet, but she'd pushed him away and held him at arm's length as she explained her feelings. It would complicate her life too much to get involved with a South African. She was only here for a year and that time was nearly up. She'd stay a bit longer until the orphanage opened, but then she'd be returning to the States.

He'd respected her wishes grudgingly, but argued that they should follow their hearts and throw caution to the wind. "Your life isn't mapped out for you, Lauren," he'd said. "There are always alternative routes one can take, you know." She'd nearly weakened as she felt his hand cup her breast once more and she felt herself flush with excitement just thinking about it again. Perhaps he was right. She knew how different her whole body felt when he was near, and when he touched her…

She put thoughts of him aside as she remembered again her grandparents. She longed to speak to her grandfather and know that he was recovering from the injuries he'd received in the accident. Before his heart attack, they had spent many days hiking together in the Blue Ridge Mountains and he'd taught her to love the outdoors. He'd always been there for her and had become like a father since her own dad died.

After some strenuous hours hiking, she stopped to catch her breath and absorb the surrounding stillness that was broken only by sharp bird calls. She looked around at the strange flora; bold protea blooms and spiky orange aloes attracted sunbirds, shimmering and darting as they hovered around the plants. If there'd been a Garden of Eden, she was sure that this would have been it. The spring heat was soporific, prompting her to lie down on a warm boulder and shut her eyes for a rest. A lizard slithered away and a family of rock rabbits scurried into the indigenous *fynbos*, resentfully giving up their places in the sun to this intruder. She tried to fight sleep, being concerned about her safety here in South Africa, but eventually succumbed with her long fair hair forming a cushion for her head.

Some time later she awoke feeling very cold and was startled to discover that the sun was almost setting. She cursed her foolishness. The gates of Kirstenbosch Gardens down below would soon be closing. She needed to make her way down the mountainside quickly as darkness was descending faster than she was able to climb down the trail. Although she felt her heart racing, she tried not to panic. *Just stay on the path and keep your eyes in front of you,* she told herself. *You don't have to worry, snakes won't be out at night.* But even as she thought that, she remembered that there were night adders and other predators. Somebody had warned her of leopards and baboons on Table Mountain and the semi-darkness seemed to bring strange noises to her ears; something howled nearby while another creature barked further off; leaves seemed to rustle ominously close by. She felt threatened by the dark African nightfall which came so quickly; it was only just light enough to see her sneakers on the path, making her breathe a sigh of relief every time she saw a white painted stone marker. Her nerves were on edge. A sudden shrill ringing exploded next to her and her heart almost stopped beating until she realized that it was her cell phone. It was a relief to have contact with someone and she hastily retrieved the phone from her backpack to answer the call.

"Hello, hello," she called, but the reception was very bad on the mountain and she could barely hear Mike Rousseau's voice asking where she was. As they had made plans to meet at Forester's Arms, she tried to explain what had happened but the crackle was so bad that she wasn't sure whether he could hear her. She couldn't waste precious time trying to be heard, so she quickly texted him a message, pulled on a sweatshirt, and continued the descent now in total darkness. She tried not to think of any lurking danger, concentrating on putting one foot in front of the other. Suddenly she heard a voice in the distance. Her natural instinct to call out almost made her do so, but caution stopped her in her tracks. She waited silently and listened. It seemed to be just one voice. She heard it again and froze. She could hear heavy footsteps on the path and then a flashlight was visible, penetrating the darkness.

"Can you hear me?" a strange voice called. The voice echoed, and only when silence returned another shout came. "Lauren." Her name now echoed up at her. She wanted to cry with relief.

"Yes. I'm here."

"Stay where you are. I'm coming to get you. Just keep calling out to me so that I can find you."

The tears were streaming down her cheeks as she answered with repeated cries of, "Here I am."

Finally, the flashlight shone on her and in the glow she could see the uniform of a park security officer with his name badge, Julius. His broad smile was comforting as he put out his big, black hand. "You're lucky. Your friend, Michael, phoned. He told me you are here; otherwise…" He shook his head. "Ay, ay, ay, come, Lauren, follow me." He led her silently in a welcome pool of light all the way down to the information center where he unlocked a gate to let her out into the car park. "How are you going home?" he asked.

"I have my car. It's in the bottom car park. I'll be fine now, thank you."

"Be careful. I think it's safer inside here than out there. You mustn't walk around by yourself at night. It's not safe. There are *tsotsis* out there, you know. You know what *tsotsis* are? They're very bad. And you're a girl; for you it's extra dangerous. Ay, too much trouble. Too many people come to Cape Town looking for work, and when they can't find it they become *tsotsis*."

"I know. It's a big problem."

"And they come from all over Africa now; Zimbabwe, Malawi, Nigeria."

"I've noticed that."

He paused for a moment and looked at her. "I hear you speaking— are you American?" She nodded and he frowned as he reprimanded her, "You're not in America now. I won't let my wife and daughters go out alone at night. Does your father know you do this?"

"My father is dead. But he would also have told me to be careful," Lauren replied. "Please don't worry, I'm going straight to my car and then I'm going to meet my friend. I made a big mistake falling asleep up there. I'm sorry you had to come and find me, but thank you so much. Please don't worry."

He stared at her with a concerned expression and then shook his head. "Your father will be shouting in his grave at you."

She smiled at him. "Julius, thank you for finding me. I promise I'm usually careful; it's just that I fell asleep. Thank you very much for your help."

He shook his head as he locked the gate after her but smiled as she turned to wave. "*Hamba gahle,*" he shouted after her in a traditional Zulu farewell, meaning, "Go safely."

She ran down the stairs leading to the lower car park and saw her dark blue Volkswagen Jetta at the far end, the only car left at the end of the day. She cursed inwardly that there hadn't been a nearer parking spot earlier, as she now had to walk about two hundred and fifty yards in total darkness, without any streetlights. Julius's warnings rang in her ears and she glanced around anxiously. There were big bushes spaced intermittently in the car park which she avoided, pleased that her car was out in the open. Remembering a safety tip given in an orientation meeting at Cape Town University, she removed her car keys from her backpack and positioned a key so that it protruded between two of her fingers, ready to stab an attacker's eyes. It seemed a futile method of defense then and now it seemed even more improbable.

Halfway across the parking lot, she heard a noise behind her. Glancing over her shoulder she saw a shadowy form emerge from behind a bush. She quickened her pace as she heard footsteps behind her on the paved road. They were getting louder and closer, and Lauren began to run for her car, not wasting time to look back again. She was almost there, relieved that her keys were at the ready when she felt her backpack slipping off her shoulder. There was no time to retrieve it and she let it drop. "They can have it," she thought, "I just need to get to my car." Thankfully she was there and tried to put the key in the door, but it was the key for the gas tank, not the door and ignition key. She quickly changed it and managed to get the door open. She jumped into the driver's seat and pulled the door closed after her, shoving the key into the ignition. The car kicked into life but as she tried to throw it into gear, the door was yanked open again and the coldness of hard metal was pressed against her temple.

"I'll shoot if you try to drive away. Get out the car quickly," a gruff voice commanded her.

She was paralyzed with shock, feeling the gun against her head. Her hesitation enraged the attacker. "I said get out," he hissed.

Lauren numbly took her foot off the clutch and climbed out the car. She faced a dark form with a woolen ski mask over his face, and an accomplice standing behind him also wearing a mask. While her attacker pointed his gun at her, the accomplice grabbed her keys, then pulled some rope from his pocket and roughly tied her hands together behind her back, before wrapping duct tape tightly over her mouth. She was too stunned and afraid to offer resistance.

"Do we take her or shoot her?" he asked. They looked at one another and shrugged their shoulders. "Might be nice, hey? Blonde. Are you blonde down there, too?" he smirked, grabbing her crotch.

The man holding the gun laughed. "I think we should take her and have a look. *Ja*, put her in the boot."

Lauren's heart was pounding wildly. The gun was used to prod her in the direction of the car trunk, then she was pulled by her hair and told to climb in; the door slammed shut entombing her in claustrophobic darkness. They seemed to drive for an eternity, sometimes at speed where she was thrown around roughly as they cornered, and sometimes very slowly. She was so afraid that her brain was not functioning; she felt totally helpless. Suddenly the car stopped and the engine turned off. She could hear voices and laughter outside the car. The trunk opened and a group of faces peered in at her. She could smell alcohol fumes coming from them as they talked to one another in a language she couldn't understand. There were six of them now; two were her attackers that she recognized by their T-shirts. Suddenly her brain began to activate and her main focus was that she needed to observe and remember as much as she could if she wanted to stay alive.

A very large man seemed to be the leader of the group, as he patted her two attackers on the backs and congratulated them. "*Bliksem*," he cursed in the vernacular, "it's a bloody good haul — nice car and a nice bit of something on the side to go with it, hey! But we must get rid of the car before any of that. We don't want anyone to come snooping. You'll have to wait a bit for us, Blondie." They all laughed and her attackers covered her with a blanket before lifting her out of the trunk and dropping her on the ground. She could smell a sharp smell of latrines that made her suspect she was in the township called Guguletu, maybe even near the kindergarten school where she worked. That was exactly how it smelled at the end of the week before the latrines were cleared on Mondays. Rough hands suddenly grabbed her feet and pulled her a distance over the hard earth into a musky shack where she was unceremoniously pushed into a corner, still with the blanket on top of her.

3

Phillip Parker's children were gathered in the living room of their old Los Gatos home at the bequest of Ned Mackay, the family attorney. They sat quietly averting their eyes, avoiding all contact, and listening to the grandfather clock ticking loudly. When they eventually heard Ned's car in the driveway, Bella jumped up to let him in the front door while Wendy and Robert rose to meet him. Howard and his wife, Tracey, looked at one another with raised eyebrows and shifted in their seats.

"I'm sorry I'm late," he apologized, "but thank you for meeting me here." He arrived with no brief case or papers, which seemed surprising. As he sat down he said, "Howard, Wendy and Isabella, I would like to offer my very sincere condolences to you. Your parents were wonderful people and will be sadly missed by all whose lives they touched. They were great philanthropists, great parents, and very simply—great people. Truly, some people slip out of life and soon it's as is they never existed. But Phillip and Edith Parker made such a huge impression on the world that they will be remembered a long time as their good work lives on. How terribly hard it must be for you to lose them both so quickly, but it was probably a blessing for them that your father went so soon after your mother." Everyone nodded politely. "Your father spoke to me only a few days ago from his hospital bed, moments before he died, with one last request—it was the last time I spoke to him." Ned looked around the room at all the faces watching him. "His last request concerned you, his children. He said that it was your mother's wish for her children to spend some time alone together to build bridges, was how he described it. To that end he requested that you three—Howard, Wendy and Isabella—spend two days at the Carmel beach house together before the will is read. He wanted nobody else to be there—no spouses, no children, and no friends. He was very specific and emphatic."

There was a collective intake of breath, followed by discontented murmurs. "Ladies and gentlemen, please don't shoot the messenger!" he said with his hands raised apologetically. "This was your parents' wish, not mine. I suggest that as today is Friday, you spend the weekend in Carmel and meet in my office on Monday at noon for the reading of the will."

***

Bella dreaded the weekend looming ahead of her as she drove by herself to the family beach house in a rental car, wanting at least that much independence. She stopped at "The Thistle Hut" alongside the road near Monterey to buy fruit and vegetables; the roadside stall had been there for as long as she could remember with greetings of *buenos dias* from workers. She made another stop at the old fish shop in Moss Landing, the smell of which triggered memories of fighting the 'fish battle' as a child. It still horrified her to see dead fish with their glassy eyes staring at her sightlessly, and the smell made her stomach heave. When the fishmonger used to place the creature on a block and chop it with his cleaver, she would always cry pitifully while Howard, the oldest, told her not to be such a baby. Her mother then always fried it the way that her father loved and he would say, "Every self-respecting Englishman eats fish and chips, now eat up. It's good for you."

"But I'm not an Englishman. I'm a Californian girl," she would wail. It varied from time to time who gave in first, but there was always a battle.

The fish were still staring at her now as she entered the shop. It was easier not to look at the whole fish, so she concentrated on the pink and fleshy salmon fillets instead. There was something comforting about the nostalgia of her mother frying fish and chips, but a relief that she would never have to eat it that way again.

She determined that the best way to cope with this enforced cohabitation with her siblings was to keep busy and distracted. Cooking a meal would help. It surprised her that her grief was overshadowed by anger and dread, which in turn made her feel slightly guilty. She wished she could have a weekend to herself at the beach house, or better still with her daughter Lauren. It was eight years since her husband, Ted, had died of pancreatic cancer and this was the first time she'd been back to Carmel. There had been so many "firsts" that she'd had to steel herself to do. Her life in Washington D.C. was far removed from her childhood days in Los Gatos, when Silicon Valley still resembled a "Valley of the Heart's Delight" as it was once called, full of orchards and canneries. Her father and mother had moved from England after World War 2 to escape the drudgery and hardship of post-war Europe. The sunshine of California was legendary and seemed an attractive alternative to gray London. Her father was an engineer who, with his partner John Keating, founded a major computer company, 'Parker Keating,' in Silicon Valley. Los Gatos was a small town in those days, but it grew fast when the semiconductor industry started pushing out the valley's fruit trees.

She had followed in her mother's footsteps and become an English teacher. Her parents had been supportive and proud when she was offered a position at Georgetown University, teaching a freshman Shakespeare class. It was there that she'd met Ted Marlowe when he was at Law School. They'd married within six months of meeting and she had lived ever since in their Georgetown townhouse, where Lauren was born a few years later. She longed for her husband and daughter now, but they both felt equally remote. Ted's deterioration had been swift after diagnosis, and he was dead before the year was out. Bella still had nightmares remembering his pain, and thinking how he shrunk into a little question mark shape of an old man.

Lauren had been a fun-loving child, but that changed when she was sixteen and her father died. From that moment, she threw herself into work and sport, never allowing herself time to reflect. It was the only way she could cope with her loss. She never vented; she just worked and drew solace from her studies and success. A little while after graduating from Georgetown University, she won a scholarship to study English-teaching in multi-lingual South Africa, immersing herself in a totally new world. It was reassuring to Bella that Lauren sounded happy again; she not only spoke of her work but about a young man she was seeing and the laughter in her voice was audible once more.

Bella was the first to arrive at the beach house and decided to try phoning her daughter again before the others arrived. It would be a little early in the morning in Cape Town, but Lauren was an early riser. She was frustrated to once more reach voice mail, but it gave her a lift to hear her daughter's voice nonetheless. "Lauren darling—it's Mom," she said, "I've tried to reach you several times but it's so difficult with the time difference. I'm in Carmel now. Wish you were here too. I'll try and call again tomorrow. Take care, darling." She felt an anxious knot inside; she hadn't been able to reach Lauren for several days now, so that she hadn't been able to tell her that her grandfather had also died. It wasn't something she wanted to leave in a message, but she might have to do so.

After quickly storing the groceries and unpacking her few belongings in the old room that she and Wendy used to share, she raced to the beach and walked in the wet sand where the incoming ripples made her jump as iciness hit her ankles. She'd forgotten the temperature of the Pacific Ocean in Northern California, and broke into a run which fell into a rhythm with the waves. She didn't have to think about Ted or Lauren, about her parents or her siblings; she didn't have to think at all. She ran until she was completely out of breath and out of view, and then collapsed on the sand, resting her chin on her knees, staring out to sea. She willed her brain to stay vacant, but the moment she caught her breath, thoughts came creeping back.

She recollected her mother discussing faith with Ted. They seemed to agree about so many things, but never religion. To her mother, it was the fabric of life and God was responsible for the good things that had happened in it. Ted had asked who was responsible for the unhappy things that had occurred, but her mother had simply shrugged. Bella thought about Howard and Tracey's zeal and fervor. They knew without any doubt what God was thinking and they were able to impart this information at any given moment. Not only did

God speak to them, but they were able to speak directly to God. At Ted's funeral they'd told Bella and Lauren that they had prayed for Ted's soul, and he would be saved. Lauren had looked confused as she asked her uncle, "From what? He's dead!"

Howard had stared at his sister with disbelief. "What have you taught your child? Has she had any religious upbringing?"

"We've taught her about love and compassion, pretty much about loving thy neighbor as thyself," Bella had replied with irritation.

"There are ten commandments," Howard had responded. "You can't just pick and choose which ones you want."

"And all this time I thought it was multiple choice!" Bella replied archly.

"It's not a joking matter, Bella. That's blasphemous," Howard had told her. "You should know better than that."

"When you are trying to grapple with grief one day, come and talk to me then. Until such time, everything you say is coming from your head and not your heart." Howard tried to respond but she pointed her finger at him and continued firmly, "Please don't tell me how to bring up my daughter, and don't try to save my husband's soul from anything. He was a compassionate man. He did good work. If there's a heaven he'll be in it. If he isn't, then I don't want to be there either. And if there isn't a heaven, then it really doesn't matter too much anyway."

These memories had been suppressed for years but now they annoyingly returned and she suddenly stamped her foot in the sand. "I don't really care whether I know the contents of the will or not. If I get excluded because I don't spend two days here, so what! I don't want to do it, and I'm not going to," she decided. She found herself instinctively looking upwards and apologizing. "I'm sorry, Mom and Dad. If Howard would apologize to me, it would be different. But he's so self-righteous, he thinks he IS God."

***

Howard drove Wendy to Carmel in his Mercedes, each of them lost in thought as the fields of artichokes and strawberries sped by. It captured their quintessential childhood memories of coming to the beach, for they always knew they were leaving school and work expectations behind when the fields turned to endless neat rows of vegetables and berries amid the dampness of coastal fog. Wendy smiled wistfully and turned to Howard. "It feels good to be here again. September is my favorite time in Carmel."

"Will the twins come down and visit you with Robert?" he asked.

"I hope so. It depends how much time they have off. They were hoping that Lauren would be here, but it was impossible for her to fly out from Cape Town in time."

Howard was silent for a moment before answering. "When last did you see Lauren?"

"At her graduation. How about you?"

"I haven't spoken to her since Ted's funeral—nor Bella either."

Wendy frowned. "Is there something else you should be telling me to complete the story?"

Howard sighed deeply. "Ask Bella. I don't think she and Ted brought Lauren up with any religious teaching whatsoever. It's unbelievable that a sister of mine could do that. Anyway, she went off like a firecracker as usual—you never know with her. One minute we were talking and the next minute she was shouting. She was very rude to Tracey and to me, and we were very hurt. She's never learnt to control her emotions."

Wendy stared out the window watching the green rows fly by. She tried to keep her eyes fixed on one row of artichokes, but they sped by too fast. It was like trying to watch a particular droplet on a waterfall. She never could. She cleared her throat and said, "It was hardly a time one would expect her to be in control of her emotions, Howard. My God, I can't imagine how I would cope if Robert were to die."

"Well, Isabella showed such hostility and scorn towards us that it felt like a slap in the face."

"I don't think I want to get involved. It's between you and Bella."

Silence returned and Wendy thought that she was beginning to understand why her parents had made this strange request for their children to spend two days together, unencumbered by anyone or anything else. She remembered her father's self-recrimination about unfinished business just before he died, and felt sure that this weekend was tied to that. What her role was to be in it she wasn't sure.

Once they were at the cottage, Howard wandered down to the beach disconsolately. He hated being without Tracey and resented this demand made by his parents, but it was the least he could do to respect their wishes. The sun was low in the sky, glowing fiery orange and tinting the gray clouds around it with color. The sea and the wet sand began to reflect the same vibrancy as he stood watching, and it felt like a revelation to him. "Thank you God. Thank you for reminding me of your presence and magnificence," he whispered.

It had been hard to follow in his eminently successful father's footsteps, and his heavenly father seemed easier to get on with and less demanding. He felt stupid and inadequate next to Phillip Parker. His mother, Edith, was his champion. She'd believed in his ability, and always assured him that he had the answers to everything inside him; he just had to give them time. He felt important to his mother, and with that confidence he could conquer anything until his father walked into the room. It wasn't actually that Phillip Parker was tough on his son. He found him difficult because the boy was resentful and brooding, making conversation difficult and slow. Time was a precious commodity. Phillip tried hard to maintain a balance between his work and family life, but success had its demands on his time. His daughters were quick and lively, although very different from one another. Each of them amused their father and delighted him with their laughter and chatter, but he found Howard to be quiet and sullen. The distance between them seemed to grow over the years, and neither of them ever managed to change that.

Howard had married Tracey late in life and she'd brought a new sense of confidence to him. He'd met her while at a Christian camp in the Sierras where he was a counselor. She had grown up on a bayou in Arkansas; her mother worked at a diner and taught Bible school, her father was a trucker. The man was on the road for most of her childhood years and then, when she was a young teenager, he drove off to Missouri and never returned.

Tracey was a very good-looking dancer, and shortly after high school she moved west to Reno, Nevada, where she was employed in revues at different casinos. The men she met there were sometimes good friends, but gay and not interested in her at all, or else they revolted her with their lecherous overtures. However, one summer she was invited by a friend to help with entertainment at a camp and that was where she met Howard. His straightforward honesty was appealing, and by the end of the week she knew that he was the man for her. He made no immediate sexual advances which she found refreshing, and when she showed interest in his religious beliefs, he was enraptured with her. He invited her to visit him in the Bay Area, and within two months he had proposed to her. Their marriage was a happy one, only saddened by their inability to have a child. Doctors had told them that often stress can be a reason preventing conception, and all tests so far had shown no physical reason for infertility. However, after ten years of marriage, Howard felt sure that it was not meant to be. He had suggested adoption, but Tracey refused and he was silently pleased about that. He felt they were a team in everything they did and thought, as if she was the part that had been missing in his childhood. Together they were invincible and he wanted nothing more to complete his life.

As he stood now, staring at the ever-changing reflections in the sand, he saw a figure so small that it looked like a sandpiper, striding and running towards him, unwittingly chasing gulls and pelicans as they scavenged for their evening meal from the ocean. As the figure grew nearer he realized it was Bella. By then it was too late to retreat so he stood his ground, watching her. The way she moved was so like his mother that he choked. If only she were as gentle, but she had their father's ways about her.

Bella was out of breath by the time she reached Howard, and she had to grasp her sides and bend over for a while until she was able to talk. "I'm heading out," she finally said as she straightened.

"What do you mean?" he asked.

"I'm leaving, Howard."

"You're not spending the weekend here like we're supposed to?" He felt an odd mixture of relief and concern.

"Nope."

"That's outrageous Bella. Why ever not? You've come all the way here—why on earth won't you stay?"

She kicked the sand under her feet and then looked up at him defiantly. "Because I can't bear it, that's why. And I want to speak to my daughter. I can't get any decent reception here. I want to go back to Los Gatos and call her from there."

"What if we agree not to speak to one another at all—would you stay then?" he asked quietly. "We're all here now, and this is what Mom and Dad wanted. Try and call Lauren on the land line in the house instead of your cell phone. That should work without problems. Come on Bella; let's make a truce for the weekend like we used to do when we were children. Remember how Mom sometimes made us stop talking to one another for a day?" She frowned and continued to stare at the sea. At length she nodded her head in acquiescence. Silently they retraced their steps and were welcomed by the warmth of the fire Wendy had lit in the living room.

She turned from stoking the fire and greeted them. "I was going to suggest we go out for dinner but I see you've taken care of that, Bella. A good idea. I ran out and bought some wine. I couldn't remember who drinks red or white. It's so nice to be back in the land of wine and wonderful fresh food. I got some lovely cheese and biscuits too." Neither Howard nor Bella said a word, so Wendy raced on to fill an awkward silence, "Shall we open a bottle now? Are you both ready for some wine?"

"I'd love a glass of Chardonnay. Thanks, Wendy," replied Bella as she tried again to reach Lauren. There was still no reply. "I don't understand why I can't reach my daughter," she said, shaking her head. "I wish there was someone in Cape Town I could call for help."

"You could always get in touch with the American Embassy," suggested Wendy.

"Yes, I suppose I could. Lauren would be so indignant though if nothing's wrong. Maybe she's away for the weekend or something. But she usually tells me these things."

"Maybe something came up at the last minute. Perhaps she's tried to reach you at home."

"No, she knows I'm in California. I e-mailed her and left her messages. Maybe there's something wrong with her cell phone. I'll just have to keep trying I suppose." She shrugged her shoulders and sighed. "I'll get busy cooking the artichokes now. The salmon shouldn't take too long, but I'm not sure what equipment we have for artichokes."

"All we need is a big pot of water and I'm sure Mom had that. Howard, do you know where the pots are kept?" asked Wendy.

"No. Not my department. I'll open the wine. Red or white for you Wendy?" He beat a hasty retreat to look for a wine opener, leaving his two sisters in the kitchen.

"The more things change the more they stay the same," muttered Bella. "Not my department...What *is* his department? Talking to God?"

Wendy found herself whistling suddenly. She called after her brother that she would have white as well and continued whistling an unrecognizable song, determined not to be drawn into the fray. Bella glared at her and then muttered, "You really have become Mom."

"I'll take that as a compliment," Wendy replied.

The evening progressed with difficulty. Wendy soon realized that she was the only one who could hold a three-way conversation, which made general chat difficult and strained. However she was relieved that at least her siblings were tolerating being in the same room as one another, even if it meant not speaking. Two days would pass quickly she reasoned, and this was what her parents wanted. Clearly her parents wanted their children to reconcile their differences. They ate their dinner in silence and any attempt at conversation by Wendy was met with monosyllabic answers. As she poured herself another glass of wine, she finally exploded with annoyance. "It's time you two grew up. We're here because our parents have died and we should be drawing comfort from one another; we're here because they want us to talk to one another and be friends; but you two continue with your stupid, petty disagreements. It's really sad that they died knowing you never outgrew your adolescent bickering. Can't you show some respect for them and look beyond your differences?"

Before anyone could reply, the telephone rang shrilly. They all looked at one another but nobody moved. Then they all moved at the same moment. Howard got there first. "Yes, that would be fine," he said after listening to the caller. "What's the purpose of it though?" he inquired. After another silence he said, "Very well then. We'll see you tomorrow."

"We'll see who tomorrow?" Wendy asked, "I thought we had to be here without anyone else."

Howard replied, "Apparently we're getting a visit from old Ned Mackay, the attorney, and he's bringing two visitors from England. He wouldn't say who or why, just that Mom and Dad had requested it. They'll be here after lunch."

4

Phillip Davis stared out of the train window as he sped towards London on the 9 a.m. express. He would be arriving at Waterloo in half an hour and would then have to battle traffic in a cab. He hoped it would be sufficient time to reach an 11.15 meeting with a solicitor situated in Holborn. It would probably be quicker to catch the underground, but these days he found that too claustrophobic. When he retired and moved from London to the old family home in East Sussex, he wondered how he had ever managed to spend 35 years living in the city and dealing with the masses of people and fumes. He and his wife, Cynthia, never returned to London unless it was to visit their son and his family, or to attend the theatre or an art show.

Phillip had been surprised to get a letter from Woods and Bailey, a well-known firm of London solicitors. His own legal dealings were with a small firm in Rye. He was even more surprised when he opened the letter and read that he had inherited an undisclosed sum of money in America, and needed to attend a meeting to find out more. He didn't even know anyone very well in America, just the people he'd come in contact with over the years on his business trips. After he'd come down from Oxford in 1961, he served articles with Smythe, Bird and Walker in the City and qualified as an accountant. Fairly soon after that, he'd been offered a job at Parker Keating and had risen through the ranks to become U.K. Director of Finance for the giant U.S. computer company. It had been a secure and successful career, affording him opportunities to travel and meet interesting people, as well as earn a very generous salary.

There was a distinct feel of autumn in the air as he entered the sober-looking offices of Woods and Bailey at 11.20 a.m. He noticed the middle-aged secretary glance disapprovingly at her watch as he approached her desk, but she quickly adjusted the expression on her face into a more welcoming smile to greet him. "You must be Mr. Davis. We've been expecting you. Mr. Bailey will see you now." He was shown into a sumptuous office with an enormous mahogany pedestal desk at the opposite end, in front of tall windows that overlooked a small park. Mr. Malcolm Bailey, a corpulent white-haired man in a pin-striped suit, arose and shook his hand heartily. "How nice to meet you," he spoke in a resonant voice and then indicated a chair, "Please take a seat. Would you care for some tea?" Mrs. Potts was dispatched to bring some refreshment and the two men settled into comfortable leather chairs where they exchanged pleasantries about the weather, traffic, and life in the city as opposed to life in the country, before the attorney cleared his throat and produced two large brown envelopes. He handed one of these to Phillip and proceeded to open the other himself. "I am giving you this to read at your leisure, in private. I'm sure you are mystified. Let me try and explain as much as I can. Ah, here's the tea. Thank you very much." They were silent as the tea was poured and served and the discreet Mrs. Potts left the room.

"It's difficult to know where to begin the story, so let me start by saying that you are likely to be shocked and surprised by what I tell you." He cleared his throat several times. "I suppose it all began back in 1939 when, as you know, we went to war with Germany. In that year, a young woman found herself in a compromised position, meaning she was unmarried and pregnant with her young man off to fight. He was missing, presumed dead, after his plane was shot down over the Channel. She was desperate; single mothers were widows, not unmarried women in those days, and she felt pressured to agree to have distant cousins adopt the child. This was not done lightly. The cousin was Mr. Edward Davis, and his wife Sarah."

"Good heavens are you talking about my parents?" asked Phillip.

"The same," replied Mr. Bailey. "And you were the baby."

"This is preposterous. I wasn't adopted."

The attorney handed Phillip an official adoption form for his scrutiny and was silent while the information was digested. After a while he added softly, "As you know, Edward died in a bombing raid on London, which you and Sarah escaped. Ironically your biological father was not killed after all, but instead was picked up by a passing German ship and spent some time in a prisoner of war camp. When he returned after the war was over, he married his sweetheart, your biological mother, and only then did she tell him about your existence. They hoped that Sarah Davis would return you to them, but she refused and insisted that they remain anonymous in your life." He paused. The only sound in the room was a clock ticking and cups clinking on saucers. "It was a difficult decision for all parties concerned. In despair, after four years of trying to persuade Sarah to change her mind, your biological parents decided to leave Britain and move to America where they started new lives."

"I begin to see how this is tying together," Phillip said pensively. "Good heavens above!"

"Sarah Davis had a difficult time financially. She stayed in touch with your parents, keeping them informed about your development but never relenting on her insistence that they remain anonymous in your life. At first she refused to accept any money from them as she wanted to remain independent. However your biological father was not only a war hero, he was also a brilliant engineer, garnering riches in California when he founded a very large company. At this point in his life, he was able to persuade Sarah to accept a very generous, regular amount of money for your education and upkeep, and to buy a home for her, in your name, outside Rye—the same home in which you now live. He also placed a large sum of money in trust for you which you came into on your twenty-first birthday."

"But that was from my father," Phillip exclaimed.

"Yes it was, Mr. Davis. But it was from your biological father, not Edward Davis."

"Good Heavens!"

"Eventually your father was able to make an agreement with Sarah. When I say eventually, that is exactly what I mean. Sarah was diagnosed ten years ago with Alzheimer's disease, as you know. At this point she didn't want you to be burdened with the expense of looking after her. She approached your father and made a pact that he would pay for her to live in the Glendale Home for Assisted Living, covering all her private medical expenses, and then only when she died, or after the death of both your biological father and mother (whichever came first), could the truth be revealed to you. I am sorry to inform you that by the strangest quirk of fate, both your biological parents died within a week of one another."

"Good Heavens. This is bizarre."

"In terms of your parents' will, you inherit $25 million."

"My godfathers! This is more than I can absorb. Twenty-five million dollars. Good Heavens!" Phillip gripped the arms of his chair in shock and swallowed hard, gulping several times. Finally he leaned forward in his chair, "Mr. Bailey, will you please tell me who my parents were?"

"I apologize, Mr. Davis. There is so much information to give you that I'm sorry I overlooked those important facts. Your father and mother were Phillip and Edith Parker."

"Phillip Parker of Parker Keating?"

"Yes, Mr. Davis. You are their first child."

Phillip stared and then frowned. "Does that mean they had more children?"

"Happily, yes. They had another son followed by two daughters. You have a brother, Howard, and a sister, Isabella, who both live in America; and another sister Wendy who lives here in England, married to an Englishman called Robert Downing. Wendy and Isabella have children, but Howard does not."

Phillip Davis stared out of the window, stunned. "I met Phillip and Edith Parker you know, on several occasions. When I was in the States on business, I was often invited to dinner at a restaurant after meetings, and she would be there too. Of course yes, Howard Parker is on the Board, but I've never met him. He was never at any of the meetings I was invited to attend."

"I've looked after your parents' affairs in England all these years. I knew your father a long time—he went to school with my father, you see. I shall miss him greatly. His payments to you have always been handled by me; I transferred the money to Sarah's account so that you wouldn't know its source. There are certain conditions in the will, however, which have to be met."

"And what are they?"

"You are required to fly to California tomorrow and meet your brother and sisters. That's all."

"Tomorrow?"

"Yes. I will accompany you, and when you are there, you are all required to spend a day together without spouses, at the family home in Carmel. They do not know of your existence; I am required to inform them and introduce you. After that, the four of you are expected to spend a day at the Carmel house together, and then drive to San Francisco for the reading of the will. I'm sorry to spring it on you like this. It's terribly sad that Phillip and Edith couldn't be the ones to tell you about your birth and adoption. A darn tragedy really. I think they hoped they would outlive Sarah Davis once she was diagnosed with this terrible disease. However, that was not to be. Such a shame." Malcolm Bailey cleared his throat before continuing, "Are you agreeable then? Can you leave tomorrow?"

"I suppose so," murmured Phillip. "I'll have to speak to my wife Cynthia and put her in the picture."

"Of course. I'll have Mrs. Potts take care of the travel arrangements right away. Do you think your wife would like to join you?"

"I doubt it. She runs an antique store that we own and wouldn't want to leave it without some forward planning."

"Will you want to spend the night in London or return to Rye?" asked the solicitor.

"Oh goodness me, I'll have to return to put Cynthia in the picture as I said, and of course I need to pack my bags. What time do we depart?"

"I took the liberty to check and there is a 1 p.m. flight we could catch from Heathrow. If it's all right with you, I'll meet you at 11 in Terminal 1 at the British Airways First Class Desk. We'll have electronic tickets so all you need is your passport. I hope that won't be a problem for you."

"Fortunately my passport is current, and by the way, I think you'd better call me Phillip."

"Very good, Phillip, and please call me Malcolm. I'm sure there's a lot going on in your head but try and get a decent night's sleep. I'll see you tomorrow at Heathrow unless there is anything else you need?" he added, rising to see his client to the door.

"Not at the moment. I'm sure when I've thought about it a bit I'm going to have a lot of questions, but not at the moment. Good bye and thank you."

Phillip Davis made his way back to Waterloo in a daze. It was difficult to know which was the harder to digest: that his parents weren't whom he thought they were; that he had a brother and two sisters; or that he had just inherited $25 million. He upgraded himself to a first class fare for his return, deciding that would be his choice from now on. Settling himself into a very comfortable seat, he removed the brown envelope he'd been given and began to read the familiar handwriting of Sarah Davis.

My Dearest Phillip,

When you read this you will already know that I am not the woman who bore you, although I have been your mother all these years and you could not have been closer to my heart if I had given birth to you myself.

Your father's second cousin, Edith Herriman, was the woman who brought you into this world. Her young man had left for the war, but he left her with child as well. She gave you up to me for adoption while she was still pregnant and so I watched your development keenly and I was there when you were born. You were placed in my arms without her ever holding you, as that was the way it was done in those days. I'm sure it was hard for her, but you brought such joy to my life and your father's. You were everything we could have hoped for and you grew into such an admirable man that I know your father would have been enormously proud had he lived to see you grown.

Phillip and Edith Parker were very generous and paid for your education as well as our home. You should never feel that they rejected you. They did not. They would dearly have loved to take you back when he returned from the war and they married, but by then, your father and I had legally adopted you, and you were everything in my life after your father was killed. I took advice from Dr. Winter, our family practitioner at the time, and he advised me against telling you that you were adopted. He said that it would only unsettle you and could adversely affect your emotional development. You were such a happy, well-adjusted little boy that the thought of undermining your well-being, especially after the trauma of your father's death, was unacceptable. Phillip and Edith honoured my wishes.

It would have remained a closed book until I was diagnosed last week with Alzheimer's disease. Now everything has changed. Darling Phillip, I have decided to reveal your true parentage to relieve you of two burdens. Nobody knows yet what causes this terrible disease but some feel it might be genetic. I never thought I would be happy to tell you that you don't share my genes. I pray that you will never find yourself, as I am doing, forgetting your life inch by inch. My distant memories are the ones I remember well — I can't quite remember how old you are now, my darling, but I think you are old enough to understand why I kept this information from you. My comfort is that you have Edith and Phillip's genes, not mine. They are of sound mind and have agreed to pay for my care as this disease progresses so that you will not be burdened with that expense. They are good people and you are a wonderful son. If I die before them, please tell them that they gave me the greatest gift possible when Edith entrusted you to my care.

Dear boy, this is a lot for you to take in. Whatever choices you make, I know you will always be compassionate and wise. I suspect that you will inherit a considerable amount of money from them one day. I trust that you will use it wisely and compassionately too. Never lose sight of who you are.

God bless you always,
Your loving mother

Phillip read the letter through several times and wiped tears from his cheeks. He slowly refolded it and placed it in his breast pocket. It felt sacred. He thought of his mother as she sat now, staring unknowingly at him when he visited her, and he wished that she had communicated this information to him earlier. Nothing would ever have made him feel differently about her, and he would have wanted her to know that. She should never have feared that he would have loved her less for not having borne him. She was his mother, and this letter in his pocket was one of the greatest sacrifices she had made for him, he recognized that. He unconsciously fingered the piece of paper and sighed deeply.

5

Mike Rousseau sat anxiously at the Forester's Arms. It had been hard to hear when he called Lauren, but her text message said that she was stranded a little way up the mountain above Kirstenbosch Gardens. A quick call to Park Security brought a return call from an officer on duty to say that she had been found safely. He nursed a Castle Lager and looked at his watch; she should be here soon as Kirstenbosch was very close by. Mike was a scientist working on his PHD thesis at the University of Cape Town, known locally as UCT. He had started out trying to develop a desalination process that would be cost-effective for use extensively in Africa, helping to solve the continent's continual droughts. However his work had led him onto more extensive ground-breaking research; converting water to fuel. His research and thesis were almost complete and he felt pleased with the results, although anxious about what the next step in his life would be. He felt it should be marketing his ideas, but that wasn't something with which he felt comfortable. Science was his field he thought to himself, not marketing. He had met Lauren on campus when she spoke at a symposium on Aids Education. He was captivated by her petite body and her long blonde hair. Her face was serious with intense blue eyes, but when she began to speak they lit up and became very animated. Her soft voice was appealing, and her American accent made her stand out from the crowd. He wasted no time introducing himself and getting to know her.

As he sipped his beer, he remembered how calmly she had responded to hecklers at that meeting. A few students had shouted insults, suggesting she take herself back to the U.S.A. and solve their messy problems instead of minding other people's business. Someone shouted, "Yankee go home." Lauren had simply waited until they stopped, and then continued saying, "I fully intend to go home and I'm well aware of many problems there too. But the fact is that Aids is a global problem, and I'm here now. If I can bring about change for the better while I'm here, that's what I prefer to do. It seems more useful than simply going to heckle at meetings. I've always believed that actions speak louder than words." The majority of the crowd applauded her loudly and there were whistles of appreciation.

He felt frustrated with her concerns about their relationship. She was clearly attracted to him, and he had made it very obvious how he felt. It was another six months at least before she planned to return to America, so as far as he was concerned there was no reason not to get involved with one another. Who knew what would happen in the future, but he was keen to see how things worked out between them now. He felt a stir as he pictured her lithe body striding out on a hike, her blonde pony tail bouncing as she walked. He thought of her lying semi-naked on the couch and smiled as he took another gulp of beer. One of these days soon he would take her home to meet his parents on their wine farm, Belle Terre.

His smile turned to a frown as he looked at his watch again and saw that it had been half an hour since the call from the security guard. He dialed Lauren's cell phone but there was no reply and he heard her voice mail message begin. He wondered whether she'd gone back to her flat to change, and decided to wait another ten minutes before calling once more. He finished up his beer at the bar and after trying unsuccessfully to call her again, decided he would make his way to her flat to look for her, stopping at Kirstenbosch on the way.

In hardly any time he pulled into the parking lot and could see immediately that there were no cars. He drove all the way around in a loop and was just heading out when he saw something lying in the road. His lights showed that it was a backpack so he drove next to it, quickly opened the door, leant over and brought the bag into his car.

He shut the door and locked it again before opening the clasp to find a wallet inside. With his heart in his mouth, he opened it to see Lauren's driver's license looking at him. He went cold. "Goddammit!" he shouted. "This can't be happening." He dialed her number one more time, willing her to answer, but he heard the phone ring in the backpack. He called security again and spoke to Julius, who assured Mike that he had let her out of the gate and she had gone to her car saying she was going to meet a friend. His next call was to the police, who were already burdened by countless cases of missing persons, stolen cars, burglaries, rapes and murders.

"We don't know that she's missing, do we?" the policeman at the desk answered. "You've found her backpack which she lost. There's nothing we can do until we have a missing person."

In a fury, Mike drove to the nearest police station and presented himself in person to the sergeant in charge that night. When he heard the same response again, he exploded. "What are you waiting for? Rape and murder? She was supposed to meet me, her backpack is lying in a car park, and her car is gone. How many more reasons do you want?"

"OK, OK. Fill in a form and I'll see what I can do." The sergeant scratched around in a drawer and finally found what he was looking for, a Missing Person Form. "I need to get some more of these," he muttered.

Mike filled it in, giving details to the best of his ability about Lauren. The sergeant took the paper and dropped it on a desk, saying, "I'll give it to the detectives when they call in."

"Why don't you call them first?" demanded Mike.

"Listen, you do your job and I'll do mine. This is the proto…um…the protocol. Now we'll call you if we need anything more."

Mike turned on his heel and stormed out the door, feeling a sense of frustration and anger. Every minute that ticked by was a minute more danger for Lauren. She had clearly been carjacked, an every day occurrence. He didn't care about her car that much, but what might happen to her made his heart race with fear. He had to think clearly…the police were not filling him with confidence. He drove to her flat first, just to make sure that she wasn't there, racing at break-neck speed and then pounding on the door. Footsteps could be heard, followed by a voice saying, "Who is it?" It was her flat mate, Barbara Dumelo, whom university housing had placed together with Lauren.

"It's me, Mike." He heard the chain and locks being undone and the door opened. Barbara stood with a Coke can in her hand and smiled at him. Without even a hello, he blurted out, "Is Lauren here?"

"No Michael, it's just me."

"Christ. What am I going to do?"

"What's the problem?" asked Barbara. "Do you want to come in?" The smile had gone from her face and she looked anxiously at him. "What's going on?"

"I think she's been carjacked."

"Oh my God! Have you called the police?"

Mike grunted. "They're worse than bloody useless. I think I'm going to get hold of the American Consul and get him to kick some arse. The police will do bugger-all unless they're forced to. Have you got a phone directory?" With haste he found the number and got through to an after-hours assistant on the 24 hour hotline.

"Are you a U.S. citizen?" the assistant asked.

"No, I'm not."

"Then I'm sorry you should go to the police."

"Dammit, listen to me. *I'm* not a U.S. citizen, but the person missing is. That's why I'm calling."

"Just a moment," the voice replied. He could hear some clicking and then, "I'm transferring you now."

"Good evening, this is a Consular assistant. How can I help you?"

With relief Mike gave his name and rattled out his story in detail, adding that the police were sitting on their hands as time was ticking away.

"Thank you Mr. Rousseau. Can you give me some details? What is the name of the woman who has been abducted?"

"Lauren Marlowe."

"What! You're sure of that? Oh my God. Stay on the line please Mr. Rousseau. I'm going to contact the Consul. He will want to be informed immediately." Mike waited a few seconds before a voice came back on the line, asking him to make his way over to the new American Consulate immediately. "It's in Tokai. Take the M3 and just keep going until you reach the 'Old Cape Road.' Turn right and you'll find us a little ways down on your right—you'll see the flag. You can't miss us. Ring the bell and security will let you in—please make sure you have some I.D. We really appreciate your assistance Mr. Rousseau."

Mike looked puzzled as he put the phone down and turned to Barb, "Boy, they're certainly 'on it.' The woman nearly hit the roof when I said Lauren's name."

Barbara nodded. "Thank goodness for that. I think Lauren's family is some sort of big deal back in the States. You'd better give me your cell phone number so that we can stay in touch. Let me know if you hear anything, and I'll do the same."

***

When Mike had repeated his story again to the Consul, he was offered a cup of coffee and asked to wait as the Ambassador was coming on the line from Pretoria and wanted to speak to him. Yet again he told his story, and finally things started to happen. "Put the Consul back on the phone please," said the Ambassador.

Mike listened to a torrent of words coming through the line, and intermittent "yes sirs," from the Consul, who then proceeded to connect the Chief of Police, the Minister of Justice and the Minister of Foreign Affairs to a conference call with himself and the Ambassador. "Gentlemen, we have a big problem and we need your immediate help," he began. "A young American woman has been abducted in the area of Kirstenbosch, probably in the car park there. Her name is Lauren Marlowe, and her grandfather is Phillip Parker, the founder of Parker Keating in the States. I want you to do whatever it takes to find this woman, as fast as possible."

There was some discussion to which the Consul replied, "Exactly. Don't waste any time. The moment the thugs know who she is—that is if they don't know already—we'll probably be looking at a huge ransom demand. I have photos of her on file which I'll email you immediately, and I've got details of the car for you. It's a dark blue Jetta, 2003 model, registration number CA 636-615. Thank you, gentlemen." The Consul replaced the phone and turned to Mike. "Thanks for your quick thinking, Mr. Rousseau. Ms. Marlowe is a

39

very fine person from a very fine family. Obviously we care about all our citizens, but some of them are more at risk than others. It's a bit like the Patty Hearst saga, if you remember that dark episode."

"I had no idea who her family is," answered Mike. "She often spoke about them, but I didn't know who they were. Maybe it would be good if her captors knew."

"No, no. She'll become a bargaining tool."

"Exactly. She'll be valuable to them. Right now, presuming they don't know her identity, she's disposable. I don't need to say anymore about what might happen."

"I'm aware of the danger she's in but the Ambassador wants to try and find her without any incident or bringing attention to her identity."

"Without any incident? What the hell do you think a carjacking and abduction is? With all due respect, it sounds like her family can afford to pay a ransom and I'm sure they'd rather have her back alive and unharmed. Why don't you ask them?"

The Consul nodded his head. "There's truth in what you say, Mr. Rousseau. The Ambassador, however, is the one to decide and he is trying to reach Mrs. Marlowe right now. Maybe that will be discussed. Thank you again for your help. We'll keep you informed."

As Mike made his way out of the consulate building to his car, his cell phone rang. It was Barbara. "What's happening?" she asked.

Mike explained and Barbara gasped. "It's too late to hush it up I'm afraid. A journalist has been here already asking for details. She was hanging around the police station when you went in and she sniffed out a story when she heard it was an American girl who'd been snagged. It'll be in *The Argus* tomorrow morning. She took that photo of Lauren and you that was on the fridge, so that'll be in as well."

"Well to tell you the truth, I think that's great. The more publicity it gets, the better, as far as I'm concerned. It'll throw the cat amongst the pigeons."

6

Phillip Davis watched the San Francisco Bay underneath him as the plane came in to land. It never ceased to thrill him flying over the Golden Gate Bridge, then the Bay Bridge, and then down to the city at the south end of the bay, San Jose, before turning around and approaching the runway from the south. Sometimes on clear days, it was almost as if the pilot liked to do a little sightseeing as a reward for the endless daytime flight from London to California—flying west after the sun, but never catching it. When the plane finally lowered enough it seemed as though the landing was going to be on water, and then at the last minute, just when one's heart was in one's mouth, the runway reached up and embraced the aircraft. Then you were in California.

It felt as if a part of him had known intuitively that he had a tie to California. He always felt a thrill being here that he didn't feel anywhere else in the world, except at home in Sussex. California had always appealed to him with its "can-do" attitude and joie-de-vivre. It seemed so much freer of expected form, allowing innovative ideas to fall on fertile ground. He was still absorbing the fact that his father was one of those innovators. He wondered what life would have been like if he had grown up here, living with his biological parents. As he felt the bump of the landing, he told himself to stop thinking about it. He and Cynthia had discussed the turn of events until the early hours of the morning, and they agreed it was important not to lose sight of who he was because of who had brought him up. When he thought of his mother, it would always be Sarah, and it made it easier in some ways that he would never meet with Edith and Phillip Parker, knowing they were his biological parents. However he was both excited and nervous to meet his brother and sisters. Being brought up as an only child had been lonely at times, and he often envied his friends who had siblings. Now that he had three of them, he felt quite anxious about the new role. He smiled thinking how his grandson had been out of sorts when a baby sister arrived and he had lost his only child status. "And he was only four!" he thought to himself. "I'm sixty-four."

Phillip and Malcolm Bailey disembarked quickly from the first class section and caught a cab to the St. Francis Hotel on Union Square. They looked forward to a good night's sleep before journeying to Carmel, but first the two men decided to freshen up and catch a cable car for a short ride to Fisherman's Wharf. Here they could enjoy a light meal; Phillip loved the local clam chowder and crab cakes, and it was invigorating to stroll around the wharf after being in an aircraft for such a long time. All in all, life felt very pleasing.

Ned Mackay, the Parker's attorney in San Francisco, fetched Malcolm and Phillip at their hotel promptly at ten o'clock the next morning as arranged. He was anxious to meet Malcolm, with whom he had communicated by letter and phone, as well as this man who had materialized in the Parker family tree. When he saw Phillip approaching, it shocked him to see how similar the son was to his father. Phillip Davis looked like Phillip Parker of twenty-five years ago. He had the same tall height and frame, as well as the angular face and a full head of white hair. He was as distinguished looking as the founder of Parker Keating, and Ned imagined how strange it must have been for his client to have watched this man through the years, knowing the relationship but being unable to acknowledge it. He marveled that nobody had ever commented on the similarity in looks. Ned introduced himself and smiled as he heard Phillip's English accent, so similar to that of the father he had never known.

It was a fine September morning and the drive down the coast to Carmel was beautiful. As they climbed into the Santa Cruz

Mountains, Ned pointed out the redwoods that densely forested the area. Once they reached the summit they had a clear view of the Pacific Ocean and Monterey Bay in front of them, blue and sparkling in the sunshine. From the crest, the panoramic view of forest and ocean made it hard to believe that this was such a densely populated area. Highway 17 was a windy road down to the town of Santa Cruz, despite being the main artery to the coast through the mountains, and Ned took it slowly around the bends. "We have plenty of time," he assured them, "so there's no need to rush. In fact we could stop for lunch on the pier here, as we're only expected after lunch in Carmel. What do you think?"

"We're in your hands," Phillip answered. "It sounds very nice to me. What about you Malcolm? Can you handle a bit more seafood?"

"Sounds good to me. Nothing like fish and chips!" he laughed.

Ned drove to the end of the pier and the men could hear sea lions barking as they climbed out the car. Seagulls swarmed around the many fishermen and a pelican watched hopefully from the railing for a bit of lost bait. Phillip felt the slight tension he'd been feeling ease as he soaked up the carefree atmosphere of this seaside town. When he turned around he could see a fairground on the beachfront that reminded him of Brighton—as he watched the roller coaster cars plying their way up and down and round about, he made a mental note that he would have to return with his grandchildren. His son, Adam, had a four-year-old boy and a baby daughter, and his daughter, Fran, had eight-year-old twin girls. He felt loathe to pull himself away from this pleasant place, but also keen to press on and meet his new family. As they ate their lunch, he found it harder and harder to concentrate on the conversation. His thoughts were elsewhere. "We have about twenty minutes or so from here to the beach house," Ned announced as they climbed back in the car. "You'll love Carmel too. I'm sure that the Parkers will show you around. You're probably wondering what they're like?"

Malcolm could tell that Phillip was getting tense and irritated by the chatter. He answered for him by saying, "It's all been so sudden. I can't imagine how he must be feeling, and likewise, it's going to be a shock for his siblings too."

"Yes indeed," said Phillip and stared out of the window at the rows of artichokes on either side of the road, indicating his desire to remain silent. Many people find silence in company an uncomfortable thing, and Ned was one of these people. He was accustomed to talk at all times and he found these two diffident Englishmen awkward. Finally he turned on the radio and they continued on their way without conversation, listening instead to Dr. Dean Edell giving advice on warts.

***

Although they all slept late the next morning, Bella was up first. She immediately tried to call Lauren but this time she couldn't even reach her voicemail. A voice announced that the customer she had dialed was unavailable at this time, and she should try her call again later. Her frustration was beginning to turn into concern. Lauren was so close to her family that the lack of communication was out of character, and if there were something wrong with her cell phone, Bella thought her daughter would have found another phone to use. She sighed deeply and bit her bottom lip as she set about making a pot of coffee, wondering who the visitors were going to be. It was all very puzzling.

The aroma of coffee awoke Wendy, who felt much revived after a good night's sleep. She pulled on her mother's bathrobe that was still hanging behind the door as she made her way into the kitchen. There she found her sister seated at the table and muttering as she punched numbers on her cell phone.

"Morning Bella," she said, leaning over to give her hug. "Sleep well?"

"I did thanks—how about you?"

"Very well thanks. What are you trying to do?"

"I haven't been able to get hold of Lauren for a few days. She doesn't even know about her grandfather yet. I've been getting her voice mail all the time and now I can't even get that. She can't make international calls easily with her cell phone, but I would've thought she'd try and call me somehow. I've tried using our land line, but that's no different."

Wendy frowned. Lauren was generally so considerate that this did seem odd. "I bet the reception is really bad down here Bella. I'm sure once we go back to San Francisco tomorrow, you'll be able to reach her."

"You're probably right." She felt reassured by Wendy's support and warmth.

They heard noises coming from Howard's room and soon he emerged as well. Looking at nobody in particular, he said, "Morning all. Are we ready for another day in paradise?"

Wendy laughed. "Mom and Dad really were lucky finding this place, weren't they? I wish I didn't live so far away and could make more use of it."

There was no mention made of their differences the previous evening, but Wendy noticed that Howard and Bella still avoided talking to one another. In a roundabout way, they all agreed to go out for brunch and be back in time for the arrival of the attorney and the mystery visitors. They strolled down Ocean Avenue and found a bistro that served a quick meal in a cheerful atmosphere. Although the crowds were beginning to make their way into town, it wasn't long before the three of them were seated at a window table, facing out onto the street. By way of making conversation, Wendy said, "I'd forgotten how wonderful service is in California. I never get tired of being told to 'have a nice day' and with a smile. Maybe sunshine does something to people." Her chatter broke the ice and her siblings laughed, but they still only spoke to her.

Wendy and Bella enjoyed window shopping as they ambled back to the house, while Howard tried to hurry them along. Finally he looked at his watch and said, "I think we need to hurry." Wendy suggested that he go on ahead and they would catch up with him shortly. Happy to escape the shopping expedition that was clearly about to ensue, he left and let himself into the house just minutes before the door bell rang. He opened the door to Ned Mackay, who smiled and said, "We're a little early. I was afraid you might not be in. Let me go and tell the other two that you're here."

"My sisters aren't here yet, but please do come in."

He walked to the car with Ned and extended a handshake as he was introduced to Phillip Davis and Malcolm Bailey. He felt a little unnerved as they walked beside him back to the house; Phillip had a familiar look about him and Howard was racking his brain to think how he knew him. They entered the living room and after the usual pleasantries were exchanged about the magnificent view, everyone sat down.

"Wendy and Isabella should be here any minute," Howard explained. "We were just in town and they couldn't resist doing a bit of shopping—a favorite pastime."

Malcolm Bailey cleared his throat and said, "I look forward to meeting them. It's very good of you to receive us at this unhappy time for you."

"Well I gather it was something that my father organized on the day he died. I'm quite baffled by it all," Howard answered.

"I'm sure you are. However I think I should wait until your sisters are here before I begin to explain what it's all about, if you don't mind," Malcolm apologized.

Howard turned to Phillip who was staring at him, and said, "Have we met before?"

Embarrassed at being caught staring, Phillip quickly looked away before facing Howard again to reply, "No, I don't believe we have."

"Are you sure? I've been trying to place you. Your face looks familiar."

"I'm sure I would have remembered," Phillip answered.

Ned chattered nervously while the other three men sat uncomfortably, wishing he would keep quiet. It was a huge relief when they heard footsteps and the door opening, followed by Wendy and Bella entering the room and saying in unison, "Sorry to keep you waiting." They placed their shopping bags on the sofa and greeted Ned, before being introduced to the visitors. Wendy was quick to offer refreshments and all agreed that a cup of tea would be very nice; she and Bella brought in a tray and served everyone. Finally Ned cleared his throat once again and began to speak. "I've been dreaming about this moment and what your father has requested me to say. The trouble is that he gave me the contents of what I was to tell you, without providing me any words with which to do it."

Wendy, Bella and Howard looked at one another nervously. Nobody said a word.

"Malcolm has looked after your parents' affairs in England for many years now, and I have taken care of things on this side of the world. Together we've been privy to a part of their lives that they sadly were never able to share with you. Let me hastily add that it wasn't their wish not to do so, but they were honor-bound. They would much rather have been the ones sitting here today and telling you what it falls to me to say," he continued. The tension was palpable.

Bella spilled her tea and muttered, "Damn it." Then she put the cup down sharply and said, "Could you please just hurry up and tell us whatever it is? My God, are we all adopted or something?"

Howard glared at her. She returned the look and arched an eyebrow at him. Wendy looked uncomfortable and shifted in her seat. Phillip put his head down to conceal a smile. The family dynamics were evident and Bella reminded him of his daughter, Fran, with her impatience bottled up in a small body. She was older, but they had the same blonde hair and strong, defiant chins.

"Yes, I'm sorry. Let me get to the point." He swallowed hard first, and then began. "The story begins with your parents in 1939, when the war broke out. Your father went off to war, unknowingly leaving your mother pregnant."

Bella gasped as she turned her head to look at Phillip. Howard and Wendy looked at her and then followed her gaze. The three of them stared at this man who suddenly was looking extremely like their father. They looked at one another with silent recognition of what was about to unfold.

Malcolm continued with the story. "You might remember being told the story that your father was missing, presumed dead. Well, your mother was in a very difficult predicament and finally agreed to have the baby adopted by a married cousin who was childless." Noticing their stares, he added, "You may have guessed by now, that the child was a boy and he was named Phillip." He gestured towards their visitor. "This is your brother, Phillip Davis."

Nobody said a word. The three of them sat as if paralyzed.

"I have to tell you that Phillip didn't know the story of his origins until two days ago. He had never known that he was adopted until I told him. I'm trying to fill in the many blanks for you, and I'm sure you're asking yourselves why this was kept secret." Wendy, Bella and Howard nodded. "It was the stipulation of Sarah Davis, who is Phillip's adoptive mother. He was legally her child and so your parents—and his—had to abide by her wishes. She agreed that only at her death or theirs, whichever came first, could the truth be revealed. I know this caused great pain to your parents, both in terms of not being able to acknowledge Phillip, nor being able to share it with you." He waited a few seconds for some response, but there was none. He finished by saying, "This is why your father—your parents—wanted you to meet here today." He gestured to all four of them. "You are all their children; you are brothers and sisters."

Phillip was the first to speak. "I know how shocked you must be feeling. That's how I felt two days ago—and still feel."

Bella gasped. "My God! You sound like Dad. You've got the same voice; you look quite a lot like him too." She got up and went over to him. "I don't know whether to commiserate or congratulate you." He rose from his chair and she leant up to kiss him on the cheek.

He held her arms gently and looked at her, smiling. "I think you must be my little sister."

By now Wendy had crossed the room and said, "I can't believe that I suddenly have another older brother." She also reached up and kissed him on the cheek. "Tell us about yourself. Where did you grow up? Tell us everything."

Malcolm Bailey and Ned Mackay quietly excused themselves, adding that they would be available if Phillip needed a lift back to San Francisco. Bella insisted that she had a car and would drive him back, and so the attorneys departed, agreeing that they would all meet in Ned's office on Monday at noon. The four children of Phillip and Edith Parker hardly noticed the two men leave. At Wendy and Bella's insistence, Phillip began to tell them how he had grown up first in London, but as a young boy his father had died and his mother had moved to a house in the country where he now lived. He told of his wife, Cynthia, and his children and grandchildren, adding that the family genes must be strong as Bella looked a lot like his daughter Fran, as well as her twin daughters, Beth and Amy. He produced family photos that Cynthia had thoughtfully sent with him, which made Wendy and Bella look at one another in astonishment. Without a word, Bella opened her purse and pulled out a picture of Lauren. "This is my daughter," she said, handing it to Phillip.

He whistled softly. "That's amazing. Who...where...?"

Wendy laughed. "They all look like our grandmother, Marjorie Herriman, our mother's mother. She died when we were very little, but I've seen pictures of her. Mom always said that Bella was like her; and I look a lot like our mother. But Bella's right. It's uncanny how much you look like Dad. I'm surprised I didn't notice it immediately." Noticing that Howard was very silent and knowing how sensitive he was, Wendy turned to him and said, "What do you think? Doesn't he look like Dad?"

He nodded his head. "I suppose he does. That's probably why I thought I'd met him before." He continued standing a little apart from the other three, and felt a strange constriction in his chest. This brother, this stranger, stood a full six inches taller than him, exuding self-confidence and good humor, completely at ease with both his sisters. In a matter of fifteen minutes, this man had simply walked in and taken possession of the status that had hitherto been his: first-born, older brother, son and heir. He felt resentment swell inside him; it felt like his father's last laugh from beyond the grave. He, Howard, was the one who had stayed near to his parents and watched over them as they grew older. God was his witness—he had endured enormous sacrifice to be a dutiful son while his sisters lived thousands of miles away, merely making phone calls and brief visits home. And now, here was yet another sibling, who had done even less than his sisters, but had walked into the bosom of the family like the prodigal son and expected to be warmly welcomed. It galled him to listen to them chattering happily about family resemblances; they all looked like somebody else and they all had children who resembled some other member of the family—all except him. He wished Tracey were here with him.

Phillip smiled at his newly found brother. He could sense tension developing between them already and wanted to stop a gulf from growing. "You have to tell me about the family I missed out on. Howard, you were the oldest of them, why don't you pull up a chair and start to tell me first?"

By now, the other three were seated at the table looking at pictures, so Howard sat down next to Wendy at a corner and looked around at all of them. "Well," he said slowly, "I can't just squeeze out fifty-eight years like toothpaste from a tube."

"Oh Howard, for God's sake," exclaimed Bella. "Lighten up. Surely you can just say something. Oh, I forgot, we weren't going to speak to one another, so never mind me."

"As you can see, my younger sister and I get on famously—always have done. I might as well cut straight to the heart of the matter. Our family always took different sides; Wendy and our father were very close; Mother and I were very close; and Bella fought with everybody whenever she could for whatever reason. She was born that way. Who knows where you would have been placed!"

Bella's eyes opened wide. "Wow! Forget about straight for the heart—that takes it straight to the jugular!"

Wendy interrupted Howard who was about to respond, putting both hands up in the air to stop him. "It's an insult to our parents, and to Phillip, to haul out all the dirty laundry. This is a good opportunity to try and act differently." She turned to Phillip and apologized, "I'm so sorry that you were subjected to that." Concentrating her gaze on her older brother, "I feel at a loss to take all this in. I'm not sure what I'm feeling, so I can't imagine what you must be feeling. It's as if your whole identity has been switched. Do you feel that?"

He smiled. "I suppose I did when I was first informed, but then after some reflection I realized that I'm still me. Phillip Davis, Phillip Parker, Phillip Whatever—they're just names. Obviously it would have been very nice to grow up with brothers and sisters..."

"Are you sure about that?" interrupted Wendy with a laugh.

"Yes, although I'm sure it would have had its tricky moments. But I was brought up by a wonderful mother who loved me unconditionally, and made me who I am. I'm very comfortable with that. Life is always full of 'ifs' but it's a waste of time to dwell on them, in my humble opinion."

"That's very accepting of you," Wendy acknowledged.

He laughed. "Maybe I lack imagination or something, but it always seems better to get on with life and play the hand that was dealt you. I've been very fortunate all my life, and suddenly finding that I have a brother and two sisters, and nieces and a nephew, is a wonderful bonus."

Bella looked at her new brother with some awe. "What an incredibly healthy attitude to life!" she remarked. "We could all learn something from you. I think I would've felt very angry and deceived if I'd been you. Do you feel that at all?"

"No, not really. I can see why decisions were made that led to my life being the way it was, and all those concerned made the best decisions they could under the circumstances. Besides, your parents—my parents—were very good to me and I did get to know them a little on my business trips to California." He laughed and said, "The only thing that is a bit of a letdown is that my success at Parker Keating was probably due to their intercession, not my ability as I'd always believed!"

He proceeded to tell them of his education and then his rise through the ranks of the firm in Britain. They all listened intently, and then Wendy commented, "That's both the curse and the blessing of privilege. You never know whether success is yours alone, or bolstered by your heritage. But I'm sure in your case, you are very able and talented, and so maybe it was both. Mom always used to say there were many responsibilities attached to privilege. I can hear her saying, 'To whom much is given, much is expected'. " She smiled at him reassuringly and then added, "Poor Mom and Dad. This must have weighed heavily on them." As she looked out the window and gazed at the ocean, she recalled her father's words just before he died and realized the full meaning of them. "Perhaps they were the ones who suffered most."

"You're right Wendy. For the rest of us, we never knew anything different and our ignorance was bliss. I believe that they were the only ones who really *suffered* from the chain of events. Their heartache must have been considerable."

"Deservedly so," retorted Howard.

Phillip, Wendy and Bella all looked at him questioningly.

"If you stop and think, they were the ones who caused the situation and their sins caught up with them. They atoned for that all their lives. You can't break the rules and expect there will be no consequences," he explained.

For once Bella did not explode. She was too shocked. The three siblings looked at one another in silence. Finally Phillip said, "What rules would those be, Howard?"

"The basic rules. The ten commandments."

"Oh here we go again," said Bella. "Isn't one of those, honor thy mother and father?"

"Trust me, I honored them. In fact I'm the one who took care of them in their old age, you might recall. But *their* behaviour wasn't honorable, so don't expect me to honor that."

"You know what I think? You did your best to make Dad miserable whenever you could. Your opportunity to work out all your frustrations presented itself after he had a heart attack. You were mean and did your best to humiliate him whenever you could because he was vulnerable. You call that honor? Kick 'em when they're down. Is that your special brand of Christianity, or are all Christians like that? And now he's no longer here, you're throwing mud at his good name," Bella hissed.

"Stop!" shouted Wendy. "You two are intolerable. Stop it right now."

Silence descended on the room. Phillip wondered whether his three siblings had received a much stricter religious upbringing than he had. He had been required to attend church at school, and he attended services with his mother at Christmas and Easter in beautiful St. Mary's Church in Rye, but that was about all. Clearly Howard was very intense about his beliefs; he wasn't sure about his sisters. After an awkward silence, he said, "I hadn't really considered making any moral judgment about any of it. As I mentioned earlier, I think everyone made the best decision they could in the circumstances, and to my mind, all concerned—my birth parents and my adoptive parents—were very honorable people."

"Hear, hear!" replied Bella, and Wendy nodded her assent as well.

The tension in the room was intense. At length Phillip suggested a walk on the beach. Wendy and Bella wanted to accompany him, but Howard remained to phone Tracey and tell her of the strange turn of events. After the initial shock, her response was completely supportive of her husband, commiserating with him and expressing her own resentment at this sudden imposition. "Why did they have to do this to us?" she complained. "After all we did for your parents, the least they could've done was be honest with us. And I suppose now this 'brother' is going to be named in the will. He comes in as a complete unknown; he's done nothing for them all his life and now claims a share of the estate. It's unbelievable. You're going to have to stand firm for what is rightfully yours, Howard."

"I will," he assured her. "There are things that have sentimental value that he has no claim to, and I'll definitely say so. You were very good to my parents, Tracey. They might not have realized it and thanked you for it, but you always knew what was best for them."

"Thank you, Howard. It was my duty and I did it for you. And I'm thankful that I was able to do it, especially as my own parents are dead. I always felt that loss and was eager to do something for your parents instead, no matter how difficult it was."

"My father was a difficult man. The whole situation that we have now is so typical of him. He had his way with my mother before they were married and then went off to have his adventures, leaving her to deal with the problems he'd caused. Everybody else has had to suffer the consequences of his actions..."

As he finished the call, Howard observed Phillip walking back up the beach with his sisters' arms linked through his. The younger brother's chest constricted with anger and resentment. In haste, he turned on his heel and retreated to his bedroom with the newspaper he'd bought earlier in town. "I wish I'd been the one who grew up without overbearing family ties to contend with," he thought to himself as he slammed the door closed. "No wonder he's such a self-satisfied bastard."

7

Lauren heard people departing, the door locking, and her car driving away; she waited until all was silent before wiggling her head to clear the blanket from her face. It was very dark, but a faint gleam of light came in from under the door and she could just see that the walls of the room were made of corrugated iron. There was almost no furniture; she could discern a table, four chairs, and some newspapers lying on the ground which was just bare earth. There was a door, and a small window with a broken pane—covered with newspaper. She got herself up onto her feet and paced silently around the shack. It was about ten feet by fifteen feet and very flimsy, with gaps at corners where a little light crept in. There were some old empty sacks lying next to the door, as well as two Pick 'n Pay plastic bags full of marijuana—*dagga* as it was called here. It was eerily silent, which made her wonder if she'd been wrong in her thoughts that this place was Guguletu. The township was never silent. It was so teeming with people that it couldn't be this quiet, even at night. She tried to see through a gap in the newspaper that covered the window. There didn't appear to be any other shacks or buildings nearby.

Suddenly there was a rattle of the lock from the outside. She raced to hide behind the door as it creaked open and closed again behind three dark figures. They saw her immediately and grabbed her. One of them roughly pulled a ski mask over her head back to front so that she couldn't see anything; the smell of it made her want to vomit. It smelled as if someone had thrown up on it, and it scratched her face with its course texture. She screamed and kicked and managed to stomp hard on somebody's foot, provoking a shout and a punch to her head that dazed her. Her heart pounded as she was shoved to the ground and kicked while trying to wriggle away. Rough hands held her down and she felt horror as first her jeans, and then her underwear, were pulled off. She tried to kick her legs frantically, but the weight of an attacker was on top of her, forcing her legs apart. Calloused hands grabbed her ankles and held them tight, rendering her powerless. Her arms, still tied behind her back, couldn't defend herself either, but felt painfully twisted by the enormous, suffocating weight on her. She heard her attacker's grunts and felt his gyrations as he kicked down his pants, and then she felt sudden unbearable pain stab her body as he plunged himself mercilessly into her. It felt as if she was going to be ripped apart and then her head began to bang on the wall as he thrust himself into her and pushed her body. Above the banging and the grunts she heard another voice say, "Hey, Zeke. Hurry up, man. We want a go too before the others miss us." With a final heave and shudder the first attacker climbed off her leaving a trail of warm liquid running down her thighs. Immediately another man took over, pinning her down and thrusting himself brutally until he too finally came to a shuddering stop. As he pushed himself up, a third man fell on top of her and began ramming into her like a jackhammer. The pain was acute and the shock so overwhelming that she started to lose consciousness; blackness engulfed her as she felt herself sinking into an abyss. When she groggily started to surface from it, someone was standing over her, coughing and spitting on her. "*Ja*, she's blonde!" he snorted, kicking her exposed body.

They all laughed and she could hear someone zipping up his pants. They spoke to one another in a language she couldn't understand, until one of them said, "Don't get too lonely Blondie. We'll be back soon." After that they left just as suddenly as they'd arrived, locking the door behind them again, leaving her lying half-naked and violated on the ground. Dry sobs racked through her body. Her groin ached and her stomach cramped with pain. Moans seemed to come from deep inside her, beyond her control, as she felt herself losing consciousness again.

She was unaware how long she lay comatose, but when she returned to her senses she was immediately alert and desperate to get the mask and the duct tape off. She needed to get free before the other men returned. Like a mad woman she rolled over onto her stomach and inched the mask up her face by rubbing her chin and forehead on the ground and against the wall. At last it lifted above her eyes and she could see again. There, not two inches away from her eyes, was a very sharp piece of corrugated iron that had come apart at the seams when her head had banged against the wall. She quickly rolled around so that the rope was up against the sharp edge, and she began to rub her arms backwards and forwards against it. Fortunately the rope wasn't very thick and she could feel it starting to loosen as the strands severed. She tried pulling her wrists apart and with a sob of relief she felt the rope fall off. Her hands were free at last. She quickly ripped the duct tape off her mouth and pulled her clothes back on over her bloodied thighs, feeling in her pocket for the envelope of dollars she'd recently received from her mother. It was gone. "Bastards," she sobbed, "they've taken my money too. Oh God, I'm in the middle of nowhere with nothing and they're coming back again." There was no time to dwell on what had happened—she needed to get out of here before anyone else returned. As if concussed, her brain froze out what had just occurred in order to survive.

She tried the door, but as she feared, it was firmly locked. Next she ran to the window, but it was stuck, so she raced to the jagged corner that had helped her cut through the rope. The gap had widened and with a bit of luck she might be able to squeeze out of the hole. She pushed hard and kicked, and sure enough—it opened wide enough for her to get out. She pulled the ski mask back over her face, the right way around so that she could see, and pulled the hood of her sweatshirt over that. Her brain was in survival mode; she needed to disguise her fair skin and she needed to get as far away from this shack as quickly as she could.

Lauren stumbled as she tried to get her bearings. She paused only a second as she decided which way to run; it was a mental flip of the coin. She was drawn to the lights in the distance, but possible danger lurked there—safety might be found away from people. Her intuition made her head towards the faint glimmer of dim lights. As she approached them, she smelled the latrines again and felt sure she was near Guguletu Township. If that were so, perhaps she could find her way to the kindergarten school where she worked. She could see a dirt trail where her car had recently been driven and decided to follow it, hoping that if she saw car lights approaching her, she would be able to dive undercover. However it was very flat and there was little plant life, just litter strewn about, so she ran as fast as she could and hoped for the best. There didn't seem to be a soul in sight.

The smell of the latrines grew stronger and soon she could see them clustered together with a crowd of people noisily lining up to use them. Lauren was sure she was in the township now and suddenly realized the need to hide her white hands inside her long sleeves if she wanted to avoid detection. She wouldn't be able to speak either. Fortunately it was dark enough that if she kept away from the occasional street lights, she might escape notice as her face and hair were hidden beneath the hood and the ski mask. It was imperative that she find help or cover before light; her concern was whom she could trust. If only she could find the school, then she would be able to find the nearby home of her friend Janet Dyani, the head teacher.

She avoided the latrine area by turning down a side alley. Her sense was that the main road lay a distance directly in front of her, but how many miles away seemed unfathomable. The township was a big place. Somewhere between where she was and that road, lay the school. Her eyes scanned all the tin shacks, hoping to find something familiar. She hadn't ever ventured too far into the township before, and never on her own as it was considered too dangerous for a white woman. She always had the protective care of Janet or a guide when she went beyond the school, or beyond the site—just outside the township—where the orphanage was being built. She didn't dare think of the dangers hidden in the darkness and shadows. There were people walking around and others standing in groups talking. There was light and noise emanating from most of the makeshift homes, which made her feel a little safer. As long as she kept her distance and moved purposefully, she felt she'd be unnoticed. She couldn't understand anything that she heard, as there were only foreign languages with guttural sounds and clicks that made no sense to her. Her heart missed a beat when someone pressed up against her and whispered something; she pushed away and hissed dismissively, hurrying on her way. Nobody followed her and her strangeness went unnoticed. She was reminded how desperately thirsty she was when she saw a communal tap in an open area at the junction of some alleys. She stood and watched a few people fill buckets and wander away, and then a young woman came and poured water in her hands to splash her face. She shouted something out and laughed, then ran after a young man. Lauren waited to see if anybody else was coming; when all seemed clear she risked revealing her white hands as she rushed and filled them with water, cupping them to her mouth. The water was brackish tasting, but it quenched her thirst and washed the dry taste of dust away. She drank frantically, spilling as she tried to get the water to her mouth until she heard someone approaching. Quickly she turned off the tap, then without looking back, hurried on her way.

She had no idea what time it was, for it was too dark to see her watch and she didn't dare pause under a street light. She had lost all sense of time; so much had happened since she'd left Kirstenbosch just after sunset and her mind was not able to think about it—as if she had temporary amnesia. She had to concentrate on survival, divorcing everything else from her brain. Turning a corner, she suddenly became aware of the sound of traffic in the distance and she saw beams of light straight ahead of her. Her heart beat faster. She was sure she'd been heading in the direction of the main road. Now if only she were also right about the school…She peered around, but every alley looked the same as the one before.

A sudden yelp startled her and she saw a little mongrel dog rush out of a door with his tail between his legs, whimpering. An angry voice shouted after it, *"Voetsak."* Lauren recognized this foreign phrase as meaning "get lost," and stored it away for future use if necessary. The dog stopped when nobody came after him, and then he turned and looked pleadingly at Lauren. When she whistled softly to him, he ran to her side eagerly. Checking that nobody was near to see her hand, she patted his little head and scratched his ear sympathetically; he licked her in response. The way he rubbed up against her leg was familiar, and it dawned on her that this might be the same little stray dog that hung around the kindergarten school at lunchtime—the one she had nicknamed "Lunch" for that reason. He appeared routinely every weekday at 1 p.m. and the children would even say, "Here's Lunch." She peered at him in the dim light, and felt a surge of excitement when she spotted his white paws, the white smudge on his nose, and the white tip at the end of his tail. He was about the same size too. She must be somewhere near the school. She leant down and cradled his head in both her hands, whispering in his ear, "Where am I, Lunch?"

His ears pricked up and his wet nose pressed against her hand, then he turned on his heels and trotted confidently along the alley. After a few yards he turned and looked at Lauren, giving a little bark. She didn't hesitate; there was nothing to lose for she didn't know where she was anyway. As soon as she drew level with Lunch, he carried on at a gentle pace further along the alley until they came to a corner. He stopped and checked that she was still following, then continued to lead her along a new wider road. They came to another junction with a communal tap and cluster of latrines. The smell made her stomach heave, but it also made her feel that they were getting closer to the school. Suddenly from the crowd gathered around the tap, two young men ambled towards her and began saying something she couldn't understand. She backed away, but one of them came closer and reached out to grab her. She hissed *"Voetsak,"* as best she could, and with that Lunch started barking furiously before biting the man's ankles. The distraction gave Lauren time to duck and head away from the crowd, who were now all laughing at the sight of a cursing man running away from a dog. In a minute, Lunch was back at her side, and then he proudly took the lead again. She felt tears well up in her eyes as she followed him, confident he knew where he was going.

They turned a few more corners and there it was at the top of the road—the school. She sobbed with relief and patted Lunch on the back. "Good boy" she whispered, and then whistled for him to follow her. Janet's house was easy to find now, and she headed there without delay, knocking sharply on the front door. There was neither sound nor light from within. She walked around the little concrete-block house, but all the windows were closed and barred; Janet was evidently not home, but just being somewhere familiar made Lauren feel safer. There was a locked, windowless concrete shed a short distance behind the house in which they kept school supplies, as space was at such a premium. They had used funds from the Parker

Family Trust to build the shed and buy supplies, and fortunately both the locks were combinations which only she and Janet knew. There was nobody in sight, so she quickly let herself in with the dog, using the flashlight that was kept on a ledge next to the door to see inside. It was very tempting to have Lunch stay with her in the shed as a comforting presence, but he might get restless and give her away. Regretfully she reached into a box of dried biscuits, gave him a couple, before tossing a few more out the shed. He ran after them and she quickly closed the door firmly shut. It was not possible to lock from the inside, but she pushed a crate filled with long-life milk, dried fruit and biscuits against the door. For the first time since she awoke in Kirstenbosch, she began to breathe normally. Grabbing some food for herself, she sat on the ground with tears streaming down her face, conscious of the pain in her ravaged body. The memory of what had happened flooded back, and she began to shiver uncontrollably.

8

Bessie Opperman couldn't believe her luck as she started to write her story for *The Argus*. As a junior crime reporter, she was constantly battling to find interesting material. There were so many rapes, murders, assaults, robberies and car-jackings that there was no shortage of material, but she had great difficulty finding something novel to write about. Her usual scouting of police stations tonight, however, had brought results: an American woman had been car-jacked. This in itself made it a little different from the norm and would rattle a response because a foreigner was involved. However, there was an even bigger bonanza when she ran a Google search on the woman and discovered that she was not just a tourist, but an exchange student on a scholarship, working in Guguletu. And now as she poured through the many search results, she discovered that Ms. Lauren Marlowe was far more than that: she was the granddaughter of Phillip Parker, founder of Parker Keating. She was one rich woman. This was a hot item on Bessie's hands, and she began to picture her future brightening by the minute. Bessie Opperman would be the new kid on the block who made it to the big time in next to no time. And then, this was too good to be true, the search engine revealed that the rich old grandfather had just died and Ms. Marlowe was no doubt going to inherit a big sum of money. The stars were all lined up for Bessie. Her report was the headline on the front page next morning.

AMERICAN HEIRESS ABDUCTED AT KIRSTENBOSCH

Little Bessie Opperman from Mitchell's Plain had made it to the top. Now she was an investigative reporter, and the adrenalin raced through her body. "God help you, Ms. Marlowe," she thought, "and I hope I can find you soon. Those *skollie* gangs have no respect for anything; for sure a beautiful young woman like you will have a rough time..."

***

Zeke and the boys finished delivering the blue Jetta to Jake's Motors, a drop-off for stolen vehicles in Somerset West. Jake Jakobs ran a motor repair shop that served as a front for his booming trade. Jettas were almost as popular as BMWs these days, and he paid the boys top price, in cash, on the spot. Jake's son, Samuel, was happy to give the boys a ride back to Guguletu in his car, lured by the promise of some fun with a blonde. Their mood was light-hearted and excited; a good night's work had been done with the anticipation of a nice reward ahead. Zeke was a little worried that the boys might be mad because he, Boy, and Tonsil had slipped back when the others had stopped for food and petrol. They had already sampled the prize, but he reckoned nobody would know who it was. Just so long as the three of them kept quiet, as agreed, nobody would find out. Blondie wouldn't know who it was because they'd covered her up. And now he was ready for more.

It was getting light as they made their way back, and by the time they reached Cape Town, the roads were busy with people going to work. They saw the newspaper delivery van weaving its way through traffic to the drop-off points, and the paper boys at corners shouting *"AR-GUS,"* and running barefoot to sell to drivers as they waited for the lights to change. They paid little attention until Zeke noticed a placard blazing the headline that Bessie had so proudly written. He whistled and raised his eyebrows. "Hey, Sammy my man, let's get a paper."

Samuel rolled his window down in preparation, and at the next stop he waited until the light was about to change before putting his arm out, signaling. The youngster came running and handed over the paper, putting his hand out for the money in return. Samuel fished around in his pocket and shouted to Zeke, "Where's your money, man?" The lights changed, and with that Samuel accelerated, leaving the newspaper boy cursing and empty-handed. The boys in the car laughed.

"Look at this! Look at this picture," said Zeke, voicing his disbelief as he read the paper. "Hey, Chinas, we struck the mother-fucking lode last night. Listen to this...Blondie is American and she's stinking rich. Her grandfather just died and left her a few million dollars. What do you think of that?"

"I think we got a fucking problem," answered Boy Booysen.

"Why you think we got a problem, man? We ransom this chick. Gen-tle-men," he drawled, "we're on ea-sy street now."

"Shit Zeke, you *blerrie* fool. You don't think the police gonna come looking hard now?" Boy responded anxiously.

As if in answer to his question, they turned a corner and were confronted by a road block. A dozen policemen were flagging cars down, and Samuel was ordered to pull over and await inspection. "Shit," he said. "Next time you boys find your own fucking way back. This is all I need."

"Hey, cool it China, we got nothing to hide," muttered Mackie Venter from the back seat.

"Well, maybe we do...And I don't like answering fucking questions."

"Ah rubbish man. They'll just check your license and the registration. You got those?" asked Tonsil Morope who sat squashed up next to Mackie.

"*Ja*. Now shut up, Chinas. No smart answers, hey."

They tried to remain calm as cars around them were searched, before two policemen came ambling over to Samuel's window and peered inside the car. Another one stood on the other side watching. They first checked Samuel's license and handed the car registration to the third officer to run a check against stolen vehicles. Samuel thanked his lucky stars that he had driven his own car, and not one from the stolen fleet at the back of Jake's Motors. Then the officer asked, "So how many people you got in the car?"

Samuel looked over his shoulder and counted. "Seven."

"Seven. And how many seat belts you got?"

"Five."

"Now why's that?"

"These guys need a ride to work."

"Are they paying you for the ride?"

"No, they my friends."

"So you're not a taxi?"

"No, no. I'm not a taxi. I got no money from them."

"Is that right? You're a good man taking so many friends to work this early in the morning. Where do you all work?"

"In Cape Town."

"Where?"

Samuel turned and looked at the boys in the back, with sweat beginning to form on his brow. "We're looking for work."

"Oh, I see," said the policeman. "You're looking for work. Well, you're overcrowded in here, so you two can climb out the car right now and catch a taxi." He pointed to Zeke and Boy, sitting on top of others, and motioned to the door. "Get out." Samuel was about to argue, but decided to keep his mouth shut as the two passengers clambered out of the car. "Once I've looked in the boot, you lot can go," the policeman said to Samuel. "Open it up."

Samuel climbed out and opened the back nervously. The others all held their breath, anxious lest there was any damning evidence of stolen goods. It appeared empty, however, and the officer gave a peremptory look before signaling to Samuel that he could go on his way. Turning to Zeke and Boy, he shouted, "You can't stand in the middle of the road. Get in the back of the van."

They looked anxiously at one another and then Zeke turned to the policeman, saying, "You arresting us?"

The officer, Sergeant Blignaut, spun around suspiciously. "Hey, smart-arse, did I say I was arresting you?"

"You told me—get in the van. That means I must go to the police station for overloading—hey that's not a big deal, man. What you taking me there for? There's no law that says I must wear a seat belt in the back! I haven't done anything wrong."

"Is that a fact? I'd like to hear what a big deal is. Tell me what's a big deal."

Zeke felt his shoulder begin to twitch. The questions reminded him of his last visit to prison; he'd been released just two weeks ago and didn't want to be there again so soon. "What you want me to say? You know what's big, why you asking me? Murder is big. I've done nothing wrong."

"What about car-jacking?"

Zeke looked at Boy in fright. They were both dumbstruck. It was impossible for the police to be on their tracks this fast, they were thinking. Neither knew what to say. Panic was written all over their faces. The three policemen looked at one another and the sergeant nodded to the corporal, "Put them in the van." Turning to Zeke and Boy, he added, "We'll be kind and give you a lift all the way to the police station, and then we'll run a check on you."

***

Mackie, Tonsil, Basie, and Abram watched through the rear window and reported to Samuel that Zeke and Boy were in custody. "True's God, they put them in the van," shrieked Mackie.

"Shit. I don't think this is worth it boys. I think we should get rid of the blonde as fast as we can," hissed Tonsil. "Maybe she can recognize us. I'm telling you, let's get rid of her."

"*Ja*, and how we gonna do that?" asked Abram.

"Don't be so bloody dumb. We shoot her, we dump the body."

"Now listen to me," said Basie. "Think carefully about what we know.

We know they got Zeke and Boy. No big deal.

We know Blondie's a rich American.

We know we gonna have a bit of fun with her, then we get rid of her, or better still, we ransom her. But, just in case maybe those boys let something slip, we need to move her first. If the police come looking, they gonna find nothing in that shed."

"How we gonna move her?" asked Tonsil.

"Same way we brought her in. We got Samuel's car, we cover her in a blanket, we put her in the boot, and we go to Mackie's place. Then we have fun."

"No way," argued Mackie.

"OK, OK, we take her to the old shack near my house. Everyone

65

says there's a *tokolosh* in it because two people died there. Nobody goes there. They're too scared of the bad spirit. We can't get her out of Guguletu right now; we might hit another road block."

"Forget it, I'm not going anywhere without what I came for," said Samuel. "If you want my car, I make the rules."

"OK. OK. You can screw her, but you'd better do it quickly," replied Basie, realizing that Samuel needed to be humored as they desperately needed his car for transporting the girl. "Then we take her away fast man, and the rest of us can do it later—as many times as we like."

"No shit," wailed Abram, "I've been waiting all night. What you afraid of, man?"

"Shut up Abram," shouted Basie. "I give the orders, *tsotsi*. I'm not afraid of anything but I'll give you something to be afraid of if you don't keep your fucking mouth shut."

By now they had reached the shack where they'd left Lauren the previous night. They looked around furtively before getting out the car and quickly making their way to the door, which Basie unlocked. He kicked it open, allowed his eyes to adjust to the light, and then pointed to the crumpled blanket in the corner. "There she is. She's yours," he said to Samuel. "Make it quick, China."

Samuel started excitedly unzipping his fly, causing guffaws of laughter from the boys. He quickly got to the corner and pulled the blanket away...There was a moment's stunned silence before pandemonium broke out. Samuel was screaming, "You lying, fucking, cheating bastards," and the other four were all shouting at one another. Samuel came at Basie with two fast fists to the face and knocked him to the ground. Then he kicked him in the face, the groin and the stomach for good measure, before storming out and driving off in his car.

Basie was writhing in the dust and moaning. Blood was pouring from his mouth where a tooth had been loosened, and he was spitting into the dirt. Abram and Tonsil were standing dumbstruck, while Mackie inspected the room, looking for evidence that would reveal how their captive had escaped. "The door was *blerrie* locked, man," he grunted as he shook his head, "I saw Basie opening it. Hey man," he said to his accomplice on the floor, "we gotta get out of here, fast. And then we gotta find the bitch. Come on, get up and stop complaining. We gotta move." Basie curled himself into a fetal position and gasped in pain, so Mackie bent down and shook him. "Listen to me, man. The police are gonna come looking faster than you think. You wanna lie here waiting for them? We don't know what Zeke and Boy are telling them. Get up."

Tonsil, sweating profusely as he recalled his part in the gang rape, noticed the gap in the walls that had appeared in the corner. He also saw the jagged piece of corrugated iron with rope and duct tape lying next to it. He pointed to the evidence and cursed, "*Bliksem*! Look at that. The bitch freed herself. How we gonna find her now?" With that he bolted for the door, followed by the other three, and they didn't stop running until they were two miles away at the first lot of shacks in Guguletu. There they could lose themselves in the surrounding sea of faces and become anonymous. Intuitively they knew to split up and take different routes to their meeting place at the *shebeen*, the beer-drinking shack that had customers even this early in the morning. Alcohol provided solace when you were out of work, and Ma Miriam sold her rough brew cheaply. Fortunately the boys had been paid handsomely by Jake, and so they could afford her better brew today, with an extra big payment if she agreed that they'd all been there last night too.

9

Back at the station, Sergeant Blignaut recorded the time—5:45 a.m. Sunday, took down all their particulars, and then began to question Zeke and Boy as to their whereabouts the previous night.

"I don't need to answer any questions without a lawyer," Zeke replied. "I've done nothing wrong."

Sergeant Blignaut stared at him for a few seconds without responding. Then he turned and called for another policeman, Sergeant Olivier, to whom he dryly said, "This piece of rubbish thinks he needs a lawyer before he answers any questions. He and his friend were riding in an overloaded car. I simply want to know where they were last night, just as a matter of interest. We need to find this American girl, and anybody who can help us with our inquiries needs to do so—without a lawyer. I think that would be considered civic duty. Don't you think that's fair, Olivier?"

"Definitely, Blignaut. Would you like me to give you a little bit of help?"

"*Asseblief*—thank you." Sergeants Blignaut and Olivier were in the habit of speaking a mixture of English and Afrikaans to one another.

Sergeant Olivier adjusted his glasses on his nose and looked the two offenders up and down. He sniffed loudly and said, "Right, first thing, you can empty your pockets out onto the desk. No arguments *julle donders*—you rubbish. Move it!"

Grudgingly Zeke and Boy moved to the desk and emptied all their pockets into two piles. The sergeants watched carefully and whistled as each young man placed wads of bank notes in front of them, which they were asked to count. Each of them had five thousand rand in five hundred rand denominations. Zeke also had a white envelope.

"Sergeant Olivier, they told me that they're looking for work. What do you think of that?"

"I think that five thousand rand is a lot of money for somebody without a job. What's in that envelope?"

"It's a letter," Zeke answered quickly and picked it up to put back in his pocket.

"Not so fast, damn it," said Sergeant Olivier. "Open it."

"It's personal," replied Zeke in a tight voice.

"Give it to me," commanded the sergeant, removing the envelope and opening it. Inside were 300 United States dollars and a card that he read aloud: *Darling Lauren, Happy birthday. I wish I could be there to celebrate with you. Love Mom.*

"Put the handcuffs on him—and the other one," Sergeant Olivier instructed. "Call the captain. Now you're going to answer a lot of questions, you bastards."

Zeke and Boy were handcuffed, booked, and shoved into separate holding cells. It wasn't long before Sergeants Olivier, Blignaut and Captain Wellington Radebe began interrogating them, starting with Zeke.

"Where did you get all that money?" Olivier began the questioning.

"I want a lawyer," replied Zeke.

"You'll get a lawyer in good time—you're going to need one by the looks of things—but right now you're going to get a kick in the arse if you don't start answering some questions. Let me ask you one more time nicely, where did you get all this money?"

"I've been working on a job at a building site. I just got paid."

"And where did you get these dollars? Who is Lauren?"

"I found that envelope lying in the street, so I picked it up. That's not a crime."

"Where did you find it? I want to know exactly where?"

"*Ag* man, I don't remember. It was in Greenmarket Square, I think."

"When did you find it?"

"Last week."

"So why haven't you changed it into rands?"

"Where can I change it? I haven't got a passport—I can't go to a bank without one. You people are all the same; you don't trust me just because I haven't got a smart uniform or something. You see me and think—this boy's lying. If I've got a uniform like you, then I can do anything I like. Just like you."

Paying no attention to Zeke's complaint, Olivier continued, "Cut the whining. Where were you working on this building site? Let's get some references for you."

"Near Greenmarket Square."

"I need a name of an employer, Zeke. Near Greenmarket Square isn't good enough."

"I can't remember. It was just day labor."

"Day labor? And you got five thousand rand for a day? Jesus man, what were you doing?"

"No, not for one day. I worked there lots of days. If you take me there, I'll show you where."

"And where were you last night?"

"At home."

"Where's home? And who was with you at home?"

"I live in Guguletu. I was there by myself."

Captain Radebe intervened. "Leave him and let's find out something from the other one. Maybe he'll be more helpful. Meantime Zeke, think about this: at the moment we have enough evidence to charge you with theft and abduction. Who knows what else we're going to find—rape, murder? Now if you decide to co-operate, things might be better for you. At the moment, your situation doesn't look good. Come Sergeants, let's go and hear what the other one has to say."

The three policemen marched out of the cell and slammed the door shut. Zeke heard the lock and their footsteps going down the corridor and he broke into a cold sweat; he had seen that there was money in the envelope when he took it out of the girl's jeans while Tonsil was raping her, but he hadn't looked too hard as there wasn't enough time. He hadn't realized that the money was incriminating dollars, nor had he seen the note with the girl's name on it. In his frustration he kicked the wall, cursing. "What the hell is Boy going to tell them?" He paced up and down the cell, trying to figure out what to say. He decided to stick to his story that he had picked the envelope up near Greenmarket Square, as that was the only incriminating evidence they had on him.

Boy was crouched in a corner of the cell when the three policemen walked in and he quickly got to his feet so that he didn't have to look up to them. Sergeant Olivier immediately began bombarding him with questions. "Where were you last night, Boy?"

"At the *shebeen* near my house."

"Who else was there?"

"Lots of people."

"Was Zeke there?"

"I don't know. I didn't see him, but maybe he was there."

"Is Zeke a friend of yours?"

"I know him a little bit."

"How long have you known him?"

"A few years."

"How old are you, Boy?"

"Eighteen years."

"You know, you could spend the next eighteen years in jail for helping Zeke abduct this girl and then stealing her car. Maybe there'll be rape or murder charges too. Now if you are co-operative and tell us where you got all that money from, it might be better for you. So tell us Boy, where did you get five thousand rand?"

"Zeke gave it to me."

The sergeant whistled. "Zeke gave it to you? That's a lot of money for Zeke to give you? Why did he do that?"

"He didn't want to have all that money in his pockets on a Saturday night. You know the *tsotsis* steal our money."

"I see. So he wanted you to carry some for him in case he was robbed, is that right?"

"Yes."

"So it's not your money, it's Zeke's?"

"*Ja*. I was keeping it for him."

"You said you know him a little bit, but I think you must be a very good friend if he trusted you with five thousand rand. When did he give it to you?"

Boy hesitated before he mumbled, "Last night."

"Where did he give it to you?"

"At my house."

"Before you went to the *shebeen* or after?"

"Before, no I think it was afterwards."

"So where was Zeke when you were at the *shebeen*?"

"I don't know."

"Let me get this straight—you saw Zeke and he gave you five thousand rand to keep for him. You went to a *shebeen*, but didn't see Zeke there, then you left the *shebeen* and you saw Zeke again. Is that what happened?"

"Yes."

"I think you're lying, Boy. Were you with Zeke last night?"

"Just at the beginning and at the end."

"So you weren't with him at Kirstenbosch?"

Boy's mouth dropped open and then he swallowed hard. "I don't know anything about that," he whispered.

"I can't hear you, speak up!"

Boy shook his head. "I don't know anything about that."

"About what? About stealing a blue Jetta and abducting the driver? Zeke said you were there too."

"No, I didn't go with him to Kirstenbosch. He went by himself."

"Did you rape the girl?"

"No Sergeant, I didn't see the girl. I don't know anything."

"So how did you get that long blonde hair stuck on the back of you shirt?"

Boy desperately started rubbing his back and peering over his shoulder which made the sergeant snort derisively. "It's too late now. We've seen it already, and removed it for evidence; a DNA check will probably tell us that it belongs to the victim because I don't think it's yours! It'll be better if you tell us the truth. Zeke is going to be in jail for a very long time, and you will be too unless you can help us. We know he's a criminal with a long record, but we're not showing much against you. The judge might be lenient if you assist us in our inquiry. If you don't, you might get the same sentence as your friend. Think about it."

The Captain stepped forward. "If the girl is dead, you'll spend the rest of your life locked away. Is the girl still alive or is she dead?"

"No, she's not dead, I'm telling you."

This was the breakthrough they were wanting. There was a long silence before Captain Radebe continued, "Where is she? Tell me now, and I'll personally recommend leniency."

Boy started to sob. He tried to speak but couldn't control himself. Sergeant Olivier strode up to him and shoved him against a wall, shouting, "Damn it. Tell us where she is."

"In a…a…shed in…in…Guguletu."

"Where?"

Boy was shaking and sobbing as he explained exactly how to get to the hiding place. A nod from the captain sent Sergeant Blignaut on his way, accompanied by three other policemen. Radebe continued interrogating Boy with Sergeant Olivier assisting him.

***

With the Minister of Police breathing down their necks, the police were highly motivated to find this American woman as fast as possible. Sergeant Blignaut raced out of the station and drove to Guguletu at high speed with his aides, followed by two other police vans. Boy's directions had been carefully given and the police converged on the shed at about 7.15 a.m. Sunday. They broke open the lock and burst inside to find nothing. "*Bliksem*, the bugger's lying," the sergeant shouted, but then he saw blood on the ground, and when he shone his flashlight, he saw the marijuana as well as a blanket, rope and duct tape lying in the corner.

"*Ja*, she was here, I reckon. But she's not here now." He radioed this information to the captain as the rest of the small force inspected the area both inside and out. Radebe was still working Zeke and Boy by interrogating them in turn and playing one off against the other. He had already dispatched another group of police to Jake's Motors in Somerset West as a result, but he cursed when he received this news. "I'm coming straight away. Search the area; I'm sending reinforcements to search the township. Anything that looks out of the ordinary, anything—no matter how small—I want to know about it. Somebody somewhere will squeal."

Within twenty minutes, Guguletu was crawling with policemen asking questions and searching the one-room houses visually from doors as they spoke to the occupants. The group at the scene had picked up the prints of Lauren's shoes getting out the corner of the house and a tracker was brought to follow the trail. They could see that she had headed towards the township from this outlying shed, and they could see the tracks from her car as it also headed in the direction of the main road, but once they reached the first houses, there were too many overlying tracks and the trail was lost.

***

Basie, Tonsil, Mackie and Abram were comfortably seated at a table in Ma Miriam's *shebeen*, drinking their favorite brew and reading the newspaper article, when four policemen entered and the room went very quiet as everyone watched nervously. There weren't many drinkers at this hour of the morning, and the policemen were able to take in the scene quickly. They questioned Miriam about how big the crowd had been the previous night, and she replied that it had been very big. They could ask her customers who were still here because they had all been here the whole night. The policemen walked around looking at the room and the last stragglers still drinking; there was a smell of sweat and vomit, as well as beer. When they got to the table where Basie sat with the other three, they stopped and stared at the cuts and blood on his face. "Looks like you've been in a fight. When did this happen?" asked a corporal.

"Someone tried to steal my money last night," Basie replied. "I hit him, he hit me."

"Did he take your money?"

"He took some."

The corporal turned to the other three. "Did you see it happen?" They all shrugged their shoulders.

"Did you report it to the police?" the corporal asked Basie.

"No, I came here and started to drink with my friends."

"How can we stop crime if you don't report it? You must come with me now and file a report."

"No really man, it's no problem. It's nothing."

"I'm telling you, we can't stop crime if we don't know about it. It's your duty to report it. Come."

He pulled Basie and took him out into the daylight where he could have a better look at his face. Tonsil, Mackie and Abram took the opportunity to slip out the back door, grabbing the newspaper on their way. Their departure was unnoticed by the other policemen who gathered around to observe Basie and the corporal.

"That looks like a nasty fight. How much money did he take?"

"Not much, just a few rand."

"He punched you like that for a few rand! How much have you got left?"

"I don't know. It doesn't matter."

"Of course it matters. Are you so rich that it doesn't matter how much he stole and how much you got left? Let's see what you got." When Basie didn't move, the corporal said, "Are you trying to hide something? What have you got in your pockets?"

Basie put his hands in his pocket and pulled out four hundred and fifty rand in notes, and some coins. The corporal nodded his head. "What's in the other pocket?" he asked.

Basie pulled his pocket inside out. "Nothing," he said.

"O.K. Now pull the first pocket out like that."

They all watched as a wad of bank notes fell to the ground, all in five hundred rand denominations. "It's very lucky that he didn't steal all that from you. Now I can see why there was such a big fight. What about in that other pocket?"

Basie hung his head, remaining silent. When he didn't move, the corporal put his hand in the concealed pocket and pulled out a revolver. "Have you got a license for this?" Basie was hunched and shook his head. "Get in the van. I'm taking you to the station."

As Basie was led away and forcibly shoved in the back of the police van, the other three took fright and ran down an alley where they debated paying a visit to the kindergarten school. It was all there in the paper; the picture of the blonde girl and the story about how she worked at a school in Guguletu. "She's going there, for sure," they all decided.

"Let's go and shoot her right now. Man, if she identifies us we're in deep *kak*," Tonsil declared.

"Wait a minute, I thought we're going to ransom her," said Mackie. "I'm not killing anybody. She won't recognize us—it was dark, man. Car-jacking is one thing, but murder—no ways."

"How about rape? You OK with that?" Tonsil inquired.

"We didn't do it. No crime there, man. Let them find her now then we can forget it. The police will go away. If they find her dead, the police are gonna be all over this place, worse than they are now." Mackie was sweating as he spoke, "I'm not looking for anybody and I don't want anybody looking for me."

"I agree," said Abram. "Man, all I've done is help take that car to Jake. Even if they catch me, hey—I'll get maybe a year. Mackie's right—once they've got her, they'll go away. I'm out of here. I'm going home."

Tonsil cursed. "You chicken shit. Go home then; I'm going to find her."

"You're mad, man," said Mackie. "If Basie or Boy or Zeke mention our names, they'll find us. If that girl is injured, or dead, they'll know who did it. And it's not going to be me or Abram." He grabbed Tonsil by the shoulders and said, "Forget it man. You're going crazy. Don't shit yourself when you smell fear. They'll find the shit. Go home and lie low; listen to me, Bro. Don't get into this any deeper. Forget the ransom and the blonde."

Tonsil pretended to agree with them. He could see that he would have to deal with this by himself; they didn't know that he'd already raped her. Instead of heading back to his own shanty, he went straight to the kindergarten and looked inside the windows. There was nothing. He'd been sure that he would find the blonde girl there trying to get help. Suddenly he noticed a sign on the door that read: Inquiries: Head Teacher, Janet Dyani—next door. He ripped the piece of paper off the door, bounded across the dirt patch that lay between the school and the next house, throwing a stone at a dog that barked at him as he ran by. He pounded on the door a couple of times until a bleary-eyed woman opened the door a crack and peered out at him. "What do you want?" she asked.

"Are you the head teacher?" he inquired.

"Yes, what do you want on a Sunday morning?"

He kicked the door open with his foot and pushed past her into the tiny house. "Where is she?" he demanded.

"What do you think you're doing? Get out of my house," Janet responded.

Tonsil grabbed her roughly by the neck and squeezed a little. "Where's the American?"

"Lauren?"

"*Ja*, Lauren. Where is she?"

"I don't know. She doesn't come here at weekends. What do you want her for?"

"It's got nothing to do with you. I want her. Now let me see your house," he said, pushing her ahead of him. "I'm gonna make sure she's not here. I think you're lying."

Janet stood aside as he searched the room, and then she said, "I'll call the police if you don't get out."

"You stupid bitch, how you gonna do that? If you try and call the police I'm gonna kill you. Now where's your cell phone?"

Janet gulped. "I haven't got one," she replied.

"Don't lie. Everybody's got a cell phone. Give it to me." He grabbed her neck and squeezed it again a little harder. "Shall I just kill you now, or are you going to give it to me?"

She reached under her mattress and found her cell phone. He grabbed it, turned it off and stuck it in his pocket. "And now I'm gonna stay here until she comes looking for you," he said. "You can go back to sleep but don't try any funny business. Whatever you do on Sunday, do it now." He took the gun out of his pocket and showed it to her menacingly.

Janet thought quickly. There was no way that she was going back to bed with this gunman sitting in the chair watching her. "I get up now and go to church on Sunday, and then I do my washing," she said.

"This Sunday you're not going to church. You can do your washing, but take all your clothes off first," he demanded. "I want to see a teacher *kaalgat*," he taunted while playing with his gun menacingly. When she didn't move, he grabbed her collar and ripped it. "Get them off," he shouted. She was trembling as she removed her pajamas with her back to him and then she felt hard steel in her back. "Turn around," he grunted. Terrified she turned to face him with a gun pointing at her. His eyes roamed over her body as he poked her nipples with the tip of the gun. "Nice," he said appreciatively. "They must give you lots of food for teaching," he sneered. Then he dropped the gun to her crotch and pushed it between her thighs. Janet was terrified and held her breath as she smelled the stench of stale beer on him. His eyes were yellow and glassy from smoking *dagga*. She stood absolutely still and waited for what would happen next. Finally he replaced the gun in his pocket and said, "I'm too tired now. Maybe later. You can give me some breakfast and then do your washing."

Janet didn't dare argue. Relieved that she'd escaped rape or murder for the present, she said nothing but did as she was told. She made two mugs of tea and cut two thick slices of white bread. She offered him milk and sugar, and jam for the bread. He ate ravenously and asked for more several times. When he'd had enough he made himself comfortable in a chair and told her to start washing. He watched her breasts as she cleared away his dishes and leaned over to pick up a mug. When she turned to walk away, he grabbed her arm and held her, while fondling her buttocks with his other hand. He liked her comfortable size much more than the skinny American, and he thought that he would enjoy watching her naked and build up some energy after a busy Saturday night so that he could have fun with her later.

He sprawled over the chair and told her to get on with her chores. Silently she obeyed and tried to think how she could overcome him, conscious of him watching her every move. Suddenly there was a loud knock on the door. She froze, hoping it wasn't Lauren. Tonsil hissed at her to keep quiet and went to answer. "Who is it?" he asked.

"Police, open up."

Janet's heart was pounding. Tonsil turned to her and whispered, "Stand right there where they can see you and shut up." She felt mortified to be seen naked by yet more men, but hoped to find a way of making the police realize that she was a captive in her own home. Tonsil opened the door just a crack to check that it really was the police.

"What do you want?" he asked. "Can't you see me and my girl are busy, man?"

The policeman pushed the door open a little further and looked around. He saw a naked woman opening and closing her mouth, trying to say something but covered in embarrassment, otherwise there was nobody else. "I'm looking for someone who's obviously not here. Sorry to disturb you two," he said with a sneer and turned on his heel. Tonsil slammed the door shut again. Janet felt tears of frustration in her eyes. She should have shouted for help; she'd lost that moment of opportunity.

He slumped back in the chair while Janet began to wash the dishes, before starting her weekly clothing wash in the kitchen sink. She could feel his eyes boring into her and as she worked, she began to plot. She would need to hang the clothes outside to dry, and perhaps she could make a break then. She knew he would be watching her though, so she thought of Plan B. He would want some more tea and food, and she could put some rat poison in the jam this time. The sweetness would disguise the taste and hopefully he would soon start to be ill. Then she could get out. But first she would try Plan A.

As she finished the washing, she turned to him and spoke for the first time since he'd attacked her. "I must put on my clothes to go and hang my washing," she said.

"You're not going outside you stupid bitch," he barked.

"But I must. If I don't hang my laundry, the neighbors will wonder what's wrong. I do this every Sunday morning."

He hesitated before answering, "OK, you can do it. But I'm going to watch you from the window. You can wave if anybody comes, but don't talk. You say you too busy today." He glared at her. "Any funny business and I'll shoot you."

She agreed to his terms and hurriedly pulled on some clothes, feeling a great sense of relief to be hidden from his leer. The moment someone came, she would run away. She gamboled that he would never dare shoot with witnesses around. Piling the wet clothes into a basket, she grabbed her bag of pegs and made her way outside, knowing that he was at the window. Her heart sank when she realized that there was nobody around; all her neighbors were at church. With frustration she realized her folly; she should have delayed coming out to do this for an hour or so. But maybe someone would come. She walked down to the shed where the start of the washing line was, and noticed the little dog Lunch lying outside. It was strange to see him here at the weekend, but he was lying in the sun and barked happily when he saw her. She bent down to pat him and remained bending over as she took in the sight of the locks. They had been opened. There was only one other person who knew the combinations of both locks. She didn't dare say anything because she knew she was being carefully watched, but her mind raced. If Lauren were inside, she didn't want her to cry out to Janet, because that would give her away. She must stay quietly inside, but how could Janet know if she was there without drawing attention to the shed, which thankfully had gone unnoticed by her attacker? She placed the basket on the ground to the side of the door and thought desperately as she fumbled with clothes and pegs. She glanced back at the window and saw his eyes watching her, but he wouldn't be able to hear her. She began to softly sing a song that they sang to the children, with a slight change of words:

Tula, tula, tula,
Be quiet, be quiet, be quiet.
There's a man with a gun
Be quiet, be quiet, be quiet.
Tula, tula, tula.
He's looking for you with a gun.

She sang the same words again, all the while hanging her clothes. Fortunately it's the most natural thing in the world for African people to sing as they work, so it didn't look suspicious. She grew bold and added another verse after glancing first at the window to ensure he was still inside.

Knock softly
If you hear me,
Knock softly

She stopped singing as she bent to get some clothes and showed no visible reaction when she heard a light tap, but her heart pounded. Now she knew where her friend was. She didn't know what was happening, or why she was in trouble, but as long as Janet kept the thug inside her house and Lauren kept quiet, she was safe. Once more she sang a song:

Be quiet little friend,
be still,
'Til I tell you it's safe
be still.
Tula, tula, tula.

She continued singing all the while she hung up the clothes, wondering whether to shut the combinations properly, but decided against it as she didn't want to do anything that would draw his attention to the shed. She kept focusing on the fact that if she kept the brute inside the house and put Plan B into action, Lauren would be safe. Suddenly she had purpose and strode back inside when she'd hung the last shirt. Tonsil was waiting.

"Take them off," he said.

"I still have to wash my sheets," she said. "I must do that quickly so that they have time to dry. When I'm finished I'll make some lunch for you."

"Why do you need to wash your sheets?"

"I wash them every week. Always. If the neighbors don't see my sheets there, they'll wonder why."

The thought of watching her bend over as she worked made him relent. "All right, but take your clothes off first."

Janet lowered her voice to say, "Please can I keep them on while I wash?"

He stared at her and sneered. "No. Take them off, bitch."

She was shaking as she began to undress once more. He stood next to her and rubbed his hands all over her body, into parts that no man had ever explored before. He soon began to breathe heavily as he felt a stirring in his crotch. "Before you wash those sheets, bend down over the bed," he said, pushing her.

"Please don't do this," she implored as she fell to the ground. "Please don't do anything to me. Please. I promised my grandmother before she died, and the priest; I said I wouldn't do that until I got married. Please don't."

He grabbed her arms to pull her up and then he shook her. She tried to pull herself away but he slapped her face hard with his open hand before shoving her forwards over the side of the bed. "Shut up. I like it better when you don't talk, and I like virgins," he said, unzipping his fly. She tried to push him away and run for the door but he tripped her up and shoved her over the bed once more, holding her down with both hands. She gasped and screamed as she suddenly felt him lunge into her body, tearing through her skin. He put one hand over her mouth and nose to stifle her. Battling to breathe under the tight grip of his hand, an automatic survival response made her bite ferociously into his palm and yank her head free as he released his grip in shock. He swore at her, and grew more violent in his assault—the pain in his hand made him want to inflict more pain on her. When she drew her fingernails roughly down his arm and drew blood, he thrust even harder. She could feel his gun pressed against her in his pocket as she continued to dig her nails into him and scratch wherever she found his flesh. It seemed to spur him on more until she thought he would rip her apart. Finally he stopped with a groan and stepped back, zipping his fly. He felt for his gun and aimed it carelessly at her, fingering the trigger. "You need sex with a virgin to cure Aids. That was lucky for me, hey! Now I'm cured. You can make me some lunch now, bitch."

Janet was in agony and filled with hatred, but she was also afraid. She had never felt so powerless and abused. Was he tormenting her with this talk of Aids, or was he really one of the ignorant who believed this terrible superstition? Did he have Aids? He was very thin, even though he was tall and had a big frame. If he did have Aids, he might as well pull that trigger.

She had been brought up by her grandmother while her mother worked, not ever knowing her father; she'd had a gentle childhood educated in a rural school, free from the terrors of township life. When she'd finished her teacher training in Cape Town, she decided to work in a township school, knowing how a good role model could influence the difficult lives of these children. She was a proud Xhosa woman in the new South Africa who'd never before had much reason to hate anybody, but she looked at this brute standing over her and felt a trickle down her legs that repulsed her. There was blood all over her and her sheets, her body was cramping with pain, and he stood there pointing a gun at her, telling her to make him some lunch. It was time for Plan B.

He took her laundry bucket to use as a lavatory. She took the time when his back was turned to make her move, grabbing a large spoon of rat poison from the box behind the detergent, and dropping it into the nearly-empty tin of jam. She glanced over her shoulder and, satisfied that he hadn't noticed, pretended to be scraping the jam out of the tin. She managed to stir the powder and jam until they were well blended, then she made a sandwich and handed it to him. He put it down on the table and demanded some tea first. She made it for him without comment, and then went to get her blood-soaked sheets and proceeded to wash them. She scrubbed them furiously, fighting back sobs and tears but watching him out of the corner of her eye. He gulped noisily at the tea and swilled it around in his mouth, scratched his crotch and then set the mug down. She watched him pick up the sandwich, examine it, and then put it down again.

"I'm tired of jam," he said irritably, "What else have you got?"

"Nothing, and that's all the jam," she replied. "I am poor. I can't afford anything else."

By now she had finished washing the sheets and informed him that she needed to go and hang them up. He grunted his agreement, allowed her to dress, and reminded her not to talk to anyone. "And no singing this time either. Just hurry up and come back here. I'll be watching you again."

There were still no neighbors about. She was tempted to bolt for it but a glance back at the house and she could see him standing menacingly on the step with his hand in his pocket, fingering the gun. As she flung the sheets over the line, she made a swift decision to use their cover to relock the shed doors. If he got an idea to open them, she feared for Lauren's life. With two quick clicks and twists, Lauren was now safe. She began to sing softly as she pulled the sheets straight:

I've locked the doors
To keep you safe
Be quiet, be quiet
He's got a gun…

She got no further with her song as a bullet whistled within an inch of her ear, straight through a sheet, and ploughed into the wall of the shed. She dropped to the ground and spun around to look at her attacker, who was busy replacing the gun in his pocket. It obviously had a silencer on it. "I told you, no singing. Next time I won't miss." He strode down until he was standing next to her, and then after glancing around nervously, he growled at her, "What were you doing to that door?"

"What door?" asked Janet, panic-stricken.

In answer to her question he fired a shot right through the door. "That one," he said.

"Nothing, I…"

"I saw you," he interrupted her. "What were you doing?"

"I'm feeling sick," she replied. "I needed to lean against something."

He glared at her and said, "What's inside there?"

Janet shook her head. "I don't know. It's not my shed." She was thankful that she'd locked the door, but hoped she could bluff her way out of this situation. He continued staring at her, and she looked him straight in the eyes saying, "I don't know what's there." She brushed past him and continued pegging her washing while he pushed the sturdy door and rattled the locks behind her. Janet's nerves were on edge as she listened, not daring to turn around. Finally he gave up.

When they got back inside she saw that the sandwich was untouched. He made her remove her clothes again and lie on the floor face down before using her pajamas to tie her hands together behind her back. She tried in vain to struggle as he did this to her, but he punched her in the head before stuffing a sock in her mouth and tying his stinking scarf over that. When would this nightmare end? It was better when she could see what he was doing instead of lying face down. He got up from tying her and kicked her exposed buttocks. He started to laugh and then kicked repeatedly. After a while he grew tired and stopped doing this. With a sigh he said, "Now, if I look in your cupboard and find something better than jam, what can I do to you? I'll think about that while I look."

She heard him tramp heavily to her cupboard and look inside. She held her breath, praying that he wouldn't see the rat poison and grow suspicious. The only food items in the cupboard were a tin of sardines and boxes of tea and sugar. He spat on the floor. "OK, so you were telling the truth. Just as well your Granny taught you not to tell lies." He returned to the chair and began to eat the sandwich, first taking a big bite and washing it down with a mouthful of tea. Janet watched him out of the corner of her eye, holding her breath that he wouldn't react to a strange taste. He took another bite which he chewed slowly, then stared at the sandwich. He lifted the top slice of bread and examined it, then put it together again and tried another bite. He took another swig of tea and rinsed his mouth out with it, then spat the tea over Janet. "This jam tastes bad," he shouted at her. "You're giving me rubbish to eat; I think I'll have those sardines instead." She could see that he'd devoured most of the sandwich before he made his way to ransack her small stack of food. She could no longer see him, but she could hear him opening the tin and chewing loudly, smacking his lips and belching loudly. He ambled over to her laundry basket and relieved himself again; her stomach heaved as she smelled the sour smell of urine and watched it spill onto the floor and trickle towards her. He was a disgusting animal who had humiliated and terrorized her all morning; she hoped that the poison would begin to take effect soon. He kicked her again as he walked past, before slouching back in the chair.

He was very quiet and Janet strained her head around as much as she could to see if he was asleep. His mouth was wide open but she couldn't see his eyes. She tried to move, but her hands were restrained by their bindings and it was difficult to shift her weight. The brute's breathing seemed to become deep and slow, and she was sure he was asleep, but being unable to move or make a sound, it didn't help her. Suddenly in the distance she could hear voices and realized that her neighbors were returning from church. Her heart began to pound with hope. The noise startled Tonsil, who rushed to the window and peered outside through a chink in the curtain. He watched as the people came closer and he moved away to stand behind the door. It began to worry him that perhaps the American woman wasn't coming here after all, and now these people were outside he didn't feel so comfortable any longer. He was contemplating what he should do about this when a sudden cramp hit his stomach that doubled him up in pain. His head began to spin at almost the same moment and he felt his stomach heave with nausea. Janet could see him writhing in agony. He was rolling on the floor, alternately pulling his knees up to his chest and then rolling onto his back. "What did you do to me you bitch?" he hissed. "I'll kill you." He groped around in his pocket until he found his gun which he aimed wildly, trying to keep a steady hand. By now he was shaking, retching, and vomiting blood, but he managed somehow to pull the trigger. The bullet entered Janet's shoulder and lodged in her right lung. She was momentarily aware of searing pain and blood spraying into her face, before she passed out.

***

Sitting quietly in the shed, Lauren had watched darkness under the door change to a thin strip of light, not enough to illuminate the shed but enough to tell her it was early Sunday morning. She had dozed fitfully during the short night, waking at the slightest sound and now she shone the flashlight around her surroundings, considering what to do. Soon Janet would be up and then she would be able to get into her house and phone Mike or the police. As she pondered how long she should wait to do this, she heard Lunch give a little bark. She strained to hear if there were any other sounds, and after a minute she was rewarded with Janet's voice starting to sing outside the door. She was just about to push the door open with relief when she heard what her friend was singing, "Be quiet because there's someone looking for you with a gun." She stayed absolutely still, almost afraid to breathe. Everything went very silent. After what seemed an eternity, she heard Janet start to sing again and was straining to make out if this was another message when she heard the muffled thud of something exploding in the wall, followed by a man's voice shouting. She was paralyzed with fear but concentrated hard to listen for Janet's singing once more; suddenly there was a man's voice right outside the door and a bullet whistled right past her, embedding itself in a box of milk powder which spilled out over the floor. Lauren froze in her tracks, keeping well away as the door shook and the locks rattled. Her heart was in her mouth until she finally heard footsteps retreating. If they were this close to finding her, she needed to change her plan in the shed. Silently she moved the boxes away from the door and piled them to make a barrier behind which she could conceal herself. If someone opened the door and searched, they would find her; but if they simply opened to make a quick check, she would be under cover. Thankful that there was food and bottled water here, she grabbed the flashlight and a bucket to use as a lavatory, then crouched terrified in her hiding place. All she could hear now was her heart pounding in her ears.

***

Bessie Opperman grabbed a camera, pushed it into her tote bag and jumped into her dark green Volkswagen Beetle. A reliable car, despite its age, it was cheap and probably unlikely to be stolen because it was so old. She turned the ignition and the car started with its distinctive tractor-like roar as she accelerated and sped off to make her first stop at Lauren's flat again. She needed to find out more about this American. The personal angle always attracted readers, and this woman was young, beautiful and rich—everything that people like to read about. She needed to find out who that young man of hers was and contact him too. A love angle would be good. She was in luck as he was there with the flat mate, and they were both only too happy to talk to her, sharing her belief that the publicity might bring someone forward with information. She suggested that Mike accompany her to her second stop, Kirstenbosch Gardens.

They set off in separate cars and made themselves known to the manager of the gift shop, who contacted the security guard, Julius. The old man was horrified when they told him of Lauren's abduction, blaming himself for not accompanying her to her car the previous night. All he could tell them was that he had seen her go down to the lower parking lot. He'd heard nothing unusual, just her car door closing twice, and a sound that he thought was the boot slamming shut. He then heard the car drive off, but he had heard no voices or gunshots. This was a small relief, but gave no lead. They thanked him, Bessie took his photo, and they went to inspect the lower parking lot. There was nothing further to see there as Mike had already found the backpack and cell phone, which had been handed to the police.

They both stood staring at the ground, wondering what their next move should be. There was absolutely no information to work with, no clue as to where that Jetta went, but they presumed that it took Lauren in it—probably in the boot. Bessie finally looked up and said to Mike, "I think I'm going to Guguletu. Do you know where the school is? If I can meet people that she worked with there, I can write a story about her work. The more people read about her and see her picture, the better. It's our best bet. Somebody will remember seeing something…" He described as best he could where the school was, and he was eager to accompany her. It would be all right to go to the building site with her as it was not quite in Guguletu, but she persuaded him that it would be a bad idea to come into the township proper. As a woman of mixed race, she could blend and go about her job, but as a white man he would stand out and hinder both her search and her ability to question passersby.

She followed him as he led her to the orphanage building site. It was a big piece of land that Lauren's family had purchased, and the foundations had already been dug. The footprint revealed that there would be about ten rooms to start with, and the first concrete blocks had been laid along the back wall. Bessie took some photos of Mike standing next to the wall, looking at the site, and then she decided to get to Guguletu while there was still daylight.

Guguletu. It made her nervous going there, but her press badge gave her a little bit of protection and if she wanted to reach the top as a journalist, she couldn't allow herself to be afraid. The next step in her career might be an overseas assignment, which could mean covering one of the hot spots in the world like Afghanistan, Iraq or Sudan, so she reminded herself of her editor's advice—get used to danger here in your own back yard first. She'd already broken the story on Lauren Marlowe and received high praise for it. If she could get the scoop by finding the American girl, she would be on a roll of success and she was hungry for that.

Mike's description of the school's whereabouts was good, and she soon found what seemed to be a kindergarten. It was strange though that he had said there would be a sign on the door, giving Janet Dyani's name as head teacher. There was no sign anywhere, but when she peered in the window, it certainly appeared to be a school. As it was Sunday at 3.30 p.m. there was nobody around to ask, so she decided to phone Mike. Perhaps he could confirm something from her description that this was the correct school. He eagerly answered the call and tried as best he could to be helpful. "Is there a small concrete house next door?" he asked. "I remember Lauren telling me that her friend was very house proud and tried to have a little vegetable garden growing in the back."

"There is a concrete house, yes. Let me take a peep and see if there are veggies here," she said as she strolled next door. "There's lots of washing on the line," she said, "and yes, there are some cabbages back here too. Thanks Mike, I'm going to knock on the door and see if this is Janet's house. I'll call you if there's anything to report."

She ended the call and made her way to the front door, where she gave a loud knock. There was no response. She tried to peep through the window, but the curtain was drawn both here and at the back. She was about to give up and try another house when she noticed a line of dark, congealed blood that had seeped under the door. She felt shivers racing down her spine as she pulled her cell phone to call the emergency police number; her heart was pounding as she gave a description of where she was and what she had found. Within minutes she heard a shrill siren getting louder and louder as a patrol car sped along, kicking up a moving wall of dust. Two policemen jumped out and asked if she had just called; they examined the blood, knocked on the door, and then kicked it open. What Bessie saw as she followed them inside would haunt her, despite the many horrors she saw as a crime reporter. The door was partly blocked by the slumped body of a man, not long dead by the looks of it, lying in blood and feces. The expression on his face was a grimace of utter agony. When she looked further, she gasped. In the gloom of the room lay a poor soul, face-down, naked and gagged, with her hands bound behind her back. The woman was on the floor in a great pool of blood that had seemingly gushed out of a gaping wound in her shoulder. It was unclear whether she was alive or dead.

Within minutes other police cars arrived, keeping onlookers out of the way, but allowing Bessie to remain when she showed her press badge. Another siren screamed its arrival and three ambulance workers rushed in to assess the situation. The man was declared dead, but the woman had a faint pulse. She was carefully covered and placed on a stretcher, then carried to the waiting ambulance amidst accompanying sounds of gasps and wails from bystanders.

Bessie had another story, but she wished she hadn't. It was with a heavy heart that she photographed the stretcher being placed in the ambulance. Things didn't look good for this woman whom she presumed was Janet Dyani; and if things looked bad for Janet, then she felt sure they were also bad for Lauren Marlowe. It was too much of a coincidence for the two incidents to be unconnected.

***

Lauren heard the sirens and commotion outside, and then the wails of people in the distance. She felt herself start to shiver uncontrollably. If only there were a window and she could see out, she thought to herself—while realizing that had there been a window, she might have been spotted earlier. There was no way of knowing what was happening. Until Janet came to let her out, she would have to remain locked in the shed.

10

With her identity confirmed by neighbors, Janet Dyani was rushed to Groote Schuur Hospital where only twelve years ago she would have been denied access because she was black, although her organs would have been permissible for transplant donation. Now, however, there was an operating room ready and available on her arrival and she was placed in the hands of some of the best surgeons in the country, who battled for two hours to extract the bullet from her lung and tried to repair the damage. Her blood group was immediately tested and she was placed on an intravenous drip to transfuse two liters of blood. This blood line was vital after such severe bleeding, but there was always anxiety that despite careful testing, the dreaded killer, the HIV virus, could be lurking in this lifesaver. Janet herself was tested for the virus and was shown to be negative; the medics took no chances though, as they knew only too well that it could be dormant. She would have to be monitored for it was evident to the doctors that she had been brutally raped within the last twenty-four hours. When she was finally wheeled into the Intensive Care Unit, she remained unconscious and sedated under police guard. Bessie had given the police a link between Lauren and Janet, and they were eager to question her as soon as possible once she regained consciousness.

**

Tonsil's body was removed to the police mortuary for identification. Captain Radebe summoned Sergeant Blignaut and the corporal who was with him earlier in the morning, and asked whether this was one of the passengers in the car with Zeke and Boy. The dead man's face looked very contorted, so it was difficult to be certain, but there was a strong resemblance and his clothes matched their recollection of a passenger. It was decided to bring Zeke and Boy to confirm the identity, and Radebe phoned the prison for them to be brought across under tight security.

There wasn't long to wait before they heard the sound of footsteps approaching as the prisoners were brought into the lobby. Radebe and Blignaut called for Boy to be brought into the observation room. This was a small room with just one chair in it, and a far wall with a large window looking into a small annex. On the other side of the window, in the annex, was a mortuary attendant standing next to a gurney that had a green sheet on it. Boy looked around nervously when he saw Captain Radebe and Sergeant Blignaut in the room, unaware of the reason for his being here. The policemen talked quietly to one another in undertones, leaving Boy sweating. Finally the captain called to the policeman guarding the prisoner, instructing him to put Boy in front of the viewing window. Then he said, "Look at this body and tell me if you recognize it." He nodded to the attendant on the other side of the glass, who immediately flicked the sheet back from Tonsil's tortured face. Boy gasped and began to wail.

"Do you know who this is?" demanded Radebe.

Boy sobbed and nodded his head.

Radebe signaled the attendant to cover the face again, and then turned to Boy. "Who is it?"

"It's Tonsil Morope."

"Was he in the car with you this morning?"

"Yes," sobbed Boy. "What happened to him?"

"That's what we want to find out. Take him back to the cell," Radebe instructed. Boy looked like he was going to faint as he swayed and began to retch, so he was pushed onto the chair and told to put his head between his knees. After a few minutes, he was hauled up and taken out, after which Zeke was brought into the observation room. The policemen followed the same procedure, leaving Zeke anxiously wondering why he was here.

"OK, bring him to the window," Radebe commanded after a while. He said to Zeke, "I'm going to show you a dead body. I need you to tell me if you know who it is." He nodded to the attendant, who gave his practiced flick of the wrist to reveal the gruesome, dead face. "Anybody you know?" asked the captain. Zeke screamed and collapsed, covering his face. A low wail began to fill the room.

"Who is it, Zeke?"

Between sobs, the prisoner replied, "Tonsil Morope."

After a nod from the captain, the body was covered and wheeled away silently. "Was he in the car with you this morning, Zeke?"

"Yes," he sobbed. "What happened?"

"We will find out after the post mortem. Thank you for identifying him for us. Take the prisoner back now," he said, addressing the guard.

Radebe and Blignaut left the observation room as well and returned to the captain's office. Radebe sat down at his desk, signaling the sergeant to sit in the other chair. He sat with his elbows on the desk and put his forehead in his hands. His head was pounding. The Chief of Police had been calling him every hour to find out what progress had been made in the case of the missing American; he had been pleased to report that the car had been recovered from Somerset West and two arrests had been made; it was a father and son operation. Zeke and Boy had been singing like canaries, but there was still no American woman found. He feared the worst when he was informed about Janet Dyani; the journalist had made the link between the two women, and much as he hated to follow a lead given by a reporter, he had to admit that there was too much going on for it to be a coincidence. He would need to find out more from the singing canaries while they were still in shock from seeing Tonsil's corpse. "Blignaut," he said, looking up through weary eyes, "We need to lean hard on those two thugs. We need to find out why this scumbag called Tonsil was at Janet Dyani's house. He must have gone there sometime this morning after he was seen by you." He said this as he leafed through some other reports, when suddenly one caught his eye. "Look at this," he said, pushing a piece of paper to Blignaut.

It read: *Questioned four men in their twenties, in Guguletu shebeen, about 7:15a.m. One, Basie, had been in a fight with about five thousand rand in his pocket, and an unlicensed gun. Booked him for that. Other three ran away out of back door. Signed; Sergeant D. Kumalo*

Blignaut looked at Radebe. "Almost five thousand rand…Another coincidence?"

Radebe picked up the phone and called the mortuary. "What were the contents of Tonsil Morope's pockets?" he asked. He nodded his head and replaced the receiver. "It's tying together, Blignaut. Guess what he had?"

"Five thousand rand?"

"Correct. He also had a gun, unlicensed, and a cell phone belonging to Janet Dyani. Now we're going to pay a visit to this Basie and see what he has to say. He was with Tonsil later than these other thugs. Let's lean on him first. And tell Dr. Meyberg in the morgue that I need the results from the autopsy as soon as possible."

Basie was summoned to the observation room and put through the same procedure as he identified Tonsil. He was visibly shaken and, back in his cell, Radebe watched the prisoner through a hatch as he vomited into a bucket. He was wiping his mouth and groaning when the door rattled open, admitting Radebe and Blignaut. "Why were you with this man, Tonsil, at a *shebeen* so early in the morning?" the captain asked.

Basie shook his head. "We were there all night. I hadn't gone home yet."

"You're lying." Radebe nodded to Blignaut who produced a leather whip, a *sjambok,* and snapped it on the floor inches from Basie's feet. It whistled as it cut through the air. "You were in a road block early this morning. Two of your friends were brought into a police station. You were not in the *shebeen* all night."

Basie began to shake uncontrollably. "Now let's start again," said Radebe. "I'll ask you a different question. Where did you get five thousand rand?"

"It's my savings," Basie replied.

"Did you get this money from Jake's Motors in Somerset West?" Radebe paused as Zeke swallowed hard. "Like your friends Zeke and Boy? Jake tells me he gave you all five thousand rand for a blue Jetta."

There was no reply from Basie, just a slight noise in his throat. Finally he said, "I don't know anything about that. Those are my savings."

"I haven't got time to waste so we will just have to ask Jake and Samuel. They've already identified Zeke and Boy. I'll have them identify you and Tonsil, and we'll see if you're telling the truth...Take him to the front holding room and bring Jake." As he walked behind the prisoner, he muttered, "If you're wasting my time you'll be sorry about it. If you co-operate and answer questions without lying, you'll find things will be better for you. Take your pick; honest and have an easier time, or lie and I'll make your life miserable."

Basie stopped in his tracks as he saw Jake enter the room. A wet patch was soon evident in his trousers as he looked anxiously about him. Radebe looked at Jake and said, "Is he one of the ones you paid R5,000.00 for the Jetta?"

Jake and Basie stared at one another for a long time in silence. Finally the captain said, "If you co-operate Jake, you'll be out of jail in a couple of years for dealing in stolen property, and you can start a proper Jake's Motors without a side business in stolen cars. But if you don't, as I warned you before, you'll be charged with abducting Lauren Marlowe. And if we don't find her soon, the charges are going to get even more serious. If she's been raped, you'll be an accomplice. If she's been murdered, you'll be charged as well. You could spend the rest of your life in jail. So tell me—did you pay this man R5,000.00 for a blue Jetta last night?"

Jake nodded and said, "Yes."

"Thank you," said Radebe. "Take both prisoners back to their cells."

Basie was weeping uncontrollably as he was led away. He knew he was trapped and just hoped his part in the rape would not be discovered as the captain interrogated him mercilessly.

"Where did you take the American woman?" he asked, "We know you were part of it, so answer me."

Basie stared at his feet but fell flat on his face as a *sjambok* cracked down on the floor behind his back, a warning delivered by Sergeant Blignaut. "Where did you take her?" Radebe screamed.

"To a shack in Guguletu," the prisoner answered quickly.

"Where was she the last time you saw her?"

"In that shed."

"Did you tie her up?"

"Not me. Somebody else did."

"Why was she tied up?"

"So she couldn't get away."

"Why was there blood on the floor of the shack?"

"Because Samuel hit me. It was my blood."

"So this wasn't the girl's blood?"

"No. There was no blood from her. Nobody hurt her."

Radebe's laugh was hollow. "Nobody hurt her! You steal her car and tie her up, and you think nobody hurt her. Did you hear that Sergeant? So we can tie you up and drive you around in the boot of a car and that would be OK because it wouldn't hurt you? Why did Samuel hit you?"

"I...I don't remember."

Radebe nodded to Blignaut who cracked the *sjambok* again. It whistled past Basie's nose within an inch. "Tell me why Samuel hit you."

"Because he wanted to see the girl, and he was mad because she wasn't there. He thought I was lying to him."

"He wanted to SEE the girl. Is that what you said?"

"Yes, he wanted to see her."

"And what did he want to do to her?"

"I don't know. Ask him."

"Oh I will, believe me. If his story is different from yours, you'll know all about it. But tell me, what did *you* do to her?"

"Nothing, Officer. We tied her up and left her there when we took the car to Jake. Samuel brought us back and she wasn't there anymore. She must've escaped while we were gone. That's the truth."

"Who else was with you and Tonsil at the *shebeen*? There were two more of you. I know that, so don't lie to me."

Basie was about to deny that anyone else was there, but thought better of it as he saw the *sjambok* being lifted and tapped in readiness for use. He backed away, hurriedly giving the names and addresses of Abram and Mackie; immediately Radebe made a call for them to be located and brought in for questioning. Within half an hour, Radebe was interrogating them, separately.

He started with Abram. "Where did you go after you left the *shebeen* this morning?"

"I went home."

"Where did Mackie go?"

"Home, I think."

"And Tonsil?"

"We all went home. To our own homes, not together."

"Not Tonsil. He didn't go home," said the captain. "Have you any idea where he went instead?"

"No. We said we were going home. If he didn't, I don't know what he did."

"Well, I'll tell you where he went. He went to a woman called Janet Dyani's house. Why did he go there?"

Abram cursed. "We told him to go home. He's so fucking stupid."

"Well not anymore. Now he's dead." Abram's jaw dropped. Radebe continued, "Sergeant, get the guard to take this man so he can identify the body for us, while I talk to the other one."

He went straight to Mackie as Abram was led away, and received a corroborating story. He then had the guards take Mackie to identify the body and returned to speak to Abram, who was now also vomiting in a bucket. Sergeant Blignaut whispered to Radebe that Doctor Meyberg was very annoyed to have the post mortem interrupted. So far he had to report that Tonsil was HIV positive, but the cause of death was as yet undetermined, and would the captain please not send anymore people to identify the body until he was finished.

Radebe turned to Abram. "Let me ask you again—why did Tonsil want to go to this woman's house?"

"I don't know why he did that. He wanted to go to the school because he thought that the American woman might go there. He wanted to ransom her. We said he was crazy to do that so he said he would go home. I don't know why he went to this person's house. I've never heard of her."

When Radebe had satisfied himself by multiple cross-checking that neither Mackie nor Abram had been at Janet's house, he left Sergeant Olivier to establish that they had also been given money by Jake Jakobs, and they could therefore be charged with abduction and car theft, along with the rest of the gang. Now he had all the perpetrators, but there was still no Lauren. He dreaded the next call from the Chief of Police who would see no progress until they had found the American woman. He felt a wave of irritation that this much concern was shown for one wealthy, white foreigner, when innumerable black women were victims of terrible crimes every day without undue concern. They simply became statistics. Perhaps when this case was closed, he would try and use the facts of it to force some changes. If he had the manpower every day that he was able to summon at this moment, he would be better able to control the lawlessness. But he was understaffed, and often the caliber of officers was less than desirable. He knew there was much corruption in the ranks that was overlooked. It all made his job very difficult, so that by contrast the successes of today were rare. He wished that the Chief could give that some recognition, instead of screaming down the phone at him every hour.

***

Lauren drifted in and out of sleep. She tried to think of a plan to get out and find help, but then she recalled how she had been raped by three attackers, or she imagined again the bullets striking the shed, and her brain froze. Not knowing who was on the outside made her terrified to bang on the door and draw attention to herself, which was the only possible thing she could think of doing. Finally she resigned herself to waiting quietly until help came to her—however long that might be. The air was stuffy and the heat of the day was stifling as it baked the shed, but at least it was safe. School would be open on Monday morning, and it surely would be safe for Janet to help her then.

11

In the morning, Bella tried again unsuccessfully to reach Lauren in South Africa. She looked at her watch and recalculated what time it would be there. At nine o'clock Monday morning in California, it was six o'clock Monday evening in Cape Town. Anxious to reach San Francisco where there might be a better connection, she mentioned this to Phillip as they drove together, following close behind Howard and Wendy. The trip back to the city was uneventful; Bella and Phillip took the time to discover that they had similar likes in music as they searched radio stations, and then discovered that they both loved Shakespeare. "I love his tragedies most," said Bella in answer to her brother's question. "I think Macbeth is my all-time favorite."

"Ah yes, the Scottish play," Phillip said. "My favorite too, but I love his sonnets most of all. I'm a romantic at heart" he laughed. "I hope you'll bring Lauren and come to England for a while so that you can meet Cynthia and my children. We can all get to know one another. How strange that Wendy lives in Brighton, not too far away." He watched Bella out of the corner of his eyes as she drove, and he felt a surge of warmth towards her. She managed so stoically, despite the loss of her husband at a young age. His sister was a strong woman, and yet there was something fragile about her. She was clearly concerned about her daughter whom she couldn't reach, and he thought he might suggest to her that she take a trip to visit Lauren.

He hesitated from doing this however, not wanting to take on a role of big brother—telling her what to do.

Wendy and Howard were meanwhile engaged in serious discussion in the other car. They had hardly locked up the house and left Carmel when Howard exploded. "I don't know how to take all this, Wendy," he fumed. "It's scandalous. We suddenly have this bastard brother and we're expected to be one big happy family! It's bizarre and totally selfish of our parents to thrust this information on us when they're no longer around. It's a cop-out on their part."

"Howard, calm down," Wendy remonstrated. "It wasn't the way they wanted us to learn about it; they were bound to keep it a secret in their lifetimes. It must've been painful for them looking at their own child and not being able to have a parent/child relationship with him. Can't you see how terrible it must have been for them? If they'd been cowards they could have kept it a secret and none of us would've been any the wiser. But they were too honest and brave ever to do that."

"I told you what I think about that. Their sins caught up with them."

"Howard, I'm going to tell you something that someone should've told you a long time ago. You've become very self-righteous." She paused, and then made a decision to continue what she had begun. "Try to see things from somebody else's point of view, not just your own. Didn't you ever listen to Mom saying there are always two sides to a story?"

"Yes, I heard Mom say that, and she was correct. There's a right side and a wrong side of every story."

"No in-betweens? Don't be so intolerant, Howard. You're so convinced of your own righteousness."

"If you know what's right, there can be only one course of action. There's no possibility of an in-between. Look at Bella—she's strayed so far from what's right that she's a mess."

"What are you talking about, Howard? She hasn't strayed anywhere at all. She's a grieving widow trying to make her life have some point. She's a devoted mother and sister—to those who allow her to come close, and she was a good daughter; she's also a well-respected teacher at Georgetown University. No mean feat. I'm in awe of her; the only person who seems to have a problem with her is you. Do you think everyone else is wrong? You have a mental block about Bella, maybe because she is so much like Dad—quick and forthright—and you always bumped heads with him as well. If I might say one thing to you; don't always judge people. Just accept them and their differences."

"Is that what you suggest I do now that I have a brother out of the blue? Just accept him?!"

"That would be a good start. You make life difficult for yourself by feeling this moral superiority to everyone else, even Mom and Dad now. It prevents you connecting with anyone except Tracey. You isolate yourself Howard. It's difficult being around you because you're always looking down in judgment on people and they can feel it—even if you don't say anything."

"What's got into you? You're usually so keen not to upset anybody that you don't stand for anything. With Bella, I know she's going to disagree with everything I say on principle, but with you, you're like a cocker spaniel with its tail wagging all the time, wanting to please everyone. Now suddenly you're like a rabid pit bull."

"You're being very harsh…"

"I could say the same about you."

"Just because I don't say anything, doesn't mean I don't think it, Howard. Just because you think or feel something, doesn't entitle you to say it—unlike you and Bella who think and say things simultaneously."

"You don't know me anymore, Wendy, and you don't take the time to find out."

"I grew up with you and I remember the person you once were; loving and compassionate. You were fun to be with once upon a time, but now you judge everything and everyone by some manmade yardstick that you're convinced is God-driven, and you find everyone except you and Tracey lacking."

"Tracey and I are Christians. That means we are followers of Christ. If you call yourself a Christian that is what you should do too. We believe what Jesus taught—there's nothing manmade about it."

"The Bible was written by people long after he died. It was written by men, Howard, not God. My idea of a Christian is what Paul wrote to the Corinthians though, that love is patient and kind. I bet Jesus was a fun-loving person. People loved being near him because he listened to them and felt their pain. Try and remember that. You chase more people *away* from religion than anything else."

"You're insulting me, Wendy. I would expect it from Bella, but not from you. If we weren't in the middle of nowhere, I'd kick you out of my car."

"And I'd be happy to get out of your car. As a sister I tell you this, your heart has grown cold and judgmental. This country was founded on freedom of religion. That also means freedom *from* religion if that's what one chooses. "

They drove without speaking all the way to San Francisco, pulling into the Union Street Parking Garage just before noon and making their way rigidly to the offices of Ned Mackay in time for the reading of the will. Phillip and Bella were already seated and chatting amiably to Ned and Malcolm Bailey when they arrived. As everyone was being served coffee, Wendy leaned over to her sister and inquired, "Any luck reaching Lauren?"

Bella shook her head and was about to say something when Malcolm Bailey began to speak. "Ladies and gentlemen, I trust you had a good time together and have digested the information that was given to you yesterday." He nodded as he looked around at them, acknowledging their smiles except for Howard, who glared icily at him. "Yes, well then it falls upon me to share your parents' wishes with you. I might add that your parents struggled with the decision of informing you about the existence of one another. It was your father's final instruction that you should meet and he hoped that you would understand and forgive any pain and shock that it caused you. Your mother and father desperately hoped that the truth would bring joy to you in time." He opened a file that was lying in front of them and began to explain the contents. Much had been left to charities that would be monitored and invested by the Parker Family Foundation yet to be formed; each child would be a member of the foundation along with four non-family members to be selected by them, and an attorney; each grandchild would receive an amount of five million dollars; the rest was divided equally among the four children, each of whom would receive twenty-five million dollars.

Howard's brain heard no more. He started doing some calculations and felt his blood begin to boil. He had no children getting five million dollars a piece. He multiplied five grandchildren by five and added twenty-five that had been given to Phillip who was legally someone else's son, and suddenly there was fifty million dollars flowing out of the pot. That was nearly seventeen million dollars he felt was rightfully his.

The Englishman was busy reading some other minor bequests in his quiet voice, when he was suddenly interrupted by the shrill tone of a telephone ringing on the desk. "I said no interruptions," muttered Ned apologetically, as an assistant rushed into the room to tell him that the call was urgent. It was the State Department trying to reach Ms. Isabella Marlowe. Bella paled as she rose and the phone was handed to her. Wendy sat holding the side of her chair tightly as she looked at her sister's face and listened to the muffled tones of a voice on the other end. Everyone was silent; watching, waiting and listening to Bella.

—Yes, this is Isabella Marlowe.

—That's correct. She's in Cape Town.

A long silence followed.

—What? Oh my God! When?

—What is being done to find her?

—No, nothing. I haven't received any ransom requests. This is the first I've heard of it. But I'll pay any ransom, do you hear me? I just want my daughter back safely.

The voice on the other end continued to speak briefly, but Bella interrupted.

—I'm catching the first flight out to Cape Town. My daughter is going to be found, and I will be there.

Bella dropped the phone and collapsed in her chair, sobbing. Everyone else looked in disbelief at one another, trying to piece together what had happened from the few words they'd heard. Wendy quickly rose and put her arms around her sister, saying, "What's happened Bella?"

Bella clung to Wendy and sobbed into her shoulder. "Lauren's been abducted. Her car was stolen and she's missing—hasn't been seen since Saturday evening."

They could hear a voice on the dangling telephone saying, "Hello, hello..."

Phillip picked up the receiver. "This is Ms. Marlowe's brother, Phillip, here. Can you please tell me what is going on?" He listened intently, with an ever-increasing frown on his forehead. When he finally replaced the phone, the state department had told him as much as they knew, including the discovery of Janet Dyani and the dead body, but adding that there was regretfully no trace of Lauren. He shared the information with the others in the room, before suggesting a course of action. "I suggest we communicate with the State Department that we'll offer a reward—a big one—for any information leading to the safe return of Lauren. Secondly, I agree with you Bella, you need to be there. I would like to accompany you if that's all right."

Bella nodded her head in agreement. "Yes, please—please come with me."

"I'll come too, Bella," murmured Wendy.

Bella nodded her head and then her body began to shake. Her face was ashen as anxiety drained her blood and reason.

Howard cleared his throat, visibly grappling with his emotions. "I think we should offer $10,000.00 as a reward. That's about R60,000. Do you agree?" he asked, looking at the others.

Bella looked at him with tears in her eyes. "Will you take care of it, Howard?"

"Leave it to me," he replied. "Actually, why don't we make it R100,000.00, whatever the dollar translation is?"

Everyone agreed and Ned set about getting tickets booked for them to fly to Cape Town that evening. There was no time to waste as they needed to be at San Francisco Airport by 4 p.m. "How many tickets are we purchasing?" asked Ned.

"I think it would be better if I remain to deal with things here. You'll have the support you need from Wendy and Phillip," Howard said to Bella. "I don't want to be upsetting you." He bit his lip after he'd spoken and added, "I'll keep you and Lauren in my prayers."

Bella closed her eyes and bowed her head. Howard wondered whether it was in silent prayer, but she raised her head and said in a shaky voice, "Ask your God why he lets such terrible things happen. I'd really like to know what he was thinking."

12

Howard watched his family depart through the security check at San Francisco Airport with both relief and regret. Robert and the twins were going back as far as London, while Wendy, Phillip and Bella would all continue from there on another equally long flight to Cape Town. He turned to Tracey and said, "What a nightmare. I feel so sorry for Bella, and very afraid for Lauren." He sighed deeply and said, "It upsets me that Bella has a good relationship with Phillip already, but she spurns me. No matter what I say, she finds fault. My conscience tells me I should have gone with her to show solidarity and offer support, but I know it would've been a disaster. We would've been snapping at one another."

"Howard, don't blame yourself," his wife responded. "She's antagonistic towards you—and me. It's not your fault that this terrible thing has happened to her, or that her husband died. You didn't wish it on her; in fact you tried to help her. If she rejects you there's nothing you can do about it."

"Tracey, you don't understand how it hurts. If only she could accept my beliefs, but she always seems to take swipes at them. She doesn't even want me to pray for her; I mean it's not as if I'm asking her to pray! You have to have God by your side, especially at times like this."

Tracey put her arm through his as they walked back to the parking garage. "We need to organize things here, and that's the best you can do. If ever she wants you, she knows where you'll be."

"Before I do anything, I need to notify the State Department that we're offering a reward for information leading to Lauren's safe return. I suppose it'll be announced through the media. Let's hope that it flushes out some information. With a bit of luck Lauren will have been found by the time Bella gets there. How long did they say it would be before they reach Cape Town?"

"Something like thirty hours, I think."

"What a nightmare, stuck in a plane and not knowing what's happening. And Lauren—dear God—I pray she's safe." He was silent as they drove along Highway 280 back to Los Gatos, lost in his thoughts. After a while he said to Tracey, "Mother always used to say that her children were the source of her greatest joy, but also her greatest sorrow. Even though Lauren isn't my child, I begin to understand what Mother meant. Do you ever wish we'd adopted a child?"

She looked startled. "No, Howard, I haven't given up on having a child of our own. I'm working with a new infertility specialist. Have you forgotten?"

"I worry about you getting your hopes up so much. It all seems unnatural to me. Either you're able to conceive or you're not. God has his reasons. Maybe we are meant to help other people's children. Maybe it's God's plan that we'll be able to help our niece."

"I'm sorry about Lauren, believe me. It's a terrible thing that's happened. But I don't think you begin to realize how much I want my own baby—I don't want somebody else's. I want our child; our flesh and blood. My body clock is ticking away so there's no time to waste, but thirty-seven is not too late, and Dr. Wilcox is the best in his field. Money is no object; whatever it takes he will do for us."

"But that's what bothers me. Babies are God-given, not doctor-supplied."

"I prefer to see it as the doctor being a gift from God, enabling us to have a baby that comes from God."

"I'll be an old man when the child would be a teenager—I'm old enough to be its grandfather. Doesn't that bother you?" he asked.

"No. I'm twenty years younger than you Howard; it's unfair of you to not accept that."

He was silent as he considered this. She had brought so much joy to his life that he could never deny her anything she wanted, and so despite grave reservations, he finally said, "You must do what you feel you have to, Tracey. You know I'll support you whatever you want to do, but please let me concentrate on finding Lauren and getting the Parker Family Foundation up and running. I have enough on my plate at the moment. Charities will soon be applying for grants, and nothing can be done until the board is in place."

She turned her head and stared out the window as her thoughts turned to her upcoming visit to Dr. Wilcox. She brooded over her unhappiness; everybody else in the Parker family seemed to have had babies with the greatest of ease and she was determined that she would have one too. Howard indulged her like the father she never really knew and there was nothing she wanted for except a child of her own. She couldn't bear to see pregnant women any longer, who reminded her of the emptiness of her own womb. Each passing year made her more desperate to have a baby.

***

Howard called the State Department, who contacted the Embassy in Pretoria. The press was notified and reporters eagerly clamored to interview Howard at home in Los Gatos, standing at his front door. Tracey was by his side as he was interviewed. On Monday night the announcement was made on all South African television and radio networks:

R100,000 REWARD OFFERED BY FAMILY OF MISSING AMERICAN HEIRESS

Pictures of Lauren were shown, as well as a picture of her grandfather. The story described her connection to the giant company, Parker and Keating. Tuesday morning's papers worldwide carried the same news and pictures, with additional pictures of Howard and Tracey at the press conference.

He closed his eyes and prayed silently that his niece would be discovered soon, and that God would keep her safely in the meantime. He also prayed for forgiveness that he had judged her harshly; it wasn't this young innocent's fault that her parents had given her no religious upbringing. He was sure that she was a very noble young woman from all reports and he deeply regretted the lost chance of getting to know her better; the thought that she might have been murdered and that he would never have that chance made him choke. He felt ashamed. "Dear God," he prayed, "please save her. So much time has been wasted and now I realize that I had a chance right in my own family to spread your influence and be a light in this young woman's life. Please give me the opportunity to be a better uncle. How could I possibly be a father if I can't even be an uncle? Please give me the chance to prove myself, and please take care of Lauren." He felt weighted by the burden of knowledge that he had not played a bigger part in her life when she lost her father, until he remembered how close she was to her grandfather and the old feelings of inadequacy began to dog him again. He concentrated on his mother's calming influence, trying to hear her voice telling him he could do whatever he chose to do, and that he should choose wisely. Fortified, he said out loud, "My father is dead. I don't have to live in his shadow."

***

Tracey was startled by an old green Chevy truck pulling up outside the front door just as she was leaving to see Dr. Wilcox. She wasn't expecting workmen. A disheveled old man approached her and removed his baseball cap nervously, placing it under his arm. "Good morning," he said politely.

"I'm sorry, I'm just on my way out," she replied. "What do you want?"

"I'm looking for my daughter," he said.

She frowned. "I don't know that I can help you."

"Tracey," he said. "I'm looking for you."

She stared at him with horror. "You...who are you?"

"Your father," he said simply. "I've been looking for you half my life. You disappeared and I didn't know where you were." He stepped towards her and she recoiled in horror.

"My God," she said shuddering, "You! Oh my God, it can't be." She shook her head in disbelief. "What are you doing here? You left my life when I was 13 — not that I even saw much of you before that — and now you just walk back as if nothing happened! Oh my God!"

"I'm sorry, so sorry. I came back looking for you but your mother had gone and died and you were gone too. Nobody knew anything about you. I searched for you, but you went and left no forwarding address."

She was stunned. "You never told Mom and me where you were. We had no idea what had happened to you. We thought you must be dead. Do you know what that was like?" Tracey stared at the man standing in front of her. He was dirty, wearing shabby clothes with a smell of alcohol about him. His nose was very red and his eyes were bloodshot. A mutt barked from the back of his truck and he turned to it shouting, "Shut it will ya!"

"I'm sorry," she said. "You made your choice many years ago. Don't try and re-write history. As far as I'm concerned both my parents are dead."

"No Tracey," he cried. "Please…"

"Go away. I mourned for you when I was 13. I'm now 37. You haven't been in my life for 24 years and that's the way it's going to stay." She turned to go, but he grabbed her elbow. With a jerk she pulled herself free, saying, "Don't touch me. If you don't leave immediately, I'll call the police and have you arrested for trespassing."

"Aw Tracey, how can you do that? You're all I have. You and Bob there and m' truck," he said, pointing to his dog. "Don't break your old man's heart. I've made mistakes but I want to make it up to you. You're all I have Trace."

She bit her bottom lip. Why did he have to turn up now? He was disgusting. She didn't have the emotional energy to deal with him. As she hesitated, pondering what to do, he sensed an opportunity and stepped forward again.

"I hated being away from my little girl, but what could I do? I had to bring in the bacon. There was no easy street for me; nothing like this," he said gesturing to her house. "It was plain ol' hard work and truckin' for your daddy. That's what I had to do to put money on the table for you and your momma. And look at you now. What a woman you are. What a place this is. You done good, Tracey. You done real good."

She felt herself shaking with shock and confusion. "How did you find me?" she whispered.

"I'm sittin' havin' coffee, readin' the paper, and guess whose picture's on the front page? I take one look and says to m'self, 'That's my girl. That's my Tracey.' I got myself straight into my truck with Bob and here I am."

"How did you know where I live?"

He laughed. "How many Howard and Tracey Parkers live in Los Gatos? It was all there in the paper — didn't take much gray matter to work it out."

"I have to go," she said, in confusion. "I have an appointment."

"I can wait," he said. "What's another hour or so after all these years?"

"No," she said with horror. "You must go. Please go away."

"What's the problem Trace? You're not ashamed of your old dad are you? Just because he's a bit down on his luck..."

"Just go away."

He sighed and turned away. "Bob, there's nothin' here for us boy. Just you 'n me again old fella."

"Wait," she said, "tell me where I can get hold of you. I need to think."

"Wherever I park my truck is where I'll be," he said.

She searched in her bag for her wallet and gave him $500. "That's all I have. Go and find a motel room."

"I sure as hell appreciate it. You're a good girl," he said. "I probably shouldn'a come here today, Trace. It must be hard for y'all with this kidnapping. I'll come back some other time."

"No, just go." She turned her back on him and slammed the door firmly shut.

Her body felt cold and shivery as she drove to her appointment. She prayed that her father wouldn't reappear and did her best to put him out of her mind as she entered the new, state-of-the-art, infertility center. Once inside, she felt a surge of relief to be safely away from the house and she put her father out of her mind. There was a calm atmosphere here and the nurses were all encouraging, putting her at ease as best they could. This was going to be very different from all her other experiences when she and Howard had been subjected to so many humiliating examinations and questions. It felt different and filled her with renewed hope. She'd undergone laparoscopic tests until she knew the inside of her body as well as the outside; Howard's semen had been examined and analyzed, both inside her and out. There wasn't anything left to examine, and yet Dr. Wilcox came with a reputation of solving seemingly insurmountable problems for which she was prepared to pay anything.

It was also a relief to be away from the oppressive gloom that existed in their home. Howard might as well have gone to South Africa because he was obsessed with following what was happening there. He was on the phone until 2 a.m. talking to the Ambassador in Pretoria, as well as the Minister of Law and Order and the Chief of Police in that country. Was there no end to it? It was a relief to go to sleep and a nightmare to wake up. She tried to prod him to work on the Parker Family Foundation to get his mind off it, but he was like a demented soul, mourning his mother and channeling his grief into futile phone calls. Tracey felt it was such a waste of time on his part; nothing he could do from here would alter the outcome of what was happening there. She felt he was on a guilt trip because of his bad relationship with his sister, but at least Isabella had been able to have a child. Even if she'd only had her for a short while, at least she'd had her. She and Howard were the really unlucky ones.

She waited for Dr Wilcox and looked around at the botanical watercolors in the room showing healthy, burgeoning ovaries inside beautiful, exotic flowers. The tranquil blues and grays and the sound of a miniature waterfall were calming, and by the time the doctor entered, she had been transported to a happier frame of mind. He smiled at her warmly and had a quick look at her chart before announcing that he would need to perform another laparoscopy. This would be to check on several things himself that were not conclusively ruled out in the existing records. He smiled at her and said, "I understand your frustration very well, Mrs. Parker. We'll get things moving along quickly here and hopefully get some results. I'll get my nurse to schedule surgery this week, if that will work for you."

Tracey nodded and smiled. "You certainly make things happen fast, Doctor. You're living up to your reputation."

"I entered this field of medicine because I believe in it, Mrs. Parker. We are making huge strides—no, not strides—huge *leaps* in what we are able to do to help couples like you. Procreation is a strong urge and the world needs parents who want their children. I feel that helping you achieve that is a gift that I've been given."

Tears formed in Tracey's eyes. "Thank you so much Dr. Wilcox. It's a relief to meet such understanding. I'll be ready for the surgery whenever you can schedule it."

"That's the right attitude. This will be your number one priority, as it will be mine. I will be able to tell you more after the laparoscopy, but I assure you that I see nothing thus far that is discouraging." He walked with her to the front desk where his receptionist took over, scheduling Tracey for surgery on Thursday, in two day's time.

She felt light-hearted as she drove home. They had recently remodeled their home adjacent to a golf course after first buying the adjoining property and demolishing that house. Howard had wanted to move into his parent's old home, an old Victorian mansion in the foothills of the Santa Cruz Mountains overlooking the little town of Los Gatos, but she disliked its "old world charm" and wanted her own new house. The architect had understood exactly what she'd wanted so that the Mediterranean style featured balconies and courtyards capturing panoramic views across the valley to the Diablo Hills. In the evenings, she loved listening to birds gathering in the eucalyptus trees and watching formations of geese flying from the ponds on the golf course. She had joined the ladies' "9-holers" and it was convenient to simply drive her golf cart out of the garden gate and be with the group. All her life needed now was a baby. She relaxed on the bedroom balcony with her customary evening glass of wine, admiring the pistachio trees which were changing to all shades of yellow, orange and red. It was a child's paradise. She smiled determinedly and said a silent prayer. Los Gatos was the perfect town to raise her family, and this was the perfect home. Howard's indifference wouldn't matter; all she needed from him was sperm and she could do the rest.

The wine and the balmy, autumn evening heightened her sense of well-being after her visit to the doctor, helping to dispel thoughts about her father. She had postponed the appointment with Dr. Wilcox because of the crisis with Howard's parents, but now she felt free of that burden and released from terrible stress. She was not about to take on a new worry about this stranger who wanted to reappear in her life. From everything she'd read, stress seemed to be a factor that very often inhibited conception and once it was relieved, women often became pregnant without any treatment. She held onto a hope that this would be so for her. The last few years had been difficult; she had overseen the care of her parents-in-law, managing the housekeepers and nurses employed on their behalf, and dealing with her father-in-law who had not been co-operative in obeying doctor's instructions. In a role reversal, she'd found herself having to play the part of a very stern parent towards them both. They, for their part, responded by behaving like disobedient children. They never seemed able to understand that what she did was for their own good. If she hadn't felt so duty-bound and loyal to Howard, she would have stepped away from the burden years ago, but she reminded herself of Ruth's devotion to her in-laws in the Old Testament, and this served as her role model. Seeing her husband's car coming down the driveway and hearing the automatic garage door open, she took another sip of wine and felt justified in expecting Howard to support her now.

He appeared on the verandah a few minutes later and kissed her on the cheek. "Another drink?" he asked. He still marveled that this beautiful woman had agreed to marry him, and never ceased to feast his eyes on her face and body. She sat silhouetted against the waning day with a mane of curly hair framing her head and her long legs curled up in the chair. He felt a wave of desire. Marriage was a gift from God to satisfy this need he felt. She looked sweetly at him and said, "I'm still busy, but why don't you join me?" As he left to get a drink for himself, she smiled.

Later, lying in bed, she was aware of a satiated silence. The birds had settled in for the night, the golfers had gone home, and all she could hear was Howard's breathing. He had fallen asleep after their lovemaking, exhausted. She whispered in his ear, "Maybe we've just made a new little Parker."

13

Bessie Opperman was feeling frustrated with the lack of progress in the Lauren Marlowe case. She wasn't alone; Captain Radebe was at his wit's end trying to fathom how to proceed. He had a gang charged with car-jacking, abduction, possession of illegal guns and illicit drugs; he had Jake and Samuel Jakobs booked for receiving stolen goods while a follow-up on them had revealed that there was another son, Willie, who was a sergeant in the police force in Somerset West. He'd already handed that information to the Minister of Police, who would set up an independent investigation into that situation. It appeared that Willie had a hand in the operation, although it was not something that the captain had the manpower to deal with at the moment and he was thankful it didn't fall under his jurisdiction. He was in a grim mood when Bessie came knocking on his door, but he invited her into his office civilly.

"What can I do for you?" he inquired.

"I went to Guguletu yesterday to visit the scene of the crime, and there are a few things that are bothering me," she replied.

"Like what?" he asked, wearily.

"Well firstly, the school children were there, as they are again today, and I think your policemen are making a difficult situation even worse."

Radebe inclined his head with a frown. "What do you mean?"

"There's only one assistant, on her own, dealing with all the children. Your guys are shouting at the kids when they come outside and go near Janet's house—they're frightening them. They could be more understanding. Why don't you put up yellow crime-scene tape, and then they won't have to shout so much?"

"Fair enough," the captain agreed with a sigh. "I'll organize that."

"Thank you. And secondly I think you might allow your police officers to let us take down Janet Dyani's washing. It might sound unimportant to you, but I can't see a need for it to remain there. I tried to remove it and one of your guys was very rude to me."

Again Radebe nodded his head. "You can take it down and give it to one of the guards. But you must please realize that they are doing their job, which is not to be babysitters or take down washing. They're there to protect a crime scene."

"Thank you Captain," said Bessie, "I'll go and do it immediately."

"I'll send a message that they can expect you."

"By the way," Bessie asked, "has the reward offer made any difference in the case? Are you getting any leads?"

Radebe looked at her with his eyebrows raised. "You're not shy about asking questions, are you? You're a chancer; you know I shouldn't give you information like that, but I can tell you that we've had some opportunists wasting our time with false leads. Still, we have to follow everything up just in case."

"Has Janet Dyani regained consciousness yet?" she asked.

"I'm supposed to be the one asking questions," he remarked, "but no, she hasn't."

Bessie smiled at him. "Thank you so much Captain. I'll keep in touch with you if I find anything of interest. I was also wondering whether it would be possible for me to visit Janet in hospital."

"What for? I've just told you that she's unconscious."

She shrugged her shoulders but looked him squarely in the eye. "To be able to get feeling when I write, I like to be able to see the scene and be accurate. Besides, I can't interfere with police work if she's not talking, can I?" Then she cast her eyes down and added, "I suppose I feel some responsibility because I helped find her. It was a terrible sight."

Radebe considered this for a moment. "Please don't ask me for anything else now," he said. "You can make one visit to see her this morning, and then please...No more questions." He shook his head ostensibly showing displeasure, but inwardly admiring the young woman's intrepid attitude.

Bessie drove straight to the vast hospital, Groote Schuur, where the world's first heart transplant was performed, and made her way to the Intensive Care Ward. Here she showed her press badge and asked permission to see Janet. She had to explain that Captain Radebe had given permission for her to do so, and when this was verified she was finally allowed to enter. There were monitors and tubes everywhere she looked, and nurses walking briskly but silently, reading charts, making notes, feeling pulses and taking temperatures. Janet was in the far corner behind a drawn curtain, with a policewoman standing guard. Once again Bessie gave her credentials and was allowed inside the curtain accompanied by a nurse and the guard.

Janet lay in a half-raised bed, with a drip in her arm and another yellow bag attached to a tube lying on the floor. She looked merely asleep, except that occasionally she frowned and groaned. The nurse said to Bessie that at times the unconscious woman seemed to open her eyes and try to speak, without focusing on anything in particular.

"What does she say?" asked Bessie.

"We can't really make it out," the nurse replied, "but it sounds like 'stay there' or something."

"Does she say anything else?"

"Not that I've heard, although a night nurse wrote in her report that the patient tried to sing. Maybe a lullaby perhaps. She was singing *Tula, tula*, which means 'Hush, hush', doesn't it? Other than that, she lies here motionless."

"Was she raped as well as shot?"

Before the nurse could reply, the policewoman said, "I'm afraid you are not allowed to ask any questions about the case. Those are the captain's orders. I think your time is up now."

Bessie knew there was no point in arguing and her head was spinning with the information given by the nurse. She left the hospital and jumped into her car, roaring down the road as she sped to Guguletu. Arriving at the school, she was pleased to see that the yellow tape was already in place and the policeman on duty gave her a polite wave. "You can take the washing down now," he said, smiling broadly. He'd obviously been told to be more personable, she thought to herself. For the first time since she'd spotted the blood under the door on Sunday, she was allowed to return to Janet's house. She felt a chill down her spine at the recollection of that discovery, and she knew without the nurse's confirmation that Janet had been raped. She was thankful that she'd seen that victim safe, but she felt despair for Lauren. Just then a little dog came running towards her barking, and she patted his head. He licked her hand, before running to the door of a shed where he lay whimpering. She wondered whether he was Janet's dog and asked the policeman, who informed her that it was a stray that came to eat at the school. He was here for Tuesday lunch.

She looked more closely at the amount of laundry on the line and realized that she needed a container of sorts to hold it. She shouted over to the policeman, "Can I look in the shed for a basket?"

He shouted back, "It's no good, the shed is locked."

She saw that it was indeed locked with two combination locks, but she also noticed a strange mark in the door; on closer inspection it appeared to be a bullet hole. Her heart began to pound. She slowly walked around the shed to see if there was a window; instead she discovered another hole in a side wall with a bullet lying on the ground below it. As she returned to the washing line, she saw blue sky through a small, round hole in one of the threadbare sheets. It was lined up with the mark in the door. Her eyes dropped to the ground, and there, covered in dirt, was another bullet. The blood in her veins froze as she put together the pieces of the puzzle; the nurse had repeated Janet's unconscious mumblings, 'stay there' and 'be quiet.' Had Janet been trying to communicate with Lauren? Did she know where the American girl was? Was Lauren under their noses in the shed? Thankful that there was a policeman close by, she strode purposefully back to the door.

"Is there anybody in here?" she said, straining to hear a response. There was none. She knocked on the door this time and repeated, "Is anyone in here? I'm Bessie Opperman, a reporter with *The Argus*— you're quite safe." This time she thought she heard something move. She decided to take a chance. "Lauren, are you there? Janet's in hospital. She told me where to find you. It's safe for you to come out now—the guy with the gun is dead." She waited a moment and thought she heard a faint noise again. "Lauren, can you hear me? If you can hear what I'm saying, knock on the door."

Bessie closed her eyes and held her breath. Then she heard it: tap, tap on the door.

She felt tears streaming down her face. "I'm going to get you out of there Lauren, but I'll have to get these locks open. Do you know the combinations?"

A strained voice said so softly that she could hardly hear, "Yes."

"You're going to have to help me here Lauren. What's the combination for the top lock? I've got my ear right here at this hole in the door. Can you speak through it?"

"23-30-27."

Bessie repeated the numbers and with shaking hands she turned the dial three times to the right and stopped at 23. Then she turned it to the left, all the way past 23 and stopped at 30. After this she turned the dial right to 27. It popped open in her hands.

"OK Lauren, good job. We're halfway there. What's the combination on the bottom lock?"

She strained to hear, but there was no sound except the dog sniffing loudly at the door. "Lauren, we've got the first lock off; tell me the next combination and I'll have you out of there in a minute."

She pushed the dog out of the way and strained to hear a voice but heard only sobbing on the other side of the door. "It's all right Lauren," she said. "You're OK. There's a policeman here too, you're in safe hands." The sobbing continued a few minutes and then between sniffs, Bessie heard, "15-32-21." She was trembling as she moved the dial. When it opened she pulled both locks off so that she could tug the door. It creaked open. In front of her was a small person kneeling on the ground. Her face was ashen and her eyes were almost popping out of their sockets, with big black rings under them. There were dried blood stains all over her jeans, and her body was shaking visibly. How different from the smiling girl she'd seen in photos, but it was unmistakably Lauren. Bessie's immediate impulse was to put her arms around the stricken young woman and comfort her, but she felt Lauren recoil. The American girl was clearly traumatized and in need of medical attention. She held Lauren's hand tenderly and whispered, "You're safe Lauren. I'm going to call for an ambulance, and then I'm going to call your friend Mike Rousseau." Lauren was shivering, but she nodded.

Bessie let go Lauren's hand and called Captain Radebe on his cell phone. "I've found her," she said in a calm voice that belied her state of agitation.

"You've what? Where? Is she alive?"

"Yes. But you need to get an ambulance here as soon as you can."

"Where are you?" he asked.

"In the shed behind Janet Dyani's house. I think she's been there all the time from the looks of it."

"I'll be right there and an ambulance will be on its way immediately. Stay with her Bessie."

"I will, don't you worry about that," she replied.

By now the guard had realized what had happened and he was on his walkie-talkie, only to be told that help was already on its way. Bessie instructed him to find a blanket for the woman, and then to take down the laundry to make himself useful. She wanted to cover Lauren and keep her out of sight from the children who would soon be coming outside for lunch. While she was waiting, she called Mike's cell phone and — once he answered — she passed the phone to Lauren. Lauren held the phone next to her ear and heard Mike say, "Hello, Hello," but she couldn't say anything. Instead she began to cry again and returned the phone.

"Mike, it's Bessie here. I've found her. She's in shock but she's all right I think. She was in the shed behind the house. An ambulance will be here any minute."

"Stay with her, Bessie. Where are they taking her?"

"Groote Schuur I suppose. I'll find out and follow in my car."

"Will you call me and let me know?"

"Of course."

"I'll be there as soon as you tell me where."

By now the policeman had returned with a blanket from the school, and just as they wrapped it around her, an ambulance arrived. The children were all peering out the window and door as their teacher's friend and helper was placed carefully on a stretcher and carried away. Their little voices could be heard calling after her, "Bye Miss Lauren," and a little dog ran beside the ambulance for a short while on its way to Groote Schuur, barking for all his might. Bessie quickly phoned her editor to update him, and he agreed to hold the printing press as long as he could to get her story into the evening paper.

***

Mike was not immediately allowed into the private ward where Lauren was taken for examination, so he stayed outside the room talking to Bessie and finding out all she had to tell. Soon the American Consul arrived and was also made to wait outside. He informed Mike and Bessie that the family were on their way and would be arriving the next morning on the British Airways flight from London. Bessie made a mental note to be there. Finally a couple of doctors emerged and spoke to the waiting trio. "She's in shock and is not talking at the moment. This can happen with trauma cases, and it's nothing to be unduly worried about. She needs to rest. Are any of you family?"

They all shook their heads and explained who they were. "Mr. Rousseau," the older doctor said, "you may go in and speak to her for a few minutes, as she knows you. I'm afraid that I can't allow you others in at the moment. It might traumatize her more."

The Consul began to ask what had happened, but the same doctor cut him off. "I'm sorry but I can't discuss the case with anybody except family and police."

"I am a representative of the United States Government, and Ms. Marlowe is a U.S. citizen. I have a duty and a right to know."

"And I am a representative of this hospital and Ms. Marlowe is a patient here. I appreciate your concern and I assure you as soon as I am able, I will tell you all I can. She has been assaulted and therefore it is a police case. That's all I can tell you."

Mike walked quietly into the room and approached Lauren's bed. She lay dazed, staring into space. When she became aware of him, she turned and looked at his face without any reaction. He didn't know what to say. Instead he reached out and held her hand in both of his, then bent his head and gently kissed her hand. She didn't respond in any way. He tried to open his mouth to speak, but choked. Finally he swallowed hard and whispered, "Lauren, I have to tell you how much you mean to me. These past days nearly drove me mad." She pressed his hand softly and then closed her eyes. "Thank God you're safe," he murmured. Soon her hand fell limp in his, and she sighed deeply as she drifted off to sleep. He watched her awhile before leaving the room as quietly as he'd entered.

He drove back to campus on a route that he would take several times each day over the next few days. He felt rage pulsing through him, knowing what was meant when doctors said someone had been assaulted; this beautiful young woman had been raped, of that he was sure—God knows by how many and whether any of them had Aids. He knew without being told that her emotional recovery would be a long process, and he didn't even want to think of the physical hurt. He was ashamed that this generous girl had been attacked in the country of his ancestors that he loved so passionately. On his mother's side they traced the family back to the first European settlers in 1652; his paternal ancestors had been French Huguenots who were granted a farm in Franschoek three hundred years ago. His forbears had been in the Cape ever since and his parents had fought for the end of apartheid. He was proud that his family was part of the fabric and history of the place. South Africans of all races used to take pride in their warmth and hospitality, but these days there were many who were as likely to kill as to befriend. Goodwill and hope were being dashed by violent lawlessness. He felt despair.

***

Howard and Tracey were awoken by the shrill ring of the phone next to their bed. Howard looked at the clock as he groggily picked up the receiver. It was 5.20 a.m. on Tuesday morning. "Hello," he said.

"Mr. Parker, this is Joan Muir at the State Department. I'm sorry to disturb you at this hour, but I wanted to inform you that your niece has been found alive."

Howard sat up in bed, now wide awake, and automatically groped for the light switch and his glasses. "Tell me everything." He listened intently and nodded. "Is there a number where I can reach her?" he asked. He scribbled this down and thanked the caller before replacing the phone and closing his eyes. "Thank you God, thank you, thank you," he uttered as he dropped to his knees beside the bed. Tracey leaned over and put her arms around him as he prayed, uttering her own silent prayers of thanks and supplication.

He finally lifted his head and she could see that his eyes were moist. She'd never seen him cry before, not even when his mother died. She felt a little stab of jealousy, but put the feeling aside and listened as he told her all he knew. He then dialed the number he'd been given and heard a strange guttural accent telling him that he'd reached Groote Schuur Hospital. Before long he found himself talking to a nurse who explained that Lauren was not speaking as she was traumatized, but that he could attempt to do so. He could hear quiet sobs as he spoke, telling her that her mother would be there the next morning. It was 1.30 p.m. on Tuesday afternoon in South Africa. Lauren spoke not a word.

14

Bella was awoken from an uneasy sleep by a gentle nudge to her shoulder—somewhere over North Africa. She opened her eyes to see Phillip and Wendy smiling at her with a stewardess and the captain of the plane standing behind them, armed with a bottle of champagne. She blinked her eyes furiously and took a moment to remember where she was as Wendy grabbed her hands saying, "Bella, they've found Lauren. She's alive."

Isabella stared open-mouthed, and tears began to roll down her cheeks.

"It's all right Bell, she's safe. The pilot has just been radioed by the police; Howard got onto it and made sure that you were notified."

"When did they find her?" she asked.

"Earlier today. She's been in safe hands for about ten hours now, and she knows that you're on the way. Howard told her that."

"Howard's spoken to her?" she asked incredulously.

"Apparently so."

Bella threw her arms in the air and cheered, "Yes. Oh thank God." Then she sighed so deeply that it seemed as if she had exhaled all the air in her body. She dropped her arms and put her head into her hands, rubbing her eyes. When she looked up, the stewardess stepped forward and said, 'Would you like to celebrate with a glass of champagne?"

Bella smiled and nodded with gratitude. "I feel as if a weight has been lifted that I couldn't bear to carry. A glass of champagne is a wonderful idea."

They all cheered as the cork popped out, and champagne was served to the small group of passengers in First Class. As she sipped it, Bella questioned the pilot for more information. He, of course, declined the celebratory drink explaining that he had only received a very crackly message to convey to her; her daughter had been safely found at lunchtime and her brother Howard had spoken to her daughter. That was all he could tell her. It was enough. She would be with Lauren in a few hours.

The plane landed at 8 a.m. exactly on time. There was a small delegation from the American Embassy waiting to meet Isabella when she arrived; they approached her diffidently as she emerged from the immigration hall, accompanied by her brother and sister. The Ambassador himself approached first and offered his sympathy and support. Bella immediately looked alarmed, "Why are you offering me your sympathy? I thought she had been found alive and safe? What are you saying?"

Phillip put his arm around Bella as the ambassador coughed with embarrassment. "She is alive and safe, let me reassure you. I offer my sympathy for the terrible time you've had, and of course the terrible time your daughter has had. She's in very good hands at Groote Shuur Hospital, Mrs. Marlowe."

"Why is she in hospital?"

"The doctors have not discussed it with us other than to say that she has been assaulted, so I can't give you any information. We have a car here to take you directly to the hospital and I'm sure they will explain everything once you are there."

Bella paled, and felt Wendy and Phillip draw closer to her. Suddenly she was aware of a woman in a bright pink shirt appearing from behind a book stand. She had a camera in her hands and began to take photos of Bella and the group of people around her. Phillip noticed at the same moment and put his hand up for the woman to stop.

The drive from the airport to hospital was tense and silent. Bella was unable to take in any of the foreign sights and sounds around her, simply staring straight ahead at nothing in particular, constantly clenching her jaw. Wendy held her hand, saying nothing. Phillip however stared out the window; he had always wanted to visit South Africa, but not under such circumstances. He watched with mild interest but suddenly jerked to the edge of his seat, shocked rigid. Alongside the motorway he saw a sprawling shanty town of houses packed close together, made from tin and boxes yet with electricity and T.V. connections attached to their makeshift structures. Poverty and squalor stretched as far as the eye could see. It reminded him of Rio de Janeiro. They continued past the endless sprawl and in the distance ahead he could see the side of fabled Table Mountain, with its tablecloth of cloud pouring over the top like an army on the march. It was reminiscent of the fog rolling into San Francisco in the afternoons. He was pleased when they exited the motorway and began driving along the N2 with its views of the harbor to the right and grassy plains to the left; there he caught sight of several zebra and wildebeest grazing nonchalantly. He really was in Africa.

The driver pulled into the grounds of Groote Schuur and Phillip marveled at the size of the hospital. It was world-renown, but he was still surprised to see a facility this large and impressive on the far reaches of the African continent. He naively had a picture in his mind of a small building in the middle of nowhere, with a few missionaries and nuns running it. He was even more surprised when they entered the building, thankful that the Consul and a doctor were there to navigate the network of buildings, wings and floors. The doctor introduced herself as Dr. Naidoo, and explained that Lauren was not responding to anybody so it was difficult to know what exactly had happened. "I hope that you'll be the catalyst and she'll speak to you," the doctor said to Bella, whose walk was almost a run as she entered the opened door to her daughter.

A young man sat beside the bed, and courteously nodded at her before removing himself from the room. Bella didn't even notice him. She ran straight to Lauren and put her arms around her. The younger woman lifted her arms to grasp the back of Bella's head, burying her face in her mother's shoulder. Phillip and Wendy looked at one another and quietly turned to leave the room, overcome with emotion. Only the doctor hovered unobtrusively in the background. The two women clung to one another silently for a while until finally Bella pulled back to look at her daughter. She saw a greatly altered demeanor staring back at her; gone were the bright, eager eyes. Lauren looked panicked and afraid. "Oh darling," Bella whispered, "what has happened to you?" Lauren stared at her mother and tears began to roll down her cheeks. Bella's arms were around her again as she rocked her gently, whispering, "You're safe now my darling. Nobody's going to hurt you. I'm here with you now."

There was a whispered murmur, "Don't leave me, Mom."

Dr. Naidoo looked startled and then smiled. This was the first time Lauren had spoken since she'd arrived in the hospital yesterday.

"I won't. I'm here as long as you want me. And if you want to come back home with me, that's what we'll do."

Lauren looked up for a moment until sobs racked her body and she again buried her head in Bella's chest. The mother held her daughter and waited quietly until eventually the sobs were reduced to sniffs and occasional shudders. She stroked her daughter's head, still gently rocking her, and whispered in her ear, "It's all right my darling."

Eventually Lauren looked up at her, spent of all tears; she was barely audible as she whispered, "It's not all right, Mom. It's not…"

Bella held her tighter and felt herself tense. Glancing over her shoulder at the doctor who nodded to her, she said, "Do you want to tell me what happened?"

Lauren sighed deeply, but kept her face buried as she began to speak. The doctor drew nearer to hear, but kept out of Lauren's sight. "Two men threatened me with a gun in my car. They were chasing me. I tried to drive away but they pulled me out and threw me in the trunk. They took me to a shed and…and tied me up. They went away, but then some men came back…" She began to cry uncontrollably again. Bella said nothing, but continued holding her and rocking her like a baby. When the tears stopped, Lauren whispered, "They raped me, Mom. Three of them." She sobbed and then whispered, "It hurt so much. I was terrified. They kicked me and hit me. I thought they were going to kill me."

"Thank God they didn't," Bella said. "Oh, thank God. You've been so brave, my darling."

Once she had acknowledged this terrible thing, suddenly the rest of the story began to pour out of her like a torrent. She told how she had escaped from the shed and run into Guguletu, avoiding contact with anyone until she found the school and Janet's house. She told how she hid in the shed and how Janet had protected her and sung songs to her. "I didn't know what was happening, but someone shot through the door and then I heard some other shots and sirens, and then all was quiet until some woman came and helped me out. I don't know how long I was in there. I was afraid it was a trick, but the woman said that Janet was in hospital so I knew I was stuck in there unless I told her the combinations for the locks." She paused and then said, "Where is Janet?"

Bella looked questioningly at the doctor as she said, "Who is Janet my darling?"

"She's the head teacher at the school."

The doctor came to Lauren's bedside and gently answered her question. "Janet was also assaulted and shot in the shoulder by an intruder. She lost a lot of blood and she's unconscious, but we hope she's going to be all right." She waited a moment as Lauren gasped, before continuing. "The police want to ask you some questions about what happened. Do you think you will be able to talk to them anytime soon?"

Lauren nodded.

"Now that we know what took place, we need to do a thorough pelvic exam," she explained gently. Lauren gave a cry of protest. "I know you probably don't want to have anybody touch you after what happened, but it's really important that we check you. Are you feeling any pain?"

She nodded again.

"I'm sorry, after all you've been through this is horrible for you, but it's for your own good. And the sooner we do it, the better." She looked from mother to daughter and then said, "Once you've been checked thoroughly, we can make a decision about releasing you. I'm sure you'd like to get out of here and go with your mom, wouldn't you?"

Bella squeezed Lauren's hand. "You can come and stay at our hotel with us. Aunt Wendy is with me, and someone else I want you to meet, but it's a long story."

"Your mom can stay with you if you like while I examine you," Dr. Naidoo added.

Lauren reluctantly agreed and a nurse was summoned to assist. Bella stood discreetly behind Lauren's head as the young woman was transferred to an examination bed. A sheet was strategically put over her while her feet were placed in stirrups. Dr. Naidoo pulled on some rubber gloves and very gently began to examine her, but Lauren screamed at the first touch of an instrument entering her body. Her legs jerked and she began to twist around on the bed.

Dr. Naidoo looked up at her and said soothingly, "Try to be still Lauren." She waited a moment or two and then tried the procedure again.

Once more Lauren shrieked. "Leave me alone," she wailed.

Dr. Naidoo removed the gloves and signaled for the nurse to release Lauren's feet from the stirrups. Her face looked grim. "I'm afraid I'm going to have to do this under an anesthetic."

Lauren turned her head away and bit her lip. She said nothing. Within minutes she was wheeled away to an operating theatre and Bella was shown into a small waiting room where her brother and sister were waiting for her, as well as a young man who introduced himself as Mike Rousseau. Bella acknowledged that Lauren had spoken of him, shook his hand politely and explained what was happening. Suddenly overcome with exhaustion and anxiety as she described Lauren's state, she tried hard to control the tears but was unable to stop herself. Mike felt uncomfortable and got up to excuse himself, but she stopped him. "No, please don't go. I know Lauren's going to need all of us in the days and weeks to come." Her bottom lip quivered as she said, "It's as bad as we all probably suspected, I'm afraid. She was raped — gang raped."

It seemed like an eternity that they sat waiting, listening to the clock ticking, drinking coffee, and jumping every time they heard footsteps. Finally Dr. Naidoo opened the door and said, "She's back in the ward. Can I speak to you a moment please, Mrs. Marlowe?"

Bella hastened outside and the doctor ushered her along a corridor to a small office, where she was shown a seat. "I'm afraid Lauren was quite brutally attacked and torn. We've repaired her very well — Dr. Goodall, a gynecologist, performed the operation. He is confidant that there will be no complications. We already have the clothes she was wearing which the police have taken away for DNA testing;

hopefully that'll help us catch the perpetrators. However, there are some other complications which need to be addressed."

Bella looked anxiously at the young doctor sitting opposite her.

"Do you know whether your daughter was sexually active before this assault?"

"I can't answer that," Bella gasped, taken aback.

The doctor continued, "We've done a pregnancy test which is showing negative. We'll need to check again in a week's time, which is the earliest that there could be a positive result if she were to conceive as a result of the assault last Saturday. We'll deal with that if needs be, but rest assured, if your daughter chooses to terminate a pregnancy that might arise, we will do that for her." Dr. Naidoo cleared her throat before continuing uncomfortably, "I wish that were all I had to tell you Mrs. Marlowe, but there is another thing we have to worry about in cases of rape."

Bella began to shake. "I don't think I can bear it," she whispered.

"I'm sorry, but there is a chance that your daughter has been exposed to any number of sexually transmitted diseases, including the HIV virus. It is rampant in this country, and unfortunately it can take six months before it shows up in her bloodstream. We have to consider her at risk in the meantime."

"You mean she might have Aids?"

"No. She is at risk of having been exposed to the HIV virus. That may or may not develop into Aids. To be honest, Mrs. Marlowe, your daughter seems to be in good health with a good immune system, so she might fight the virus on her own if it were transmitted to her. However, there are anti-viral drugs available that we could start administering immediately, which would lessen the potency of the virus if it were present."

"Well, let's do it," said Bella.

"They are extremely expensive," said Dr. Naidoo.

"Please do whatever you have to do at whatever price. Money should not be a deterrent." She paused and added, "Please do the same for this friend of hers, Janet. I'll pay all the costs."

"Very well, Mrs. Marlowe. I'll not waste another minute. It would have been best if we could have started the anti-retroviral within twelve hours, but that wasn't possible. The window of opportunity at

the moment is seventy-two hours for best results after exposure—
we're right about there. Medical research is moving rapidly all the
time though. Now I suggest you go to a hotel and get some sleep—just
leave a number where we can reach you. Your daughter is going to be
very drowsy for some time; she won't miss you. Get some rest while
you can."

Mike stayed behind at the hospital, but the others made their way
to a hotel that the Consul had organized for them on an old estate
amongst the vineyards of nearby Constantia. The Cellars Hotel was
cool and elegant, housing antique Cape Dutch furniture as well as
some fine European pieces. They were greeted with warm politeness
and shown to their rooms in an adjoining building, where the
entrance hall and their rooms were filled with flowers arranged in big
round vases. The scent of roses and tuberoses permeated the air, and
the staff graciously brought their guests tea and sandwiches. Wendy
took the opportunity of phoning Robert and Howard to tell them
what was happening; it seemed like a year since her mother's funeral
but it was only just over a week. Phillip called Cynthia, then he lay on
his bed, marveling at how he had suddenly acquired a big family and
his life had been turned upside down. The brief glimpse he'd had of
Lauren haunted him; she was very like Fran, but the tortured
expression on her face spoke of enormous fear and agony. He was
still thinking of that brief glimpse as he drifted off to sleep. Bella and
Wendy were likewise asleep in their respective four poster beds in
adjacent rooms. Never had any of them been so exhausted.

***

Mike sat quietly next to Lauren's bed, watching her as she lay
drifting in and out of anesthetic-induced sleep. The nurse on duty
had explained to him what findings surgery had produced and also
the problems that still needed to be addressed. He stared at Lauren's
unconscious, pale face, horrified by the knowledge of what she'd
endured. In the stillness of the hospital hush, he began to absorb the
full implications of what it meant for Lauren in the future. As he had
been writing her into his future, the implications included him now
as well. If she had been exposed to the HIV virus, he would be at risk
in a relationship with her. Condoms only minimized the exposure,

they didn't remove it—and he knew that. Enormous anger welled up inside him against the perpetrators of this heinous crime, while at the same time he felt a rush of tenderness as he looked at Lauren's inert body, so frail and helpless.

He remembered her speaking about Aids education when he'd first set eyes on her at that meeting months ago, and he considered the irony of the situation now. She had tried so hard, but ignorance and violence were walking hand in hand out there. When leaders announced that they were safe because they showered after unprotected sex with an HIV+ woman, what hope was there of educating the uneducated masses about Aids?

15

Janet Dyani continued to remain unconscious. Dr. Naidoo was baffled by the case and began to suspect that the emotional trauma suffered by the patient was even greater than the physical injury. God alone knew how the poor woman had been terrorized before the journalist had found her. It was now three days that she'd been lying comatose, occasionally stirring to mutter a few words over and over, before relapsing into a coma. She was fed oxygen because of a collapsed lung, but the injury to the shoulder had become infected. Antibiotics were added to the intravenous drip.

The patient's mother, an elderly woman who simply called herself Mama, had been contacted and made her way to the hospital. Apparently Janet's neighbours had taken her in until such time as the police would allow her to stay in Janet's house. The suffering on Mama's face as she gazed at her daughter touched the doctor deeply. The woman stood silently, overwhelmed by the strangeness of a hospital environment with its antiseptic, steely appearance, and disconsolate at the plight of her daughter. She was transfixed as the nurse ushered her into the ward but bowed her head politely when introduced to Dr. Naidoo, shaking hands and touching the elbow of her right arm with her left hand as a sign of respect.

"I think it would be very good if you could talk to Janet, Mama.

I hope that she might hear your voice and maybe start to respond. Do you think you can do that for us?" she asked.

Mama nodded her head and slowly moved closer to the bed where Janet was raised into a semi-seated position. The mother gently cradled her daughter's hand in her own, kissing it delicately as she bent over. She began speaking in Xhosa very softly, close to Janet's head, and then began to sing softly. Dr. Naidoo felt tears well up in her eyes which she had to fight hard to restrain. The hardest part of her job was dealing with emotions rather than injuries and disease. She blinked hard and turned her head away.

Mama's soft voice was suddenly interrupted by loud beeping from one of the monitors attached to Janet's body. Dr. Naidoo and the nurse on duty moved quickly to check the screen; Janet's heart beat had begun to fluctuate as Mama sang, which had set off a warning. As they watched, the graph returned to normal but they heard a faint murmur from the patient, who opened her eyes and tried to focus. Not a sound escaped any of the onlookers as they watched the patient, willing her to regain consciousness. She stared in the direction of her mother's face for a few moments, prompting Mama to begin singing softly again. Janet's head rolled slightly to the side, still with her gaze trying to focus on her mother. As they watched, her mouth dropped open, her eyes glazed over and the monitor screen flattened to a straight line.

***

Dr. Naidoo sat at her desk writing her report with tears streaming down her face. She had studied and worked hard to get where she was, and it was clear that Janet had also risen from humble beginnings to educate herself and become a productive member of society. She felt outraged by the futility of people's good efforts when she saw them destroyed so frequently by wanton brutality and evil. So much had been accomplished trying to build a new South Africa, but what was the point when thugs could do so much harm and undo the good?

Her thoughts were interrupted by the phone ringing. It was Bessie Opperman, asking for an interview. She was outside in the hallway and entered the doctor's office looking visibly shaken. When she saw Dr. Naidoo's tears, it was as if a tap had been turned on and she too, began to cry. The two women sat opposite one another with a box of tissues between them, not looking at one another, but releasing all their grief for this unknown woman as well as their sad country.

16

The time had come for Bella to break the news to her daughter about two more deaths. She knew how sad Lauren had been about losing her grandmother, and she dreaded telling her now that her grandfather had also died. He had played such a big part in her life since her own father's death. Bella discussed with Wendy, Phillip and Dr. Naidoo whether they should withhold the news until she was stronger, but Lauren had begun asking after her grandfather and demanding to see Janet. Dr. Naidoo called Bella early the next morning and requested she come as soon as possible to break the news. It was the first time that Bella had seen her daughter up and about. She entered the ward and felt her heart miss a beat at the sight of Lauren walking around in pajamas. She looked much brighter after the surgery and a good sleep, but there was a nervous wariness about her that concerned Bella. She ran to her daughter now and embraced her gently saying, "I'm sorry I wasn't here when you came around from the anesthetic my darling. Your doctor told me to go and get some sleep myself and they would call me when you awoke."

"It's OK, Mom. I knew you'd be here soon, and Mike was with me when I came round."

Bella looked at her daughter and stroked her hair. "He seems very nice…"

Lauren cut her off. "Yes, he is, but I don't want to talk about that now. Please tell me how Grandpa is doing?"

Bella took her daughter's hand and led her to a chair before seating herself on the adjacent bench. "I'm afraid, my darling, that he didn't make it." Again she stroked Lauren's hair and held her hand, "Grandpa died last week."

"What? Why didn't you tell me?" Lauren wailed.

"I tried calling you many times, but I just got your voice mail. I didn't want to leave the news in a message," Bella replied softly.

Tears welled up in Lauren's eyes. "Grandpa's dead! I can't believe it..." She put her arms around her mother and whispered, "He was such a presence—even when he was 90!" She held her mother tightly as her tears began to flow. Finally she whispered, "I'm so sorry for you, too, Mom. God, I know what it's like to lose your father."

Bella nodded her head. "He was a most amazing man and he lived his life to the full. But he was ready to go when the time came and there's some comfort in that. Wendy was with him when he died, holding his hand. She said that he had just been speaking about you and how proud he was..."

The tears continued to pour down Lauren's cheeks. She looked at her mother and said, "Did he know what happened to me?"

Bella shook her head.

Lauren buried her head in her hands as her mother knelt on the floor in front of her, embracing her daughter. After a time, Bella said to her, "I have something for you of Grandma's. She wanted you to have it." Lauren looked up as her mother handed her a gold chain with a small locket attached to it.

"I remember that so well," Lauren murmured as she held it in her hands. "Grandma wore it all the time. I always wanted to look inside when I was little. I suppose I can look inside now." She fingered it lovingly, picturing how it hung on her grandmother's chest, and then gently opened the lock. Bella moved behind her daughter to see as well, searching for her glasses to do so. "It's a picture of Grandpa in his army uniform on one side, and a very young Grandma on the other!" Lauren exclaimed. "Oh wait, look, there's another picture here sticking out underneath it." She removed the picture of her grandmother where it was obviously worn from being lifted over the years. She strained her eyes to see the small photo, and exclaimed, "It's a baby. Which one of you is it?"

Bella looked hard at the pictures and felt a lump in her throat as she thought again how hard it must have been for her mother, keeping this painful secret. She shrugged her shoulders in response, saying, "I'm not sure."

She decided to avoid telling about Janet's death until such time as her daughter asked again. Lauren needed time to deal with this sadness, coming so soon after the terrible experience she had endured. Fortunately there was a distraction when Wendy and Phillip knocked on the door; Lauren stood to hug her aunt, but frowned as she looked at Phillip. He smiled and put out his hand to her. "I'm Phillip Davis," he said. "I can see you're wondering what on earth I'm doing here. Who is going to explain?" he asked, looking at his two sisters.

Bella turned Lauren back to the chair where she'd been sitting, placing herself again on the bench. Wendy and Phillip sat on the edge of the bed and they all looked at one another expectantly. Finally Phillip said, "It's a complicated story Lauren, but actually I'm your uncle!" He proceeded to tell her the story of his birth and adoption, as well as his happiness at finding an unknown family. The sisters felt tenderness towards the man. He was so open and unguarded with his emotions; they couldn't help but love his warmth. Lauren stared in amazement as she listened to the story, and she too was touched. As she watched him talk, she could see an uncanny resemblance to her grandfather; it was bizarre, hearing that she'd lost someone dear to her, and then having him seemingly re-appear in a younger form. Her eyes drifted to the chain still clutched in her hand and she nodded knowingly. "I think you might be interested to see this. It belonged to my grandmother and she always wore it," she said to Phillip. He had a sudden intake of breath; seeing a familiar picture of himself and realizing its significance in this locket, struck his heart more than any words could do.

Lauren frowned and then turned her head to look out the window, gazing at the view of Table Mountain. In a moment it was as if nobody else was in the room; her thoughts retreated to the same place they kept tramping. The events of the past few days replayed themselves like a video and she couldn't find the stop button. She seemed to stay disconnected for some hours as Bella sat by her side. Wendy and Phillip left after a while, and Mike Rousseau arrived at lunch time as the trolley with her food was wheeled in. Bella took the opportunity to slip out for some lunch in the cafeteria while he was there. Lauren was still sitting in the chair, with her eyes fixed expressionlessly on the mountain top.

He picked up the plate and placed it next to Lauren. "Come on now," he said, "Chicken Groote Schuur, served to delight your palate with a little bit of potato and peas." She turned and looked at the plate and then at him, before shaking her head. "Come on, Lauren," he said. "You have to eat something. If you won't eat that, what about this jelly and custard?"

"It's jello, not jelly!"

"Maybe in the States; here it's jelly. But if you'll eat it, I'll call it jello."

They stared at one another unflinchingly, until he said, "Take your pick, chicken or jello?"

"Jello."

"That's an excellent choice," he said and smiled. "My guess is that you are about to taste an exquisite blending of raspberries and strawberries, drizzled with the finest Crème Anglaise made on the premises this morning by the chef." She began to eat rather gingerly. "Am I right?" he asked.

"Wrong," she replied. Lauren ate half of the dessert only and as he placed the plate on the trolley she said, "Mike, thank you for visiting me, but please don't feel you have to come."

He spun around almost dropping a plate, and said, "Lauren, I would rather be here with you than any where else. I resent the time that I have to be back on campus."

She bit her bottom lip and whispered, "Thanks." Then she looked up at him and said, "But it's the end of the academic year and I'm sure you've got stuff you have to do."

He sat down next to her and held her hands. "Let me worry about that, OK? My thesis is almost finished and I have only thirty exam papers to mark for the group that I tutor. No problem. Everything is under control."

She turned and looked out the window, and once more he felt her presence slipping away from him as she retreated to the world that haunted her. He didn't know whether it was better to leave her alone in it so that she could deal with the demons, or to try and draw her back to him. He sat holding her hands, imagining that he could transmit strength to her if he concentrated hard enough, and thinking how even a scientist could hope for an inexplicable miracle.

Later that afternoon when Bella returned, Lauren asked to see Janet again. Dr. Naidoo was called and, in consultation with Bella, decided that she would have to break the news about the friend's death. She began by saying, "Lauren, I'm afraid that Janet wasn't as fortunate as you. I told you that the assailant shot through her shoulder and into her lung, didn't I?" Lauren nodded. "Well, I'm sorry to tell you that Janet Dyani died yesterday without regaining consciousness."

The news was like a body blow to Lauren, who collapsed on the bed and buried her head in the pillow. Loud sobs racked her body as she wept. "She died because she tried to protect me. He was looking for me and he killed her instead. Poor, poor, Janet." Apart from involuntary gasps, she lapsed into silence again, shaking from shock. At length she moved to the open window and gripped the sill tightly, peering down at the ground five floors below her. Bella moved nervously to stand next to her; for the moment Lauren seemed unaware of anyone else in the room. Tears streamed down her face, even when she shut her eyes tightly. "It's a nightmare," she whispered finally. "Why, why, why? There's no sense in it at all. She was such a good person...This can't be true."

Bella put her arm around her daughter to try and comfort her, and for a long time Lauren simply cried in her mother's arms. "There are no answers to these questions, darling. We can beat ourselves up asking them, but it doesn't help. Life is very precious and sometimes we only realize that when we see how quickly it can be lost. The only thing I've ever figured out from my questioning is that we should appreciate what we have, and who we love, while we have them."

Lauren breathed deeply and a few lingering sobs caught in her chest. "She was such a fine person. I was privileged to have known her and worked with her, Mom. I'll never forget her..."

Dr. Naidoo was reluctant to allow the police to interview Lauren, but Captain Radebe was insistent as he was being pressured from higher up the chain of command. She delayed as long as possible, saying that her patient was in shock and not fit to speak to police, but finally she was forced to relent, especially when Lauren expressed eagerness to do something that would help apprehend the attackers; Janet's death triggered a desire for revenge in her. Captain Radebe tried to put Lauren at ease, and was happy that her mother and the doctor stayed at her side during the questioning. Bella winced as she heard all the details her daughter bravely described in a very matter-of-fact tone. Lauren seemed robotic, never saying how she felt, just what she saw and heard.

Captain Radebe, accompanied by Sergeant Olivier, was armed with a microphone to record the interview. The captain prompted her at times as Lauren's thoughts seemed to drift, gently bringing her back to the story. He pressed for descriptions of her attackers, but she replied that it was dark and she had been covered with a blanket and then a ski mask. However she did recall that the two men who had grabbed her in the parking lot were also two of the three who had raped her. She remembered their T shirts which were gray; one had a South African flag on it, and the other had a black emblem of an elephant and 'BIG FIVE' written on it.

"Did you hear any names mentioned, Lauren?" Radebe asked.

She shook her head. Then suddenly she looked up and said, "Yes I did. I did hear a name—I remember—let me think a minute. It was..." She took a deep breath and shuddered. Bella held her hand protectively. Shaking, Lauren continued, "When one of them was attacking me, one of the others called him something that sounded like Geek—or Zeke. That was it; he said, 'hurry up, Zeke.' I remember now."

"That's very useful, Lauren. You've identified one of the attackers and the good news is that we already have him in custody. I'm sorry that we had to trouble you, but you've been most helpful. With this information and DNA evidence, the case will be buttoned up soon."

***

Phillip and Wendy volunteered to take care of the reward payment for Bella, who only left Lauren's side to sleep or to give Mike time alone with her. Captain Radebe gave them Bessie's name and

Mike organized a meeting with her, arranging to bring her to The Cellars Hotel, where Lauren's family was staying. Phillip and Wendy were sitting on the patio when he arrived with Bessie and made the introductions. They shook hands and Phillip thanked her profusely for what she had done, saying, "From what I can gather, it was your perseverance and alertness that were responsible for finding my niece."

Bessie smiled demurely and replied, "I was at the police station when Mike first reported her missing. It was just lucky that I was there at that moment and got onto the case."

"Well exactly," Phillip said. "It was your presence of mind that found Lauren. We are deeply indebted to you." He pulled a cheque from his pocket for R100,000 and handed it to her.

Wendy shook Bessie's hand as well and said, "We can never really repay you enough for finding her, but this is a start. I imagine when Lauren is stronger she will want to meet you and thank you herself."

"I would like that," said Bessie, "but I know she won't want to be bothered for some time. Thank you all very much for the cheque—I really appreciate it. Please tell her that I would like to meet her and thank her for all the good work she has tried to do here in Cape Town. She has such great vision and generosity; I hope these terrible events don't make her lose those qualities."

Phillip invited the guests to join them for lunch and as they all sat dining in the sunshine on the verandah, Mike re-iterated how Bessie had found what was under the their noses all the time. "There was a policeman standing twenty-five yards away from the time that Janet was found. He never knew it."

After lunch, Phillip and Wendy watched as Mike walked to his car with Bessie. They commented on his pleasant, easy demeanor but Wendy added cautiously, "He seems very devoted to Lauren yet I fear that there's a difficult road ahead for them. It'll take a lot of time for her to heal. I hope he's a patient man."

***

They kept Lauren in hospital for observation another day, at which point Dr. Naidoo decided that the patient would benefit from being discharged to stay with her family. Bella consulted with the doctor and the rest of the medical team, and they decided it would be preferable for Lauren to share a room with her mother for the present time, until they had a better idea of her emotional stability. Anxiety about security and being alone were to be expected. The Cellars Hotel was set in beautiful grounds with gardens and vineyards surrounding the buildings, as well as a swimming pool and tennis courts. Most importantly, there was a security gate. Lauren would be able to recuperate, cocooned in a protected environment. Bella asked when they could return to the U.S.A., but was informed that the police required Lauren to be on hand until the case was closed.

Dr. Naidoo also felt there were strong medical reasons why Lauren needed to remain in the country. "We need to ensure that she doesn't have any adverse reaction to the anti-viral drugs we're administering, and we also need to do a pregnancy test towards the end of next week." She bit her bottom lip and cleared her throat. "In about six week's time, it will become evident whether there is any HIV virus that might be converting to positive. It would be helpful if you remain here until such time."

"What happens after that?" asked Lauren.

"Well, if you start running a fever and getting a rash in six weeks time, that would be an indication of a conversion. We'll test again at that point regardless. If there is no conversion, we'll wait six months until March next year, at which point if there is still no indication of the virus, we would consider that you are all clear. But I would like you to remain here for at least six weeks."

17

Mike came to visit Lauren every afternoon and evening, and they walked in the safety of the hotel gardens. Sometimes Lauren would talk, but most times she was silent and listless—in contrast to the dynamo he had come to know before this nightmare had started. She showed some interest in what he was doing, so he spoke to her about his work, but after a while he would notice that her thoughts were elsewhere and then he would stop. He brought her books, but she seemed to remain on the first chapter of the first book constantly. She complained of headaches when she tried to read and seemed to want nothing more than to lie next to the pool for most of the day. She grew nervous as it grew darker, and at night she chose to eat dinner in her room rather than in the main dining room, as this would involve walking across a parking lot.

Bella and Mike spoke about their observations, and she informed him that as soon as she got Lauren back home she would have her start therapy to deal with the trauma. Mike felt himself getting angry, but tried to contain it. He didn't like the talk of taking Lauren away, and furthermore he didn't believe in automatically deciding that therapy was needed. He considered keeping quiet, but then decided he needed to voice his opinion. "With all due respect Mrs. Marlowe," he began, "I think we should see how Lauren manages healing herself first. Human beings have an enormous capacity to recover from terrible atrocities. They've done so since time began."

"Are you suggesting that just because people survived without therapy in the dark ages, there's no need for it now?"

"No, I'm a scientist Mrs. Marlowe, I'm not promoting the dark ages. All I'm saying is that we shouldn't prescribe if we don't need to do so. Think of a bird that flies into a window. It's stunned and might seem lifeless, but after a while it'll start to shiver. If left alone, it will continue to do so until it's re-orientated itself, and then it'll fly away. If somebody interrupts that process however, rushing to pick up the bird when it is stunned or when it starts to shiver, the natural healing process can be interrupted and the bird can be thrown into shock again."

Bella stared at him for a while and then said, "So you wouldn't take the bird to a veterinary doctor?"

"If it were visibly injured I would, but otherwise, no. I'd let nature have a chance to do its work. If it couldn't, then I'd let science lend a hand." As Bella seemed to consider this he added, "Think of trees that are injured as saplings—perhaps they've had a rope tied around them that cuts into the bark. They absorb the injury and grow around it, remaining strong and beautiful. Give Lauren a chance to do the same."

"You make a compelling case," she said, nodding. "I remember when her father died, she dealt with that remarkably and you're right—people kept telling me she needed therapy and that I needed therapy; it made us both mad. But this is different..."

"Give her a chance, Mrs. Marlowe. Give her time." He watched Bella and recognized the same intent concentration he saw sometimes in Lauren. "You know I want her to recover as much as you do."

***

The days passed without much variation until the call came from Dr. Naidoo to say that it was time for the pregnancy test. Lauren was thrown into a panic as Phillip drove them to Groote Schuur and she entered the laboratory where the blood would be drawn. Bella was at her side, holding her hand. "Breathe deeply, darling," she said.

Looking pale as a nurse tied a tourniquet around her arm to enlarge a vein, Lauren looked the other way so that she might avoid the sight of her blood being sucked into the syringe. Bella, however, felt as if she were going to faint, and quickly sat down with her head between her knees.

They were both relieved to return to the waiting room where Phillip was waiting to drive them back to the hotel and the long day's wait for a result. They all watched the clock continually, and nobody felt much like doing anything. Conversation consisted of a few words spoken here and there; books were picked up and put down again; they kept close to the land-line phone while Lauren checked her cell phone frequently to make sure she hadn't missed a call. It was four o' clock before the phone finally rang. Dr. Naidoo was on the other end asking for Lauren. The room was charged with tension as everyone watched her face to try and get a reading of the results. She, however, was stone-faced as she listened to the doctor.

"I'm sorry to tell you, we have a positive result," Dr. Naidoo announced in a strained voice. "As I have explained already, we can terminate the pregnancy for you if this is what you choose to do. And of course, if so, we should do it as soon as possible. Let me know what you decide."

Lauren replaced the phone and looked down. Her bottom lip quivered. "I'm pregnant." She excused herself as she closed the bathroom door behind her and locked it.

Mike and the family sat frozen for what seemed an eternity. When Lauren finally emerged from the bathroom, she looked as if she were in a trance. "I want to get rid of this thing inside me immediately." Nobody else moved, but Lauren. She strode across the room and grabbed the phone, making arrangements to be at Groote Schuur the following morning at 6:00 a.m. without anything to eat or drink for twelve hours beforehand.

***

When Howard received the call from Wendy, he and Tracey were getting ready for bed. "No, no," he cried. "She mustn't terminate it. Please don't let her do that. It's a baby's life we're talking about Wendy, not a bunch of cells. It's a God-given life."

"Howard, be reasonable," she answered. "This is the result of rape. Why would Lauren wish to nurture this pregnancy and have the child? And who knows what diseases it would inherit? If you could see the state she's in you'd understand; she just couldn't deal with a pregnancy now."

"She'll be even more scarred if she has an abortion. Tell her not to worry about this; Tracey and I will adopt the child. Please tell her that—we'll give it a loving home, no matter what. It's an innocent baby and it has our blood in its veins. " At this point Tracey gasped and waved her hands in horror. Howard put his finger to his lips, silencing his wife.

Across the world in South Africa, his sister's eyes opened wide. "Are you serious about that?" she whispered into the phone.

"I've never been more serious in my life. Wendy, you have to stop her from doing this. We've had enough deaths in the family; please don't add a murder to it."

She wanted to scream at his comment, but instead she answered in hushed tones, "I'll tell Lauren of your offer to adopt, but I can't promise anything. I just wanted to let you know what was happening."

"Thanks Wendy, I appreciate that. Would it help if I spoke to Lauren?"

"No, I don't think so. She's not speaking much to anybody."

"Please tell her that she's in our prayers."

Howard replaced the receiver carefully and looked up at the ceiling with his hands together in prayer. Tracey, however, wasted no time as she stormed at him. "How can you make a decision like that without consulting me? And don't just tell me to 'shush' because you're on the phone. I'm not a child. I've told you Howard, I do not want to adopt! What part of that don't you understand? I will not adopt this child who'll very likely be born with Aids, as well as having a criminal for a father. How dare you presume that I would? How dare you?"

Howard had never seen his wife so angry before. He tried to placate her by putting his arms around her, but she shoved him away. "You can call your sister right back and tell her that you were mistaken. You'd better do it before she passes on your message to Lauren. I deserve an apology from you."

Howard threw his hands in the air with exasperation. "I can't believe you're being like this. We have everything in the world to offer a child; and this would not be just any child we'd adopt, it's a member of the family—whether you like it or not. If you were to get pregnant and the child were born with a disease, you would keep it, wouldn't you? It's not for us to pick and choose, Tracey; we have to take what God gives us. We've wanted a child, and God is giving us one. It's not the way we expected him to give it to us, but he works in mysterious ways."

She stared at him coldly. "God is not giving this baby to us. You're making too much of it; it's not our problem. God is helping us to make our own baby with a little bit of help."

"And you don't have a problem with how that all happens? I go off into a little cubicle and do things I've never done with a clear conscience—and then somebody else shoves that up you and there we have our baby. You think that comes from God?"

"It's humiliating enough going through all this infertility treatment without you debasing it." Her eyes flashed as she added, "I'm telling you one more time, you can say what you like but I will not adopt Lauren's baby. You will have to choose between that baby and me."

Howard took a deep breath and sighed. "I'm afraid I've promised, and I've given God my word as well," he said as he turned out the light. "Please don't make me choose," he whispered in the darkness.

***

It was many days before Lauren would speak after the termination of the pregnancy. If she had felt ravaged before, her spirit now seemed to have been sucked out of her as well. She barely ate anything, wanting to be left alone in her room where she simply lay on the bed. Sometimes she slept, and sometimes she stared at the ceiling, re-living her terror. The six pills she took daily made her gag as she swallowed them. They were bitter reminders that stuck in her throat, but she took them dutifully, visualizing them as bullets fighting the virus and winning the battle. She thought of Janet constantly, and wept for her. One night she dreamed so vividly about her friend that she awoke startled and shaken. It felt as if Janet had been in the room with her. In the dream, Janet had been singing cheerful songs to rows of children as she handed them books and pencils. They were all sitting up in neatly-made little beds, holding out their hands. When she reached the last child she turned and smiled beatifically, saying in a loud voice, "Now you can begin to learn. Lauren will help you."

Not one word escaped Lauren's lips though, until four nights' later when she picked up the phone and called Mike. In little more than a whisper, she asked him to find Bessie Opperman. Despite her grief, she wanted to meet this woman who had started the trail that led to her. Bessie was a link in the chain of events that she now wanted to face.

Thankful to see Lauren have some focus again, Mike organized the meeting as quickly as he could get hold of Bessie. She was very eager to meet Lauren, who seemed enigmatic to her, so was quick to respond and come to the Cellars. When Mike introduced them, they shook hands tentatively. Bessie was unusually nervous to see this victim again — it was not something she normally did in her job. She was used to simply getting the story and moving on, but this saga had her in its grip and she was unable to let go. Seeing Lauren reminded her of Janet Dyani; she couldn't rid the image from her mind of that poor woman's body in a pool of blood, lying on the floor. She began to have serious doubts about her ability to be a crime reporter if she were so deeply affected by what she saw, a thing she dared not admit even to herself.

It was more than courtesy and gratitude that drove Lauren to meet Bessie; it was curiosity. She hoped that hearing the reporter's side of the story would fill in some blanks for her. She was in a constant nervous state. There seemed to be such a fine line between order and chaos, and while she understood that her family was trying to protect her, she also felt a desperate need to regain control of her life which seemed to have descended into hopeless disarray. She knew that Bessie had also rescued Janet, and she needed to know more about that. The uncertainty of the story added to her fear. Whatever the truth was, she wanted to know it and Bessie was the one who could tell.

They sat outside on a bench under an oak tree and Lauren coughed nervously before saying, "I know my family has thanked you, but I wanted to do so myself."

"I'm glad you're here to do so," exclaimed Bessie. She took hold of Lauren's hands gently. "I'm ashamed that this happened to you in my country, and it's terrible about your friend, Janet. I am so sorry Lauren."

"Bessie, please don't say that you feel shame. What happened to Janet and me could have happened anywhere."

Bessie nodded. "That's generous of you to say that, but the chances were much greater here than anywhere else. We've become the crime capital of the world."

Lauren nodded her head. "I know that and people warned me when I came here. Somehow I never thought it could happen to me. It was just statistics. Now I'm one of them. And Janet too." She looked steadily at Bessie. "Was she conscious when you found her?"

Bessie put her head in her hands to hide her face, but her body began to shake softly and she was unable to conceal her anguish. "You don't want to know. It was terrible," she cried.

"I do want to know, Bessie." Lauren had tears pouring down her face too. "Everybody avoids talking about it, but she was my friend. She died because she tried to protect me. If I'd never come here, Janet Dyani would still be teaching in her little school. She would still be alive. Please tell me everything you know."

Bessie squeezed her face in a grimace as she looked up at Lauren. Very softly, she said, "The poor woman was unconscious. The attacker had — had — tied her up." The young reporter closed her eyes and shook her head. "She was face-down on the floor, naked, with her hands tied behind her back. There was blood all over the place. Everywhere. She'd been shot in the shoulder." Bessie blew her nose before adding, "He was dead already. Apparently Janet poisoned his sandwich. He was there a long time terrorizing her...She had to endure the bastard torturing her for several hours."

"He was waiting there for me, wasn't he?"

Bessie nodded. "I'm afraid so. Janet was very brave and cunning. She used her wits to kill him, but I'm afraid he..." She was unable to continue as she was once again overcome with emotion.

Mike had sat quietly all the while, but he now quietly interjected his thoughts. "Both of you are feeling guilt when that's the last thing you should be feeling." He shook his head and looked at each of them in turn. "Bessie, you shouldn't be feeling responsible for the crime in the country. You're reporting it, not committing it! And Lauren my love, all those 'ifs' can drive you mad, but they can't change anything. *If* you hadn't come to South Africa, yes, everything would have been different. But you *did* come here. And that was my lucky day, I might add. And you came here for the noblest of reasons. You're justified in feeling lots of things, but guilt—definitely not. This is a story about three brave women; the two of you and Janet." He put an arm around each of them, "Please believe me," he added.

Lauren nodded her head and whispered, "Thank you for being honest with me Bessie. I knew she was raped—oh God I can't bear to think of it. I know how afraid she must have been."

"If only I'd found her earlier," said Bessie.

"You have to stop saying 'if only'—don't beat yourself up," Mike said.

"I suppose I'll accept that in time," remonstrated Bessie, "but I can't help how I'm feeling now."

"Hey Bessie, you're amazing. Your reporting is good and factual. I can see how emotional you are, but you've not allowed it to cloud your work. What a gift that is. Don't ever stop feeling; it's your passion that makes you so good. You never gave up on your story and thank heavens you didn't. I'm indebted to you too," he said as he kissed the top of Lauren's head.

"That's the best thing anyone has ever said to me," Bessie answered. "Thank you."

"What I find so hard to understand though," said Lauren "is why they did it." She looked at Mike and Bessie with a frown. "I know there aren't answers, but that's what drives me mad. Why? Why did it happen?"

"It's hard to find reasons for these awful things, Lauren. When terrible things happen to good people, it makes you question everything you've ever believed in," said Mike. "But there just aren't any answers."

"There aren't answers, but there are reasons—if that makes sense!" responded Bessie. "These thugs were all street children.

They've grown up with no education and maybe no parents. No guidance. They've brought themselves up probably, and the only thing they've learned is how to survive without anything. There are so many of them. They're very poor people who know no better, and can hope for no better. The only way they know how to live is by stealing, and rape or murder just happen along as by-products. For them life is cheap. It has no value. I see it every day as a crime reporter. There's almost an entire generation like that. Some of them were born during the struggle and some of them later. They're victims too. I don't know how or when we can ever re-integrate them into society. But Lauren, you're doing the very best thing by teaching a new generation and helping build an orphanage to house some of the street children," Bessie said.

"You sound like Janet. That's what she believed in too. She always used to say 'look to the future, Lauren. Look to the future. It's no good complaining about the past and wringing our hands. That won't fix anything. Teach the children, and teach them English.' She always said that it was all very well having eleven official languages, but if we couldn't speak to one another it didn't do much good. If I heard her say that once, I heard it a hundred times."

"It's the irony of it that beats the hell out of me. These bastards attack the people who help them." Mike hit his fist against a tree with frustration.

Lauren sighed. "It does feel hopeless. What good does it do that I'm teaching forty children and housing another forty, when there are millions more who aren't being helped? It's not even a drop in the ocean."

"Don't say that," Bessie answered quickly and emphatically. "If there were more like you the drops would grow. Everything starts out small, but it has to start somewhere. There are others like you— if it weren't so, *that* would be hopeless. Don't stop doing what's good just because there's lots of bad stuff out there. Your ex-president, Bill Clinton, said the lesson from globalization is that those in wealthy countries must work to empower people in poorer nations. You're doing that, Lauren." She stood up and gave a faint smile as she reached out her hand, "I'm so glad I spoke to you here today." The two women shook hands again and then embraced. "God bless you Lauren."

Lauren and Mike walked Bessie to her car and watched as she drove off until she disappeared round the corner. They wandered out into the vineyards in silence, where Lauren stood kicking stones in the path disconsolately before looking up at him, "I feel totally empty," she said. "The point seems to have gone out of my existence."

He put his arms around her gently and whispered in her hair. "Lauren, please don't shut me out." He felt her body start to shiver and he automatically held her tighter to try and warm her. She pushed away from him. "I don't want to Mike, but I'm numb. It's horrible, I can't feel anything. My body has been used and violated; and the child inside was my innocent baby. I didn't stop to think before I did what I did."

"Lauren, whatever choice you made about that was going to cause you concern. There was no right or wrong decision there; you just had to make a decision and I really believe that the choice you made was valid and sensible. Trust me; it's perfectly natural for you to be feeling like this after all you've been through. Feeling numb helps you to protect yourself. Please don't shut me out though. Let me keep coming to visit, and we'll take it a day at a time."

"I look forward to you coming," she said, "but I feel guilty."

"Not more guilt! What on earth do you feel guilty about?" he asked.

She sighed. "I suppose one day I'll get over this shock; but you must know, I might be infected with HIV. We won't know definitely for ages. It'll always be hanging over me—and if you get involved with me, it'll be hanging over you too. It isn't fair to you."

"Lauren, what do you mean '*if* I get involved?' I *am* involved with you. There isn't a waking moment that I'm not thinking of you—and most of my sleeping moments too. I know HIV is an issue, but it's an issue for both of us, not you on your own. You're not alone in this."

"You say that, but it's not that simple Mike."

"It's as simple or as complicated as you make it. For a start we don't know that you are HIV positive. If you are, there are treatments—and research is being done all the time. We'll deal. And as for you and me, if I were lucky enough for you to feel about me the way I feel about you—well, that's what condoms are made for."

She blushed and looked down. "If I'm HIV positive, I'm not sure I'll be able to have children."

"Sure you will."

She looked at him and shook her head. "Not if we're using condoms!"

He smiled and cupped her face in his hands, whispering, "There are ways and means...You realize that you're making me a very happy man just contemplating all of this?"

She moved towards him and buried her face in his chest, clinging to him. "I just can't imagine ever wanting to have sex after..."

He held her tightly. "And we won't until you want to do so, however long that takes. What's important is that you tell me what you feel, and likewise I tell you." She nodded, still with her head in his chest. "And I'm telling you now Lauren Marlowe, that I love you."

She looked up at him and stared into his eyes. "What would I do without you? I love you too, very much."

18

Captain Radebe felt empowered by the swift success of the Lauren Marlowe case. He was able to demonstrate to the Minister of Police that with sufficient manpower and support, crime could be solved quickly and criminals apprehended. With more successes like this, the police would be able to put a stranglehold on the increasing crime rate, making it a safer place for all citizens of the country, not just the ones who could afford fancy alarms and security systems. The wanton brutality in the Janet Dyani case upset him more than most cases, especially when he read reports and realized that a policeman had checked the house in the morning and seen Tonsil Morope there, as well as Janet. With hindsight it was possible to see that the woman had been so terrified that she was paralyzed. If only she'd called out to the policeman at the door the story would have been different, but it happens frequently that victims are too shocked to act or react. She was a good woman from all accounts, and it must have taken great courage and resourcefulness to poison Tonsil. It was clear from the autopsy that he had died an agonizing death and that section of the case had been closed. The verdict was death by poisoning administered in self-defense.

The police laboratory did HIV tests on Zeke and Boy. The results came back negative. Tonsil, however, was HIV positive. Captain Radebe and Dr. Moodley each read and signed the reports, commenting on the statistic that—according to some—about one in three of the population being infected was mirrored in this case. "It's possible that Lauren might not get infected, even though one of her attackers was," Dr. Naidoo said to the captain. "However, if she was infected, the antiviral drugs will help her chances greatly."

Lauren's evidence helped wrap up the rest of the case. Zeke broke down under questioning, admitting that he was the first to rape the American woman, followed by Tonsil and Boy, who also confessed to the crime. This was confirmed by DNA found on Lauren's denims. The laboratory was able to separate the DNA and matched it to Zeke, Boy, and Tonsil. The T shirts described by Lauren as worn by Zeke and Boy were found in the clothing removed from the prisoners when they were first booked—so they were charged with car theft and abduction as well as rape. The entire gang was charged with theft, as well as possession of illegal arms and drugs, and the case was brought to trial within six weeks.

Lauren was required to attend the court proceedings despite the fact that Dr. Naidoo strongly advised against it. The recorded account gathered by Radebe, combined with Dr. Naidoo and Bessie Opperman's evidence, should have been sufficient to prove the case, but the prosecution was taking no chances. Supported by Mike and her family, Lauren made her way into the courtroom and bravely took the witness stand. There was hardly a dry eye in court as the frail young woman looked at the prosecutor with haunted eyes. In a quiet, steady voice she identified the T-shirts and her own clothes when these exhibits were shown to her, and then described to a hushed audience the ordeal that began in Kirstenbosch. When questioned, she stared hard at her assailants in the dock but was unable to identify them. Instead she began to shiver uncontrollably as she shook her head and was gently led away. Despite this lack of recognition, the evidence for the prosecution was so compelling that the case was over in five days with a guilty verdict for every member of the gang. They all received very lengthy prison sentences while Zeke and Boy received additional sentencing for charges of rape. Lauren was not even called back to the witness stand by the defense lawyers, for they realized it would not further their case in any way.

In Somerset West, Jake's Motors opened up a cesspit of corruption in the police force, resulting in the charging and dismissal of five policemen involved in a car theft scam. Radebe felt satisfaction about that too; it was time for some house cleaning in the police force, but difficult to achieve. Corruption is insidious and covers its tracks well.

***

There was great relief when the case was over and with a bit of closure, Lauren's mind began to edge away from the attack. She began to fret about the kindergarten school, and made her first difficult trip back to Guguletu. With her eyes averted from Janet's house and the shed, she steeled herself to open the door and face the children. Their joy at seeing her was expressed with happy shrieks and hugs as they rushed towards her, shouting "Miss Lauren." It prompted her to get back into the routine of teaching twice a week, although every day was an ordeal as she approached the school. Isabella had insisted on hiring a driver and a car for them, and although it felt strange, Lauren knew she couldn't manage on her own yet.

No matter how much she was assured that it wasn't her fault, she fretted over Janet, feeling guilt-ridden that her friend had suffered so badly at her expense; she was concerned about Janet's mother and how she was coping; she worried about what was happening with the building of the orphanage. There was so much else to worry about that she was able to forget her own horror—during the day at least. But when she turned out the light each night, the torturous memories returned.

Her car was returned to her possession after the case closed. Captain Radebe brought it to her at the Cellars Hotel and smiled broadly as he handed over the keys. "Most people never see their stolen cars again because they change hands so fast and get stripped down very often. We fight a losing battle, so I'm very happy to return yours to you."

Lauren thanked him and felt touched at his concern, but she also felt revulsion as she looked at the Jetta. Panic hit her full force and she felt so ill that she had to walk away from the car. Bella and Wendy ushered her away as Phillip walked with the captain to the awaiting police car, thanking him for the excellent police work that had been done. "Not at all, not at all," Radebe said as he put out his hand.

"Please call me Wellington. I think we have become friends now," he said smiling, as the two men shook hands.

Rejoining his sisters and niece, Phillip spoke his thoughts aloud. "I've been doing some thinking about a few things. Firstly, I believe we should get rid of this car—sell it or donate it to somebody in need. What do you think Lauren?"

She nodded. "I never want to see it again."

"Right, I'll take care of it. Do you have any thoughts on what to do with it?"

Lauren was looking at her feet and murmured, "I really don't care. Donate it to some charity, or maybe use it for the orphanage."

"OK. The other thing I was thinking about was that we should probably put together a board of trustees to look after the orphanage you're building," he said. Lauren looked at him with sudden interest as he continued. "Sooner or later you'll be leaving, and if you don't have a body of people overseeing everything, all the good work that you've done could fall apart. Nothing should ever be dependent on only one person."

Lauren nodded. "I suppose you're right."

"Can you think of any suitable candidates for trustees?" he asked.

"Not immediately."

"Well, I've actually been thinking about it over the last few days, and I have a few suggestions to make," Phillip said.

Bella and Wendy smiled at one another. This was exactly what their father would have done—set about solving a problem and at the same time engaging Lauren in something constructive to move her forward. It was in the blood. "Phillip, you're ready to nominate board members to a board that hasn't been created yet!" Bella laughed.

He smiled and said, "Yes, it is a bit presumptuous on my part, but they're just suggestions. The thing is that I've met people of such high caliber since I've been here. I think that Dr. Naidoo and Bessie Opperman would be very good if they were interested, and maybe Captain Radebe. He seems a sincere man and very eager for the right thing to be done. Having an honest cop on board would be good."

Bella felt a load start to lift from her shoulders. Lauren showed enthusiasm and direction for the first time since the attack, and there was a difference in her walk and demeanor as she chatted about establishing a board with her uncle. He was a blessing in their lives.

She would miss Phillip and Wendy when they returned to their families in England, but in the meantime, it was good to see her daughter focusing on work again and she felt gratitude towards her oldest brother for his help and understanding. Each day Lauren healed a little more.

Howard, on the other hand, had berated her for allowing Lauren to terminate her pregnancy. His anger was so palpable when he heard that the abortion had taken place that Bella chose to put the phone down on him. "He only ever sees things through his own eyes," she fumed to Wendy, when Lauren was out of the room. "He can't have a baby of his own, so he wanted this one from my daughter, no matter what the cost was to her. That's what it boils down to—forget all his religious clap trap—he's a selfish, mean-spirited ass."

Wendy grimaced. "Bell, I don't think he's being selfish at all. I think it really is because it's against his beliefs and he feels so strongly about them. It's a huge commitment on his part to offer to adopt."

"So he thinks my daughter is immoral, is that what you're saying?"

"That isn't what I said at all. I'm sure if he were here and could see her, he would be more understanding."

"There are thousands of babies who could be adopted. Why doesn't he do something about them?"

"Because this is family," Wendy replied. "Adoption isn't foreign to us."

Phillip, all the while, was gentle and caring as he worked with Lauren and their two heads were constantly huddled in discussion. All the suggested people were honored to be on the Board of Trustees and within two weeks they had written a mission statement and set up a working committee to ensure the orphanage would be well-managed financially, and also that their staffing needs would be met. It was Lauren's suggestion to name the orphanage 'The Janet Dyani Home', and to have Janet's mother present at a ribbon-cutting ceremony at the opening next May. She also wanted a monthly amount paid to support Mrs. Dyani, who had been deprived of the income that her daughter had sent her regularly. "And," Lauren added with a smile, "I'd like the orphanage to adopt Lunch! That little dog also needs a good home and it'll be fun for the children to have a pet."

Phillip insisted that Lauren get a new car and begin driving as soon as possible. "You have to get back in the saddle again," he told her. "This is not a city where public transport is a viable option, so if you're staying here for several more months, there's no other option for you. You've got to drive and I'd like you to start doing it again while I'm here with you." Bella was thankful to have the supportive input and Lauren responded well. She put her arms around her uncle and hugged him; when she lifted her head, he could see that she'd been crying just a bit.

Lauren and Phillip paid daily visits to the building site, checking the plans and progress. They also met with their new-found committee several times and began approaching government officials about the selection process for orphans to the new orphanage. The files were so numerous that it was difficult to know how to start. "We need to be building hundreds of orphanages," Lauren wailed. "I get this sinking feeling again just looking at all these faces in the files. And who knows how many more there are who've slipped through the cracks?"

"Don't think about it Lauren," Phillip said firmly. "You need to concentrate on what you're doing and do it well. You'll be lighting one little candle, but one candle can light another, and another, and another. Just concentrate on one candle at a time."

The days were busy, but it was at night that Bella worried about her daughter. She often woke to hear her crying and groaning in her sleep, and in the morning Lauren looked exhausted. Bella tried to persuade her daughter to return to the United States, but this was not an option that Lauren would consider. The earliest she would return was May, after the opening of the orphanage. Bella decided for her own peace of mind to apply for leave from Georgetown and stay in South Africa with her daughter until Christmas, returning to work for the new semester in January. She knew, as a parent knows, that her daughter's well being was at stake and that was more important than anything else. With this in mind, she rented a furnished cottage in a gated community opposite the American Consulate; both women felt relief as they moved into a place they could call home for a while. There was room for Wendy and Phillip as well. It was safe, beautiful and restful, built in Cape Vernacular style, with a beautiful view of the Steenberg Mountains all around and a golf course in front. There was a pool in the small garden where a flock of spotted guinea fowl came to visit daily. Lauren took pity on a little outcast that was always bullied by others in the flock. She thought wryly about this pecking order—even birds can victimize an individual; she made a daily ritual of putting seed down for the weakling when the others were distracted elsewhere.

In early November, Dr. Naidoo called and reminded Lauren that it was time to test her blood again. The doctor was pleased that there had been no feverish outbreak or rash, and encouraged her patient to get the blood work done as soon as possible. Lauren needed no reminder as the necessity was imprinted on her brain. If there were no evidence of the dreaded virus in her blood at this point, she was probably going to be all right, although there would be a further test in March just to be sure. It didn't bear thinking what would happen if the test were positive. And so she found herself eager to get to the appointment, but wanting to delay it at the same time. As long as there was no definite answer, she had hope.

Bella accompanied her to Groote Schuur once more and afterwards they drove back home in silence, awaiting the results. It was going to be a long day but Dr. Naidoo had promised to call as soon as she knew anything. Lauren was fidgety and unable to concentrate. She snapped at her mother's suggestion of going for a walk, and when Mike called to ask whether they had the results, she was abrupt with him. At 5 p.m. her phone rang. Lauren's hand was shaking as she answered, and her voice was barely audible. Bella watched without moving or even breathing. It seemed like an eternity for a simple answer to be given; yes or no. Finally, as Lauren ended the call, she dropped her head into her hands. Bella's heart stopped. Had she been in denial? It hadn't seemed possible that her daughter could be HIV+. She was stunned, totally unable to react.

Lauren looked up, with tears streaming down her face. "It's OK, Mom," she said. When her mother didn't react, she said again, "It's OK, Mom. It hasn't converted. I think I'm going to be all right."

19

The time finally came to say goodbye for Phillip, who was returning home after nearly seven weeks away; a time in which he had learned to be a brother. He felt sadness saying goodbye to his sisters and niece, but happy to have his reality returning as he stared out the plane window, circling over London. The grey cloud cover was such a contrast to the brilliant African sunshine that he had just left behind, amid promises to return for the opening of the Janet Dyani Home in May. His previous, comfortable life seemed distant since his whole existence had turned upside down. There had been so little time to reflect amid the whirl of action that only now, as he returned to England, was he able to try and think of himself in a new light. His mother's letter had said that he should never lose sight of who he was, but he wasn't the person he thought he was; everything about him was different—and yet he was the same. In this quandary, he felt a surge of joy seeing Cynthia waiting for him. The familiarity of her glowing face and small figure, bundled up in her old brown parka, warmed his soul. Her embrace was a quick shot of reality. As they left the airport and drove through the wet streets, they talked of what had transpired in the past month, but all the while he fingered the letter from his mother which he carried in his pocket. It explained everything, yet left him with so many questions. He felt an overwhelming need to see her and so on impulse, before returning to Rye, they stopped at the rest home.

Sarah Davis was slumped on a couch in a corner of the communal lounge and he went straight to her, avoiding the outreached hands or stares of her neighbors. She raised her head when he called her name and smiled weakly. He felt frustration as he smiled back. There was so much in her head once upon a time, and so much that he wished she'd told him. Now it was either trapped or gone forever.

"Mother, I have just returned from abroad," he said as he bent down to kiss her cheek. "I met my brother and sisters."

She smiled sweetly and vacantly at him.

"They are Phillip and Edith Parker's children. I've been in California and South Africa"

Phillip willed her to respond and grasped her hands firmly. "Do you remember Phillip and Edith Parker?" he asked.

There was a heavy silence as his mother continued staring at him; then she looked down at her lap and fell asleep again. He continued sitting in front of her, holding her hands before he leaned down and kissed the top of her head, whispering, "I love you Mum." His eyes glistened with tears as he left the room and Cynthia linked her arm supportively through his. No words were necessary; he just squeezed her hand.

They drove in silence until they reached the fields of Sussex, with sheep grazing peacefully as far as the eye could see. Phillip turned to his wife and sighed, "It's really good to be home. This is where I belong."

"It's good to have you home. You know I married Phillip Davis because I fell in love with him many years ago, and I still love him. I'd hate him to become someone else."

"He's the same man you married; he just comes with rather a lot of complicated family relationships now. You've acquired a strange bunch of in-laws I'm afraid."

***

Wendy left three weeks after Phillip, eager to return to her husband and children but anxious about leaving her younger sister and niece. She felt the lifelong weight of parental admonitions to look after her sister; they had always considered Wendy the level-headed and strong child and consequently had come to rely on her through the years. Even with their death, that dutiful requirement remained with her. "I'll be back for the opening of the orphanage," she promised, "and I'm just as far away as your phone if you need me. I can be here the next day."

"We're fine Wendy," Bella assured her. She was thankful for the support and practical advice that had been given and saddened by the parting; their lives had been thrown together again in such extraordinary circumstances, drawing them very close to one another. It was sobering to realize that life was now continuing without that familiarity and support.

20

The Rousseau farm lay in the Franschoek valley, not far from Cape Town. It was overflowing with long rows of vines nestled against a backdrop of majestic mountains. Their farm, Belle Terre, had been in the family for three hundred years and produced superb varietal grapes. With their father's approval, Mike and his brother David had developed a new venture in the past few years, producing an excellent pinotage wine on their distinctive Cap Rouge label that carried the blue and yellow family crest on a red background. Mike had proudly given Phillip and Wendy each a bottle of this prize-winning wine before they'd returned to England in early November, as well as giving Isabella and Lauren a whole case of it to ship back to the States. He explained, as they drove to the farm for Christmas, that the dark red background was chosen because the family name was derived from the French word for red. "My brother has the Rousseau red hair," he said. Turning to Lauren he added, "I take after my mother's side of the family, who originally came from Holland. We simply get on with the job and do the work," he laughed. "The French side has all the 'savoir faire'! David's the real wine-maker. I'm just a part-timer. He studied viticulture at Stellenbosch University and he's keen that I do the same. I'm too much of a scientist though."

"But wine-making is a science, surely?" remarked Lauren.

"It is," he agreed, "but it's an art as well. David has the flair."

Mike had been eager to show Lauren and her mother his own little piece of Africa as he called it, but the time had not been right for Lauren until now. As they drove up the long avenue of oaks to the old Cape Dutch homestead, Lauren understood why he was so passionate about his home. It was breathtaking. The white gables shone impressively in the dark thatched roof, while the shuttered windows and teak door were wide open and beckoning. There was a vast lawn bounded by lavender bushes in front of the house, and a big rose garden to the side, with a cottage nearby in the same architectural style.

Two young children on a bicycle waved happily as they drove past, shouting in Afrikaans. Three more children ran alongside the car waving and shouting, "Happy Christmas." Mike waved and greeted them in Afrikaans, turning to Lauren and explaining that they were children of workers on the farm. He had known them since they were born and Christmas and New Year were very big events around here. The children's excitement was evident as they screeched and laughed loudly. "There'll be lots more of that in the next few days," Mike continued. "Be ready for some crazy people!"

Lauren turned to look at her mother seated in the back of Mike's Land Rover and the two women smiled at each other, pleased to be spending Christmas together here on the farm and meeting Mike's family the first time. For Bella, her daughter's smile meant the world. It was three months since Lauren had been savagely attacked and Bella wondered sometimes, in the dark of the night, whether her child would ever be totally happy again. She marveled at the patience and wisdom of the young man driving the car; his advice to first give Lauren time to heal on her own had been valid. The security of being loved, feeling safe, and doing something positive, was having a beneficial effect—as that moment of happiness in her smile had revealed. She was reminded of her own feelings of joy when she first met Ted at Georgetown; Lauren and Mike had that same electric charge. Their happiness was contagious and it made her feel almost as if her husband were here with them too.

Even before the car came to a stop in the gravel driveway, a tall gray-haired woman dressed in jeans and a striped shirt, rushed out the front door waving and smiling. She carried a young child on her hip who stared somberly, still heavy with sleep from which he had recently awoken. "Here are Uncle Mike and our guests, Ryan. Say hello." She placed the child carefully on the ground and embraced her son as he climbed out the car. Then she turned and said, "You must be Lauren." With that, she embraced the young American woman and said, "I'm Martie Rousseau. Welcome to Belle Terre. I'm so happy to meet you—and goodness me, you're as beautiful as Mike said you are!" she laughed, giving her son a playful jab in the ribs.

Lauren blushed and smiled. "I've been looking forward to meeting you too," she replied.

"Mrs. Marlowe," Martie added, turning to Bella with a hug, "I'm thrilled that you're also joining us for Christmas." It was impossible not to feel instantly warmed and welcome. "Come, come inside and let's make some tea or coffee. Let's get you comfortable and then I'll show you around. My son David and his wife Tina are joining us later; this is their son, our first grandchild. He's three, aren't you Ryan?" Ryan looked shyly at them and buried his head in his grandmother's knees, showing only his reddish blonde curls. "My husband sends his apologies that he isn't here to greet you—he's at a meeting in Stellenbosch. But we'll be having dinner together tonight. You'll get to meet them all then."

Mike laughed as he put his arm around his mother. "My mom is a great organizer."

Bella and Lauren smiled. They both started to speak at the same time and then stopped. "I've been looking forward to this," Bella started again. "I'm excited to have a warm Christmas with no snow."

"No snow, but plenty of ice in your drinks," Mike laughed.

Ryan turned and stared again at the two strangers. "What's snow?" he whispered to his grandmother.

Lauren spoke gently. "I'll have to find a picture and show you, Ryan. It's pretty, but very cold. It's a bit like rain, but it's little white flakes instead of raindrops."

"Hey big guy, aren't I getting a hug today?" asked Mike. He picked up his nephew and the two of them began to laugh as Mike deposited Ryan on his shoulders, holding the boy's legs firmly as he raced up the stairs to the front door. He turned to Lauren, Bella and his mom, saying, "Come on, ladies first!"

And so began Lauren's introduction to Mike's little piece of Africa.

The two days before Christmas were spent exploring the farm and the little town, as well as helping with preparations in the kitchen. Martie Rousseau was an impressive cook, ably assisted by a warm, smiling woman named Chooks. Chooks and her husband March were retired and lived nearby, but she liked to come back and help Martie for special occasions. They had worked side-by-side for many years; at first she had been employed as the family's cook, but as Mike and David grew up, Martie began to spend more time in the kitchen herself. Between the two of them they had an extensive menu of old Cape cooking; Afrikaner recipes from Martie, and Cape Malay recipes from Chooks. They began to put their skills to work with a small catering business which soon grew to be almost more than they could handle. As Franschoek became the gourmet capital of the country, so their business thrived with weddings and other functions taking place in ever increasing numbers. At one time Belle Terre, itself, was even used as a wedding venue, which proved very lucrative. Both women had enjoyed the challenges but were happy to retire when they became grandmothers at about the same time.

Chooks beamed at Lauren. *"Jurre!"* she exclaimed. *"Jy's mos baie maer.* You're very thin," she repeated in English when she realized that the young woman didn't understand Afrikaans. "We must fatten you up. Doesn't your *ma* feed you?" she laughed, patting Lauren. Then she added with a big grin and a grunt, "We must fatten your mother too. I thought there was lots of food in America. That's what people say — bloody Americans eat too much. But just look at the two of you — you're as thin as that drain pipe outside there!" She laughed, happily continuing to chop onions. "I'm going to teach you to make *babotie*. That's Michael's favorite food. It looks like you've caught his heart jus' fine, but the stomach is the way to keep his heart. You listen to me, Lauren. Me and March, we've been married forty-six years now. Hanky-panky; that's once a week maybe, but food is three times a day at least. You can't live on love and fresh air."

Lauren blushed as Martie chortled with laughter. Her old friend and helper always spoke out where others feared to go. Nobody else would've dared make such an explicit comment to Lauren, given the terrible experience she'd had, but this old woman was the salt of the earth; she and her people had survived because they simply got on with life, regardless of its trials. Lauren would need to get used to such forthrightness from her by degrees, Martie thought. "All right Chooks, I think that's enough," she said.

True to her word, Chooks taught Lauren to cook *babotie*, a mingling of curry and spices with ground lamb and a savory egg custard. It was unlike anything she had ever tasted, but delicious and she felt pride in her creation. Cooking was a new experience for her. She had never really done much in the way of food preparation, other than putting frozen food in the microwave or making a salad. She would never have believed it possible that it could be such a pleasurable occupation, but Martie and Chooks made it so. When she watched David, the winemaker, at work, she saw the same sense of adventure and delight in bringing ingredients together to produce a wonderful new flavor. Martie and Tina had an organic vegetable patch and herb garden in the back, fenced to keep the dogs out. Everyone was enthusiastic about what they did and it was clear to see why Mike was such a positive person.

He took her for a long hike on the farm and the surrounding area, and up into the nearby mountains. It reminded her of the Santa Cruz Mountains in California, near her grandparents' home. The healthy glow in her face was evidence that she was finding peace again, and when Mike suggested she accompany him to Knysna in the New Year, she agreed to go. March and Chooks's youngest son, Pieter, was the same age as Mike. The two boys had grown up together and the Rousseau family had paid for Pieter to attend Art School at UCT at the same time that Mike studied there for his B.Sc. Pieter was a very talented artist making a name for himself in the South African art world, with a studio in Knysna amongst a colony of other young artists. He would be home for Christmas, but invited Mike to visit his studio for the opening of his latest exhibition in early January. It would be very interesting Lauren thought, and would take her mind off saying good bye to her mother after Christmas.

Martie and her husband, Dawie, enjoyed showing Bella and Lauren the family tree which was printed on a chart and hanging on the wall of the dining room. The American women were surprised at how extensive the information was, going back ten generations in South Africa alone. The mix of nationalities was similar to many American families they commented, and it was interesting to see how emigration from Europe had spread out in different avenues, but for the same reasons and at similar times. Mike laughed at their reactions, saying, "You see I could just as easily have ended up an All-American boy if my ancestors had gone west instead of south, and by the same logic, you could have been South African."

"I guess we're all citizens of the world really," Lauren replied. "Globalization makes patriotism a bit silly."

"In some ways, but we all love what's familiar to us. I mean, your father could have married anyone, but he chose your mother. He loved her, not any of the other women he might have chosen!" he laughed.

They all smiled at his analogy but Lauren persisted with her argument. "That isn't a good comparison at all, Mike. My father didn't fight other men to prove that my mother was better than their wives! That's the trouble with patriotism; people go to war over it."

"OK, you're right about that. But loving your country because you grew up there is like loving your family," he said. "Come on Lauren. Tell me I'm right."

She reached up and kissed him on the cheek. "You're right. Let's not go to war over it. All I can say is that you have a lot more relations than we have, but we might catch up if we find anymore previously unknown ones!" laughed Lauren.

"You'll see plenty of the relations tomorrow at Christmas dinner," exclaimed Mike. "Don't even try and figure out who belongs to whom."

Christmas proved to be as noisy and festive as anticipated. There were countless cousins and children and they all spoke a mixture of Afrikaans and English. While chatting over cocktails before lunch, Lauren asked Mike's dad whether any of the Rousseaus spoke French, at which point he laughed loudly. "They stopped doing that not long after they arrived in South Africa, I'm afraid. It's a shame, isn't it? They had to learn to adapt and Dutch was the lingo spoken here at that time."

"So is Dutch the parent language of Afrikaans?" Lauren asked.

"I suppose you could say that. But nowadays, you know, we've had to adapt again and you'll find more and more English spoken around here. I went to an Afrikaans school and university, but Mike and David went to English institutions. Even at Stellenbosch where

David went to university—it's Afrikaans, but lots of the work is in English. You have to adapt you see, and English is a language spoken almost everywhere in the world." He looked at her and winked, "Just think, Mike would never have been able to ask you out if he only spoke Afrikaans!"

The Rousseau children, as well as many of the workers' children, were anxious for the arrival of Father Christmas and as they played on the lawn, they kept watchful eyes on the side gate. Suddenly there was a shriek as one of them spotted a flash of red and they all went running in that direction. Father Christmas opened the gate and called out, "Ho, ho, ho! Happy Christmas everyone. Now let's see which children have been good this year?" He made his way to a garden bench stroking his white beard as he looked around at the eager faces. "Hmm, you look like a good bunch. Let me see what I have in my sack."

The young children all rushed to sit as close to Santa as possible, while the older ones hung back. They were a little embarrassed, but not ready to dismiss this tradition quite yet. Father Christmas stretched his arms and rubbed his back before he sat down, saying, "I get so stiff riding in that sleigh, and it's been a bumpy ride this year. I think it's global warming causing thunder storms over the equator."

One of the older children sniggered. "Where's your sleigh?" he asked.

"Same place I always park it. And it's a secret! I don't want the reindeer disturbed by too much attention. They're having a little rest right now. Is that young Willem asking questions?"

The child nodded. Father Christmas said thoughtfully, "Come over here, Willem Moolman, let me look at you." He looked the boy up and down and said admiringly, "You've grown a lot, I can see that. How's the rugby ball you got last year? Scored many tries with it?"

Willem looked amazed. He nodded, and then said in a less confident voice, "It was very nice thank you, Father Christmas."

"So it got lots of use did it?"

Willem nodded again.

"Well, let's see what we've got in store for you this year." He delved into his sack and retrieved a box wrapped in red paper, which he handed to the excited young boy. At the same time he called for Anita, Chooks's granddaughter, to collect a large silver parcel with green ribbon. There were cries of pleasure and amazement as he called on all the children and chatted to each of them in turn, before giving their gift to them. At length he stood up and waved, saying loudly, "I'm glad you've all been good this year. I've had no complaints. That's the way I like it. Now I must leave you because there are still a lot of presents to deliver and time is short. I must be on my way but I'll be back next Christmas." He picked up his empty sack and made for the gate again, stopping to look at Lauren. "Look at this lovely lady. I haven't seen you here before. Welcome to Belle Terre." He blew her a kiss and then slipped through the gate before disappearing into the orchard.

There were thirty adults sitting down to lunch at the huge table stretched out on the back verandah, and twelve children at a separate table close by. Traditional roast turkey seemed strange on such a hot day, but both Lauren and Bella enjoyed all the cultural similarities nonetheless. Before everyone started eating, Dawie Rousseau asked for silence as he began the meal with grace. "Dear Father, we thank you for the wonderful meal you have provided us, and we thank you for the loving hands that prepared it. We also thank you that on this special day, you have brought Lauren and her mother to us. We thank you for our many blessings and pray that we always remember to share our bounty with others. Amen." He opened his eyes and looked around the table, raising his glass, "Happy Christmas!"

There was an answering chorus of "Happy Christmas," and clinking of glasses, and then everyone began feasting. Lauren leaned over and whispered in Mike's ear, "Santa, I find you irresistible." She kissed him on the cheek and then added, "I have a very special Christmas gift for you, but I'll give it to you later when we're alone."

He put an arm over her shoulders and whispered in her ear, "If I'd known it would have this effect on you, I would've worn my fancy dress a lot sooner."

She giggled and said, "I want you without fancy dress though, in your birthday suit not your Christmas one."

He looked at her with his head inclined. "For once in my life I'm speechless! What did you just say?"

"I said that I have another gift for you, but I have to give it to you in private. I think you'll like it...You've mentioned a few times that you would!"

"Any clues?" he asked.

"Well, it might ruin the surprise if I give you too many."

"Lauren, are you saying what I think you're saying?"

She put her finger over his lips. "I think you've guessed right, but no more clues. Just come to my room tonight."

Wiping his brow he laughed and said, "This sweat is not entirely from that hot, red gown." He found it very hard to concentrate on anything other than Lauren's words after that. People spoke to him, but his thoughts wandered and he paid little attention; he found himself in a tricky situation. There was nothing he wanted more than Lauren, but he wasn't expecting this bonanza and had come unprepared. As it was Christmas day, there would be no shops open to buy condoms, and he knew he couldn't chance it without; apart from an unwanted pregnancy, Lauren was not by any means in the clear from HIV. She'd passed the 3 month mark successfully, but they couldn't be sure yet.

He was distracted briefly when the Christmas pudding was lit. Everyone laughed and cheered as his mother ran out from the kitchen carrying a flaming dish and singing, "We wish you a merry Christmas and a happy New Year." The flame finally died down and all the guests applauded. Lauren was intrigued that the old English custom had found its way to Africa, and was still lovingly continued even in the heat of summer. Despite her English grandparents, she'd never tasted plum pudding before and felt more inclined towards the English trifle that was offered as an alternative. Mike wouldn't let her escape however, and gave her a piece with brandy sauce. "Trust me, it's good."

David Rousseau laughed as he watched her face. "She needs more brandy sauce on it, Mike," he said as he poured dessert wine for those who wanted it. "You've got to look after her, bro'!" Then he added, "Can you tear yourself away for a few minutes and help me get some more wine from the cellar?" As he got no response from his brother, he prodded Mike and repeated the question, adding, "Hey, anybody home?"

"Oh sorry, I'll be right there." Mike excused himself and followed his older brother to replenish the wine. They made their way into the temperature controlled building in the winery adjacent to the house, and both men sighed with relief as they felt the welcome rush of coolness. "Man, you don't realize how hot it is until you get inside here," Dave said. Then he looked at his brother and added, "What's eating you Mike? You went very quiet during lunch. Is everything all right?"

"Yeah," replied Mike. "Everything's great."

Dave looked at him a long while and then said quietly, "Well, remember you have a brother if ever you've got a problem. OK?"

"OK, thanks," said Mike. They both stood staring at the rows of wine bottles in silence. Finally Mike cleared his throat and said, "Actually, have you got any condoms to spare?" He felt his face redden.

Dave was tempted to laugh at his younger brother's discomfort, but this was no laughing matter. "Hey, what are you getting yourself into? There's a lot at stake here, man. I know she was a victim, but until you know for certain she's not HIV+, why take the chance of making yourself a victim as well?"

"I'm not going to take a chance. That's why I want the condoms. There are no bloody shops open today and I think she's just given me the green light. I've been waiting six months for this moment Dave; I don't want to wait another day."

Dave grunted and put his arm over his brother's shoulder. "What do you mean—wait another day? I really wish you would wait at least another three months until you know for sure what her situation is. Listen to reason, man."

"I know, I know. But there's no way I can wait that long now that she's ready…"

Dave sighed deeply. "I'm not happy about this Mike." They sat in silence for a while before Dave said, "The only reason I'll give you some condoms is because I don't want you having sex without them. But you'll have to come around to our place this evening and fetch them. I don't just carry them around on me."

The hours seemed to drag until evening fell and guests went home. Mike and Lauren felt like teenagers who were eagerly anticipating forbidden sexual pleasures. When their hands touched, they felt nothing but each other's hand, and when their eyes met, they saw nobody else. When finally he crept into her bed, Mike was desperate to feel his body naked next to hers. There were no words necessary as they embraced and explored each other. Her fears of engaging in sex had dissipated and her mind was aware of nothing except this man and the sensations she was feeling. It was all good.

***

Bella waved until she could see her daughter no more as she snaked her way through the security line at Cape Town International Airport. The three months since she'd arrived seemed like an eternity. Her heart felt very heavy leaving Lauren behind in this strange country, so full of such contrasts. The warmth and beauty of the Rousseau home was a haven amidst the violence of Cape Town and it was clear to see what a beneficial effect Christmas at Belle Terre had produced in Lauren. As Mike and Lauren were driving her to the airport, she'd watched the shanties sprawled on either side of the motorway; after the pleasant interlude on the farm, they brought her sharply back to the reality of her daughter's life here. When she hugged her goodbye, she whispered in Lauren's ear, "I'll be back in May, but I can't wait for you to come home again." They held onto one another tightly for a moment and then Bella pulled away before she could break down and cry. "Look after yourself darling."

When her mother finally disappeared from sight, Lauren felt herself tremble. Her lower lip quivered uncontrollably as she buried her face in Mike's chest. He said nothing; just held her tightly. At length he led her by the hand back to his car and they drove in silence most of the way to Knysna. The orphanage could wait until their return to Cape Town. The scenery helped to distract Lauren from her sadness and when they arrived in the little coastal town about four hours later, she was intrigued by the expansive lagoon and the rocks at the mouth of it. "Those are 'The Heads' and just about every artist in Knysna has painted them at some point in time," Mike told her. "This part of the country is known as the Garden Route because an enormous proportion of the world's flowers come from around here."

The natural beauty of the land was evident in all the artwork she viewed at the gallery where Pieter's work was displayed. There was a woman artist who painted studies of flowers in oils, and another woman who painted abstract acrylics—evoking such anguish and passion in broken African figures that Lauren could barely look at them. Pieter painted water colors of Knysna Heads, Table Mountain, and an exquisite pair of paintings that depicted vineyards and Cape Dutch buildings which she immediately recognized as Belle Terre. She and Mike knew instantly that they were going to buy them, and although the exhibition only opened the following day, Pieter promised that he would put red "sold" stickers on them. "We'll have to flip for who gets which," Lauren said, "I'd be happy with either." Mike said nothing.

They promised to return the following evening for the opening, and headed further up the coast to Plettenberg Bay where they were spending a few nights. Their hotel room seemed perched on the edge of the Indian Ocean with views, from the huge picture windows, of long white beaches extending to the left and right of them. In the distance they could see a spit of land which Mike explained was a nature reserve called Robberg. "And that, Lauren, is where I'd like to take you hiking tomorrow. It's my favorite place on earth and I want to share it with my favorite person in the world."

The next day was warm and sunny. After an early morning swim in the Indian Ocean, they set out early so that they could get all the way to the end of Robberg and back before it got too hot. It was a long hike and at one point they had to swing over a narrow chasm, holding onto an iron chain embedded in the rocks. Way below them the sea rushed into an inlet and beat against rocks, spraying foamy water high in the air. Lauren felt unafraid, but rather exhilarated. The wild ocean on the other side of Robberg was called Nelson's Bay and it lay far below them. They paused to rest on a steep cliff, standing slightly apart and staring at the pounding surf, aware of nature being in charge of this vast continent. Seagulls swooped and cawed around them, and rock rabbits scurried in the sun, but the two of them were the only people in sight. Civilization seemed a million miles away. At length, Mike pulled her close. "Lauren," he said, "I always knew that I would come here to ask this question." He paused. Each of them could hear their own heart pounding louder than the waves. Their future was like a third person standing between them.

She looked up at him and he said, "I don't know where we would live, but I can't live without you. Will you marry me, Lauren Marlowe?"

The only sound was the surf and the gulls, as she stared at him silently. "Lauren," he finally said, "Can you give me an answer any time soon?"

"We don't know for sure that I'm in the clear, Mike. Why don't we wait until we know in March and you can ask me again then?"

"I'm not asking again in March, I'm asking now. Whatever happens, I want to marry you."

She turned away to hide the tears in her eyes. "You know that I love you, and that I've never been so happy in all my life as this past week. But I can't tie you down to me if I turn out to be HIV+. We can't ignore the possibility that's still sitting out there."

"Let me be the one to decide..." he began, but Lauren cut him off before he could continue.

"No Mike. I am the one to decide. I love you too much to marry you if I'm HIV+. We're using condoms now but I don't want that for the rest of our days, and then somewhere down the line you have a wife who develops full-blown Aids and dies. You will have wasted years of your life on a lost cause." She turned around to face him. "All I can promise is that if I'm still free of the virus in March, and if you still want me to marry you, I will undoubtedly say yes."

21

In California, the New Year started with much promise for Tracey. The gray, dreary days of January were spent in consultation with Dr. Wilcox, who directed the functioning of her life and her body. He continued to be very optimistic about the outcome of their efforts; after her excellent response to medication, he was able to obtain twelve eggs by the beginning of February. Howard did his part privately, but with much embarrassment, and Dr. Wilcox put all the components together. He was happy to report that seven of the eggs had been fertilized, and Tracey was ready to return to his clinic the next day to have the embryo transfer take place. There had been prior consultation about how many of the crop should be transferred into her womb. The doctor had recommended placing two or three inside Tracey, while freezing the remainder for future use if needed. There would be no guarantee that all — or any — would implant themselves, but if they all did so, then there was a risk factor to be faced with multiple births. Dr. Wilcox had broached the subject of selective pregnancy reduction.

"What exactly do you mean by that?" Howard had asked.

"I mean that if we transfer three embryos and they all implant, there is a heightened risk involved in multiple pregnancies. Patients often consider terminating one of them to give the other two a better chance of survival."

"Oh my goodness, how would you do that?" Tracey had inquired.

"It's a delicate procedure where we use ultrasound to guide us, and then we inject a needle containing a solution of potassium chloride through your abdomen, into the fetal heart. This causes it to stop beating. Your body then reabsorbs the fetus. Although it's delicate, it's been performed many times very successfully. It's quite safe."

"Never!" Howard had jumped out of his chair and pounded his fist on the doctor's desk. "It's bad enough that we've created life in this artificial way; we cannot destroy it willfully. That's murder."

"But Howard," Tracey had interjected, "Consider that by terminating one embryo, we give the other two a better chance to live."

"No, Tracey. I can't agree to that. I'm having a hard time accepting that there will be four other embryos languishing somewhere waiting to be born, but to actually kill one. I simply can't agree."

"But I would only be about seven weeks pregnant. It wouldn't be like killing a baby."

"There are no buts about it. It's a life Tracey. Whether it's seven weeks or seven months or seven years, it'll be my child, *our* child. Do you honestly think that's an acceptable thing to do? I'm appalled."

"Of course we can simply transfer only two embryos now," Dr. Wilcox had intervened. "This is what I would recommend in your case. We have a slightly smaller chance of impregnation, but we'll still have five in reserve to try again—if we need to do so. And if both implant, I am very confident that you are healthy enough to carry two babies almost to term."

Howard and Tracey had looked at one another—and then nodded in agreement.

The eleven days after the transfer took place seemed interminable. Tracey and Howard tried not to discuss it much, but their thoughts were constantly wound up with the matter. Tracey tried to visualize what was happening inside her body and willed it to accept the offering it had been given. Howard was relieved that his sperm had done the job and somehow felt a father already, just knowing that he had made embryos. On Valentine's Day, they got the call. Both embryos had implanted. Tracey was expecting twins on November 1st, All Saints' Day. When he looked at his wife, Howard experienced emotions entirely new to him. He was filled with a need to protect her and these new beings that were his children. Life had never felt so good before and his only regret was that his mother wasn't here to share his joy, although his unshakeable belief was that she knew about it wherever she was. He almost believed that she had willed it to happen.

With all other aspects of his life under control, Howard turned his energies to the Parker Family Foundation. Ned Mackay had been a unanimous choice to be on the Board of Trustees, in addition to the four brothers and sisters. Howard had also obtained agreement to approach two women who were chairpersons of Non-Profit Organizations—one in Washington D.C. and the other in San Francisco, as well as a financial advisor from an investment banking firm in New York. With this group in place, work began on investing and managing the money, as well as assigning portions to charitable operations. It had taken a lot of Howard's time and he felt pleased with the outcome. An office was formed in Woodside, California, convenient for San Francisco Airport and Silicon Valley, and this was where Howard spent much of his time.

As he drove home from work one afternoon a few days later, the green hills alongside Highway 280 uplifted his soul and the clusters of daffodils on the Stanford hills were an affirmation of new life to him. His parents had gone, but life continued with its awesome rhythm. He felt gratitude that God had finally allowed him to procreate. He began to hum automatically, and smiled when he realized it was his mother's favorite hymn, 'Onward Christian Soldiers.' He was still humming as he entered the driveway to his home and was surprised to see an old green Chevy truck parked outside, with a mangy-looking dog sitting in the front seat. He opened the automatic garage door and drove in with a frown on his face. He wondered whether this was the new gardener Tracey had employed, and if so, why the man was audacious enough to park his dirty truck right outside the front door. There was a parking lot at the side for deliveries and workmen. This matter would have to be addressed immediately. His surprise was even greater when he entered the kitchen and saw a disheveled old man in denim overalls and a plaid shirt sitting at the table, smoking a cigarette and drinking a cup of coffee in a polystyrene cup.

The old man jumped up and quickly stubbed out his cigarette in the sink. He stepped forward with his hand outstretched. "I'm Joe Billings—Tracey's ol' man. Pleased t' meet ya. I think you mus' be my son-in-law."

Howard stared at the man in silence, ignoring the proffered hand. "Will you please refrain from smoking in my house?" he said and turned on his heel, slamming the door behind him. He marched straight to the bedroom where Tracey was lying prostrate on the bed, with a cool cloth on her forehead. Her face was quite ashen. "Tracey, is that specimen in the kitchen really your father as he claims to be?"

She nodded and wept. "I thought he was dead. I told him to go away but he came back. Please make him go away Howard. I can't bear it."

"You're sure he's your father?"

She nodded vigorously. "Tell him to go away."

"When last did you see him?"

"He came here in September when he read about Lauren in the paper. I gave him some money and he went away."

"But when did you see him before that?"

"When I was thirteen. He disappeared after that. We gave him up for dead. He can't just presume to walk back into my life now. I don't ever want to see him again. He's disgusting…He reeks of tobacco and alcohol. I want him out of my house."

"All right Tracey, stay calm. I'll deal with this," Howard said. "You need to calm down. It's not good for you to get into such a state in your condition. Think of the babies."

"I am thinking of them. I don't want them growing up with that awful man anywhere near them."

"All right Tracey, all right." Howard stepped aside quickly, as she leapt from the bed and rushed to the bathroom where he could hear her retching. The stress was clearly aggravating her morning sickness. Feeling helpless to assist her, he closed the door quietly and went to his study where he slumped at his desk with his head in his hands. He did what he always did in a crisis; he prayed.

"Dear God," he said silently, "please show me what I should do. This man is repulsive, but he is my wife's father. We have an obligation to take care of him, but Tracey is so angry with him and it's not good for her to be so upset." He squeezed his eyes shut and tried to let God enter his head. In the silence that engulfed the room, he was only aware of his heart beating in time to the grandfather clock, which had come from his parents' home. As he listened to the old clock, he felt aware of his mother's guiding voice telling him that he would always know the answer to things from within himself. It was an epiphany. "God is guiding me through my mother," he thought to himself. And he knew the answer, much as he was trying to escape from it. He knew that he couldn't turn his back on the old man; he had to help him. It was up to him to show this man the error of his ways. Perhaps he could lead him to God. He would have to show him God's way and God's laws; that was why God had sent this man to his house. He lifted his head and smiled. After a while he arose and moved to the window, where he stared into the distance as he tried to decide how to deal with Tracey. She needed to also see this as a divine opportunity.

He was tempted to return immediately to the kitchen, but his conscience forced him to deal with the more difficult task—Tracey. He hesitated momentarily before making his way slowly back to the bedroom, where his wife now lay curled in a fetal position. She lifted her head and looked questioningly at him. "Has he gone?"

"Not yet, Tracey. But don't worry. Everything is absolutely fine."

She rolled over and straightened herself. "You are so wonderful Howard," she murmured, "I couldn't have managed without you."

Howard sat on the bed next to her and stroked her hair. "You're having such a rough ride with this pregnancy, but it will all be worth it. The nausea can't continue much longer, hopefully." He smiled at her and kissed her damp brow. "I've been doing some thinking Tracey, about your father." She stiffened. "I think God wants us to do his work with your dad. I firmly believe that the reason why he found us is because God sent him here to us."

"Howard, the reason he found us is because he wants money. I've given it to him once for God's sake, and he's back again. He'll just keep coming back. Tell him to get the hell out of here, once and for all. If you love me, you'll do that for me."

"No Tracey. We can afford to take care of him, and we can't afford to have this on our consciences if we don't." He sat back and folded his arms. "He's your own flesh and blood. He's our babies' grandfather. It's quite clear to me that we have to try and save his soul for God. It'll be very testing, but we have to do it."

She was weeping and shaking her head as she moaned, "No Howard. I hate him. You don't understand."

"Then this is a God-given opportunity for you to be reconciled. Don't send him to his grave without giving him a chance." He leaned over and patted her. "We'll put him into the guest cottage so that you don't have to see him all the time." When she didn't respond, he nodded his head and sighed as she sobbed into her pillow. Without another word he left the room.

***

The old man sat dejectedly in the kitchen. His daughter had screamed abuse at him and his son-in-law had snubbed him. He'd been living in his truck and eating dog food with Bob for the past week until his next social security check arrived. He wasn't afraid of doing that again if he had to, but he had in his heart to reunite with his daughter and belong in a family once again. His son-in-law didn't look a very friendly sort, and Tracey was hysterical. Seemed like there was a baby on the way and women were likely to be irrational when they were pregnant. He remembered Tracey's mother, Trudy; she had remained irrational all her days. He felt bitter remembering how she had disapproved of his drinking and smoking. They were always arguing about it but she didn't understand how lonely it was for him on the road all the time.

"Well get another job and be a decent father," she would complain. "You're a bad influence on Tracey. For myself, I can do without a husband."

"The trouble with you is that you spend too much darn time at Bible school," he used to say, "an' then you forget how to live 'cause you's always prayin'.

Finally, while he was away, she moved without telling him. When he returned, there was a note on the door that all his stuff was in storage and his wife and daughter had left. He found her at work, but she refused to give him any information—just that she wouldn't live with him anymore and Tracey had gone to live with her aunt. This he realized now was a lie. He sent money regularly to her bank account for child support, but he didn't have the money to hire a lawyer. He hoped that she would eventually weaken, but she never did. Trudy had been such a happy, beautiful woman when they first met, but as soon as they had a baby and she got all tied up with them Bible school folks, she felt he wasn't good enough. When she died, he lost his last hope of finding Tracey until he saw her picture in the paper. "Well, Trudy would be proud of her daughter now," he thought to himself.

He looked up tensely as the door opened and his son-in-law entered once more. He pulled up the straps of his overalls and tucked his shirt in at the back. "I was jus' leavin'," Joe said.

"No, no, please stay." Howard replied. "I'm sorry I was rude earlier, but you took me completely by surprise. I thought, like Tracey, that you had died many years ago."

The old man relaxed slightly. "It broke my heart that she never known her daddy. Her momma would'n let me see her all those years. She was a mighty mean woman, I can tell ya." He explained at length what had happened, and Howard listened sympathetically, considering that it might just be true.

"I tell you what Joe," he said when the old man had finished his story. "I think God has had a hand in all of this. I should ask you, do you believe in God?" he asked.

Joe shifted in his seat and swallowed hard. "Yes," he said. Then he frowned and added, "But I don' git why he's made life so hard for me. Some folks have it real easy-like, and then there's others an' they gits nothin' but trouble. Why would God do that if he's sittin' up there watchin' it all? That's what I don' git."

"Everybody has their own troubles, Joe. Sometimes you just can't see them. But God always gives us a way out of our troubles if we would only see the way that he gives us. I believe that he brought you here so that we can help you—but you also have to help yourself." Howard looked at the old disheveled man and wondered how Tracey could possibly be related to him. The first things necessary were a shower and some clean, decent clothes, as well as a shave and a haircut. Personal hygiene was clearly not Joe's top priority. "Are you prepared to help yourself, Joe?

"Course I am."

"Then you must be prepared to accept God into your life and let him lead the way." Howard put his hand out and touched the old man on the shoulder. "We have a little cottage in the garden and you can stay there for the time being, until we figure out what to do with you. But there are some house rules that I insist you abide by."

"Whatever you says."

"Good. First thing, there will be no smoking inside either house. There's a back porch at the cottage, and that's the only place where you may smoke.

Secondly, don't park that truck outside my front door. There's a parking space near the shed where I park my golf cart—I'll show you where. The workmen use that; please park there.

Thirdly, please don't come into the main house unless you're invited. This is our home, the cottage will be yours on loan—let's be good neighbors. Oh, and no guests. We're only having you to stay, no hangers-on.

Lastly, I'll buy you some new clothes. I expect you to shower, shave and wear clean clothes every day. Cleanliness is next to godliness, remember.

Also—that dog. I don't want it running around in my garden. Make sure you keep it with you all the time, and clean up after it."

Joe stared at Howard. "Bless my soul that's mighty gen'rous of you," he said. "Could be you's right and that God is tryin' to help me after all."

"Trust me Joe, he is."

"An' I can tell you I'm mighty handy around the house. Anything needs fixin', I can do it for ya. All ya have to do is holler."

And so Joe Billings moved to Los Gatos, into the first home he had known in over twenty years. Life had certainly taken him to some strange and interesting places in his time, but never to such a comfortable one.

22

The orphanage building began again at a rapid pace in the New Year and was reaching a point where Lauren needed to start considering furnishings. After much agonizing, she had handed over the difficult task of selecting Aids orphans to the Child Protection Agency as she couldn't bring herself to play God, admitting some and denying others. She also decided to use some of her inheritance to buy a house in the Cape Town suburb of Gardens, which she planned to convert to a halfway house. It was a 1920's brick house with the typical old South African "servants' quarters" in the back. In total it would house ten orphaned teenagers who came out of the state system at sixteen, but were unequipped to live on their own satisfactorily. It would also provide room for two teachers who would help supervise the teenagers and give them guidance for a further few years, ensuring that they continued their education. She set up a fund to pay for their education as well. Lauren had seen this system work in Durban and favored the homey, supportive atmosphere it provided. It was her hope that the Parker Family Foundation would provide more funding for many more such homes; it seemed imperative, given the number of orphans in the country. Without help, many of them ended up incarcerated within a year of their leaving an orphanage, as they had no means of supporting themselves—if they had been lucky enough to be in an orphanage at all; many children were simply street children and joined gangs.

Mike was equally as enthusiastic as Lauren about the orphanage and halfway house, which she decided to name 'Parker House' after her grandparents. She was in the process of submitting a formal application to the Family Foundation for enough funds to buy two more properties in Cape Town, and three each in Johannesburg and Durban. She was also asking for money for an education fund to be used by the residents. So far she'd heard nothing and time was going by fast. It was the end of February already; only three more months before she was due to return. Life back in the United States seemed remote. She had put all thoughts of her own future on hold until March and the next blood test—and it was suddenly very close.

Hard work helped keep her mind off her anxieties and she threw herself into readying Parker House for its occupants. On Thursdays Mike met with his professor; recently they had been meeting very late, making overseas calls regarding Mike's thesis. It seemed a good opportunity to work in the home as there were no interruptions and she could get things done. With only the radio for company, she was busy painting the kitchen when she heard knocking at the front door. This caused her to frown with irritation; it was hard to complete a task with people continually knocking on the door, usually asking for work. She decided to take no notice and continued painting. She was up on a ladder, painting the ceiling, when she heard a strange creaking sound in the vicinity of the living room. She climbed down the ladder and turned the radio down; there it was again. It sounded like the door being forced open. Her heart stood still. There was nothing in the house to steal, only her, and she was totally unarmed.

Silently she opened the kitchen door and crept out, closing it after her. She had the key to the "servants' quarters" in her pocket, and dashed out into the dark, overgrown garden, silently letting herself into the room and locking the door behind her. Her heart was pounding with fright and all the nightmares of last September were back in a flash. She was programmed to panic after her ordeal. There was an old bed standing on bricks in the room and she crawled under it, out of sight should a flashlight be shone through the window. She looked at her watch which glowed in the dark; it was 11.30 p.m. It was very silent as she lay for a long while, wondering when it would be safe to come out. There was no sound coming from the house, and no light anywhere. She decided to stay where she was until morning, but at midnight a sharp ring penetrated the silence. Her body began to shake momentarily until she realized it was her cell phone. "Why didn't I think to use it?" she asked herself. Her brain had frozen again. In a whisper she answered it. It was Mike.

"Where are you?" he asked.

She tried to whisper to him, but he said, "Lauren, I can't hear you. What's going on? I'm standing here in the kitchen of Parker House and it's unlocked. Where the hell are you?"

With relief she shouted out loud, "I'll be right with you," as she crawled from under the bed and opened the door. She ran across the dark space to the kitchen and threw herself into his arms, shaking as she clung to him.

"What is it?" he asked. The concern was audible in his voice as he hugged her and whispered in her ear, "What's upset you so much?"

"There was...There was somebody trying to break in," she said. "I ran to hide in the back room and I've been there for half an hour. Thank heavens you came, Mike."

He stiffened as she spoke and quickly locked the kitchen door. "Come with me," he said, leading her by the hand as he began to turn on all the lights in the empty house and lead her from room to room, checking all the doors and windows. There was no evidence of any attempted break-in until they reached a side bedroom. There they found glass lying on the floor, where someone had broken the window and tried to force the burglar bars apart.

Lauren froze. She began to shake again and Mike quickly put his arms around her. "It's all right. We'll call the police. I'm here with you and there's nobody else in the house. If they came inside through the back door, they realized there was nothing to take except your radio, a ladder and some paint. None of that seemed to take their fancy."

"It could've happened all over again," she whispered. "I can't stand it."

"It didn't happen again Lauren. And we're going to make sure it never does. First thing tomorrow, we're getting a burglar alarm installed here and a night watchman too—if you would like." He held her as she sobbed, and stroked her hair gently. "You're safe my darling and we're going to keep you safe."

"I can't help thinking of Janet," she said through her tears. "Most people are poor and they can't afford to have burglar bars and alarms. What's the matter with this place when you have to go about your daily business looking over your shoulder all the time? You can't live in fear like this. It's insane."

Mike kept his arm around her as he called the police. It was 2 a.m. before anyone showed and then the officer looked annoyed. "Nothing's been stolen and nobody was assaulted. What am I investigating?"

"I would've thought it's fairly obvious," replied Mike, bristling. "There's been an attempted break-in and entry; look at the bloody broken window."

"A broken window isn't big on the crime list around here, sir. A kid could have thrown a stone," the officer commented as he kicked some of the broken glass with his boot. "But let's see…It would be useful to have a police report for the insurance. A window this size costs lots of money to replace," he said. "I'll tell you what; you can go to the police station and file a report, or you can pay me R300 for the service and I'll do it now."

Mike clenched and unclenched his fists several times before answering, "Yes, I need a report, you're right. Why do I have to go to the police station for it though?"

"You don't. I said that I can do it for you on the spot for R300."

"Yes, so you did. I'm sorry, what did you say your name is?"

The officer looked warily at him and then replied, "I didn't."

"Oh," said Mike calmly, "Who do I write a cheque to?"

"No cheques sir, only cash."

"I don't have R300 on me Sergeant. But I tell you what, why don't you give me your name and address and I can send it to you when I've drawn the cash tomorrow?"

The policeman cleared his throat. "I'll come with you to the ATM? We can go now."

"Sergeant, it's late and we all have work tomorrow morning. I appreciate you trying to quicken things up, but I need to get this lady home. She's had a rough night. I think it would be much easier for us all if you just wrote down your details here and then gave me a police report." Mike handed him a piece of paper and pen from his pocket and waited. When the policeman handed the paper back there was a barely legible scrawl that read S. Mabele, with an address in Guguletu. "What does S stand for Sergeant?" asked Mike.

"Sipho," he replied. "Sergeant Sipho Mabele."

Mike repeated the name. "I tell you what I'll do for you. I'm going to mention this to Captain Radebe who is a personal friend of mine; I'm sure he'll be very interested to hear about your investigation methods and how you wanted to save me a trip to the police station. Excellent customer service you offered"

The sergeant snatched the paper away and opened his mouth to speak, but Mike pointed to the door. "Get out," he said. "Two crimes were committed here tonight, and yours is the greater. Get out." They watched him depart and clamber into the police car where another policeman sat waiting for him. "Bastards," muttered Mike. "I bet they're both in it, deep as shit. I won't forget that name, Sergeant Sipho Mabele." He quickly wrote it down himself.

The following morning, Wellington Radebe shook his head and sank in his chair as Mike relayed the previous night's events. "Thank you for reporting the matter, Mike. He's so cocky and stupid that he even gives you his name! I'll deal with it immediately. We have to weed these corrupt officers out of the force, but it's difficult to catch them. I really appreciate your information. Will you be prepared to give evidence if necessary?"

"Of course I will," Mike replied.

"And I think you must definitely get an alarm installed there. I'll come over and take a look at the security of the place. Is Lauren OK?" he asked.

"She's shaken up by it. I'm afraid it opened up some wounds for her."

Radebe nodded. "In my experience, victims of violent crimes never get over them completely. They often learn to get on with their lives, but their trust has been broken and it doesn't take much for that to show." He sighed and looked down at his hands. "She's strong and brave, and you're very good to her, but I'm afraid she's scarred Mike. She's probably suffering from Post Traumatic Stress Syndrome."

Mike tapped his foot with impatience. "I know," he replied.

"Perhaps she should get Dr. Naidoo to recommend a counselor. Or she can speak to my wife, Faith, if you like. Faith works in Guguletu with the Rape Crisis Trust. "

Mike continued tapping his foot.

"It's just a suggestion, Mike. You know Lauren better than I do."

Mike stood up and took a deep breath. "Thanks Wellington, I'll give it some thought." He took his leave and drove home with a heavy heart.

Lauren had been too distraught to return to her own place and had spent what was left of the night pacing the floor in Mike's living room. He had slept intermittently, but was aware of her moving around every time he awoke. Only at 8 a.m., as he was leaving, did she finally fall exhausted into his bed to sleep. There would be no teaching for her today. As Mike made his way back, he considered the question of therapy to help Lauren. She had come such a long way in the healing process, and it was only to be expected that fear would trigger a perfectly natural response. It was just two days until she had the next blood test and he felt sure that the outcome was weighing as heavily on her mind as it was on his own. That tension must have added to the stress she'd felt last night. He questioned himself about his reluctance to therapy. "I should be more open-minded about it," he thought to himself, "especially as a scientist. I have this feeling though, that it's often like picking a scab off a wound. I think Lauren is doing fine without anybody opening up her scabs."

He, too, was awaiting the results of her test to make the next decision about his career. His thesis had aroused great interest in several overseas academic institutions, and in the past fortnight he and his professor had been fielding calls from France, Britain, Canada, Australia and the United States. This past week had brought offers of visiting fellowships from Cambridge and Edinburgh Universities, as well a Fulbright Scholarship to do more research at Stanford University in California. He would be receiving his doctorate later in the month, and then he had the world to choose from. His decision would be based on Lauren, but he hadn't told her any of this for fear of placing unfair pressure on her.

She slept most of the day and stirred when he opened the door, but she didn't fully awaken. He watched her as she lay asleep; her face scrunched up in a frown at intervals, as she groaned softly. Her dreams were troubled and he wasn't surprised when she awoke a little later still feeling exhausted. "Stay with me tonight, Lauren," he said, putting his arms around her.

She nodded and answered quietly, "OK."

"Why don't you move in with me?"

She pushed away from him and answered quickly, "Let's deal with the next two days first. I can't make any plans until then…"

He nodded and thought to himself, "I can't either."

23

Tracey refused to visit her father in the cottage. It was as if he didn't exist. She felt that she owed it to her babies to protect them from the harmful effect his presence had on her, not to mention the second hand smoke. Howard, however, took care of everything. He hired Maria, their housekeeper Rosa's younger sister, to clean house, do laundry and cook for Joe. He visited every evening when he returned from work to ensure that all was well, and he also took the opportunity to have Joe join him in daily prayer and worship. It seemed fitting to him that he do this for Tracey, as she had overseen his own parents' needs in their old age. But as the scriptures told him, he didn't want his right hand to know what his left hand was doing, so he told nobody about Joe. Only Rosa and Maria knew the old man was there, and they befriended him.

At times it almost seemed as if God was giving him another father and he felt a good relationship developing. The old man cleaned up well and looked very handsome; it was easy to see a strong resemblance to Tracey with the same fine, strong bone structure, blue eyes (although his were bloodshot), and lean body. Joe thankfully accepted the bounty he was given, and was very grateful. Every day when Howard visited, he thanked him again and again, saying, "Dear God, I don't know how I would manage without you. You're my savior."

Howard would assure him that it was Jesus who was his savior, but he never tired of hearing the old man's thanks because they showed he had come to see the way of God in his life. Joe listened as Howard recited, "I am the way, and the truth and the light. Nobody comes to the father except through me," and Howard always smiled as the old man would repeat after him, "Jesus is my Lord." It began to weigh upon Howard that he ought to be taking his father-in-law to church. He and Tracey had struggled to find a church that satisfied their needs when they were first married. His parents had been Anglicans, switching to Episcopalians when they moved to California. The Parkers had been stalwarts of the parish where he had been raised, but as an adult he began to find it all too flexible; he saw it as a religion that was user-friendly rather than God-driven. It took courage to leave the Episcopal community and incur his parents' disappointment, and there was a time when he felt like a ship without a radar system until he and Tracey found something suitable; a religious community that wasn't elastic in its outlook. They abided by God's Laws alone, and didn't tweak those laws to suit their own needs.

The problem now was Tracey. She wouldn't tolerate her father's presence, and when Howard suggested to her that the old man attend a Men's Group breakfast with him, she nearly choked. "Don't embarrass us, Howard," she had pleaded. "He can barely speak properly let alone use a knife and fork the right way…" It would have to wait a while, he decided.

One evening he made his way over for his customary visit, but as he shook off his umbrella and stood it at the door, he could smell smoke. It was evident that the old man had been smoking inside and when he questioned him, Joe nodded shame-facedly. "It was cold and raining," he replied. "Me ol' chest sure don't like being out in the freezing rain."

Howard took a deep breath to try and control his rage. Finally he said, "You really let me down, Joe. I've taken you into our home and I haven't asked much of you in return. Look what I've given you, and you can't do this one thing that I asked of you."

Joe's eyes began to water. "I'm real sorry Howard. I've been real good about it, but it was mighty cold today, and rainin' cats an' dogs.

193

Can we jus' make it that on rainy days I smoke inside? Jus' rainy days, that's all?"

"Dammit, no Joe. Not ever." Howard decided it was better to skip prayers this evening as he felt his blood pressure rising. He glared at his father-in-law then turned on his heel, grabbing his umbrella before striding up the hill. The wind was blowing hard and turned his umbrella inside out, just as Bob came bounding after him. He jumped up on Howard with a ball in his mouth, eager to play. The rain had kept him inside. Howard shoved with his elbow, but the dog ran in front of him and placed the soggy ball at his feet, barking and nudging it closer, getting in Howard's way. He picked up the ball and threw it wildly away, only to discover, with horror, that it landed in a flower bed into which the dog then plunged headlong. In disgust, Howard rushed into the kitchen without closing the door and washed the saliva off his hands. As he dried them, out the corner of his eye he saw Bob dash into the kitchen, leaving muddy paw prints in a trail as he presented Howard with the soggy ball again. He had an incredible urge to kick the dog, but kicked the ball instead, just as he looked up to see Tracey enter the kitchen.

"Get that creature out of here," she screamed. "Look at all the mud. Rosa has just cleaned the kitchen floor."

They were both startled by a sharp whistle. Joe stood at the door. "I've a good mind to take that animal to the pound if there's any more trouble," Howard shouted at him.

"No, no. Don't do that. I'm sorry," he said, "I'm just tryin' to get Bob back. Sorry to disturb you. Sorry. It won't happen again." He whistled again and turned away, shuffling down the hill in the rain to his cottage, with Bob following him. Tracey turned on her heel and left.

Howard stared out the window at the damaged flower bed. It would be dark soon, so Tracey wouldn't notice, but he decided to get rid of the evidence in the meantime while there was still enough light to see. In the morning he could get the gardener to replant the bed. Grabbing a rain jacket, he rushed out with a garbage bag to gather the broken plants and felt he'd done a fairly good clean-up job in the garden before tackling the kitchen floor. It was annoying that he hadn't had time to change, but he needed to keep the peace and get it done before Tracey realized what had happened. As he emerged from the flowerbed however, while turning around to check for more evidence, he felt something squishy underfoot. He knew by the smell what it was and cursed out loud. These were his favorite Italian loafers; he would never feel the same about them again and might as well toss them in the garbage along with the broken plants. What a disastrous evening; what a setback. He was still angry as he tossed the bag into the garbage, but he also felt slightly ashamed that his anger had got the better of him.

He wondered whether he was being unreasonable about the smoking on wet days, and decided to discuss it with Tracey. "No Howard, you are quite right. It's bad for everybody else's health, and I don't want that cottage stinking of smoke. Besides, if you give an inch, it'll soon be a yard. If he insists on pursuing that filthy habit, then he has to suffer for it. That's all there is to it," was her reply.

He felt justified once more.

When Maria arrived the following morning with her sister, there was a note from Howard. It read: 'There will be no smoking in the cottage. Please empty and remove all ashtrays and garbage, and get rid of the smell of cigarettes.'

Tracey was in the adjoining room and listened as Rosa read it out loud. The two of them discussed it in Spanish, with some universal interjections of disapproval, before Maria made her way down to the cottage. Joe was seated in front of the TV and greeted her warmly when she arrived; he already had the coffee brewing. "*Buenos dias*," she said in reply. "You make trouble with *Senor* Parker and the cigarettes?"

Joe rolled his eyes in response.

She laughed loudly as she poured coffee for them both. "What you can do? He no like smoke."

"I guess I got to do it outside. That's what he says."

"When is raining?" she asked.

He nodded his head.

She shrugged. "When is raining *amigo*, you come see me and my famly. We no care at our house."

***

Howard drove home from work the following evening in blinding rain, admonishing himself for losing his temper and determined to be more in control. He was also fighting hard at work as he objected to Lauren's appeal for money in South Africa, but the rest of the committee was in favor and ready to vote on it. His windscreen wipers were working at top speed, yet it was still difficult to see the road in front of him. When Mother Nature unleashed a wild Pacific storm, she left no doubt about her power. He crept along the freeway with everyone else, concentrating on the tail lights ahead of him. It took him an hour to get home, twice the normal time, and it was with relief that he finally turned into his drive. As he reached the top of the long drive and visibility cleared, he cursed. The green truck was parked right outside his garage, blocking his way. He immediately put his hand on the horn and blasted continuously, while letting down the window and shouting at the same time, "Joe, move this contraption of yours." The rain flew in his face.

His cell phone rang and it was Tracey. "Is that you outside Howard?" she asked.

He felt unsure how to answer. "I'll be with you in a moment, don't worry," he said, hoping she wouldn't question him further. The best thing to do, he decided, was to leave his car where it was and make a dash for the garage. There was no point in trying to attract Joe's attention, as he couldn't or wouldn't listen—and there was no way that Howard was running down there in the rain.

He fumed all through dinner, not paying much attention to Tracey's chatter. When he saw the rain slackening, he excused himself and dashed down to the cottage. Without knocking, he barged in and shouted, "What the hell is your damn truck doing outside my garage? Are you purposely trying to make me mad? I assure you, you're doing a very good job of it if you are."

The dog was lying asleep sprawled across the bed, and Joe was lying stark naked in the bath with one leg dangling over the side. He had a beer bottle in his hand and was just switching the hot tap off with his big toe. The bathroom door was open so that he could watch the TV from where he lay. "Oh shit," he said under his breath, quickly putting the bottle down and pulling himself out the bath. He reached for a towel, which he threw over his shoulders, and hurried over to Howard, who was still standing in the doorway. The younger man tried to avert his eyes, but he couldn't help noticing how large the older man's genitals were and he was aghast that his father-in-law was not the least bit embarrassed. He was speechless as Joe apologized to him and strode out the door with only a towel, now over his head. The old man bent down to retrieve the key which he had hidden underneath the chassis, and then the green truck sputtered and lurched forward as its owner steered it down the drive to the workman's parking lot. With horror, Howard looked up and saw Tracey watching from an upstairs window.

A few minutes later Joe reappeared with the towel thankfully around his waist. "I'm sorry," he said immediately. "You see what happened was I took Maria and Rosa home cause it was raining too hard for them to catch the bus. An' then I gits back an I thinks I'll jus leave m' truck close until the rain stops so's I don' get too wet m'self. And then I forgot. That's the honest truth. I'm sorry."

Howard took a deep breath. He still felt angry, but he couldn't attack the man when he'd been doing a good deed. "I see," he said. "Well if it happens again, please don't block my garage—or Tracey's either for that matter. And Joe, Adam and Eve started wearing clothes when they left the Garden of Eden. It's more becoming. Please don't walk around naked."

"Oh, I...I'm sorry. I didn't think about it. I's in such a hurry to move m'truck. Sorry, sorry."

"All right, never mind. Get dressed and let's say prayers. We missed them last night."

Joe was shivering. "Sure," he replied, looking wistfully at his bath.

***

Later, when Howard made his way upstairs, Tracey was pacing up and down in their bedroom. She looked up as he entered and eyed him coldly. "This is outrageous. I've reached my limit with him."

Howard tried to put his arms around his wife to calm her, but she pushed him away. "You don't begin to see how hard this is for me, do you? This first trimester of pregnancy is a difficult time, Howard. Just because you want to try and reform that old swine, I have to endure breathing the same air as him, and now he's walking around the garden naked! What if somebody saw him? Thank heavens it's dark and raining and there's nobody about, but you just don't know what he'll do next. And that dog of his has been running around the garden barking again today. It's too much, Howard. The dog needs to go, and he should go too. I can't stand it anymore. Trust me, the man is bad. Anybody who can run out on their family like that is bad. There's no hope for him, he's a sinner."

Howard was tired himself, and anxious about his wife's well-being. He looked at her face and noticed the strain around her eyes; she had been doing a lot of crying. "OK Tracey, I'll get rid of the dog, but let's just give your father time to repent before we send him on his way. I'll get him set up in an apartment somewhere and get him out of your hair, but just give me a chance to make sure that he has come to accept Jesus into his life first."

"You promise you'll get rid of the dog?" she asked, looking at him searchingly.

"I promise."

The next morning dawned bright with not a cloud in the sky. The storm was over and Howard felt his spirits lift as he surveyed the vista from the patio. The spring flowers were looking bedraggled from the battering wind and rain, but they were trying their best to recover with the sun's warmth. The golf course looked soggy, but it would be a perfect morning to hit some balls on the driving range before he left for work. It would help take his mind off his problems, he told himself as he made his way down to his golf cart.

As he opened the door to the shed, he thought he heard a strange noise. He stopped and listened, but there was nothing. He was just about to load his golf clubs, when he heard it again. It was a scratching sound. He put the clubs down and went around to the back of the shed; Bob had his nose down and was digging frantically to get under the fence. He looked up at Howard and barked anxiously, causing the Egyptian geese at the water hazard to take flight. The dog sat down and whined as he watched them soar into the sky. Howard paled. Without hesitation, he removed the strap from his golf bag and attached it to Bob's collar. He yanked it, dragging the animal to his car. Gone were thoughts of golf for the day; he had more important things to take care of. Snatching his keys and wallet he headed off to the pound.

24

Lauren awoke early. Already the day was hot like the end of summer often is, as if an accumulation of heat from the previous months was ready to explode. The night had been warm and she'd slept fitfully, watching the clock at every turn, anticipating the alarm. She had a 7 a.m. appointment with Dr. Naidoo to have a blood test; her mind could think of nothing else, yet she wanted to forget all that hung in the balance. No event in her life before had ever filled her with such anxiety. She turned and watched Mike as he slept next to her, drinking in the image of his face. She loved him dearly, but she was single-minded in her resolve to leave him immediately if her test came back positive. She wasn't sure what she would do with her life instead, but she knew that she wouldn't allow this man to be shackled to her problem, no matter how much he protested. In fact the only plan she had been able to put into action was being ready to return to the United States at the weekend, without telling him, if she proved to be HIV+. She had taken Bessie into her confidence and they had discussed plans for the orphanage and halfway houses. Lauren was thankful that Phillip had helped her set up this group that would administer to the needs of both places when she was no longer around

Silently she made her way to the bathroom and got herself ready to leave. She kissed Mike lightly on the forehead as she grabbed her keys next to the bed, and he opened his eyes half way. She kissed him again and he smiled, closed his eyes and went back to sleep. She marveled at how well-adjusted he was. He had been so good to her — and for her. He would always be the greatest love of her life.

She was trembling as she climbed the stairs to the laboratory. Dr. Naidoo was already there, looking equally tense. Normally she would not still have been involved with a case at this point, but her personal interest in Lauren and all she was working for, kept her on the case. She, too, knew what lay at stake. She had tried to dissuade Lauren from any drastic action like leaving Mike, assuring her that advances in medicine were such that she could live many, many years with the virus without it developing into Aids. Children were also possible, she added, using artificial insemination. Lauren was adamant, however, that it would be like giving Mike only half a wife. Her obstinacy left Dr. Naidoo frustrated.

Normally Lauren turned her head away when blood was being drawn. Today she stared in fascination as the small syringe filled with red liquid that held her future within. She watched as they capped it and released the tourniquet from her arm. It was done.

She arrived back at Mike's flat as he climbed out the shower. She made some coffee and watched him calmly putting a towel around himself as he walked into the kitchen. "You're back quickly," he said, putting his arms around her. It was 8 a.m. "What a lovely surprise," he whispered in her ear as he undid the buttons of her shirt and slipped his hands around her back to undo her bra. She didn't resist as he slipped her clothes off while dropping his towel, and soon they were back in the unmade bed. As she felt his body on hers, she wondered how she would ever find the resolve to leave him. They kissed passionately and their love-making had an urgency which left her sobbing uncontrollably afterwards.

At length he said to her, "Can I ask you something?"

She pushed him aside. "No, not now. We've both got things to do. I'll see you back here later, but I'm going to be late for a meeting if I don't run."

He watched as she pulled her clothes back on and charged for the door. She was in her efficiency mode now. "Call me as soon as you hear anything," he called after her.

Mike got up at a more leisurely rate and perused *The Argus* while eating his breakfast. There were four more rapes in Cape Town yesterday he read, and then he scanned the statistics that were quoted. There were forty times more rapes in Cape Town than in the average European city, and one and a half times more in Cape Town than the national average. He glanced at the top of the article and saw that it was written by Bessie. Rape had become her pet cause, ever since she'd found Janet and Lauren. She continued to say that the Rape Crisis Trust reported rapes were becoming more violent as well as more frequent, and an additional nugget of information was that there were more people killed each year from violent crime in South Africa than were killed in 9/11 in the U.S.A. It would be good to get Lauren away from here he thought to himself, but he just hoped that she would allow him to remain in her future.

The day dragged. He called Lauren at lunchtime to suggest they meet at the cafeteria on campus for lunch. "I can't Mike," she replied. "I'm up to my ears with paperwork here. We're finalizing the list of orphans and teens going into the homes."

Mike frowned. "You have to eat Lauren. I'll come there if it's easier."

"No honestly, I'm busy with the committee and we're just having sandwiches while we work. I'll see you later," she said with finality. He ended the call, frowning as he replaced the phone in his pocket.

Arriving back first at his flat, he found himself checking the time at regular intervals. He was anxious to call her, but she'd shown such irritability that he was loathe to do so. When she finally walked in the door, he spun around to try and read her expression. "I've heard nothing," she said, anticipating his question.

"Have you called to ask?"

She shook her head.

"Well let's do so." She opened her mouth to argue, but he walked away and used his own phone to reach Dr. Naidoo, who exclaimed with relief, "Mike, thank goodness you called. I've been trying to reach Lauren for the past hour and her phone has gone dead. Are you with her?"

"Yup, she's right here."

"Can I speak to her Mike? I know it affects you both, but legally I must give her the results."

"OK, I'll hand you right over." He passed the phone to Lauren who was ashen. Her hand trembled as she reached out, and their eyes met as their hands touched. He swallowed hard and said, "Your phone isn't working."

He turned away and shut his eyes, concentrating on her voice. He heard her gasp and quickly spun around. She began shaking, crying and laughing hysterically all at the same time. No words would come out of her mouth as she dropped the phone and covered her face. He felt at a loss.

"Lauren," he said softly, but she couldn't hear him through her sobs. "Lauren," he repeated loudly, "please tell me what she said."

She threw her head back and ran her hands through her hair, before stretching her arms out to him. Tears streamed down her face as she looked up and whispered, "It was negative."

25

Joe was delighted to wake and find that the rain had stopped. He was very pleased to have had a proper roof over his head in a storm, but he still had to brave the elements to enjoy a cigarette. He didn't dare break the rules and incur Howard's wrath again. He'd taken Maria and Rosa back to the house that they shared with their mother, *Senora* Nunez, and five other brothers and sisters as well as their children. *Senora* Nunez was a happy woman who loved having her family near, and an extra person was always welcome. She'd smiled broadly at Joe and said, "I hear my daughters talk about you. I happy I meet you—thank you. You drive my daughters." He liked her immediately and smiled with pleasure at such a warm reception. They lived in an old Victorian house painted bright yellow and situated near the freeway in San Jose. He'd been welcomed into the home, despite difficult communication. He spoke no Spanish and their English was very broken, but they'd invited him to eat tamales with them and nobody had minded that he smoked. In fact two of the brothers smoked with him and he was happy to share his cigarettes. There was a small store across the road that sold '*Cerveza*' and he had bought beers for them as his contribution. It had been a happy evening and Bob lay quietly at his feet, wagging his tail when anybody threw him a nacho. He promised to visit again as he left to a rowdy chorus of *"Adios."*

He scratched his head as he looked around him now. Bob was usually here badgering him for breakfast. He put his head out the door and whistled, waiting for the dog to come bounding. Nothing happened, despite more whistles. Nervously he stepped out of the cottage. He dared not go to the big house and ask if Bob was there, but that seemed to be the only explanation. There was no sign of him outside and the gates were closed, so he wouldn't have run off. Besides, he would come back when he heard the whistle. Hesitantly he made his way to the big front door and pressed the bell. His heart was pounding, both with anxiety about seeing Tracey, and concern for Bob. He heard footsteps and then the door opened. His daughter stood looking at him and she was more beautiful than he had ever remembered. She stared at him unblinkingly before saying, "What do you want?"

"Trace, I know you don' wanna see me, but I...I," he swallowed hard. "Well two things; I jus' wanna tell you how sorry I am for all the hurt when you were young. I love you Trace an' I wish you'd let me explain."

"My husband told me what you said. I don't believe you."

His face scrunched and he shook his head. "All I can say is I'm sorry. Your mother lied to us both, Trace. It's not me that's a liar. Your mother told you that your daddy was dead, but she knew I weren't. She said I was bad. She didn't want me to see you no more. Your momma always thought she knew what God wanted, but I tell you, be careful of people who tell you what God wants, because they's really telling you what *they* wants. They just try's to make it like that's what God wants." She stared at him, but said nothing. Finally he said, "I was wondrin' if you've seen Bob."

"Who's Bob?" she asked.

"Bob's my dog. My buddy."

Tracey flushed. "Oh, that dog! No," she replied, shaking her head as she closed the door.

He stared at the door for a moment before wandering down the drive, whistling every now and again and looking for signs of Bob. As he reached the fence, a voice on the other side said, "You looking for the dog?" A maintenance crew member from the golf club was looking at him. "I saw it about twenty minutes ago. It was there digging at the fence," he said, pointing further along at the shed. "A man took it away in his car."

Joe's heart was pounding as he rushed to his truck and started the engine. He knew where the pound was and that was where he headed now. The dog was his best friend and companion in the world; Bob was his family. He had tears streaming down his face as he made his way to Santa Clara in heavy traffic, and there, just as he expected, was Howard's black Mercedes parked outside. He rushed inside the office and saw Howard writing a check and smiling. He heard him say, "Thank you for taking care of that for me." Joe shouted at the top of his voice, "No, you can't do that!"

Howard and the clerk both turned to face him. Joe shouted again, "Don't you put my dog down, you murderer."

Howard went red in the face. "The dog was a menace and I warned you Joe. You can't say we didn't warn you."

The clerk intervened. "Excuse me sir, are you claiming the dog?"

"You haven't…you haven't…you know…put him down?"

"No. We keep the dog for at least a week or so if there's nothing wrong with it. You can claim it if you fill in the paperwork that says you won't disturb this gentleman again. You must take responsibility for the dog. You'd better have a look at the adoption papers."

"But he's my dog. I'm not adopting him."

"Joe," Howard said sternly, "I'm sorry, but if you take the dog back, you'll have to leave. It's the dog or us."

Joe stared at his son-in-law and finally said, "You're an ass-hole." Then he turned his back on him and said to the clerk, "Can you get my dog now?"

As the clerk left the small office to fetch Bob, Howard said coldly, "I mean it Joe. You can't bring that dog back."

Joe turned and looked Howard in the eye. "I mean it too. You're an ass-hole an' I won't be comin' back." The only sounds were the dogs barking outside in the pound as the two men glared at each other. "You hear them dogs?" Joe said at length. "They're God's creatures too, jus' like you an' me."

***

When the Nunez sisters arrived for work the next day, Tracey informed Maria that she would no longer be required after that day, as the cottage would be empty. She would be paid a month's wages in *lieu* of notice, and she should clean the cottage thoroughly today. As an afterthought Tracey added, "You'll find a lot of clothing there still. If you want any of it please take it, otherwise it's going to Goodwill."

"*Gracias*," she replied and smiled at Rosa, who said, "thank you." They spoke in Spanish to one another and laughed happily. Joe would be pleased to have his new clothes back; he'd moved in with the Nunez family last night and was hoping to start work on a construction site with Ernesto Nunez. There was no need for Mrs. Parker to know that.

***

It irked Howard that Lauren wanted more money for her pet project in South Africa. It was annoying that she had inveigled money out of his parents while they were alive, but there was nothing he could do about that. However, that was enough to his mind. There were so many other worthy causes closer to home, where money could be dispersed from the Foundation without going out of the country. His argument was that it was chasing good money after bad. His siblings did not agree with him, needless to say, and as the remainder of the Board was siding with them, he had been over-ruled. Wendy and Isabella had made the argument that this was in keeping with their parents' wishes, as they had clearly indicated an interest in children's causes at home and in South Africa. Phillip had made the suggestion that they needed to define their mission so that there would be more unanimity in future, but meanwhile one million dollars had been designated to the 'Lauren Project' in South Africa.

As Howard sat in his office with a view out onto the rolling green hills of Woodside, he saw nothing but oppressive rain and cloud. Yesterday's sunshine had gone, and he felt a weight of annoyance burdening him; it was not only the Board's decision, but also the memory of Joe. He was appalled at the man's ingratitude and rudeness. Nobody had ever used such language to him before and he felt it was totally out of line. While it was a relief that the old man had left, Howard couldn't help feeling that he had failed in bringing this man to God. That was a disappointment that wounded him. "He was just taking advantage of us," was what Tracey had said in response. "We were quite within our rights to get rid of the dog."

For once he wasn't comforted by her reassurance.

26

Neither Mike nor Lauren wanted a long engagement, and when Mike announced that he had accepted a Fulbright Scholarship to attend Stanford University in September, the decision was made to marry in June before he left. This gave them three months to plan. It was difficult to decide whether they should have the ceremony at Belle Terre, or in the Georgetown Chapel, Washington D.C., as both places had strong associations for each family. Lauren knew that Mike would dearly love to be married on the farm, but he was generous enough to say that it was the bride's prerogative to decide. She felt that while it was a link with her father if she married in the chapel where her parents had married, Belle Terre had nothing but happy associations for her, whereas her father's memorial service had been in the Georgetown Chapel and that was a dark day in her life. In the end, the farm was chosen as the venue and Isabella planned on flying to South Africa for the opening of the orphanage in May, remaining for the wedding in early June. The rest of the family planned on doing the same, except for Tracey, who would not be able to travel at that point.

Martie Rousseau and Chooks were delighted at the opportunity to practise their wedding planning skills again, and there were countless emails and calls flying between Franschoek, Cape Town and Washington D.C. There were many practical decisions to be made, beginning with whether they should they marry in church or not. Lauren preferred a civil wedding, although she wasn't averse to a church wedding if that was important to Mike. Mike had been brought up in the Dutch Reformed Church, and definitely wanted a church wedding. Lauren, however, spoke no Afrikaans, which was the language spoken in the DRC, so that became an issue. Lauren also fretted about who should walk her up the aisle. If she were to be traditional and have a man do this, the logical answer would be one of her uncles, but this was problematical. She felt closer to Phillip, but she'd only known him for three months and it would be an affront to Howard. She wanted her mother to do it, but Bella wasn't sure she wanted to do so.

Even the weather became an issue. June, being the middle of winter, was not the best time for a farm wedding as Cape winters can be cold, wet and windy. Ideally they would have wished for an outdoor affair, but this would not be possible unless they waited for summer. Martie tried to persuade them to wait, but neither Lauren nor Mike would hear of it. They began to taste the difficult dynamics of wedding planning, but endeavored not to become overburdened with the issues. When Lauren became agitated, Mike—always one to cut to the core—said, "Whatever we decide, some will be pleased, and others won't. Hopefully everyone will be gracious enough to simply enjoy the day and celebrate the happy occasion with us."

In the end, they agreed to compromise. They would be married in the local Anglican Church, the religion of Lauren's grandparents. If her mother wouldn't do the honors, she would ask both Phillip and Howard to walk her up the aisle, and the wedding party would be held indoors in the tasting room of the winery, which could accommodate 120 people. It would make a very warm, festive setting although the numbers would be limited. They anticipated that many overseas guests would not attend—but if they did, it was possible to erect a marquis tent and have multiple heaters outside.

Once the guest list was settled and invitations were sent out, Lauren could concentrate on getting a wedding dress and seeing to the final arrangements for the orphanage and halfway-house. Bessie took her to a seamstress who was a family friend, and there Lauren was able to look at pictures, choose her fabric and style, and leave everything in the capable hands of Fatima Suleman. All she had to do was show up for fittings. The result was everything she could have hoped for.

March also saw Mike receive his doctorate in a special ceremony for graduate students at UCT. Lauren sat with his family and felt great pride as she watched him capped; years of hard work were being recognized. It made her realize how modest this man was. He had a brilliant mind and had achieved so much while still so young, but he never spoke about himself or his work. He always seemed more interested in what other people were doing. She held back as his parents rushed forward at the conclusion of ceremonies. This was their moment as much as his in a way; they had reared him to be the person that he was, and they'd supported him throughout his life. She was new to the line-up. When he finally made his way to her, she held out her arms and hugged him, whispering in his ear, "Dr. Rousseau, I feel like a very lucky woman."

"I feel lucky too!" he replied. "How about after dinner at my place?"

"Are those Doctor's orders?" she asked and smiled.

"Definitely."

***

In April the orphanage was finally complete, ahead of schedule. Everything worked like clockwork and the furnishings arrived that Lauren had previously chosen. It was an emotional day when the nursing staff took up residence and prepared themselves for the children's arrival in May. Although the official opening had not yet occurred, Lauren felt that she was handing over the reins to the resident team of four health care workers. It was with mixed emotion that she greeted and welcomed them to The Janet Dyani Home. Her friend should have been here for this moment, and all the moments that were to follow. If anybody believed in providing for children to improve the future, it was Janet. The women that she greeted had been selected for their dedication as well as their training, and their excitement was evident as they toured the building and examined all the facilities. The children would be in good hands. Janet would have approved.

Lauren also felt relief that the details of hiring cooks and janitors would no longer be her responsibility. She had enough on her plate with the wedding, and it was important that these women, Esther, Frieda, Promise and Sandile, employed the people with whom they would be working.

27

Howard was in the middle of a conference call with the Board when an administrative assistant rushed into his office, looking very anxious and waving a piece of paper at him. He frowned at her and mouthed, "Not now," but she shook her head and pointed to the paper. He put his phone on mute to read what she had placed in front of him, and he was stunned. Tracey had started contractions and had been rushed to hospital. She was not quite four months pregnant.

He left his assistant to explain the situation to the members of the conference call, and drove as fast as he could to Good Samaritan Hospital in Los Gatos. Within half an hour he was standing at his wife's bedside, where Dr. Wilcox was in attendance with Tracey's regular obstetrician, Dr. Lu. Dr. Wilcox introduced Mike to Dr. Sandra Lu; he had taken care of the infertility treatment, but she was looking after the pregnancy. They had already monitored the contractions and the babies' heart beats. The babies sounded strong, and so they had gone ahead and given Tracey medication to stop the contractions. "She is going to require almost total bed rest for the rest of the pregnancy," Dr. Lu told them. "I understand that this creates difficulties, but it is imperative that we put as little stress on the uterus and cervix as possible. Tracey, you will be able to get up for bathroom purposes, and to make your regular visits to my office for check-ups.

Other than that, you need to remain lying in bed. And I'm afraid there must be no sexual intercourse for the rest of the pregnancy."

"What are the chances of saving the pregnancy?" asked Howard.

"It's difficult to say. It's at an early stage; in another two month's time the babies will just be viable, although we would want them to develop longer than that if possible, to give them a better chance of survival. We'll do our best, Mr. Parker. If there is some abnormality with the fetuses, then there is not much we can do and nature will take its course. But we've checked the heartbeats and they're strong, so that is a very good sign. I would like you to remain in hospital for a few days Tracey, so that we can monitor you, but I would also like to run some scans and tests on the babies. I'll schedule you for an ultrasound tomorrow. "

Tracey was pale with shock. "This can't be happening," she whispered. "It's so unfair."

Dr. Lu looked at her for a moment and said, "You need to relax as best you can Tracey. We're going to do everything we can to help you hold onto this pregnancy, but you have to do your part too. You need to obey my instructions about total bed rest and no intercourse, but there's something else. You need to have a positive attitude. It will help us all, especially you and the babies. And you, Mr. Parker, your job is to help your wife be positive."

Howard nodded. "God is in charge," he said to Tracey. "Have faith."

The scans and tests showed healthy, normal babies at the right stage of development. However when Dr. Lu examined Tracey, she suspected cervical weakness and scheduled a cervical length scan for the following day. This confirmed her diagnosis that the contractions had been caused by an incompetent cervix.

"What does that mean? Am I going to lose my babies?" asked Tracey.

"Hopefully not. There is a well-used remedy to help you. It requires a general anesthetic, but it's a quick procedure where we place a stitch in the cervix to help it do its job. We call it a cerclage. I've scheduled surgery for tomorrow morning early, and I feel confident that we'll then have control of the situation. You'll be home in a few more days—I hope your husband is useful around the house," Dr. Lu laughed. "If he isn't, he'd better learn fast."

Howard had been busy getting the household organized while his wife was in hospital. She arrived home to find their bedroom changed around so that their bed was closer to the bathroom, and he had ordered a new mattress for her that could be raised to different heights. Flowers and baskets of fruit adorned the room to welcome her home, but most important of all, he had re-employed Maria Nunez to attend to her five days a week. Maria would cook all meals and help Tracey with whatever she needed. At Dr. Lu's recommendation, a physical therapist would visit three times a week to try and help Tracey maintain some muscle tone with exercises that wouldn't strain the abdomen. Her hairdresser agreed to pay a home visit once a month, and Maria would be on hand to help with everything else.

Howard had thought of everything and he was much relieved to see Tracey settle down comfortably when she got home. It was evident that she felt more confident having the cerclage in place, and they were both delighted when Dr. Lu suggested that it would be easy for her to pay a house call on Tracey once a week on her way home, as she lived just a block away. There would be no need to leave the house; they simply had to hunker down and wait. Everything was in good hands.

Rosa and Maria's English had improved greatly. When asked, they admitted to taking lessons. Maria explained that their family had taken another lodger who was English-speaking, and part of his rent was to teach the whole family English. Tracey found herself looking at Maria with new eyes. She was the younger of the sisters and very striking in her appearance. She seemed to have taken a new interest in her looks and instead of tying her dark hair in a bun, she had cut it to shoulder length. Her dark brown eyes were expressive and animated, showing to advantage with the new hairstyle. Her features were fine and delicate. When she smiled, her face lit up and her perfect teeth would have been a good advertisement for any orthodontist, but they had lined themselves into position without any help. Slender and tall, she was very strong; a perfect companion for Tracey under the circumstances, especially as the young woman had a very pleasant disposition.

It was an unwritten rule that they never discussed Joe. Often Tracey would read or watch TV, but sometimes she enjoyed Maria's cheerful chatter. The Mexican woman told about her childhood in Guadalajara, and how she had moved to San Jose when she was ten, after her father sent enough money for her mother and sister to join him. Her brothers and father had come to California ahead of them, working at first in the Central Valley as farm workers, but eventually making enough money to move to San Jose and get work in construction. She had spoken no English at all when they first arrived, and school was terrifying. But it soon became easy because there were so many other Spanish speakers that their life settled into a very pleasant existence in the Hispanic community. It was like being in Guadalajara, except they had a nicer house, more money and food.

When some of Tracey's church or golf friends came to visit, Maria would bring them up to the room and soon became quite comfortable serving refreshments very elegantly laid out on trays. She watched and listened and absorbed. One day, as a distraction, Tracey decided that she would get Maria to help her clear some space in her wardrobe so that she would have place for maternity clothes which she had ordered from a catalog. Maria was holding up two outfits awaiting instructions, when on a whim Tracey said, "What size are you Maria?"

"I don't know Mrs. Parker. My mother, Rosa and me, we sew our clothes." She shrugged her shoulders. "We just make them fit," she laughed.

"Try on that yellow skirt and blouse, Maria," she said. "Go on, please," she added when she saw Maria hesitate. "I would like you to try them on. Go into my bathroom and see if they fit. Then come and show me."

Maria giggled like a young girl and disappeared behind the door. Tracey waited and heard more giggles. Finally the door opened, and out stepped a transformation. Gone was the worker in utilitarian black jeans and white T-shirt; in her place stood an elegant beauty. It was as if the linen skirt and blouse had been made especially for her; the fit was perfect and the young woman blushed as she stood self-consciously before her employer. Tracey was stunned. She indicated that Maria should turn around and show off the back of the outfit.

"Maria, do you have a boyfriend?" she asked, as the young woman turned to face her again. Maria nodded and laughed.

"What's his name?"

Maria looked down at her hands and smiled. "Jose," she replied.

"If you would like that outfit, please take it. I would love to see Jose's face when he sees you wearing it," she added. "You'll have to tell me what he says."

The two women were laughing when the door opened and Howard walked in. His eyes went from one to the other and then back to Maria. She felt herself blush again, as he too looked admiringly at her. "What's going on?" he asked, bemused.

"We're just talking about clothes," Tracey replied.

He faced Tracey again as he said, "I'll be back in ten minutes—just going over to the golf club quickly. Can you stay that long Maria?" he asked, looking once more at the young woman. She smiled and nodded, and Howard closed the door in confusion.

When he returned, Maria was back into her own clothes and had dinner ready for them as usual. It only needed to be popped into the microwave when they wanted to eat, and then the plates could be left for the morning when she was back at work. Howard thanked her courteously and watched in amazement how shapely she was in her black jeans as she walked down the drive to catch a bus. When he went to bed that night, he lay for a long time without sleeping. He put his hand out towards Tracey and touched her breasts; they had grown full with pregnancy and he experienced a rush of desire as he felt her nipples harden to his touch. But she pushed his hand away, saying, "No Howard. We can't."

He sighed and turned away.

The following day was his usual Wednesday morning golf game. He played terribly; his drives felt unco-ordinated and his putting was even worse. For this he blamed the sleepless night he'd had the night before and hoped the rest of the day would improve. There was another teleconference meeting with the board, which he could take at home, before he made his way to Parker Keating for the remainder of the afternoon.

He parked his golf cart and was strolling up the drive when he caught sight of Maria in the garage. He watched as she bent to pick up parcels from the trunk of the car; she was wearing a short denim skirt which revealed skimpy underwear when she leaned over. Her legs were long like Tracey's, lean and tan; her buttocks were firm and small; she moved with ease, quite unaware of being watched. He stood absolutely still, watching but hardly breathing. When she reached up to close the trunk, her shirt lifted with her arm and he willed it to go all the way up so that he could feast his eyes on her torso. All too soon she dropped her arm and he felt frustration that all he saw was three inches above her waist. When she turned around to retrieve the parcels on the ground, she saw him standing watching her and smiled shyly, remembering the flush of excitement she'd felt wearing the yellow outfit the previous day and seeing his appreciation.

He frowned and asked why she wasn't with Tracey.

"The physical therapist is here," Maria replied. "When she comes, I go to the store to buy groceries."

Howard raised his eyebrows and said, "You drive my wife's car?"

"*Si*, yes Mr. Parker. She tells me I must do it. You don't like me to do that?" she asked.

Howard looked at her and shrugged. She was nervous in his presence and took some deep breaths to calm herself. Watching her breasts rise and fall made him want to scream with frustration, but he steeled himself. "If it's OK with her, it's fine with me," he said as he helped her carry the bags inside. He hurried off immediately to shower and change before his call; Tracey was busy with the physical therapist doing her exercises, and nodded at him as he rushed into the shower. He kept the water cool, gradually reducing it to cold and praying for guidance. He stayed in the shower until he was shivering and made an important decision; he would try to avoid Maria.

Refusing lunch, he made his way to his study and connected to the teleconference call. Isabella was already on the line when he joined in, but as yet they were the only two. The others would be there momentarily.

"Hi Howard," she said, when he announced his presence. "How's Tracey doing?"

"OK," he replied. "I think everything will be fine. She's stopped having contractions, and we have somebody looking after her fulltime when I'm not here. How's Lauren?" he added.

"Everything is ready for the opening next week—I'm leaving tomorrow to be with her—and then it's full steam ahead for the wedding. Has she spoken to you about that yet?"

"About what?" he asked.

"About walking her up the aisle? She said she was going to ask you to do that."

"Oh," he replied. "No, I haven't heard from her yet." He was about to add that it would be difficult with Tracey confined to bed, but just then he heard Phillip and Ned come onto the line, followed almost immediately by Wendy. It wasn't the time to discuss it.

When the call was over, he bade goodbye to Tracey who smiled happily and announced that she was going to be swimming in future, as recommended by the therapist.

"But how will you manage getting up and down the stairs?" Howard asked.

"I hope that either you or Maria will carry me down, and then I can use a wheel chair to get to the pool. Apparently the water will offer wonderful support and I'll get much better all-over exercise without any strain on the uterus."

Howard frowned. "I think it would be better if we move you downstairs into the fifth bedroom, Tracey. Then we can get you downstairs once, and set you up comfortably without continual danger of negotiating the stairs."

She thought about it for a while and nodded her head. "I'll ask Maria and Rosa to organize it for me."

He kissed her on the cheek and tried to slip quietly out to the garage without seeing Maria. She was in the kitchen with Rosa however, so he kept his head averted as he made his way past them in silence. As he was about to walk out the door, she stopped him with a question. "You want me to cook dinner for you tonight, Mr. Parker?"

He turned to face her hesitantly, and found himself staring at her breasts again. Her nipples were showing their presence through the T-shirt. He blinked and turned away saying, "No. I'll be out for dinner."

Howard climbed into his car and headed north to his office. He would have to speak to Tracey about getting Maria to wear a uniform of sorts, something unrevealing. Satan was lying in wait for him and he had to be strong. Meanwhile he began to think of the news that Lauren wanted him to walk her up the aisle. This changed things and he was glad that he'd been prevented from saying he wasn't planning to attend the wedding. His prayers had been answered; Tracey was in good hands, so he could leave her for a week, and then he would be able to get away from Maria and get a grip on himself. It was diabolical that he kept thinking of the woman and imagining her naked body; his own body was reacting in strange ways when he saw her and he felt ashamed of his unclean thoughts. Getting away was going to be a God-given gift. He wouldn't go to South Africa for the opening as it would make his trip too long, but he could surely be away for a week. If needs be, he would hire a nurse to be here around the clock for the duration of time that he would be away. He smiled when he thought that Lauren had chosen him to give her away and vowed to be a better uncle to her from now on; he'd been given another chance to do this.

Tracey felt much better at the prospect of swimming. It was boring being confined to bed, and she made plans eagerly to move downstairs so that she would have easy access to the pool and the garden. Now that the weather was getting warmer, she would be able to lie outside on a *chaise lounge* and get some fresh air as well. Maria was instructed to find her bikinis, and the following afternoon when the sun was on the pool, she decided that it was time to make her move. Howard had already left for Woodside, so she told Maria that she needed to be carried downstairs. The woman looked aghast.

"No, Mrs. Parker. It is not possible. I not so strong to carry you." She stood with her mouth agape and shook her head. "If I drop you…" She threw up her hands in horror.

"I want to go downstairs and swim, Maria, and I want to do it now. I've been dreaming about it. You don't know what its like to be shut up in a bedroom all the time," she said.

Maria continued to shake her head. "No," she said again.

Tracey flushed. "Then I'll walk down myself," she replied. "I'm going to wear this bikini, and you can wear the other one. You must be ready to get in the water if I need you. And when I get out the pool, I'll go straight to the other room. Please ask Rosa to make sure its ready."

Maria watched as Tracey took off her pajamas, pulled on the bikini, and marched downstairs to the pool, shouting, "Hurry up, I need you there."

As soon as she had settled the pregnant woman in a chair, she rushed to inform Rosa of the plans, and then to change into the bikini so that she could help Tracey in the water. Fortunately she wore the same size as her employer, except for the bikini top which was too small—but nobody would see her other than Mrs. Parker. She'd never worn a bikini before and felt herself blushing as she pirouetted in front of the mirror, trying to see her back view. Jose would laugh when she told him, she thought.

***

Lauren's email was waiting when he got to the office and he read it eagerly. She hadn't received an answer from him, but presumed he would be attending her wedding. He cleared his throat uncomfortably and read on. As Bella had indicated, she did indeed want him to give her away in the absence of her father and grandfather. He breathed in deeply and smiled before hitting the reply button with his sentiments about being honored to do so. He had a lot to get organized in the next three weeks; first he needed to break the news to Tracey and then find a nurse who would live in for a week. Perhaps Maria and Rosa could also be persuaded to stay over in Los Gatos while he was away. And then he needed to buy a ticket to South Africa.

Tracey objected strongly when he broke the news to her. "How can you leave me Howard?" she cried. He felt his resolve weaken with her tears, but suddenly she looked up at him and said, "How can I be so selfish? Of course you must go. It's your family. With a nurse, and Maria, and Rosa, I'll be fine. And Dr. Lu is just around the corner. You must go and do your duty. Don't worry at all about me and the babies."

He hesitated, but decided to take her words at face value. "Thank you for being so supportive," he replied. "You know I wouldn't have gone if you'd wanted me to stay."

28

It had rained all week, but on Opening Day the sun came out and shone on the gathering of people as they arrived at the new building. Everything inside was gleaming and the children in the orphanage were wide-eyed when they saw a stream of strangers inspecting their new home. Lauren was delighted to have her mother there, as well as Mike and the Rousseau family. The Minister of Health was present, as well as Janet's mother, and of course Phillip and Wendy. Wellington and Faith Radebe, Bessie Opperman and Dr. Naidoo, all felt equally as proud as Lauren did. They were all moved to tears when Mrs. Dyani spoke in Xhosa, praying for the soul of her daughter—now with her ancestors—as well as the wellbeing of these children, who would live in the home that was named after Janet.

Lauren spoke next and remembered her grandparents, Phillip and Edith Parker, who had made all this possible. She thanked them especially, but also all the members of the Board who had helped build this dream. Wendy fought back her tears as she reached over and squeezed Bella's hand. It was impossible to express in words the pride that they both felt for this young woman, understanding the journey she had made to get here. She looked so frail, but they knew the strength that lay hidden in her small frame.

Finally the Minister of Health stood up. She was a sturdy woman, clad in a long dress made from a bright African print with a matching bandana on her head. Around her neck were cascades of colorful beads that shone in the light as she moved theatrically to emphasize her speech. She spoke at length about the problems of Aids in South Africa, emphasizing that education was equally as important as looking after innocent victims. "If we could educate people successfully, we would begin to beat this disease, and then we wouldn't need the orphanages," she announced. "But we need to educate at the highest levels as well as at grass roots. We need to overcome ignorance, misinformation and superstition. Nobody must ever again believe that a shower will protect them from this virus! People must *know* how this disease is transmitted—and how it can be prevented. Men must know that having sex with a virgin will not cure Aids, and that if they rape someone, they will be hunted down by the police. Our women and children must be protected from ignorance and violence." She turned and smiled at Lauren. "Ms. Marlowe, the people of Cape Town—the people of South Africa—thank you for the inspiring role model you have been in the face of adversity. Your philanthropy and dignity have touched the lives of more people than you realize, and we thank you. I wish your friend Janet Dyani was also here today, but we honor her by naming this beautiful orphanage after her. She will live on in our memories as a brave and good woman, an innocent victim of senseless violence. And now, it is with great pleasure that I declare The Janet Dyani Home open."

29

As the plane left Dulles Airport, Howard put his seat back and savored the pleasure of peace at last. He looked out the window and marveled at the prospect of flying such a great distance across the Atlantic Ocean and finding himself in Africa. He had been to Europe many times, and to Asia and Australasia a few times on business, but he'd never set foot on this mysterious continent. Everyone who had ever been to South Africa spoke of its grandeur and delightful mix of first and third worlds, but he hardly knew what to expect. What a relief it was to be rid of his guilty thoughts for a while and he eagerly scanned the entertainment programs offered in first class, settling down for the long haul to the other side of the globe.

He spent a restful night in the comfortable flat bed, opening his eyes to see the sunrise peeping through the window shade. Eagerly he looked out and was overwhelmed by the red glow of the sun on dry earth below; this was Africa. He wished Tracey were here to share the moment with him. For hours he watched deserts, mountains, forests, rivers, and occasional signs of habitation pass beneath him, until finally the plane began its descent. Then he was entranced by the sudden appearance of fertile agricultural land, green as far as the eye could see. The pilot announced that they were flying over the wine lands of Western Cape Province, and they would be landing in ten minutes. He felt his heart beat faster as he tightened his seat belt and sat upright, still watching in awe. Soon the ocean appeared, and then he saw it—the flat-topped mountain that he'd seen many times in pictures rising up over Table Bay. He had arrived in Cape Town.

When he emerged from the customs hall, he looked around for a familiar face to meet him—but there was none. He scanned the boards being held up with names on them, and finally saw 'Mr. Howard Parker' being held aloft by a uniformed man with a name badge, 'Petrus'. When Howard acknowledged him, the man leapt forward eagerly, saying, "Welcome to Cape Town; I've come from The Cellars Hotel to fetch you. Here, sir, let me take your bags— please follow me." Howard followed and was led to the curb where a big white Mercedes soon pulled up. Petrus opened the back door for him and stood aside, waiting until Howard was safely inside before placing the bags in the boot, as he called it. When Petrus was seated in the front, the driver locked all the doors and closed all the windows automatically before they pulled away and departed for the hotel in Constantia. "You must make sure you always lock the doors," the driver said over his shoulder.

Howard stared around him in amazement. They had no sooner left the airport and driven onto the motorway, when suddenly there were corrugated iron shacks lined up next to one another, row after row of them, and each one smaller than his shed at home. Some were made with boxes and boards, but there was electricity running to most of these hovels, and many had cars parked outside. Washing was hanging on barbed wire fences and children were running alongside the busy motorway, waving at passing cars. Towering over it all was the side of Table Mountain, with mist twirling over the top of it. "You see the table cloth coming over the mountain," smiled Petrus. Howard noticed for the first time that the man had no upper front teeth, but this didn't prevent him smiling the biggest of smiles. "This part nearest us is Devil's Peak," he explained, "and the devil is smoking today. That's why we've got all that cloud coming up." He laughed happily and added, "Around the other side of the mountain is Lion's Head. We can't see it from here."

It wasn't long before they arrived at The Cellars, an elegant and comfortable hotel in the district of Constantia, Petrus informed him. When he checked in, the receptionist handed him two letters; one was in the familiar hand of his sister Wendy, but the other he didn't recognize. He was shown to his suite in the annex on the first floor, where a big basket of fruit awaited him with a small bottle of wine. Petrus offered to order a tray with tea or coffee. Howard had stayed in many gracious hotels around the world, but this was in a class of its own. It had old world charm with quiet, efficient service. The spacious room overlooked a vineyard and was decorated with numerous antiques and delicate watercolor paintings; a huge bowl of flowers adorned a period writing desk. On the far side of the room was a comfortable sofa and chairs, grouped around a TV set. He was standing at the window as Petrus placed his suitcases on a stand, when there was a knock at the door and another smiling face delivered his tea. With a quiet, "Morning sir," the tray was placed on a coffee table and the uniformed woman departed. The only sound came from large birds outside on the grass, strutting around digging for worms with their long beaks. They looked like ibises, but as they lifted off into the air, their sound was like a loud laugh as if they were all sharing a joke. Petrus looked up and said, "We call them ha-de-dahs, sir. I hope they don't wake you in the morning. Is there anything else I can get you?"

Howard shook his head. "No thanks," he replied.

"If you need anything, just dial 0 and ask."

As Petrus departed, closing the door quietly behind him, Howard kicked off his shoes and lay on the bed to read Wendy's note and enjoy the refreshments.

Dear Howard,

I'm sorry we couldn't all be here to welcome you in person, but we have to be in Franschoek for the wedding rehearsal. It's a shame that you had to miss it, but I'm sure Phillip will be able to fill you in on anything you need to know. I hope you find everything to your satisfaction at the hotel. Please rest after your long flight so that hopefully you'll feel refreshed and can enjoy the rehearsal dinner tonight at 7.30 p.m. It is being held in the Cape Malay restaurant at our hotel where we're all staying together. We're looking forward to seeing you and we're so pleased you were able to make the trip. I'm sorry Tracey can't be here with us too, to share the joy.

Love,
Wendy

Howard smiled as he folded the letter and put it next to his bed. If only Bella could be more like Wendy, he thought to himself, but he was resolved to remain on good terms with all the family, come what may. "I'm not going to fall into old patterns," he told himself. He opened the next one and quickly looked at the signature. It was from Lauren.

Dear Uncle Howard,

Thank you so much for flying all the way from California to South Africa to be at my wedding, and especially for agreeing to walk me up the aisle with Uncle Phillip. It means so much to Mom and me, and we both appreciate it greatly. I know that even though my father and grandfathers are no longer with us, I am very fortunate to have two uncles to represent the family on this happy day.

Thank you again. I look forward to seeing you after far too many years,

Lauren

Howard was stunned. He scrunched the note into a little ball and threw it into the trash. "I've been brought here under false pretences," he thought to himself. "It was just a ruse to get me here." He got up and paced the room, feeling his heart pounding. Suddenly his thoughts turned to Tracey. "I need to phone and tell her that I've arrived safely." It would be almost midnight in Los Gatos, but he needed to speak to her.

She answered almost immediately. "I can't believe how long it's taken you to call," she said.

"I've just got in, Tracey. It's one heck of a trip, but I'm here safely. How are you? Is everything all right?"

"Everything is fine. Rosa got her brother to help move my mattress downstairs and I'm very comfortable down there. I can feel the babies moving now, Howard. I thought I could before, but Maria laughed and said it was just gas!"

"That was very rude of her," he replied.

Tracey laughed. "Oh, not at all. We have fun together and she makes me laugh. Without her I would die of boredom."

"I see," he said. It was an uncomfortable thought and he didn't want to be reminded of Maria. He had other things to discuss. "Well, you'll never guess what I've discovered here."

"What?" she asked.

"I've been hoodwinked again. I might have guessed that it was too good to be true."

"What Howard? What's happened?"

"I thought I was being given the big honor of walking Lauren up the aisle…"

"Don't tell me that she's changed her mind?"

"No. But she's asked Phillip as well. She wants us both to give her away! I ask you—she barely knows him. It's an insult. I've a good mind to refuse."

Tracey thought about it a bit, then said, "Now Howard, I'm sure you're disappointed, but it's not as if you have known her all that well either. Maybe Lauren is trying to unite the family by asking you both. Try and see it like that. I wish I could be there to make you feel better about it, but try not to get upset. It'll take two minutes to walk up the aisle and then the whole thing will be in the past tense."

Howard was silent for a minute. "You don't think it's very rude?" he said at last.

"I think it'll be a bit strange having two men walking her up the aisle; but I suppose that's been done before. She's a strange girl, and it's an unusual situation."

Her voice and words soothed him, and he took a deep breath. "Maybe you're right."

"Call me again tomorrow night after the wedding, Howard. It'll be my Saturday morning. I'll be thinking of you."

He felt a little better after the call, and much better after a shower and a nap. He was ready to meet the family again.

***

He was seated between Wendy and Martie Rousseau at the rehearsal dinner and was glad to have his sister on hand, for he found it very difficult to understand Martie's accent; her husband was quite impossible. Thank heavens Mike spoke perfectly clearly, as did his brother and sister-in-law, but the parents sounded very guttural most of the time. And as for the woman called Chooks, he hadn't a clue what she was saying, but he laughed politely when she laughed, which made her laugh even harder.

He excused himself after speeches had been made as the jet lag was taking its toll. Isabella shook his hand as he was leaving, saying how glad she was that he had come to South Africa; Phillip and his wife Cynthia rose to wish him good night, together with their children, Fran and Adam. He looked around for Lauren and found her in a corner, with her fiancé and a group of young friends. "Good night," he said, "don't you think you should also be getting a good night's sleep for the big day tomorrow?"

A young friend snorted into his beer as he laughed, saying, "Are you saying there won't be much sleep tomorrow night? Or are you saying he needs to build up his stamina?"

Howard wanted to snap back with an answer but restrained himself. He remembered Tracey's admonition that he should try not to get upset, even when all the young people started laughing. Mike put out his hand and touched Howard on the arm, saying, "Don't worry about this bunch. They're some old friends who've had a bit too much to drink."

"The wedding is tomorrow," Howard remarked. "I thought that's when the festivity starts."

The same young man took another gulp of beer and said, "I think Mike and Lauren started their festivity a little while back, didn't you Mikey?!" Once again everyone laughed and Lauren blushed. "Anyway, we like this American idea of yours, having a rehearsal dinner. It means we get two night's drinking instead of one."

Another young man chimed in, "And maybe Mike and Lauren can rehearse tonight as well. Last time before you're a married man, mate. It might not be so much fun when it's legit!"

Howard raised his eyebrows and left the room. Lauren ran after him apologetically, explaining that these were old university friends of Mike's who were groomsmen and ushers. "They're very nice, Uncle Howard, just being silly with all the booze."

"They're very crude, Lauren. Matrimony is a sacrament—and the act that goes with it is a holy one. Why am I giving you away if you've given yourself away already?"

Lauren stopped in her tracks and pulled away from him. "I didn't ask you to give me away. I asked you to walk me up the aisle, as a gesture of family support."

Howard stared at her, taken aback. "I might be old-fashioned Lauren—call it what you will—but the point is that marriage is a not a laughing matter."

"Who's laughing? I quite agree with you Uncle Howard. Mike and I have had excellent role models to teach us that. We're not taking it lightly. I appreciate your concern, but please rest assured we're very serious in our commitment to one another." The smile was gone from her face. "See you tomorrow," she said and returned to the party.

Fortunately the day dawned clear and dry, although cold. As the wedding was only in the late afternoon, Phillip suggested a trip up the cableway to the top of Table Mountain in the morning. "There's nothing much for us to do here and we'll probably get in everyone's way. Besides which, they say that you have to make the most of the opportunity to go up the mountain when the weather is clear. It can change at any minute, I'm told."

Howard joined Phillip and his family as they set out early to try and beat the long lines for the cable car. The drive into the city was interesting, especially when Phillip pointed out the hospital where Lauren had been taken last September, and on the other side, further up the road, there were zebra and wildebeest roaming around the unspoiled open space at the foot of the mountain. They drove through tree-lined suburbs with beautiful homes, such a contrast to the shacks he had seen the day before, until they arrived at the cableway. The state of the art machinery had them at the top of the mountain very quickly, while rotating so that everyone had panoramic views. It was degrees colder at the top, but the views were spectacular. He could see Devil's Peak and Lion's Head that Petrus had mentioned, as well as the Twelve Apostles—a set of peaks running parallel to the Atlantic Ocean. Howard stood gazing in awe at nature's grandeur, picturing himself on a map standing at the southern tip of this vast continent. All of Africa was behind him.

He joined the others for a guided tour around the top of the mountain, on an easily marked trail. The wild flowers were beautiful, even at this altitude, although the guide recommended a visit to Kirstenbosch Gardens at the foot of the mountain. Flora at the lower level were even more spectacular, she promised. She pointed out a trail that could be climbed to get down the mountain to Kirstenbosch, but warned them to watch for weather changes and baboons. Almost on cue, a troop of baboons clambered across the rocks just below and barked their annoyance at being disturbed. Phillip turned to Howard and said, "It makes me shudder to think of Kirstenbosch."

"Why?"

"That's where Lauren was abducted. Well in the car park, actually. She'd been walking in the Gardens."

"Oh yes," Howard responded. "I didn't realize it was down there." He found himself walking with Phillip and chatting easily about the wonders of this mountain. He found that he actually rather liked the man; it was strange to think that they were brothers. He remarked that it was odd to think of Phillip being a grandfather, while he was only just about to become a father for the first time. "It'll keep you young," Phillip replied, laughing. "I find that the young always challenge one to think. They won't simply accept what one says. I'm not sure I was like that when I was young, but that's the way it is now. It's good, really." Howard thought about his exchange with Lauren the previous night, and wasn't so sure. Some things are sacred.

***

The Franschoek Valley put on a glorious face for the wedding. As Howard arrived at Belle Terre, he looked around in amazement. He had no idea that any part of Africa would look like this; it was almost European with majestic mountains surrounding well groomed vineyards and oak trees, and the most unusual gabled architecture he'd ever seen. The vast thatched homes looked solid, yet ethereal. He was even more amazed to discover that this house was hundreds of years old, Phillip wasn't quite sure of the number. When he saw his brother's surprise, Phillip nodded his head. "Yes, I was surprised too," he said. "The Rousseaus are a very old South African family. Something like three hundred years since the first ones came here from France. They've been on this farm ever since. It's going to be hard for Mike to leave, but maybe they'll come back when he's finished at Stanford."

He and Phillip were shown into the front room to await Lauren, who was getting ready here at the farm for the short drive to the church. Mike and the rest of the Rousseau wedding party had already left. The room was full of brightly shining antique copper and silver, as well as large wooden pieces of furniture glowing with the deep patina that comes from years of polishing. The high ceilings and tall windows gave the room stature to accommodate everything with space to spare, and big Persian rugs covered the old yellow wood floor. They sat listening to a mantel clock ticking while waiting for their niece—otherwise everything was quiet. At length, the clock chimed the quarter hour and the two men looked at one another; they were due at church in fifteen minutes.

And then the door opened and there was a rustle of silk. Lauren entered the room and both men rose to their feet. She looked like a porcelain doll as she stood smiling nervously at them, with Isabella making last minute adjustments to her veil. Her hands were shaking slightly as she clutched her bouquet of white roses and lilies. The photographers and videographers were busy recording every moment for posterity, but the tableau was one that Howard would never forget, regardless. His sister and her daughter looked beautiful, but the look on Bella's face was what choked him; it was emotion packed. In that moment he understood something about his sister that he would not be able to put into words if he tried; for the first time in his life he felt empathy with her.

The little church was adorned with white flowers and as the doors opened, the organ struck the first chords of the processional music. Phillip, Howard and Lauren began slowly walking up the aisle to where Mike was waiting at the altar and there were murmurs of appreciation in the congregation. All eyes were on the bride, who felt a sudden calm and smiled serenely at her mother, and then her fiancé. There was hardly a dry eye as the couple took their vows and the priest pronounced them husband and wife; when Mike kissed his bride there was spontaneous clapping from family and friends.

Howard, however, began to feel uncomfortable. He looked at the program and saw that someone called Bessie Opperman was reading from the Koran, and somebody else with an unpronounceable name was reading something from the Upanishads—Hindu scriptures. He had nothing against Muslims and Hindus in general, but the inclusion of their scriptures at a Christian wedding was outrageous.

Regardless of what Phillip had said about the young challenging one to think, they didn't have the answers to everything. He would teach his children the right way—the only way. God's way.

The tasting room had been transformed with bowers of protea, erica and other indigenous flowers; pale pink fabric was draped along the high ceiling in great swathes to soften the room and connect it to the marquis tent. Belle Terre wine flowed freely. The guests were happy; the speeches were entertaining and heartfelt as Dawie Rousseau welcomed his new daughter-in-law into the family; Mike and Lauren were radiant as they took to the dance floor. Before Phillip could do so, Howard quickly rose and asked Bella to dance. She looked surprised, but her face softened as he put his arm around her waist. "This is a first," she said and laughed.

He smiled at her. "It's another day for a truce, Bella. Agreed?"

"Agreed. Mom would be pleased."

Taking his surrogate father role seriously, he gallantly proceeded to dance with Lauren and then Martie Rousseau. Wendy watched with pleasure and amazement as her brother played the congenial guest and relative. She whispered to Robert as they danced past, "I wonder how long this will last? It's too good to be true."

Martie led Howard over to introduce him to Reverend Matthew Jackson, the young Anglican minister who had officiated at the marriage ceremony. She left them talking and took her leave to mingle with other guests. Howard cleared his throat and complimented the young man on the homily he had delivered. "Thank you," Matthew replied. "You've come a long way for the wedding. Your niece must be very special to you. She's a remarkable young woman. I'm sure you're very proud of her."

Howard cleared his throat again. "Yes—yes, I am."

"She's done such good work amongst society's most needy," Matthew said. "She professes not to be a Christian, but I defy anybody to show me someone with more Christian behaviour than Lauren Marlowe—I beg your pardon—than Lauren Rousseau!"

Howard's eyebrows shot up. "I'm surprised that you agreed to perform the ceremony if she isn't a Christian."

Matthew shrugged. "Mike is a Christian—she wanted it for him. And frankly, one doesn't draw people to the church by turning them away. She was very honest about her beliefs and I respect that. She's a good woman, intrinsically good. Actions speak louder than words, I feel. Her actions are all God-affirming, even though her words aren't," he said with a laugh. "A lot of 'good' Christians are just the opposite; all talk and no action."

Howard frowned, and then he asked the question he was burning to ask. "Tell me, Reverend Jackson, what's your opinion of the readings today?"

"I thought they were beautiful."

"But they weren't Christian!" Howard clenched his jaw with indignation and his face reddened as he said, "It's quite wrong to have non-Christian readings in a Christian place of worship."

Matthew Jackson sipped his drink as he looked hard at Howard. "Actually, I think we need to listen more to what others have to say, wherever we have the chance to hear it. Lauren and Mike are inclusive people; they're global citizens." He took another sip and continued, "Intolerance has done more damage in the history of the world than famine, disease and drought combined, and all in the name of God." He accepted some more wine from a passing waiter and continued, "In 1 John 4:7, the Bible says: *'Beloved, let us **love one another**: for love is of God; and every one that loves is born of God, and knows God.'* The readings today were about love."

"But they weren't Christian," Howard persisted. "It doesn't matter that they were about love. They weren't Christian and this was a Christian wedding."

"Any faith without love is fanaticism, Mr. Parker." He smiled politely at Howard and excused himself to dance with the bride.

***

Reverend Jackson's rebuke rang in his ears and colored the next couple of days which were spent sight-seeing with a guide in the wine country and Cape Town. The city seemed a mixture of colors, creeds and languages which he found unsettling. It was the mix of first and third worlds that he had been told about. There were little black street children begging on corners, and countless vendors at the side of the road every time his guide stopped at a traffic light, selling wire ornaments and toys, flowers and fruit, or newspapers and magazines. All this made him happy to be staying comfortably in

Constantia where he could retreat at night with the security of an armed guard at the gate. There were quite as many mosques as there were churches, and the days seemed to be punctuated by the Imams' calls to prayer, as well as the noon day gun firing from Signal Hill. The guide proudly explained that the eighteen pounders used for this were the oldest guns in the world in daily use, and they had been firing since about 1806. Originally they were to signal the harbor that a ship was approaching for provisions, as Cape Town was the half way station to the East from Europe in those days, before the Suez Canal was built. The noon day signal, the guide added, was implemented as a time keeper for ships to check their chronometers in the nineteenth century, and had apparently remained a daily ritual in Cape Town. Howard was amazed to discover that there was a castle in the city which had been built in the seventeenth century by the Dutch, and that there were slave quarters which now housed a museum. The older wine estates also had relics from slave days, which astounded Howard. He had only thought of slaves being taken from Africa, not brought here as well. His guide informed him, however, that no slaves had ever been taken from South Africa.

Isabella was planning to fly to a private game park in Limpopo Province, and invited Howard to accompany her. Phillip and Wendy were there already with their families; Lauren and Mike would also be joining them as part of their honeymoon before leaving for California in early July. He was sorely tempted to extend his trip as he felt he had seen nothing of the country, and barely any wild animals. When he heard his wife's voice on the phone however, he knew he was needed at home. He would come back to South Africa with Tracey one day and enjoy the sights with her. Even better; they would come with their children. He would have his own family.

30

Howard was unable to settle comfortably on the return flight. He was confused. The past few days had caused him some unpleasant moments, and yet overall his experience with family members had been better than usual as there had been no flare-ups. He was pleased with himself that he had made the trip, and gratified that Bella and Lauren were appreciative of his efforts. Phillip had turned out to be pleasant enough—in fact he liked the man who couldn't be blamed for the sins of his parents. It was just difficult to accept that they were brothers.

What troubled him was the great latitude given by Reverend Jackson to Lauren and Mike. If he could have done so, Howard would have liked to debate more with the priest. It was not proper to have other religious prayers in a Christian church, no matter what the man said. It would be like putting cherry into an apple pie because they were both food, and still thinking it was a cherry pie. If you wanted cherry pie, it wouldn't be right to serve apple pie, and vice versa. And then there was the matter of Lauren's abortion. Everyone seemed to gloss over that fact, including Reverend Jackson, although perhaps he didn't know that piece of information about her. If you respect life and accept that it is God-given, then it follows that it is only for God to take it away. He hoped that Lauren had begged God's forgiveness and atoned for her sins, and he fully intended to discuss it with her when she came to California. It was his duty as a caring uncle and good Christian.

He slept fitfully, dreaming of crying babies and anguished mothers. One of the mothers was Tracey with a dark haired woman next to her who turned to look at him; it was Maria, feeding Tracey's child. The baby's mouth was plugged on her nipple but the other breast was exposed, full and pale, with a dark center like the core of an exotic flower. He awoke with a start and an uncomfortable feeling of tightness in his pants. He felt himself sweating. Damn Maria.

The flight home seemed interminable. After changing planes in New York, the day went on and on as they chased after the sun; when the plane finally descended over San Francisco Bay and he saw the Golden Gate Bridge, he sighed with relief. Everything looked so normal. The stretch limousine that awaited him hit Highway 101 and sped past billboards, prosperous cars, and corporate headquarters of household names. Howard felt happy to be back in the environment he understood. Glad that he had done his duty, he was excited to be returning to Tracey.

She had just come in from the pool when he arrived home and walked into the downstairs bedroom. Maria saw him and discreetly slipped out to the pool house to change. Tracey's hair was wet and she was clad in only a towel, which dropped as she turned to greet him. It was so long since he had seen her standing naked that he was taken aback; her pregnant stomach was more than just a bulge now; her navel had popped out; her breasts were much larger with pale blue veins running through them, converging on her pink nipples. She was radiantly healthy and happy as she greeted him with her arms outstretched. He felt his chest constrict as he took her in his arms and caressed her body, running his hands over her belly. "You are beautiful," he whispered in her ear and carried her to the bed.

She held onto him as he gently placed her down, and said, "Keep your hands here and you'll feel the babies move." She pulled his hands onto her belly. It was such a powerful reaction he felt to the tiniest of movements that it brought tears to his eyes. "It's a miracle, isn't it?" she said. "One of them seems to move a lot, and the other one is more laid back."

"How can you tell?" he asked with amazement.

"They just feel very different."

"Have you had any more contractions?" he asked.

She shook her head. "Everything is absolutely fine."

His hands moved up from her belly and cupped her breasts. She smiled and he took it as a welcome sign as he leaned over to kiss them, but she pushed him away and held him at arm's length. "No Howard."

He hit the pillow under her head in frustration and said, "Tracey, why can't I kiss your breasts? Dr. Lu didn't say anything about that as far as I remember."

"I'm sorry Howard," she replied, "but I know how quickly you'll go from kissing my breasts to other things."

He looked so dejected that she put her arms around him tightly and whispered, "Just once can't hurt, can it? It felt like forever that you were away."

A month of pent up anguish flooded him as he ripped his clothes off and pressed his wife against him. She responded passionately as they rediscovered one another's bodies and it wasn't long before they were oblivious of Dr. Lu's orders, making love despite the twins occupying space between them. Finally, exhausted, Howard fell asleep in Tracey's arms, but she lay perfectly still. "Dear God," she prayed, "please don't let anything happen to my babies. I shouldn't have weakened. I'm sorry."

The next morning Howard awoke very early, but refreshed. Tracey was still asleep next to him and he lay watching her, considering himself very blessed. Marriage certainly was a great gift and sacrament. He arose quietly and decided to leave early for work in order to catch up on the backlog. After a quick shower and breakfast, he waited until he saw the Nunez sisters walking up the drive and then took off for Woodside. He felt reassured that he could look at Maria without any reaction, and he was glad that Tracey had instructed her to dress more modestly. Both sisters wore white collared shirts and khaki trousers. Rosa would never make a man look twice, but it was as well to have them both dressed with more decorum.

He turned out the drive and caught sight of a green truck, just turning the corner ahead of him. It looked like it could be Joe's truck. "I bet he's hanging around here again wanting more money. I must tell Rosa not to allow him into the house," he thought to himself and immediately called home on his cell phone. Maria answered the phone and when he gave his instruction, she replied politely, "Mrs. Parker's father...he..."

Howard cut her off. "Don't ask questions Maria. He is not to come into our house, no matter what he says. Do you understand?"

He found his mind straying at work. The Reverend Jackson's comments still concerned him, and the reminder of Joe was another source of bother. Both these men had been offensive in their remarks to him, and he didn't want anybody telling him anything about God's love or God's creatures. He did so much for charity, and he had personally tried to help Joe; nobody could have tried harder. At length he decided to go home early and play a few holes of golf, as it would help get his mind off these things and ease the jet lag.

The house was very quiet as he made his way up to his room and began to change, until he heard laughter coming from outside. He looked out the window and saw Tracey, giggling and floating on her back in the swimming pool, her stomach raised like a buoy above her. And then he saw Maria emerge from the shadows. He was transfixed. The bikini she wore covered very little of her body, and the things he had guiltily dreamed about were suddenly there for him to see. Her breasts, as he'd suspected, were exceptionally large for the rest of her body; consequently the two small triangles forming the bikini top barely covered her nipples and all the roundness of her breasts was exposed. As she walked into the sunlight, he saw that her legs were long and lean, and her waist was slender. She stood still, raising her arms to tie up her hair into a ponytail before putting a toe gingerly into the water, and then as she turned around, he gasped. The bottom of her bikini was a thong, revealing her virtually naked buttocks. They were round and firm and smooth. His disapproval was extreme, but he couldn't stop staring, try as he would to look away. Thoughts of golf were forgotten as he spent the afternoon at the window.

Later that evening over dinner, Tracey made an announcement. "I'm sorry Howard, but I'm going to be sleeping by myself downstairs. You will have to go back upstairs. I don't want any more possibility of things getting out of hand again. God has given us these babies, and at this stage I'm an incubator looking after them—I want these babies more than I've ever wanted anything in my life. Nothing is going to diminish their chances of survival."

"Tracey, I promise that I won't make love to you again until after they're born, but please don't keep me out of your bed," Howard begged.

"No, I'm sorry. I know that the flesh is weak," she said with finality.

He had decided to tell Tracey that Maria needed a new bathing suit if she was to swim in their pool, but somehow the opportunity to do so didn't seem to arise. Howard found himself drawn to working at home many afternoons, and it was as if he couldn't help himself as his feet made their way upstairs to watch Maria at the pool. She was the most beautiful woman he had ever seen—other than Tracey—and the thought entered his head that if God had made perfection and put it here, was it wrong for him to look at what God had made?

Dr. Lu arrived three weeks later for her usual monthly call to check on Tracey. Maria showed her into the room and stepped outside while the doctor performed an examination. Dr. Lu smiled at Tracey as she removed her stethoscope from her black bag, saying, "I must be the only doctor in the United States who makes house calls."

Tracey smiled too. "I'm very fortunate. Thank you."

"It feels good, actually," replied the doctor. "It's a little reminder of days gone by and how doctors used to be. Thank goodness we have technology and medicines that are more up to date though." She placed the stethoscope on Tracey's stomach and began moving it around to listen for heartbeats. "There's one," she said, "a nice strong, steady beat." Then she moved it around some more, and frowned.

She made no comment, but asked Tracey if she'd had any vaginal bleeding or cramps. Pleased to hear that she hadn't, the doctor did a pelvic examination before saying that she needed to do some scans in hospital as soon as possible.

Tracey was stricken with anxiety. "What's the matter?" she asked.

"Hopefully nothing, but I'm having difficulty picking up the second heartbeat."

Maria drove Tracey to Good Samaritan and stayed with her in the waiting room. "Do you want me to call Mr. Parker?" she inquired with concern.

"No. There's nothing he can do." Tears welled up in Tracey's eyes.

***

When she got home, Tracey closed her bedroom door and refused to speak to Howard. It was Maria who explained to him what had happened, as best she could. "The doctor she come, and she say Mrs. Parker must go to hospital for scans. When I bring her home she is crying, crying, crying. She tell me one baby is dead."

"What?" shouted Howard. He tried again to speak to his wife, but she wouldn't allow him into her room, nor would she answer when he spoke to her. In desperation, he phoned Dr. Lu who explained that one baby had died in utero. "It sometimes happens and we don't know why," she explained gently. "There is no course of action we can take. It would endanger the other baby, so one baby grows while the other atrophies. I'm very sorry. Mrs. Parker will have to continue with the pregnancy and give birth to both babies when the time comes."

"Isn't there anything you can do?" Howard asked heavy-heartedly.

"Not a thing, Mr. Parker. All we can—and must – do, is to be very supportive towards Mrs. Parker. It's a very difficult situation emotionally for her. I know it is for you too," she added hurriedly, "but we have to be careful that she doesn't stress so much she endangers the live baby."

***

After three days when Tracey would admit nobody but Maria into her room, he called Wendy in despair. "She's six months along now and the surviving baby is viable," he explained. "She needs to hang on as long as possible but she also has to carry the dead baby until the live one is born. The pregnancy has been high-risk all along, but now it's very precarious. Poor Tracey, she's inconsolable; she won't speak to me; she won't eat. I'm at my wit's end. She won't even let me into her room. If she doesn't look after herself, we might lose this baby, too."

"Do you want me to come and help?" Wendy asked. "Is there anything I can do?"

"I don't know Wendy. I don't know what to do." He shut his eyes tight, remembering how he had made love to Tracey on his return from South Africa a month ago. He blamed himself, but he couldn't tell his sister this. It didn't matter that Dr. Lu had explained nobody was to blame; these things happened she had said, adding that Nature only allows the fittest to survive. Dr. Lu didn't know what they had done; what *he* had done. Tracey had begged him not to make love, but his hungry flesh had made her weaken. He knew he was to blame for the death of his child and he knew that Tracey blamed him as well. "I don't think there's anything you can do either, Wendy."

"Lauren and Mike will be arriving in California soon. They're with Bella in Georgetown at the moment. Maybe Tracey will speak to Lauren," Wendy suggested. "Lauren's young, but she has wisdom and compassion after all she's been through. She might just be able to reach out to Tracey."

"Perhaps," Howard replied doubtfully.

He replaced the receiver and his head sunk to his chest. "Dear God," he prayed as he covered his eyes. "Forgive me for being selfish and weak-willed, but please don't punish me by taking away everything I love. I'm a terrible sinner, but please...Spare our innocent baby...Please don't let Tracey hate me..." He couldn't pray any more as he quietly sobbed, grief-stricken and ashamed.

31

Lauren watched her husband's face as they flew into Dulles International Airport. She pointed out the Potomac River, the Washington Monument and the White House as they flew over Washington, D.C., and he smiled excitedly, recognizing landmarks, but feeling disbelief that he was actually seeing them. She remembered her reactions arriving in Cape Town, seeing picture postcards come to life and how surreal it had felt. It was hard to believe that it was eighteen months since she had left home and such terrible things had happened, but here she was back again, a married woman, and happier than she'd ever been in her life.

Isabella was there to meet them and as they walked out the terminal building they were assaulted by a wall of heat. Mike gasped in disbelief. "Man, is this hot and humid or what?" he exclaimed. "This is something else. I thought Africa was hot..."

Bella and Lauren laughed at his shock. "Africa doesn't have the sole rights to heat," Lauren replied. "We've got it too."

As they crossed the Potomac, driving over Key Bridge into Georgetown, Lauren turned to him and said, "You're on *my* home turf now. Growing up in a townhouse is a bit different from a farm; not too much space to call your own, but we love it and there are lots of perks."

"Home is where you make it," he said and smiled.

Bella glanced over her shoulder and said, "You remind me of my mother when you say that. She always said you should bloom where you're planted."

The traffic congestion was unlike anything he had ever seen. As they drove along busy M Street, cars seemed to cruise around looking for parking like predators—until Bella turned onto a quieter tree-lined street with old Georgian buildings on either side, seemingly untouched by the centuries. Her home was beautiful; three storeys with a small private garden at the back, opening out from French doors in the living room. Antique furniture filled each room and every surface was adorned with photos of Lauren and Ted, as well as Phillip and Edith Parker. Lauren was overjoyed to be home and her eyes glistened with emotion as she showed her husband around the house.

The days were packed with sightseeing and meeting old friends. Mike marveled at the quietness their home offered, surrounded by busy Georgetown. The university dominated the top of the hill with its old buildings and campus dating from 1789; the residential area was very gracious while the shopping area was frenetic. Lauren took Mike for a drink at the "Tombs", a below-ground level pub just off-campus which she explained was the Georgetown equivalent of "Forester's Arms" at UCT. They did the tour of all the Memorials and Monuments in Washington D.C. and then began exploring the various Smithsonian Museums, which fascinated Mike particularly. He loved seeing Lauren's enthusiasm as she showed him her hometown and he realized that he'd forgotten she was actually an American. This was her home. He was so used to her being part of his world that she had ceased to be a foreigner. He wondered whether he would fit into her country as well as she had done into his.

Bella had organized for the three of them to take a couple of days fly-fishing in the Blue Ridge Mountains, before Mike and Lauren headed off to California. This was a place that they had visited every summer when Ted was still alive, and afterwards Lauren's grandparents used to bring her here. It was peaceful and unspoiled, and Bella felt increased warmth towards her son-in-law. It was comfortable being together and gave a very pleasing sense that the family had grown.

Mike watched his wife fishing in her waders, standing next to her mother as they both concentrated on rhythmic casting in their quest for trout. He had never seen her more relaxed and happy. Gone was the haunted expression that sometimes crossed her eyes; instead he saw the bright face of the woman he'd known before her ordeal. He knew that their happiness together was a contributory factor, but being back in her own environment was playing its part.

They grudgingly left the wilds and returned to Georgetown, where there was a frantic message from Wendy awaiting them on the answering machine. "I've been trying to reach you on your mobile without any luck. Please call me when you get this. Howard and Tracey are having problems. One of their babies has died. I'll explain more when you call."

It came as a terrible shock after the carefree days they had just enjoyed. With a six hour time difference it was late at night in England, but Bella decided to call anyway. Wendy was relieved to hear from her sister and explained what had happened, adding that Lauren might be able to bring them some comfort when she got to California.

Bella frowned, before replying, "That's asking a lot of my poor daughter."

"Don't be like that Bella," Wendy said. "Don't kick them when they're down."

"It's not that." It was hard to disguise the irritation in her voice. "The thing is, neither of them ever listens to anything from us. I'm not saying I don't feel sorry for them, but be realistic. They're both so rigid in their beliefs, poor Lauren can't be expected to make a difference."

"Just offer love and sympathy. It's not a time for proving points Bella."

Lauren's eyes filled with tears when her mother explained what had happened. "That must be so hard," she said, and Bella felt herself redden. Compassion is a terrible thing to lose, she told herself, and for a moment her old knee-jerk reactions had tripped her up.

Lauren and Mike both felt some trepidation as they left Dulles to fly to San Jose. Their honeymoon was over, and it was time to get on with the next chapter in their lives. For each of them there were unknowns, but they felt excitement that they were now starting the rest of their lives together and as they walked into their tiny campus apartment at Stanford, they looked at one another and smiled. This was their first home together.

Before visiting Howard and Tracey, Lauren insisted that they look around the campus and the town of Palo Alto, where Stanford was situated. They had a few days to settle before Mike began work, and Lauren had a month before starting her job at Planned Parenthood. He was eager to explore the wealth of art work on campus and was moved by the Rodin sculpture garden with the Gates of Hell, as well as the Burghers of Calais. He'd seen these figures from a distance in London and France, but to be able to walk up to them and touch them seemed a privilege. When he entered the chapel, he was overcome and sat quietly in a pew, looking around at the stained glass windows with light filtering through them, bringing them vibrantly to life. Lauren sat next to him and held his hand. His thoughts were of his family that he'd left behind, and his bride sitting next to him. His future had come to a turning point and he'd taken the first steps along a new road; he knew in that moment that he would never return to live in the land of his birth. He would be the first in a new line of Rousseaus in America, starting anew — just as his ancestors had done centuries ago, when they moved from France. It was in his blood. He could make his future anywhere he wanted to, just as they had done. His future would be where his wife would be happiest, and it was very clear that she had come home.

The drive down to Los Gatos was surprising as they drove along Highway 280. Mike had not expected to see such a lot of open space and rolling hills. Lauren explained that most of it belonged to Stanford, which was why the university was called 'The Farm.' She pointed out where the San Andreas Fault ran through Crystal Springs Reservoir, and he marveled aloud at the golden hills punctuated with giant oaks and evergreens, with cows and horses meandering around. "I can't believe such a bucolic scene is in the middle of Silicon Valley," he remarked.

Lauren laughed and said, "You're a Californian already. They say that it's only when people see the summer hills as golden and not brown that they've become Californian. In the winter these hills will be as green as anything you've seen in England." She turned to him and smiled. "This is where my mom grew up, and I spent lots of my childhood here with my grandparents. It's my other home—I'm lucky I have so many!" She drummed her fingers on the steering wheel and added, "Unfortunately, I don't feel quite so at home with Uncle Howard and his wife. They're all right I suppose, just a bit..."

"Narrow-minded?" he asked with a laugh.

She turned and glanced at him, laughing. "How did you gather that so quickly?"

"Just something Matt Jackson told me. He and your uncle had a little altercation apparently."

"What about?"

"Oh it got up your uncle's nose about us having Hindu and Muslim readings at our wedding. Matthew gave him a few revs, and then because the wine had loosened his tongue, he told me about it. It's quite funny really."

Lauren shook her head. "He and my mom have always bumped heads ever since they were children. Anyway, poor guy, I wouldn't want to be dealing with his problems at this moment. His wife is difficult at the best of times, so I can only imagine what she's like now with this sadness."

As they drove up the drive to Howard and Tracey's house, Mike whistled. "This is quite a place they've got here."

Rosa answered the door and showed them into the living room, explaining that Mr. Parker would be back from work soon. When Lauren asked if she could see her aunt, Rosa replied, "I ask my sister. She is with your auntie. She will ask her. Your auntie no see nobody."

In a few minutes Rosa returned with her sister. It was hard to believe they were related; one was stocky and homely, while the other was stunningly beautiful. She smiled sweetly and said, "I am Maria. Mrs. Parker say please come in."

Mike and Laura both got up, but Maria stopped them. "Sorry, she say only you," and she pointed to Lauren. "I am very much worrying for Mrs. Parker. She no like to eat, she no talk, she no wash no more. Nothing." Lauren followed Maria to her aunt's room; she was shocked when she entered. Tracey lay in bed looking ashen faced, with dark rings under her eyes. Her hair, which Lauren remembered as being a shining mane, lay dankly in greasy strands on her shoulders and her expression was lifeless. She looked up as Lauren entered and stared at her, then closed her eyes as tears streamed down her face.

Lauren glanced at Maria, who left the room quietly. Instinctively Lauren moved forward and sat on the bed next to her aunt. The young woman put her arms around the older one and held her gently; Tracey stiffened momentarily, before placing her head on Lauren's shoulder and sobbing. There was nothing that either of them could say to ease the pain, and Lauren felt her own tears falling too. "Thank you for coming to see me," Tracey finally said. "I didn't mean to break down, but just seeing you...You're so brave and strong. I'm so weak; I feel like part of me has died. I can't even feel joy about the one that's living. I just feel so guilty. I killed my baby."

Lauren found herself searching for words of comfort. She knew the indescribable emptiness her aunt was feeling, and there was nothing anyone could say to alleviate it, but she couldn't understand the guilt. She had felt guilt, she still felt guilt, but she had made a decision to terminate a pregnancy. This had been out of her aunt's control. She continued holding her as Tracey's sobs grew weaker, and at length she said, "I know it sounds hollow, but you will heal with time, and in the meantime you have another little being you have to concentrate on. You can't blame yourself for what has happened. All you can do is accept it, and make the most of things as they are."

Tracey shook her head. "But I do blame myself, and I blame Howard even more. I begged him to stay away, but...I shouldn't have weakened. I know that's what caused this to happen. Dr. Lu said we weren't to do it and she was right." She pushed herself away from Lauren and said, "I haven't admitted that to anyone, but that's what's driving me crazy. I was to blame." She slumped in the bed and blew her nose loudly.

"It seems highly unlikely that you caused this to happen. Think about it, Tracey. I suppose that you were cautioned about...you know, not having sex, because the doctor didn't want you to start having contractions again. Is that right?" She looked at her aunt until finally Tracey looked back at her and nodded.

"Well, you didn't have contractions did you? You're still carrying the baby. The baby's heart stopped beating—that's what happened—but it wasn't because of anything that you did. Who knows why that happened—we'll probably never know, but you didn't cause it to happen."

Tracey stared at her as she spoke. "God is punishing me for giving way to desire. I wanted that baby so much and I should've been more grateful for the gift God gave me. It's Howard's fault too. He made me do it."

This didn't make sense to Lauren and she felt like screaming at such illogical thinking, but she was quiet as she thought how best to respond. "I don't know what's between you and Uncle Howard, but do you really believe that your God would be spiteful like that? I don't know much about these things, but don't you believe that your God is loving and forgiving?" It felt very strange for Lauren to be talking about God; she was in uncharted waters. "You see, I don't think that this is about you at all—nor Howard. Sometimes we forget we're all part of the animal kingdom, although we're at the top of the chain. It's just biology. Only the fittest are able to survive, and sometimes nature creates imperfect specimens. It's a miracle that you have another little being growing inside you that's probably perfect. He or she needs you to take care of it; otherwise you will be to blame if something happens because you refuse to take care of yourself. That little life is totally dependent on you at this stage."

Tracey began to cry again. "I'm a bad mother already; maybe that's why I had such difficulty getting pregnant. I wasn't meant to be a mother. My parents were worth squat; they both lied to me. And now I'm just as bad."

Lauren was exasperated. "For God's sake, you're being totally self-indulgent. Get a grip on yourself—and reality. You're wallowing in self-pity. If you think you'll be a bad mother, you probably will be. Why don't you just trust that you'll do everything in your power to be the best mother that you possibly can be? My grandmother, your mother-in-law, always used to say to me, 'if you look down you'll see the dirt, but if you look up you'll see the stars.' Why don't you try looking up Tracey?"

The two women stared at one another for a length of time. Lauren was concerned that she had pushed the limit too far—she hadn't even seen her aunt since her father's funeral—but she couldn't undo what she had said. At length Tracey said, "I think I should take a shower.

Please ask Maria to come here." She blew her nose again and said, "Thanks Lauren."

When she returned to the living room, Howard was seated with Mike. He jumped up when she entered and welcomed her, quickly adding, "How was she?"

"She was pretty bad actually Uncle Howard. But she talked to me, which was good. She's feeling very guilty, which is ridiculous, but you know...people can't help what they feel."

"I knew it. I bet she's blaming me too, isn't she?"

Lauren nodded. "It's silly and unreasonable."

Howard looked uncomfortable. "It's not at all unreasonable. There's more to it than you know. We're guilty, both of us. But I'm guiltier than she is; in fact I'm altogether at fault here, if the truth be known."

"Uncle Howard, she told me everything. You're both crazy. For God's sake, you had sex—you're husband and wife. It's not the end of the world. That's what husbands and wives do. I know the doctor told you not to, but Tracey didn't go into labor or anything; the baby's heart stopped beating. That's totally unrelated. She's still carrying the baby, so having sex didn't make her have contractions. And sex didn't make the child's heart stop beating. It wasn't anything that you and Tracey did."

Howard went red in the face and Mike found his mouth quivering as he tried to suppress a smile. Lauren's face looked very earnest. At length her uncle cleared his throat and said, "How dare you speak to me like that? Show some respect."

"I'm trying to reassure you that you and Tracey shouldn't be blaming yourselves. I'm sorry that I used the word 'sex,' but unfortunately that's what you're both beating yourselves up about. There are other words I could use, but you'd like them even less."

"That's enough," Howard exploded. "I don't need advice on such matters from you young lady. In fact you're the one who should be feeling the most guilt around here."

Mike arose and took Lauren by the arm. "We're leaving," he said. As they got to the door, he turned and looked at Howard, "That was totally uncalled for. I might be new to this family, but let me tell you something, you're a self-righteous, narrow-minded prick and I have no qualms about telling you so."

As they went out the door, Howard shouted after them, "Don't bother coming back."

Mike turned and glared, "There is absolutely no danger of that."

After they left, Howard sat slumped in a chair staring into space, remembering Phillip's words about the young forcing us to think by challenging everything. The exchange with Lauren and Mike was evidence that Phillip was wrong; the young knew no barriers of decorum. He could feel his heart pounding as rage consumed him. He was still seated there when Maria knocked on the door to say that Mrs. Parker wished to see him. He bounded along the passage, stopping only when he reached Tracey's bedroom door. "Come in, Howard," she called when she heard his footsteps. She was sitting up in bed in fresh pajamas, looking pale but with her newly-washed hair gleaming about her shoulders. "I'm sorry," she whispered. "I know this has been just as hard for you as it has been for me. Can you forgive me?"

He sat on the bed and took her hands. "I'm sorry too, Tracey."

"There's nothing to be sorry about. Your most extraordinary niece made me see that I was torturing myself over something I wasn't responsible for—and neither were you. But we mustn't chance our luck again. We still have a baby alive and well—and kicking very vigorously." He put his hand on her stomach and she said, "You won't have to wait long to feel it move. It's a busy baby."

"Thank God," he whispered.

"I hope Lauren will come and visit often. I feel ashamed that I didn't meet her husband. Are they still here?"

He looked away. "No. They had to leave." He cleared his throat and said, "They won't come back. I don't want them back in this house."

Tracey looked shocked. "Why?" she asked.

"Tracey, I accepted that you didn't want your father in the house. Please just accept that I don't want my niece and her husband here either." He drummed his fingers with agitation on the window ledge. "That young woman forgets herself. She discusses things that are none of her business and that she knows nothing about. I will not have her interfering in my life. Besides, I don't need advice from someone who had an abortion. And as for that husband of hers, he's barely in the family and already he's shooting his mouth off."

As he left her room, he wondered why he didn't feel happier. Tracey was at peace and she'd absolved him of guilt, and yet he felt alone and dejected. There was something about any dealings with his family that always set his nerves on edge, and now Mike had teamed up with the rest of them. "You'd think they'd be more sensitive at such a difficult time in my life," he thought to himself.

32

Lauren was very quiet as they drove back to Palo Alto, and remained silent all through dinner. She seemed preoccupied when Mike attempted conversation, and long after they put the light out he was aware of her lying awake. He had drifted off to sleep when he was awoken by the muffled sounds of her suppressed weeping, prompting him to roll over and put his arms around her. "Hey, forget about that arse hole. He's missing a few vital ingredients; a heart and a brain." Mike continued stroking her hair, trying to calm Lauren.

"I just hate it that he's bringing up something I'm trying to forget. I thought I'd moved on, but I feel like it's all come to the surface again."

"Lauren," he whispered in her ear, "you have moved on. Listen to me, you are a brave woman and you made a wise choice. Howard doesn't have the right to express his opinion. In any civilized society it's accepted practice that a rape victim has the option to terminate an ensuing pregnancy—and that's what you were Lauren, an innocent victim."

"I know, but I took a life. That was another innocent victim."

"It was a few cells, Lauren."

"Christianity says that it was a life. I thought you were a Christian?" she said.

"I am. I'm also a scientist—and those two things are compatible." As she lay quietly in his arms, he added, "Your uncle is cruel, Lauren. He isn't a Christian's bootlace. I can't stop you seeing him, but please don't ask me to accompany you. He seems to have a great capacity to judge others without looking too carefully at himself."

"I know," she agreed. "Poor Tracey, imagine being married to him."

"We all make our choices," Mike replied, "and then we live with them. What do they say? Marry in haste, repent at leisure!"

They lay quietly together in one another's arms, finally going back to sleep in the early hours of the morning—only to be wakened by the phone's shrill ring, like a cricket chirping. Mike awoke from a deep sleep and was momentarily confused about his whereabouts. It sounded like the old phone on the farm, perhaps because he had been dreaming about his old home. Lauren stirred and fumbled as she reached across the table to find her cell phone, but it was Mike who found it first on his side of the bed. A familiar voice said, "Hi, sorry. Did I wake you? What's the time there?"

"Bessie, is that you?" Mike asked groggily. "Where are you?"

"In Trafalgar Square. I'm at South Africa House."

By now he was wide awake. "What?" Mike replied. "What's going on?"

Lauren sat up in bed and stared in puzzlement, trying to piece together what was happening from her husband's responses. As he rang off, he sighed deeply and sunk his head in his hands. "Shit," he said.

"Tell me what's happened," Lauren demanded. She shook him as he appeared dumbfounded.

"Bessie was attacked in Cape Town three weeks ago. She was on a job and some guy followed her when she got out of her car in Long Street…"

"Oh my God. What happened?"

"He pushed her into a dark alley and…Fortunately somebody heard her screams and came to the rescue. The bugger took off but he cut her up badly with a broken bottle."

Lauren went cold and closed her eyes. When she opened them, Mike had put his arms around her and was whispering, "She's O.K.

She's O.K." He hugged her and stroked her hair, adding, "I think she's lost her nerve, by the sound of things. She headed off to London to attend a conference, and then on a whim decided to come and visit us. She was able to get a visa in London and was checking that it would be all right with us."

"When is she coming?"

"Tomorrow."

***

Lauren watched passengers appearing on the closed circuit TV screen as they cleared customs and made their way to the arrivals hall at SFO. Some looked exhausted and irritable after their long flights, while others seemed eager and excited. She searched for Bessie's face amidst them and gasped when the South African woman finally appeared on the screen; Bessie had large dressings on her forehead, chin and left cheek, while her neck was in a brace. She walked with apparent discomfort. It was helpful to have had this brief preview of her friend so that Lauren could hide her shock when they greeted one another moments later. They hugged and smiled, then hugged again, both lost for words until they were in the car heading south down Highway 101 when the words finally began to flow.

"I am so sorry," Lauren said. "Thank God somebody stopped the guy, but it looks like he did quite a bit of damage."

"Oh Lauren," Bessie sighed, "I was so shit-afraid and angry. But you know what the worst thing was—I was absolutely bloody powerless. I didn't have the *fokking* physical strength to fight him off. All this stuff on my face is only part of it. He broke a bottle and kept slashing me with it; he'd ripped most of my clothes off me by the time somebody came and he was threatening to cut off my nipples. He was trying to make me…" She shuddered and stopped for a moment, then began again in a hushed voice. "He was trying to force me to…" Words failed her as she sobbed.

Lauren felt herself shivering, while trying to concentrate on driving and Bessie's horror at the same time. Her friend continued, "I can't handle it anymore, Lauren. All the reporting I've done was gruesome, but I always tried hard to remain objective about it.

Suddenly, I…I can't do it anymore. I believe it's an important job, but it's not safe. Crime is rampant and the attacks against women have become more and more violent. I really believed in what I was doing—and I was good at it—but now I'm not sure it serves any purpose at all and it just puts me in the line of danger." Her agitation was evident as she blew her nose and searched for her dark glasses before adding, "The editor was very kind and sent me to a conference in London, to give me a bit of a break—you know—but I've lost my nerve. *Jus*, I don't think I can go back to journalism. I'm telling you— I'm a mess, man." Lauren put out her hand to her friend. "I knew you would understand, Lauren," Bessie continued, touching Lauren's proffered hand. "Most of my male colleagues just say that I'll get over it and everything will be fine. But how the hell would they know? It was—how can I explain? It was a sense of being totally powerless against the *blerrie* bastard that haunts me. And they won't catch him…That's for sure. The police are useless—*fokking* useless!" She shook her head and shuddered. "He's out there doing it over and over again, whenever and wherever he likes. Him—and hundreds more just like him." A frightened Bessie Opperman from Mitchell's Plain had displaced the accomplished journalist.

"I know," Lauren answered. "The fear revisits you when you least expect it, and often at night in dreams. I have this recurring nightmare where I'm being chased by three men, and sometimes I dream I'm in that shed again, or in the trunk of a car. I think you did the right thing to get away, and I'm glad you've come to us. I hope you can stay for a while."

Bessie had tears in her eyes as she said, "Thank you Lauren. It's nice to be somewhere where I feel safe."

There was a deep bond between the two women that they both valued. Each could draw strength knowing the other understood her perfectly, without explanation; their nightmares were different but their emotions were the same. It was also good to have first hand news of the orphanage; Bessie described how Faith and Wellington Radebe visited the place at least twice a week. They were providing strong role models for the children and took personal interest in each child. Parker House was also functioning smoothly and Wellington visited there every week as well. This was reassuring news, and

Lauren expressed eagerness about returning at Christmas to see the progress for herself. Final arrangements were also being made for the purchase of halfway houses in the other big cities.

It was fun to show Bessie her first glimpses of the United States and Lauren hoped that the distraction would help her friend heal. There was some time before she began work at Planned Parenthood and she enjoyed having a South African visitor, despite the horror story Bessie brought with her. Mike was initially afraid that it would be a setback for Lauren, but instead she seemed to find new strength as she offered comfort and reassurance. They spent time reminiscing over things they missed from South Africa, and Lauren made *babotie* as a surprise. Each day they did some sight-seeing; there was so much to see and Bessie fell in love with San Francisco immediately. People had said it reminded them of Cape Town, but she saw no similarity at all other than it was a beautiful city next to water. The hilly streets and quaint architecture were unique, but most of all she loved the carefree, tolerant attitude that seemed to be the pulse of the city.

Bessie began to formulate an idea that perhaps she could persuade *The Argus* to let her remain here for a while as a foreign correspondent; the editor was disposed to helping her as she had done so well in her job, and he was sympathetic about her feelings since the attack. With this in mind, she wrote an article which she emailed back about the homeless problem in San Francisco, comparing it to Cape Town's street people. She was delighted when she received news that it was going to be printed in *The Sunday Argus*, and the editor asked her to write more articles that would be run as a series. Her next article was about how San Francisco had made her change her pre-conceived notions about the U.S.A. Far from being the wasteful, materialistic metropolis she had expected, there was a recycling ethos that seemed ingrained in the sense of civic responsibility; it was a clean city with excellent public transport and allowances for the handicapped. She wrote too about the wonderful mix of people who were proud to call themselves San Franciscans, living and working happily side by side. She added that she felt uncategorized as she went about her business; she was simply a person, not a Cape Colored woman. She called it the 'City with Soul.' She threw herself into observing and writing, and with the friendship of Lauren and Mike to strengthen her, she began to breathe more easily.

With a couple of month's employment ahead of her, it was clear that Bessie needed to find other accommodation. She and Lauren began to search on Craig's List, another innovation that Bessie found fascinating. It was possible to find just about anything on this website and, within a few days, she was able to sublet a room in an apartment for two months. The rent was reasonable, the location was excellent, and Bessie settled into San Francisco life. Her observations and views were recorded and helped earn her keep as *The Sunday Argus* ran a popular series on the 'City by the Bay.' She joined a Rape Survivors' Support Group and as she listened to other victims tell their stories and try to work out their fears, she began to formulate another idea for her future; she would write a self-help book that would put her skills and experiences to some good. She had no difficulty selling her idea to publishers and soon Bessie Opperman was doing what she knew best; she was writing from her heart. This was her therapy and salvation.

As the weeks passed she grew stronger emotionally until she felt fortified to return home in pursuit of her career. She would write about the rampant crime, corruption and violence in her country, and shame the police and other authorities into addressing issues, rather than ignoring them. Anger flamed in her eyes as she thought of the safe, comfortable existence lived by some of those who had been leaders in the struggle against apartheid; their new status, complacency and greed made them ignore the dangerous plight of ordinary people, trying to go about their daily lives. There had to be a new struggle, and it would start with the power of the written word. As nostalgia overcame her, she made plans to return with Mike and Lauren at Christmas; the flat-top mountain standing guard over the city at its feet was calling her. She longed to hear familiar accents and be among her own people again. "I'm a visitor here in San Francisco, albeit a grateful one," she thought to herself. "I've regained confidence and direction here, but Cape Town is where I belong; it's my home."

33

Tracey and Maria had begun swimming again in the afternoons for the weather had become increasingly hot in early September, as it so often did in Northern California. It was a relief for Tracey to float in the pool and feel the weight ease off her when she did so. Maria was not a good swimmer, but these months with Tracey had given her more confidence in the water. She enjoyed the relaxed attitude that seemed to have developed when they were outside in the swimming pool, and the two women talked quite freely about many personal things that they didn't discuss indoors. It was while they were swimming that Maria informed Tracey she had missed her period and thought she might be pregnant.

"But Maria, are you married?" Tracey was shocked.

Maria blushed and said, "I marry on Saturday."

Tracey looked at her. "I don't understand. You got married last Saturday?"

"No, Mrs. Parker. I marry this Saturday."

"Why have you kept it a secret? Tell me about Jose, and tell me about your wedding."

Maria blushed. "He is good, he is very kind. He wants to be a good father. When I tell him maybe I'm pregnant, he cry Mrs. Parker."

"I see," said Tracey. "Well, are you happy Maria? Do you love him?"

Maria nodded. "Yes, and he love me. I am very happy."

"Where does he work?"

"He work with my father and Ernesto, my brother. They work in construction."

"And where will you live?"

"With my mother. He live there now. My mother, she like him too. Everybody like him."

"Have you seen a doctor?"

Maria shook her head. "Not yet. Is too early."

Tracey swam to the side of the pool and made a mental note to speak to Dr. Lu about taking Maria as a private patient. As she lay out on the chaise lounge, Tracey asked, "What are you going to wear? Tell me about the wedding?"

Maria smiled. "My mother, she make a dress and a cake. That's it. We marry at Sacred Heart Church, and then we have a party at our house."

"What about Jose? Does he have family nearby?"

Maria blushed and looked at her hands. "They not come. They live in Mexico."

When they went inside, Tracey pulled out her check book and wrote a check for $1,000.00 which she handed to Maria. "This is my wedding present for you and Jose," she said. "If I were allowed out of bed, I would invite myself to your wedding, but please be sure you bring me photos and a piece of cake! I am very happy for you Maria. You deserve much happiness. You're a good friend to me."

Howard had been watching from his usual place upstairs and it was evident that the two women were discussing something seriously. He watched as Maria ran her hands over her stomach while talking to Tracey, and he saw her nipples harden in the cool water. They showed right through the bikini which almost floated away as she swam. When the women went back inside, he waited until he heard the Nunez sisters leaving before going into Tracey's room. She turned and smiled as he entered.

"I've just had the happiest news. Maria is getting married on Saturday."

Howard paled. "Maria? Married?"

Tracey laughed. "You look so surprised. Did you think this was her only life, looking after me?"

"I…I guess I hadn't thought about it. I presume she'll continue working, will she?" he asked.

His wife considered telling him about Maria's suspected pregnancy, but decided against it. "Yes, while I need her, I'm sure she'll stay," Tracey replied.

The heat wave continued and the following afternoon was stifling hot. Howard's heart was pounding in his chest as he made a decision that he, too, would have a swim that afternoon. After all, it was his swimming pool. When lunch was over, he made his way around the back of the property to the pool house, where he was quietly changing into his bathing suit when the toilet door opened. Maria appeared naked in front of him. From two feet away, she was beautiful beyond belief. He felt a throbbing in his groin; as he stood up, he almost brushed against her breasts. She gasped. Howard was also naked, paralyzed with embarrassment as Maria stared at his erection and began to giggle.

"What are you doing here?" he asked, suddenly trying to cover himself.

"I, I…I go here," she gestured to the toilet, "but my bikini is there on the bench." With that she rushed past him to retrieve it. She was close enough that he could have reached out and touched her. He could smell the scent of her body and as she reached over to grab her bikini, he longed to stop her so that he could gaze at her more. She was more beautiful naked than he had dreamed and he couldn't bear to think of her getting married.

"Maria…" he said, as she turned her back on him to put on her pants, "I'm sorry…I didn't know you were here." At a loss for words he was riveted by the sight of her bent over, stepping into her bikini. He had always fantasized over her breasts, but the rest of her body was more than he could ever have imagined. The sight of it now was driving him insane; as he gazed at it, he desperately wanted to touch the darkness of her most private place. He wanted to help her when she struggled to do up the clasp of her bra, but realized it would be inappropriate. She grabbed a towel and ran out of the pool house, without looking at him again.

Shaking, he pulled on his bathing suit and collapsed on the bench. His chest tightened as if it were being squeezed in an old fashioned laundry wringer. When he looked down at the embarrassing wetness in his trunks, he was glad that nobody was there to see him. "If you have sinned and nobody sees, have you really sinned?" he thought to himself wryly. He couldn't bear Tracey to find out about the incident and sat for a long time wondering when it would be safe to come out. He could hear the two women's voices outside. It seemed that the best idea was to remain where he was until he heard Tracey return to the house, and then she would never know what had happened — unless Maria told her. Thus he spent a hot, stuffy afternoon sitting in the unventilated pool house, remembering a glimpse of beauty, recalling how she had giggled at the sight of his naked body, and unable to forget his shame.

As he sat idly waiting to get out, his thoughts ran their oft-traveled path of remembered hurts and slights. He spent time mulling over the fact that his child that was about to be born, had been cheated out of its birthright. His parents' will had left $5,000,000.00 to each grandchild — including Phillip's children whom his parents had never met, not to mention Lauren. It was almost like rewarding her for her sins. It wasn't fair to his child — and anymore children he might have. It was so typical of his father, he thought, favoring everybody else. There had to be a way to address this oversight and he decided to discuss the matter with Tracey.

At last he heard Tracey make her way back, with Maria walking beside her to support her. He used that moment to grab his clothes and make his retreat as well, without ever having a swim to cool off. He planned to ask her opinion about the will over dinner, but as they ate she asked what he had been doing all afternoon. "Thinking about some things," he said. He explained his concerns about the will as it pertained to their child, fully expecting her to be as indignant as he was. But Tracey merely said, "With all due respect, your parents weren't to know that you would have a child after they died. Maybe you can speak to your brother and sisters about it. It would be nice if they could be fair about it and see your point of view for a change." Before he could say anything more she returned to her previous question, adding that she'd thought he was going to join her for a swim.

"I changed my mind," he said. "I didn't feel like it when I got thinking about this."

Tracey pushed her food away without eating and said, "Howard, I don't understand you. Why are you lying to me?"

He looked pained. "I have never lied to you in my life. You know that's against my principles. What on earth are you talking about?"

"Will you tell me what you did this afternoon?" she asked again.

"Exactly what I told you, I tried to figure out what to do about the will."

"Where were you?" she asked.

He sighed. "I don't understand what this is all about. Are we playing 'Twenty Questions?' Why am I being cross-examined?"

"Because I know you were sitting in the pool house. It doesn't need a rocket scientist to work out that you were in there—watching Maria undress. The question I have is whether you meant it to happen, or whether it was an accident. It seems so odd that you would sit there all afternoon and not come out. Were you waiting for her to go back in again? She was afraid to do so and borrowed some of my clothes to go home. What were you doing in there?"

He looked away and said, "Tracey, I'm such a fool. Of course it was an accident. Do you think that I would try and spy on Maria? I was embarrassed. I was also changing and she saw me naked as well. It was awful. I couldn't face coming out again."

Tracey shook her head. "You still have to see her again sometime. Wouldn't it have been better just to come out immediately?" She watched him eating his food and tried to picture what might have happened in the pool room. He clearly didn't want to speak about it anymore, and she couldn't quite decide whether his red face was caused by embarrassment or guilt.

Having avoided Maria all week, when Saturday came, Howard felt listless. He played golf, but couldn't concentrate on the game. All he could think of was Maria with another man. It irritated him that Tracey was so happy about it, and he was even more irritated when she brought up the subject of Lauren. He reminded her that they both had bad apples in the family.

"Howard," she said, "it's like comparing bad apples with perfectly good oranges! My dad was a bad man and he was a lousy father. Lauren is a good woman and a caring niece—and I like her. I really want to see her again and I want to meet her husband. If you don't want to see her, well don't. But please don't stop me. Just give me her phone number and I'll call her."

"I don't want them in my house again."

Tracey glared at him. "Will you at least tell me what the problem is?"

There was ice in his voice as he replied, "She was very rude. She said totally inappropriate things to me. Her husband was even worse; he slung some nasty names around. And as I recall, Lauren is the sinner in the family."

"Lauren? A sinner?"

Howard looked at his wife in amazement. "Am I the only one who remembers that she had an abortion?"

"Perhaps you are. Everyone else is trying to forget the nightmare," she replied.

"It's not for us to forget sins, Tracey. Only God can wipe the slate clean."

"Why don't you leave it to God then, instead of acting on his behalf? Worry about your own sins, and let Lauren's be between her and God. At least Lauren doesn't sit in a pool house lusting after someone she isn't married to, ogling naked bodies. Or is that not a sin?"

He exhaled loudly in disgust. "I don't believe that God considers embarrassment a sin, although obviously you do. I've told you what happened Tracey." He stopped and glared at his wife. "Anyway, Lauren doesn't even believe in God."

Tracey lay back on her pillow and closed her eyes. "I'm not interested in what Lauren does or doesn't believe—and I find your excuse very hard to believe."

"Excuse me, are you accusing me of lying?" he asked.

She opened her eyes, looked at him wearily and sighed. "I think I am. I'm not a fool, Howard. Maria is a beautiful young woman with an amazing body. She's gorgeous. I know you're frustrated because we can't have sex at the moment; I just can't believe that you—of all people—would forget the vow you made about forsaking all others, and take advantage of an innocent woman who is my friend. You know that she changes in there when we swim. I'm just not sure what you were doing there."

"This is outrageous. I went into my own pool house to change so that I could have a swim in my own swimming pool. I didn't know Maria was in there. I can't believe you're accusing me of breaking my marriage vow because we saw each other naked! You're as bad as the rest of my family. They always think the worst of me. I thought that my wife would always be my supporter."

"I want to believe you Howard. Please don't ever give me cause not to do so; don't ever lie to me. My father did that, and then he tried to tell me that it was my mother who lied. All I ask for is the truth at all times."

"Oh, so now I'm like your father. And it's OK for you to make judgments about your father, but I can't state facts about Lauren?" he said.

She closed her eyes again and murmured, "I wish you would grow up—before *you* become a father."

***

Maria was radiant when she arrived at work on Monday morning, and immediately gave Tracey a box containing a large piece of cake. "And the photos are here," she said, eagerly handing them over. The Polaroid shots showed her looking beautiful in a long, white, lace dress. Her husband was a tall, good-looking young man, dressed in a white tuxedo and smiling very proudly with his arm around his bride.

"Are there any pictures of your family? I want to see them all." Tracey asked.

Maria looked confused for a moment, as she pulled more Polaroid pictures out of an envelope. She sorted through them and pulled out a few in which she pointed out her mother, brothers and sisters. The others were wives, nephews and nieces. "Where is your father?" Tracey asked.

"He is…dead, Mrs. Parker."

"But I thought you said your father would be at your wedding…"

"Oh," Maria said, reddening. "My mother she has new husband. He not my father, but he very good man for my mother. Very good man, but no pictures of him," she said hastily, gathering up the photos and replacing them in an envelope on the bedside table, before helping Tracey make her way to the bathroom. "Today I must send these photos to Jose's parents." Then she giggled and whispered shyly to Tracey, "My period it start yesterday. No baby!"

"Maria!" Tracey stopped and stared at the young woman questioningly. "Are you happy or disappointed?" she added.

"I am happy Mrs. Parker. And Jose, he happy too. We have no money for children now. We want to save."

Tracey smiled. "That's very sensible, and I'm also happy because I hope you will stay and help me when my baby is born. Will you?"

Maria nodded.

Later, when Maria left to fetch breakfast, Tracey reached over for the photos to have another look at them. Their happiness was evident as all the family looked close-knit and very proud. Suddenly her hands froze as she looked at a photo that Maria hadn't shown her. It was a picture of the bride and groom with Maria's mother and Tracey's father. She stared at an image of the man who was anathema to her, smiling proudly at the camera, with Maria leaning on one arm and Maria's mother on the other. He was clean-shaven, dressed in a dark suit and tie, and looking very handsome. Underneath was written, Mama, Papa, Maria.

Tracey was stunned and stared at the picture without breathing for a few seconds. The sound of approaching footsteps triggered a response and she quickly pushed the photos back into the envelope, and then threw it onto the table again. When Maria entered with her breakfast she couldn't bring herself to look at the woman, rolling over and saying she didn't feel like eating, asking to be left alone.

She lay on her side and stared into space. How could this be? Her vagabond father, Joe Billings, was Maria's step-father? When did this happen? Maria was her step-sister? Questions flooded her brain, but she was too shocked and proud to ask them.

There was to be no time to ask anything however, for later that day her waters broke. Howard was summoned and drove her to Good Samaritan. Here they were met by an anxious looking Dr. Lu, who proceeded to do an examination and announced that she would have to perform a caesarean section immediately. It was seven weeks early, but there would be more danger to the baby by waiting even a day. Tracey was wheeled to surgery with a pediatrician and neonatologist on standby, and an anesthesiologist to administer an epidural. At 3:35 p.m. Gabriella Mary Parker was born, weighing only 4.5 pounds, but giving a healthy cry to announce her arrival. She looked her mother briefly in the eye, before being rushed to an incubator. Her misshapen twin was quietly taken away.

The brief glimpse that Tracey had of her daughter's blue eyes choked her with emotion. Her incubation days were over and now she could resume life again, but a new life as a mother. What she'd longed for had finally been realized, and tears poured down her cheeks as she watched her baby breathe her first breath. Everything was going to be all right, and as Lauren had said, she was going to do everything in her power to be the best mother she could. A sense of responsibility that she had never known before overwhelmed her. This little person was entirely dependent on her.

Howard, too, was in awe as his daughter was lifted from his wife's womb and her life began right there in front of his eyes; he felt numb. Tracey's words rang in his ears and he prayed that he would be worthy of being a parent. At that moment, he remembered his own father and felt himself grow cold.

Flowers and greetings arrived in armloads, but visitors were restricted to family. The following day Tracey was sitting up in a chair with Gabriella at her breast, when the door opened and Lauren walked in with a bunch of yellow roses and a gift for the baby. She looked embarrassed and offered to return later, but Tracey stopped her from leaving. "Lauren, I'm so pleased to see you," she said. "Please stay—I don't mind if you don't. We're two women. Come and meet your cousin."

Lauren knelt on the ground next to the chair and was overcome. She'd never seen a new-born baby before, and Gabriella—though tiny beyond her wildest dreams—was perfect as she suckled on her mother's breast. She stared in silence, as Tracey watched both Lauren and her daughter. There was a smile of contentment on her face. Finally Lauren looked up at her and whispered, "She's a little miracle."

Tracey nodded. "All my prayers have been answered. I never thought I would be able to have a baby…"

"And now you have the most beautiful baby that ever there was," Lauren said as she leant over and kissed both Tracey and Gabriella.

Tracey put her hand out and held Lauren's. "I've wanted to call you, but I didn't know how to get hold of you. I'm so sorry that you and Howard had a disagreement. I don't know what it was all about. Did he say something hurtful?"

Lauren shrugged dismissively.

"I'm so sorry. I wish he weren't like that, but...Anyway, I would really like us to get to know one another better Lauren. I...thank you so much for coming to see us," she said, looking down at her baby. She squeezed Lauren's hand. "Please give me your phone number and as soon as I'm up and about again, maybe you'll let me come and visit you."

"I'd like that very much. I want you to meet Mike."

"I'd like that too. I need to make sure he's good enough for my niece!"

"He is, I promise. It was my lucky day I met him."

Tears welled up in Tracey's eyes again. "I felt that way about Howard once. And I still do—but he can be very judgmental and rigid. I couldn't bear it if he were like that with Gabriella. I can't have that happen to her."

Lauren frowned and said, "You're probably the one person who can help him. He's a good man, but he's complicated. From what I can make out listening to family chatter, he and my mom have always bumped heads, just as he and Grandpa did. I think it was hard for him growing up in the shadow of Grandpa—who was so successful. He wanted to be like him, but he wasn't. He was more like Gran; she was wonderful too, but in a different way. Maybe it was easier for the girls because they didn't have perceived pressure on them to be successful like their father, and Uncle Phillip didn't ever live in his shadow. He was like me, he didn't have a father—or thought he didn't. From what Mom and Aunt Wendy say, when Uncle Howard married you he seemed to find what he'd been looking for. You're very good for him."

Tracey gave a half smile. "You've heard a lot of stories, I can tell. There's always more than one side to a story, though. It seems that families can harbor grudges for a long time and it's hard to change that. We can try, but it's hard. Oh dear, what a world am I bringing you into my little Gabriella?" she said softly.

"She's a new beginning, Tracey. She's going to be her own person and you're going to be a wonderful mom."

"And Howard…"

"is going to be a loving father." Lauren finished the sentence for her. "She's a gift to the whole family as well."

"The gift of unconditional love," Tracey said and smiled at Lauren. "I think you must have always had it, Lauren, that's why you know what it's all about. You're so sure of yourself and compassionate. You're right; I won't try and plan her future, she can do that herself. I'll guide her, and feed her, and educate her, —but…"

"Just love her," Lauren said.

There was a slight noise at the door and both women looked around. Howard stood watching them silently. They weren't sure how long he had been standing listening to them, or how much he'd overheard, and eventually Lauren broke the awkward silence by standing up and saying, "Congratulations Uncle Howard. You have a beautiful daughter."

He cleared his throat and nodded.

"I was just leaving," she added quickly, gathering her purse and keys.

Tracey watched the door close and turned to look at her husband, saying, "It's time to put your stupid pride aside. Go after her and thank her."

He opened his mouth to speak, but thought better of it. He left the room quietly and closed the door, then stood watching Lauren walk down the long corridor. As she waited for the elevator, she turned to look at him. He raised his hand slightly and waved; she returned the gesture before disappearing through the opening doors.

***

Dr. Wilcox came to visit Tracey in hospital, to congratulate her and see the baby. This had been a very intriguing case for him and he was aware that there were more embryos in the wings. However, as he had kept abreast of what had happened during the pregnancy, he was of the opinion that further pregnancies would be ill-advised for Tracey. He told her this now, while the memory of the difficult time was fresh in her mind. She nodded her head and sighed. "I suppose I should be happy to have one child at least. I thought it might never happen. It would've been nice for her to have a brother or sister though."

Dr. Wilcox cleared his throat and said, "There are ways of achieving that Tracey. We have the embryos; they don't need *you* as their incubator. A surrogate mother could do the job. It's quite possible anytime you're ready."

Tracey's face lit up with hope. Her thoughts immediately turned to Maria and she wondered whether it would be something her friend would consider. But then she thought of Howard. "I doubt my husband would agree to that," she murmured.

"Think about it, Tracey. You don't have to make up your mind now or anytime soon."

"What happens to the embryos if we don't use them?" she suddenly thought out loud.

"With your permission, we would destroy them."

Tracey paled. "I know my husband would never agree to that. We would have to do that without him knowing."

"I'm afraid I can't do that. Legally you both own them, so you would both have to give permission to do anything with them — whether you use them or destroy them."

"Oh dear," Tracey sighed. There was a long silence and then she said, "I'll think about it. You never know with Howard…"

***

Gabriella had to remain in hospital another few days, until the doctors were confident that her lungs were coping. On the day that she arrived home, Rosa and Maria were beside themselves with excitement to meet the baby. They presented Tracey with a pink sweater that their mother had knitted, as well as a miniature rocking horse that their stepfather had made. Both were works of art. "I used to have one just like this," Tracey exclaimed looking at the horse, "when I was a little girl, my father made one for me." Suddenly she stopped speaking and looked away. She felt tears in her eyes, and was unable to stop them pouring down her cheeks. At length she composed herself, and as she looked down at her daughter, she said, "You're a very lucky little girl."

Maria and Rosa both wanted turns holding the baby, as Tracey looked on. At length she said, "Please thank your mother and your father very much. I appreciate their kind thoughts."

Maria looked at Tracey. "I like to take pictures of you and Gabriella for them. Is OK for you?" she asked, pulling a small disposable camera out of her pocket. When Tracey nodded, Maria had her hold the baby and then took numerous photos from different angles, as well as close-ups of each of them. "Beautiful. My mother and father, they will be happy when they see. Thank you."

34

The christening was scheduled to take place the following month in October, when Phillip, Wendy and Bella would all be in California for the Parker Family Foundation board meeting. Howard was pleased that they were all staying for his child's baptism, and decided to broach the subject of the will at that time. He spent a great many hours thinking what he was going to say. Sometimes he rehearsed in front of the mirror, between brushing his teeth and rinsing; other times, he sat at his desk and spoke to an imaginary audience. He didn't want to be side-swiped by any comment from Bella, and he wanted to be sure that his argument came across clearly and logically. He suggested that Tracey listen to his speech, but she was pre-occupied with Gabriella and didn't give him her full attention. It would have to be a solo effort, he realized.

The day of the board meeting finally arrived and he practised over and over as he drove to Woodside, trying different inflections for better emphasis. He felt very confident when he arrived in the boardroom and eagerly awaited his chance to raise the topic. As the meeting was ending, he made his move, inserting his request into 'other business' at the bottom of the agenda. All eyes were on him as he cleared his throat, took a deep breath, and launched into his speech. "I'm sure you will all agree with me that the newest member of our family, Gabriella, would have brought great joy to her grandparents—much as your children did, Wendy and Bella. However, because of timing, she was not included in their will as your children were, and even yours Phillip—whom they never knew at all. Had they been able to foresee her arrival—and the possibility that there might even be more to follow—I'm sure they would have made provision for them." He looked around the room at his sisters and brother, giving them time to absorb his words. "I would like to propose that in fairness, an equal amount should be put in trust for Gabriella, with money from the Foundation. I believe that our parents would've wanted her to have it."

After considerable silence, Phillip was the first to speak. "Unfortunately I don't believe we can legally do that, Howard. The will has been finalized and the Foundation was established for charitable organizations, clearly laid down in the will."

"But the money came from our parents," Howard replied with anger.

Bella and Wendy looked at one another, but before either could speak, Phillip continued. "I see your point entirely, and I think you are perfectly justified in hoping something can be worked out for your child." He smiled and said, "It's such a natural, basic instinct to look after our offspring. There's nothing we can do about the Foundation paying out, but in fairness, I would like to make a bequest to Gabriella myself—I'll still have more money than I ever imagined possible."

Bella and Wendy immediately began to suggest that they would also contribute, but Phillip shrugged them off. "There's no need."

Suddenly Bella slammed her fist into the palm of her other hand. "If we're talking about fairness, then let's *make* it fair. There are four of us. If each of us gave $1,250,000—Gabriella would have her $5,000,000."

Howard shot back at her, "You want *me* to pay? I think you're missing the point. My family is the one that's been short-changed."

"I'm suggesting you make a contribution to your daughter's trust fund, along with the rest of us," she replied. "Don't be paranoid. It's pathetic."

"Please, please, please," Wendy intervened, "can you two try and communicate civilly? Let's not fall back on old habits here; stop it, please. Howard, you can decide whether to contribute or not, but I think I can speak for the three of us—we'll each contribute a quarter of the amount."

Howard slammed a book shut and began to argue. Just as Bella opened her mouth to reply, Phillip suddenly banged both his fists on the table. "Enough! For God's sake, you force one another into roles you should've outgrown forty years ago. Wendy's always the peace-maker trying to break up the two of you bickering. Why don't you try to see one another as strangers meeting for the first time, just as I met you last year? Imagine you know nothing about one another and show some respect. You're so unforgiving. My God, you wouldn't speak to anyone else the way you speak to one another. I begin to understand why Cain killed poor old Abel!" There was a stunned silence as they all stared at him, and then Phillip continued. "We're all born with brains, but we should try to develop them into minds during the course of a lifetime. An open mind is best. You can look for the worst in one another, or the best; rest assured you'll always find what you're looking for. It's all depends on your angle of perspective."

Wendy began to laugh. "Phillip, you've taken up your role in the family dynamics at last. Welcome to the club—you passed the entrance exam! All the other slots were taken, but nobody took the 'wise' position. We left that for you."

Phillip shook his head. "Thanks all the same, but no. It's been a tough test and I'm not sure I've passed it yet. It seems very difficult being a blood relation in this family, but I'm not taking any slot and I'm not going to react every time one of you tries to yank my string. That's my point. It's time to leave those positions you made for yourselves as children and see one another as adults." There was silence in the room as he added, "Life isn't a puppet show."

35

As the family stood around the baptismal font, Mike listened carefully to the prayers being said in a language vastly different from his childhood church-going days. There was comfort in knowing and understanding the traditions, for it gave him a sense of belonging despite being a stranger in this new land and family. His own family seemed very far away with their familiar mannerisms and warmth; he felt a rush of emotion remembering his father, so rooted in his farm and its vines. He was the quiet anchor and historian, yet also a man of vision. His brother David still felt it necessary to give his younger brother advice even if it wasn't taken, and his mother was always bustling with activity and enthusiasm. She was acceptant and supportive of all her family's endeavors and they all drew strength from her. He observed Lauren's family now and noted how Howard and Tracey stood stiffly apart from everyone else, anxiously clasping their new daughter. Bella meanwhile, stood between her daughter and sister, and her fingers unconsciously drummed on the closed prayer book she was holding. Her thoughts were clearly elsewhere as she went through the motions of being at the christening. Wendy watched the baby all the time, smiling and occasionally dabbing her eyes. His gaze softened as he looked at his wife who was concentrating intently.

Lauren, for her part, was mystified by the ancient rites and prayers of the baptismal service. As she listened, she too watched her aunts and uncles with their eyes closed in prayer, and her mother staring at her feet, drumming her fingers. What were they thinking? They were so predictable in their reactions to one another, yet not having her own siblings to help her understand, their behavior seemed unfathomable. Her thoughts strayed to the Rodin Sculpture Garden at Stanford where she loved to linger on her walks through the campus. 'The Gates of Hell' never ceased to intrigue her as she studied the details of tormented souls, struggling to get out of a nightmarish pit, but she was always more moved by the attitude of a lone figure seated atop the gates, contemplating the damned. Perhaps it wasn't what Rodin had in mind when he cast the massive work of bronze, but the composure of 'The Thinker,' soul-searching as he stared with chin resting in hand and elbow on knee, displayed wisdom that made him a survivor in Lauren's estimation. He stared without any self-righteousness etched into him; he'd risen above the quagmire of violent hatred and jealousies that had trapped those other souls in their own undoing. He would not be entering those gates of hell.

As she turned her gaze to Gabriella, Lauren was filled with a sense of both the transience and tenacity of life; it was just over a year since her grandparents' lives had ended, but here was new life, with their blood and genes, beginning afresh. Lost in her thoughts, she only half heard the prayers; all the words about redemption from sin seemed incongruous with this innocent baby as their focus. Like a fairy godmother, she wished Gabriella none of the things that were being talked about. Instead, she wished the child's days would be lived to their fullest so that no matter what tribulations she encountered along the way, she would always love and be loved.

Then Lauren looked at Mike; he was watching her. They smiled.